THE
Big Wander

BOOKS BY WILL HOBBS

Changes in Latitudes
Bearstone
Downriver
The Big Wander

THE
Big Wander

Will Hobbs

Atheneum • 1992 • New York

Maxwell Macmillan Canada
Toronto
Maxwell Macmillan International
New York   Oxford   Singapore   Sydney

Atheneum
Macmillan Publishing Company
866 Third Avenue
New York, NY 10022

Maxwell Macmillan Canada, Inc.
1200 Eglinton Avenue East
Suite 200
Don Mills, Ontario M3C 3N1

Macmillan Publishing Company is part of the
Maxwell Communication Group of Companies.

First edition

Printed in the United States of America

10   9   8   7   6   5   4   3   2   1

Library of Congress Cataloging-in-Publication Data
Hobbs, Will.
The Big Wander / Will Hobbs. — 1st ed.
p.   cm.
Summary: Although his older brother decides to return home to Seattle, fourteen-year-old Clay continues his search for his uncle through the ruggedly beautiful Southwest canyon country.
ISBN 0-689-31767-0
[1. Southwest, New—Fiction.   2. Uncles—Fiction.
3. Horses—Fiction.   4. Navajo Indians—Fiction.
5. Indians of North America—Fiction.]   I. Title.
PZ7.H6524Bi   1992
[Fic]—dc20   92–825

For my mother

I'm glad I shall never be young without wild country to be young in. Of what avail are forty freedoms without a blank spot on the map?

—ALDO LEOPOLD

Map by: Virginia Norey

1

Clay Lancaster rolled the window down and drank in the wind and the rolling red desert, the clouds impossibly tall in Arizona's turquoise sky. He read the billboards aloud to his brother Mike at the wheel of the pickup.

PRAIRIE DOG VILLAGE!

GENUINE INDIAN MOCCASINS!

LIVE TWO-HEADED CALF!

Clay had never seen so many billboards in his life as lined Route 66. Dozens, even hundreds, advertised the same few roadside attractions. You started seeing the signs hundreds of miles away and you came to think of them as companions on this thin strip through the big emptiness.

Ahead, a long-promised trading post appeared on the red horizon, with a dozen tepees circling a cluster of gift shops disguised as a fort.

"Chief Yellowhorse Village coming up, Mike. Hey, that last sign said something about rattlers. Slow down."

"Slow down—that's a good one," his brother Mike said

1

with a smile, coming a bit out of the daze he'd been in ever since they left Seattle. "Clay, we could've raced a tortoise into Arizona and lost."

"C'mon, Mike, your Studebaker has character." To Clay everything about their trip was perfect, even the way the truck backfired going down the hills. They were on the loose at last and four days into the Big Wander.

"These places are all phony as wooden nickels," Mike scoffed. "The Indians in the desert didn't live in tepees."

"There it is again—BABY RATTLERS—hey, Mike, let's take a look at 'em! I bet it's time to check the oil again anyway."

It was always time to check the oil. They'd left a plume of blue smoke behind them all the way down through Washington State and Oregon and practically the whole length of California. The truck was new, bought especially for this summer out of Mike's savings for seventy-five dollars. Well, not exactly new, Clay thought, but new for them. Its original red showed in places, but mostly you'd have to say it looked rusty, which came close to matching the color of the desert and seemed a lucky thing at the moment. Another lucky thing about the truck was its age, Clay thought, it being a '48 model, same as me, and that makes us both fourteen.

They walked onto the wooden porch of the trading post and Clay's eyes looked past the cigar store Indian to the footlocker with BABY RATTLERS spelled out large. As Clay knelt and cautiously began to lift the lid, a pair of little boys came streaming out of a station wagon and bounded onto the porch, their parents trying in vain to call them back. Twins, Clay figured. They froze big-eyed as Clay peered through the opening into the box. "These rattlers are a little different from the ones back home," he reported to Mike. "Maybe they're desert rattlers."

A little smile came to Clay's face as he looked from his

brother to the buzz-headed twins, crowding as close as they dared, deliciously terrified and hair-triggered to run. Their older sister was stepping onto the porch, curious to find out what was going on.

"Careful," Mike warned.

Clay's right hand started into the box. The blond girl and her little brothers gasped.

"Clay!" Mike shouted.

"I think I can get one behind the head," Clay said calmly, and his arm disappeared inside the box. The twins took two steps back and eyed their escape routes. Even Mike backed up a little.

Clay reached inside, carefully, carefully. Suddenly it wasn't so easy for anyone to tell what had happened, with all the rattling and commotion and Clay's elbow flying back. But the sudden look of terror on his face said it all—he'd been bitten!

Now, Clay thought, crying out in pain and throwing the lid open, springing in one motion on the twins with two of the rattlers in his right hand. The boys screamed and fell back against their sister and their parents who were backpedaling nearly as fast, until they all spied the baby rattles in Clay's hand—a pink one and a blue one.

"Hey," one of the twins exclaimed, "those are *rattles*, not *rattlers*!"

By now everyone was laughing with relief. The twins took the rattles from Clay's hand, wanting to hold the "snakes" too and shake them menacingly. Clay was much more aware of their sister, who looked to be about his age. She was watching him, and she was smiling. Her glistening hair, curling into a flip at her shoulders, shone about as bright as the sun.

"Are you fellas on your own?" their father inquired. Clay had never met a Texan before, but he recognized the accent from the movies.

"We sure are," he answered proudly. "My name's Clay and this is my big brother Mike and we're on the loose."

Both parents looked a little confused. "You're on the loose," the mother repeated, sounding a little concerned.

Mike was standing back and seemed to be enjoying this. Clay thought he'd better explain. "We've been talking about a big trip for a long time, just the two of us, for the summer after Mike graduated. He's starting college in the fall—at the California Institute of Technology."

The man whistled and raised his eyebrows. "Good school."

"Where're y'all from?" the girl he liked asked cheerfully. Her hair was blonder than blond. To his amazement, she was speaking to him.

"Seattle," Clay answered, enchanted with her accent and hair and everything about her. She was shining that warm, sweet smile on him.

She must be wearing perfume, he thought, and as they started to talk he could feel its delicate scent wafting through his nostrils and overcoming his brain, making him dizzy. Tropical flowers, that's what it is. Like they have in Hawaii.

A miracle was happening. He was usually so shy with girls. . . .

Her name was Marilyn, which awed him, because the only Marilyn he'd ever heard of was a blonde too, and her name was Marilyn Monroe. As they talked, he started remembering Marilyn Monroe in one of the most memorable scenes of one of his favorite movies, *River of No Return*. He could see her now, struggling to keep her feet on that lurching makeshift raft out in the middle of the rapids. He'd often pictured himself rescuing a girl in just such a situation and earning her eternal gratitude.

2

By a great stroke of luck, her father wanted to treat him and Mike to milk shakes at the soda fountain, and in a heartbeat Clay was sitting next to Marilyn at the counter. "We're going to see everything, go everywhere, do everything," he declared. "At the ends of the roads we're going to take off with our backpacks." He hoped Mike was hearing this—he needed to be reminded—but Mike was a few feet away at one of the tables and busy talking to Marilyn's father.

Marilyn had the bluest eyes. She looked interested in what he was saying. What did she think of him?

"We call our trip the Big Wander," he told her. "I can't believe we're finally on the road after thinking about it for so long. What makes it even better, we have this uncle we haven't seen for a couple of years. . . . Nobody know's what's happened to him, and we're out to find him. Did you ever hear of Clay Jenkins, the rodeo star?"

"I guess not," Marilyn said apologetically.

"He was All-Around Cowboy in 1956. That means he was the world's best. Here, I've got a few pictures in my shirt pocket." He showed her his favorite first, Uncle Clay under a black cowboy hat with that trademark smile all over his face, standing by a fancy pickup that had his name and a bucking Brahma bull painted on the side. Then he showed her the one with Uncle Clay in all his sequins and bangles standing in front of bright lights that spelled out MADISON SQUARE GARDEN.

"That's the biggest belt buckle I ever saw."

"That's for All-Around Cowboy," Clay said proudly. "He did it all—he rode bareback broncs and saddle broncs, bulldogged steers, even rode the bulls. He hit all the big-time rodeos, like Pendleton, Cheyenne, the Calgary Stampede. . . . Wait, there's one more."

Clay took another photograph from his pocket and held it out. Uncle Clay's face didn't show very well under his black Stetson, and his chipped tooth and three-day beard made him look a little like an outlaw. He wore jeans, a long-sleeved plaid shirt, and a silk neckerchief, and he was leading a burro.

"He doesn't look the same."

"Well, it's our most recent, from two years ago. He's older—it was taken after he left the rodeo. The last we knew, he was trying to make a living as a uranium miner."

" 'The Lonesome Trail,' " she read from the border at the bottom of the picture. "Where is he now?"

"That's just it," Clay said. "We don't really know, and that's what's going to make it interesting. All we know is where he was when that picture was taken—near Grants, New Mexico, at the Bluewater uranium mill. And he was leaving there. He could be anywhere from Tucumcari to Mexican Hat." They were just names off the map, but they sure sounded good when he said them.

"Mexican Hat. Why do they call it that?"

"Because people wear sombreros a lot there, I'm pretty sure."

Clay noticed Mike's smirk, but Mike kept on talking to Marilyn's parents, telling how they'd saved up for the trip and assuring them that their mother was all in favor of it.

Before any time at all, their milk shakes were dry and they were standing outside shaking hands and saying good-bye. Clay noticed someone in the station wagon, a boy a year or so younger than Mike. "My brother," Marilyn explained. "He's not in a very good mood. I think he's just tired of our trip and being jammed in with all of us."

Awkwardly, Clay reached to shake Marilyn's hand. It wasn't anywhere to be found, but finally she produced it, which was a relief.

"Good luck finding your uncle," Marilyn was saying.

"You too," he replied, and flushed as he realized it hadn't come out right.

She chuckled, and then her family all turned for the station wagon.

"Did you get her address?" Mike asked under his breath.

Clay felt his face flushing red and his throat going tight. It was all he could do to wave as the station wagon pulled out. "What was I supposed to—"

Mike was shaking his head. "I'd swear your last name was Pigeon."

"It's not like I'll ever see her again. . . ."

"You never know, Clay, you never know. You could have written her at least."

I could have, Clay thought. Why didn't I think of that?

"You were too wound up to think," his brother said. "I saw you. You've never kissed a girl, have you?"

" 'Course I have."

"Yeah, right. That's why your face is bright red. You're the worst liar I ever saw. All good things in all good time, Clay Pigeon. Look, you're tall, you've got that dark hair, and you're handsome—the girls are going to be knocking down your door."

"Sure, Mike."

"You check the oil while I make a call, okay?"

It was time for Mike to disappear into a phone booth again and talk, talk, talk with his girlfriend, Sheila. Every day, and sometimes twice, Mike would slide into a phone booth and then afterward drive in a trance for a hundred miles. Clay had a bad feeling. He didn't even want to think about it. The Big Wander was supposed to be better than all the old days put together when they were hiking in the Cascades, swimming rivers, busting salmon and steelies, messin' around. But Mike's heart wasn't really in it.

The oil was down a quart—no surprise. At least we're on the way, Clay thought. Fifteen hundred miles from home and out in the middle of Arizona. Maybe Mike will snap out of it. The only trouble was, he'd been this way all spring, like he'd even forgotten he had a brother and the Big Wander was coming up. In the days just before the trip it was a matter of holding your breath and ducking out every time Mike seemed to be getting worked up to making a speech or something. If it hadn't been for the blowup with Sheila, Mike might've called the whole trip off.

Back on the road, Mike didn't speak for a long time, except to mutter, "In search of the 'Real West' . . ." Clay didn't want to ask him what he was getting at. As the shadows grew long and they drove through the Painted Desert, Clay could see the Real West out there, glowing and magical, beyond the billboards. Mike was missing it, but there was no budging him when he was in a funk like this.

Eventually it was starting to get dark, and KOMA was beginning to come in. KOMA would make his brother feel better. They'd never heard such a great radio station. It played all the great songs and it seemed to reach about everywhere, as if most of the country was in the neighborhood. The deejays would announce dances from Tyler,

Texas, clear up to Aberdeen, South Dakota, and from Columbia, Missouri, all across to Needles, California.

"*Ricky Dare here, riding your way on the big signal coming at you from Ok-la-homa City, Ok-la-homa, playing the songs you want to hear when you want to hear 'em, and that's right now. From John in Cody, Wyoming, for Betty Ann in Casper, here's Gene Pitney and 'Only Love Can Break a Heart'. . . .*"

Unfortunately for Mike, the signal faded just as the song began. Mike was in the mood for sad songs, sad love songs. Clay glanced at his brother, who was reaching for the dial and trying to get that song back. Mike was hurting, it wasn't hard to tell.

It wasn't as easy to talk to Mike as it used to be. For the last year it seemed like all his brother thought about was his girlfriend Sheila. There hadn't been time for him and Mike to do things anymore.

Now that Mike and Sheila had broken up, you couldn't just ask what had caused the big blowup. Clay felt bad for him but really was thankful it had happened and Mike had wanted to get out of town. Otherwise all those old plans for the big road trip would have been just a pipe dream. The phone call from Uncle Clay had helped too, but the call wouldn't have been enough.

I'd be mowing lawns this summer, Clay thought, and Mike would be pumping gas and hanging out with Sheila. We wouldn't be together out in the middle of the desert heading for New Mexico and points beyond, that's for sure.

Clay started to write a postcard.

"Who you writin' to?" Mike was still trying to tune KOMA back in.

"President Kennedy."

"Oh, yeah? No kiddin'? Just thought you'd stay in touch with the president?"

"Well, you know, I think he's the greatest . . . and I always kind of wanted to write to him." Clay was a little embarrassed now, but at least his brother was back poking fun again. "I figured out that we wouldn't be doing this trip if it weren't for him."

"How'd you figure that?"

"Well, I think it's because of President Kennedy that Mom got the idea about going to Guatemala for the summer, about helping other people—you know."

" 'Ask not what your country can do for you . . . ,' " Mike began, imitating the president's voice and Boston accent to perfection, " 'ask what *you* can do . . . for your country.' Is that what you mean?"

"Yeah, sort of. If she hadn't come up with such a great idea for her own summer, she might not have been so easy on us about being gone so long—you know, if we were leaving her home by herself."

"So we have the president to thank? Pretty farfetched, if you ask me."

"And just think if we find Uncle Clay! Then she'll really be proud."

Mike tried the radio dial again. "That's just a long shot, you know."

"We'll find him. I have this feeling."

Mike hooted. "You didn't even find out where he was when he called!"

"I know, I know. . . . I could hardly hear a thing. It was a bad connection. Really bad. I just couldn't think."

"Yeah, I know, you got so excited. Well, we know he was in Bluewater a couple of years ago, that's a start. Clay, you have your own unique style, I'll have to give you that."

Mike had a big grin across his face. Clay was sure that the farther Mike got away from Seattle the better he would feel. This was beginning to be just like the old days. And the whole summer was stretching out in front of them.

Clay returned the grin, brandished his ballpoint, and went to work on his postcard:

10

Dear President Kennedy,

My brother Mike and I are big fans of yours. My mother wanted to join the Peace Corps, but she's a teacher and couldn't be gone for two years. But this summer she went to Guatemala with a church group called Amigos.

Mike and I, we're out looking for our uncle. You may have heard of him—Clay Jenkins—used to be a famous rodeo cowboy. Keep up the good work.

Your friend,
Clay Lancaster

"I had to kind of squeeze it in," Clay said as he finished up.

"You think he can read your chicken scratch?"

"Do you think it will get to him if I just address it to the White House in Washington, D.C.?"

"Sixteen hundred Pennsylvania Avenue. I don't see why he wouldn't get it, and he ought to like that eight-foot trout lashed to the horse. Probably don't see many of those in Washington."

3

Oklahoma City was coming in strong now. It was getting dark. Mike liked to drive at night because the radio came in so much better, especially KOMA. Ricky Dare was playing "Return to Sender" and Mike was singing along. Clay hoped his brother would start looking more on the bright side of breaking up, the way Elvis seemed to in the song. Elvis was torn up and everything, but he didn't sound like he was going to *die* from it.

But wouldn't you know, the very next song was "Sheila." "Blue eyes and a ponytail" and all that. As soon as the song started, Mike was shot through the heart. Well, Sheila's eyes really were as blue as you'll ever see, and she did wear her hair in a ponytail. She did after the song came out, that is.

Clay knew not to try to talk to Mike during "Sheila," and it got even worse when Ricky Dare followed with "Breaking Up Is Hard to Do" as if he were broadcasting Mike's life story.

"I wish they'd play 'The Loco-Motion,' " Clay suggested, hoping to derail his brother's train of thought. "Or 'The Twist.' Hey, do you know why Chubby Checker named himself Chubby Checker?"

" 'Fraid not," Mike mumbled. His eyes seemed so lost in the distance Clay wondered if he'd get them into a wreck.

"His hero's Fats Domino."

"So?"

"For somebody who's planning to be a scientist . . . ," Clay teased. "Fats . . . Chubby; Domino . . . Checker. Get it?"

"So where'd you learn that? I thought you were born yesterday."

"Day *before* yesterday."

"You heard it first on KOMA and the Ricky Dare Show— here's Gene Pitney with 'The Man Who Shot Liberty Valance,' from the new movie starring John Wayne and Jimmy Stewart."

Mike was still talking, but Clay shushed him and hung on every word through the whole song. "New song, new *movie!*" he yelled when it was over.

"You sure are nuts for Westerns," Mike commented, acknowledging Clay's big moment. "Haven't you heard that Westerns are going out of style?"

"Sure," Clay scoffed. "Never happen and you know it. I wonder who the song's talking about, who was the bravest of them all? John Wayne or Jimmy Stewart? Probably John Wayne, that's what I think. I sure would like to see that movie."

"Horse operas . . ."

"Big doings Saturday night at the fabulous Black Mountain Playhouse in Red River, New Mex-i-co. Music by the Road-hogs—don't miss it! And don't forget you heard it right here on KOMA, coming your way out of Ok-la-homa City, Ok-la-homa!"

"Red River," Mike reflected. A sudden awareness came to his face and he said with a sly smile, "Maybe Marilyn will be there."

Clay felt a pang of hurt and surprise. Why was Mike going to bug him about Marilyn again?

13

"I'm not kidding, Clay! Her folks told me they were going next to Red River, New Mexico, to stay for a couple of days before they go home. They said they always go there—it's up in the mountains or something. So where's Red River? Check the map, pick up your jaw, and put on your dancin' shoes! Black Mountain Playhouse, Red River, New Mex-i-co."

"Checking . . ." Clay fumbled with the map.

"Anywhere near Gallup or Grants? Maybe Uncle Clay will turn up at the Black Mountain Playhouse, in the band or something."

"Found it. Red River's north of Santa Fe."

"Sounds good to me. Can we make it by tomorrow night?"

"I think we can do it . . . and still go over to Bluewater on the way, see if anybody there has any leads on Uncle Clay."

"On the back of the map—read me the population of Red River."

The best part was, Mike was coming out of his daze and thinking about what was ahead of him instead of what was behind. "Here it is. Five hundred fifty people."

"See? If she's not at the dance, you'll bump into her on the street."

He didn't want to talk about it. He felt too good and too sick to speak. Maybe he really would see her again!

They pulled off Route 66 somewhere near the Arizona–New Mexico state line onto a dirt track and found a little clearing for the night a quarter mile back among the yucca and cactus. The tailgate of the pickup served as their kitchen table. "What's for supper?" Mike asked enthusiastically.

"Chicken dinner," Clay beamed, and produced a tall can with a label picturing its contents.

"A whole chicken. I see. What goes with it?"

"That's it."

"You're kidding."

"It's precooked. You want to heat it up on a stick?"

"I'm hungry. Let's just eat it."

Clay was dismayed to find it looked so awful, with big globs of jellied fat adhering to it.

Mike pulled off a drumstick. "The bones have turned to rubber, like the whole thing's been soaked in formaldehyde." He ate the drumstick. "Well, I did ask you to take care of some food for the road. Clay, this is the best cold and greasy canned whole chicken I've had in my life."

Afterward they lay in their bags on their backs and watched the stars a long time without speaking. Mike wasn't going to say anything. Clay knew he must be missing Sheila really bad, going over the breakup and regretting. It was his job to keep his brother's mind off his ex-girlfriend or girlfriend or whatever she was, and on the Big Wander. "Mike," he asked tentatively, "do you think we'll really put a man on the moon before this decade is out, like President Kennedy said?"

"Possible," Mike murmured.

"Do you think we'll find Uncle Clay?"

"Possible."

"Do you think he still wears that big buckle, the one he won for being All-Around Cowboy?"

"Possible."

"Do you think you'll let me drive tomorrow?"

"*Im*-possible."

Clay smiled to himself. He loved it when things were going like this, more like they used to be before Sheila. Just him and Mike, off on their own together. "Mike"—he nudged him in the ribs—"you know that singer Don Ho?"

"Yeah."

15

"What if he named his son Westward?"

Clay couldn't see Mike's face, but he knew there had to be a smile on it.

"Or Tally or Gung," Mike suggested. "Maybe Heidi for a girl. Heidi Ho."

"How about Land? I'd like that for a name. Land Lancaster."

"Possible, but not Land Ho. Good night, Clay."

"Good night, Mike. Thanks for everything."

"I haven't done anything. Well, maybe I let you talk me into this Big Wander of yours. That was some dinner you set out. . . ."

Clay let his brother drift off, and then he balled up his jacket for a pillow and took in with deep satisfaction the faraway whistle from the Atchison, Topeka, and Santa Fe Railroad, and the sage smell of the dry desert air. It was altogether different from the deep woods scent of western Washington. He always felt hemmed in by the woods; he preferred the sea. This desert was like a dry ocean, big and open, with a big sky and shapes enchanting in the far off. It was pleasant waiting for shooting stars and listening to the cicadas drill their shrill signal into the night, half expecting a sidewinder to slither across your bedroll. And it all lay in front of him, this summer and these landscapes from another world, rolling into it with his big brother and eating out of tin cans.

4

"Fifty miles to Bluewater, New Mexico," Clay announced as Mike fished the truck key out of his pocket. "Maybe Uncle Clay's still around there somewhere."

"Tell me again about when he called," Mike said as he pulled back onto the highway. He turned off the radio, which was spitting static as always in the mornings. "Maybe you'll come up with something better than 'Restaurant Hay.' Just try to remember."

"I've been trying, believe me. The connection was terrible; at least I couldn't hear a thing. He was surprised it was me—he thought it was you. He said I sounded a lot older."

"Well, we haven't heard from him in two years."

"He asked about Mom, probably he asked to talk to Mom. I thought since I couldn't hear him, the best thing to do was to tell him all I could, so I told him how she'd just left for Guatemala."

"What else did you tell him?"

"Oh, you know, how she got all fired up about Amigos. I said she was going to be giving used eyeglasses to people with bad eyes, and all that stuff. I told him they didn't have any telephones where she was going, so he couldn't call her

17

there. I told him she wouldn't be back until the end of August."

"But what about him? Nothing about what he's been doing? Just that he was calling from some place called 'Restaurant Hay'?"

"It only sounded like that. Mike, you wouldn't believe how hard it was to hear. It sounded like he was calling from Timbuktu."

"Come on now, you've looked over that map a hundred times. There isn't any town named that. You're going to have to try harder."

"Really, Mike, that's what it sounded like."

"Are you more sure of the 'restaurant' part or the 'hay' part?"

"The 'hay' part."

"He didn't mention the name of the state. . . ."

"Probably he did, but I didn't hear it."

"Did you ever ask him to repeat the name of the town or the state?"

Clay didn't answer.

"I just can't believe, after we hadn't heard from him for so long . . ."

Clay's stomach was in knots. Mike didn't understand, he'd had this same conversation with himself a hundred times already. If only—"Wait, Mike. I remember something else. Something about horses."

"Well, that's better. What was it all about?"

"That's all I can remember—something about horses."

"Say, that's a surprise. A guy who's been in rodeo half his life mentioning something about horses. But then again, it gives us something to go on. Every time we see somebody with a horse, we can show him one of those pictures in your pocket."

*   *   *

The foreman at the Bluewater mill told them Uncle Clay had taken off to do some uranium prospecting. "Your uncle didn't take to punching the clock and working for wages. He got himself that pack burro and started prospecting. Moved on pretty quick as I recall. He was heading for Moab, Utah. Lots of uranium discoveries up there."

Clay asked, "You're sure it was Moab?"

"He wasn't around long, but you're curious about what a man who's enjoyed some fame will do when he's out of the money. To tell you the truth, I don't think he knew what to do with himself. He was starting all over in life."

"On to Moab," Clay said cheerfully as he got back into the truck. "See, Mike? We're hot on his trail."

"Via Red River, New Mexico. Don't forget about that. What's the name of that band they keep talking about— Polly and the Wogs?"

"The Roadhogs."

"Say, Clay, did you hear the one about the horse that decided he was fed up with the same old menu out at the barn?"

"No . . . ," Clay replied suspiciously.

His brother had a huge satisfied smile on his face. "Well, he decided he'd go into town and treat himself at a fancy eatin' place. And what do you guess he ordered?"

"What?"

"Restaurant hay!"

The Studebaker's old motor wasn't hitting on all six cylinders. The truck felt like a bucking horse as they climbed into the mountains in the dark, into the pines and spruce trees and cool mountain air. One headlight was blinking in and out, but they made it to Red River, all excited because they'd been pushing for Red River most of the day and here they were.

Was she here too? Clay wondered. Was Marilyn here?

The Black Mountain Playhouse wasn't hard to find. The music had already started, and they could hear it coming from down by the river. Their momentum carried them right to the big hall made of enormous logs.

A dozen kids were waiting in line, but nobody could get in until some people inside left. "It's packed in there," Clay heard someone say. "It's because of KOMA. There's people here from all over."

They bought their tickets and waited in line. The band was playing good stuff, mostly right off the radio: "Big Girls Don't Cry," "Good Luck Charm," "Duke of Earl."

At last they were next and you could see into the dance floor. "These Roadhogs are pretty good," Mike was saying. "Hey, Clay Pigeon, there's just as many girls here as there are guys. Tonight I want to see you make your big move."

"Yeah, sure, Mike," Clay mumbled. He kept wondering if Marilyn might actually be inside.

"Okay," the guy taking tickets said. Mike went on in, and Clay looked in one hand and then the other for his ticket stub.

He checked again. Clay started to fish in his pockets when he realized what had happened to his ticket. He'd been chewing on it. He'd absentmindedly stuck it in his mouth and turned it into a wet ball, like a spitwad.

"Hey, get a move on," the guy behind him said, a guy with a greased-back ducktail.

"Really, I had one."

The ticket-taker acted like he was a giant pain but let him go over and buy another one, then let him in.

Mike was waiting just inside the dance. "What's been keeping you? Marilyn?"

Some things you just don't tell your brother. Like how could you tell him you got so excited you ate your ticket?

Mike was looking around, and then he just up and asked a girl to dance. A slow dance—"Stranger on the Shore."

20

Then a fast one with a different girl. Mike made it look so easy, but that was Mike.

To Clay's surprise he saw Mike thanking the girl after "Hey Baby" and coming back over. Mike didn't say anything, but it wasn't hard to tell he wasn't feeling as good as he'd been on his way to Red River now that he was here. Sheila? Clay wondered. He's missing Sheila?

Mike pointed out a girl and tried to make him go ask her to dance, but he wouldn't. Not that way, not with your big brother pushing you. And besides, as soon as he did they'd play a slow one, he was sure of it. Slow dancing was torture, plain and simple.

"I think I'll go play the pinball machines," he said.

Mike shrugged. "I'll see you around. I'm gonna go make a phone call."

Clay played the pinball machines a long time, but he wasn't any good. He couldn't concentrate. He kept watching the door. It was getting late. The dance had to be about over. The music was so loud and he felt so lonely.

When he glanced back, there she was. Marilyn. Standing just inside the door with her brother, looking out across the dance floor toward the bandstand. The Roadhogs were starting into "The Peppermint Twist." He could dance to that!

He fairly flew down the arcade and up to her and said, "Hi Marilyn." The surprise in her face was perfect. "You wanna dance?"

The music was so loud, she probably didn't even hear what he said, but she understood. In a second they were out there dancing. The Twist was so easy. You just make like you're putting out a cigarette on the floor. Lead with one leg, keep putting that cigarette out, keep your weight on that foot, then shift to the other one. Unlike with those slow dances, you never have to worry about stepping on her feet. You just keep drying the small of your back with that imaginary beach towel. Hips going all the time, forward, back, up, down . . .

21

hey, she was having a good time too, and her smile, well, she made you feel like the sun was shining on you alone.

"How did you—," she asked breathlessly when the music stopped. "Were you just coming here? That was way back in Arizona where we met you!"

"We heard about the dance on KOMA. My brother thought it'd be fun. He heard your father say you were going to Red River. We just took a chance."

She smiled. "Dad said your mother is in Guatemala for the summer. Is that true?"

"Sure is."

"What about your dad? Is he there too?"

"My father died a long time ago, in the Korean War."

"I'm sorry."

"Last dance," the band was saying, and the music began soft and slow as the lights went way down. Clay recognized the song—"Sealed with a Kiss." A slow one, way too slow! What was he going to do now!

She seemed to be waiting for him, and she was swaying a little with the music. Everyone else on the floor was starting to dance. It's now or never, he thought. His hands barely seemed to belong to him as one met her hand and the other closed behind the small of her back.

He would be safe if he barely shuffled his feet. He would get by. He thought he'd gone to heaven she was so pretty.

Clay rested his cheek in her hair. Tropical flowers. He'd never forget that scent. "I want to get your address," he whispered. "I'd like to write you about our trip."

"Sure," she said. "It would be fun to get a postcard from one of those places you mentioned."

Halfway through the song he brought her in closer and she held him tight in return. As the music was fading he glanced up and noticed, under the light by the door, her brother waiting and his brother smiling.

5

In Chama, New Mexico, in Durango, Colorado, and in Monticello, Utah, Mike phoned Sheila. Always he talked for a long time. Other towns along the way he'd tried, but he didn't always catch her at home. Clay was worried. How could Mike concentrate on a Big Wander in between phone calls? What was going on with Sheila? And another thing— how long would his brother's money hold out the way he was dishing out quarters? It felt like Mike was way out on a big rubber band that was about to snap him back maybe all the way to Seattle.

Finally the Studebaker backfired its way down into Moab, an oasis of bright green cottonwoods along the Colorado River. Clay's heart leaped at a glimpse of a man with whiskers and a straw hat leading a packed burro down the side of the wide main street. "Man with a burro!" Clay shouted. "It's him!"

Mike took a better look. "Too old. Uncle Clay's in his early forties, and that guy has to be in his sixties."

"But he might know him," Clay declared, and so they stopped to find out.

"Never heard of him but I can find him for you," the

man said. "Got a nose for what's lost, me and Pal both, that's the name of my friend here."

Clay was running a knuckle down the burro's gray muzzle from just below its eyes, ringed with white, to its nose, all white like the burro had stuck its face into a bag of flour. "Pal," Clay repeated.

"Likes you, I'd say," the old-timer said. "Try the insides of her ears."

Clay extended his forefinger and the burro's closest ear swiveled to meet it. "She sure has long ears."

"About three times as long as a horse's. Of course she can hear a lot better too. Her eyes, you'll notice, are set more to the side of her head—she can see all four feet as she's walking. The name's Hubcap Willie, what's yours?"

"Clay Lancaster, and this is my big brother Mike."

They shook hands, and Clay went to scratching Pal's other ear.

"You collect hubcaps," Mike said, indicating several that were sticking out of the pack, along with pots and pans.

"Sure do. Find 'em, sell 'em, anything I can get my hands on."

"You make a living doing that?" Mike looked skeptical.

"After a fashion. Hubcap Willie's been a lot of things in his life, and he's only gettin' started. Fought in the First War, owned a sheep ranch in Australia, flew for the Mexican Air Force, run cows, run whiskey, run a dude ranch, skinned cat, married seven times, owns a gold mine."

"How come he isn't mining it?" Clay asked.

"You mean, me?"

This was getting confusing. "You said 'he.' "

"Never said 'he.' Don't try to confuse me, boy. For one thing, his mine's in Mexico."

"There, you said it. You said 'his.' "

24

The old-timer scratched his head, then proceeded slowly. "Mined originally by the Indians, then by the Spanish with the Indians doing the dirty work, then by me."

"That's better," Clay said. "Now I know who we're talking about." Out of the corner of his eye he saw Mike smirking.

"Anyway, his third wife's people ran him off and it wouldn't be too healthy to go back."

You just did it again, Clay thought, but I won't mention it. "What's 'skinned cat'?"

"Drove a Caterpillar tractor in the woods—loggin' work. Don't know much, do you? Now, you boys would appreciate finding your uncle who is lost?"

"We didn't say he was lost," Mike said. "We just don't know where he is. He's the kind of guy who's always moved around a lot."

"What kind of work's he do?"

Mike shrugged. "Maybe prospecting, but who knows."

"Anything he does he's good at," Clay explained. "Uncle Clay could've been anything, that's what my mom says and she's his sister. He left home during the Great Depression when he was fourteen, the same age as me, and he did all kinds of jobs. Mostly ranch work. He always sent money home too. When he came back to Washington he worked on a salmon boat for a couple of years. He fought in the South Pacific near the end of the war, and after that he started following the rodeo circuit. Got to be a star—Clay Jenkins."

"Never heard of him. Learned rodeo in the army?" Willie asked with a grin, "or was it on the salmon boat?"

Clay liked this old guy. "He and my mom grew up on a ranch in eastern Washington—a little town called Starbuck."

"Never been there."

Clay handed the old-timer the most recent photograph,

the one with the burro. "Last we know of him he was prospecting for uranium."

Hubcap Willie studied the photograph a long time. "One of the Men Who Don't Fit In," he pronounced finally.

"We knew that," Mike said.

Now Hubcap Willie studied Mike awhile. "And you're a college boy."

Clay thought the old man was pretty sharp. "Mike's a whiz at math and science," he said proudly. "He's going to the California Institute of Technology in September. He might even be an astronaut."

Mike laughed, embarrassed to have his dream talked about.

"Wouldn't let them send me up in one of them tin cans," Hubcap Willie said gravely. "You know the first one to go up was a monkey."

The burro started braying.

"*Monkey*, Pal, not *donkey*."

"I thought you said she was a burro," Clay said.

Hubcap Willie eyed him suspiciously, as if he were confusing things again. "Same thing, burros and donkeys. Desert canaries. All the same animal."

"I'd go," Clay said.

"Go where?"

"Up in a rocket. To the moon."

"What for?"

"I dunno, just to go. To beat the Russians."

"Beat 'em to what?"

"I dunno," Clay said with a shrug. "Just so they don't get there first."

"So you haven't seen this man," Mike said, taking back the photograph.

"Not yet, but there's plenty of uranium prospectors in this country. Somebody will have seen him. Seek and ye shall find, College Boy."

"We've got all summer," Clay said.

"I wouldn't say that," Mike corrected him.

Clay couldn't believe what Mike had just said. It was supposed to be until they found Uncle Clay or their money ran out, whichever came first. And Mike had agreed they could work along the way to keep the money coming in, the way Uncle Clay had always done.

"Big brother here isn't as hot onto the project as little brother. Well, searches can take a considerable time. Hub-cap Willie himself searched six years for his mine before he found it. But we'll see what we can do."

As Mike fired up the Studebaker, he said, "We don't need him."

"I kind of like him—and his burro."

"I think our friend's got a pound of shrapnel in his head, probably from the combat he saw in the Mexican Air Force."

At the Moab uranium mill across the muddy Colorado, a brawny fellow with a handlebar mustache remembered Uncle Clay. With a hearty laugh he said, "Uranium prospector? Not hardly. I remember a card game where he staked his Geiger counter and lost it, then said he didn't care to be digging around anyway for something that might end up in a bomb. He wasn't in town for any more than two or three weeks as I recall, before he took off."

"Took off for where?" Clay asked.

"I just can't tell you," the foreman said. "But word was he was seen in Mexican Hat a month later, leading his burro down the road."

Clay's heart jumped. He'd told Marilyn his uncle could be in Mexican Hat, and he was only making it up! "But what happened to his truck?" he asked the foreman. "He had a fancy truck with a bucking Brahma bull painted on the side."

27

"Funny thing—he practically gave it away here in Moab. Sold it for maybe half of what it was worth. Sold it to a kid in town who was a local hotshot in rodeo and was just starting to compete on the circuit. I'll tell you, that was one happy kid. I remember your uncle saying he was so tired of the road, he'd be happy to stick to where a burro would take him. Imagine how many hundreds of thousands of miles that man drove and how many towns he passed through in his life. I guess I'd be sick of the road too."

"Thanks," Clay said. "Thanks a lot. We'll try Mexican Hat."

"Uncle Clay could be out of the country by now," Mike said as they climbed back into the Studebaker. "He could be in Canada for all we know."

They drove up into Arches National Monument to take a look around. Mike said he needed to do some thinking and wandered off by himself. Clay took off in another direction. He'd always wanted to find some petrified wood and so he started watching the ground closely. He liked this redrock country. Everywhere you looked, domes and arches and buttes and fins and canyons, with the Colorado River cutting right through it all. It reminded him of Monument Valley, where some of his favorite Westerns were filmed. He didn't know where Monument Valley was but he sure wanted to go there some day.

A distinctive triangular shape caught his eye, lying on the sandy soil held by the occasional scrubby trees, piñon pines and junipers. Not an arrowhead. He knew a shark's tooth when he saw one and this was a shark's tooth, only it was made of a stone.

Back at the truck, Mike admired the shark's tooth only a moment. He was too preoccupied to appreciate it properly. As they drove back to Moab to look for a campground Mike didn't even speak.

The only place to camp turned out to be right next to

Hubcap Willie. Mike circled the whole campground but every other spot was taken. "That's all right," Clay said. "He won't bother us."

"That desert canary better not start singing in the middle of the night."

In the evening Clay wandered over and showed Hubcap Willie what he'd found.

"Sure enough shark's tooth," Hubcap Willie agreed. "Petrified. Trade you for it."

Clay wondered how much it might be worth. There was no telling. "Like what?"

"A fifty-six Chevy and a fifty-four Buick."

The tooth was rarer than he'd thought. Lucky day! Two cars for one fossil. He and Mike could sell both of the cars, or keep one and sell one and the truck. . . .

The old-timer fetched two hubcaps from his collection. "They're beauties."

"Oh," Clay said quietly. "No, thanks, I don't think I'll trade." He took to scratching the burro's ears. The burro sure was on the pudgy side, he noticed. Must be a big eater.

"I'll go three, but that's the best I can do."

"I kinda want to keep it." He was already thinking of who he wanted to give it to.

"Say, Pal takes a shine to you, I can see that. Of course she'd run with anybody that'd scratch the insides of her ears."

Clay fed the burro a peppermint off his palm. "Pretty good," laughed Hubcap Willie, displaying the stub of a finger on his own left hand. Clay liked the burro's huge brown eyes, the fat white belly and legs, and the thin, dark stripe that led all the way down her spine from the bristly mane to the paintbrush of a tail. "Kind of a funny marking," he said aloud.

"Sure enough. Every donkey's got it, all the way back to the one that carried Mary into Bethlehem, or so the story goes. The cross of Bethlehem, they call it. Shows up really good on a gray burro like Pal. Long piece down the spine, cross member across the shoulders."

"I might like to have a burro some day. Like my uncle."

"Your uncle's no fool. A burro can carry as heavy or heavier'n a horse, did you know that?"

"Really?"

"No question. More endurance, more alert to danger, more surefooted even than a mule, and only a camel can tolerate thirst better than the burro."

"Is it hard to pack her?"

"Not once you know how. There's an art to packing right, that's for sure. You don't want an animal to be rubbed raw, even if a burro does have a tougher hide than a horse, which is why the flies don't bother 'em nearly as bad. And the load has to be perfectly balanced."

"We're going to Mexican Hat tomorrow—where my uncle went."

"In that case, I wonder if you and your brother wouldn't mind giving us a lift down there tomorrow."

"We don't have a trailer."

"Don't matter. Done it plenty of times with a pickup."

6

"The air's so dry out here, my fingertips are cracking open," Mike was saying. "Never seen anything like it."

"Mine aren't," Clay said.

"I guess that makes you a desert rat. You like the heat too, I guess."

"I don't mind it. That's what deserts are supposed to have. The good part is how it cools off every night. Every morning you're starting over."

"Yeah, the nights are okay."

Mike's nose was peeling pretty bad too, but Clay wasn't going to point it out. His brother sure burned easily with his sandy hair and fair skin. And new freckles were showing up on his forearms.

Clay took a look over his shoulder through the cab window into the bed of the pickup. Every time he glanced back it still seemed strange to see somebody there, but Hubcap Willie and the burro sure made a picture. The burro's knees were folded underneath and those long ears were standing straight up and alert. Her huge eyes, those delicate eyelashes, and that expression around her mouth and whiskers seemed to say, "I sure put up with a lot."

That brushy switch of a tail was beating a rhythm almost like Pal was counting the time of this latest trial in her life.

It hadn't been as easy to get the burro into the truck as Hubcap Willie had indicated, and Mike hadn't made it any easier saying with his eyes "I told you so" a half-dozen times at least, and then saying it out of the corner of his mouth for good measure. But now that they were rolling, if "rolling" could describe the motion of their bucking horse of a truck, you'd have to agree that hauling a load this colorful sure seemed like the kind of thing to be doing on a Big Wander. Well, Mike wouldn't agree, but that's because he was just being disagreeable this morning.

They asked around about his uncle in Mexican Hat, a tiny town perched by a suspension bridge over the San Juan River where it narrowed and entered a canyon. Upstream, lots of cottonwoods; downstream, all slickrock. At the store, the café, the gas station, nobody had ever laid eyes on the man in the photograph with the chipped tooth and the three-day beard.

Nobody here wore sombreros after all, Clay noticed. They wore cowboy hats, some straw and some felt like the Stetson his uncle favored. He'd like to get one of those himself, black with that deep middle crease.

Mexican Hat, it turned out, was named after a formation balanced high above the river on a skinny rock pedestal. He'd seen it himself on the way into town but had thought it looked exactly like a flying saucer. He hadn't mentioned the resemblance to Mike because Mike was stewing, and Mike kind of let you know when he wasn't in the mood to be jollied up with commentary like "Flying Saucer, Utah, would have made an even better postmark." Clay had seen plenty of weird town names as he scoured the map for Restaurant Hay. Truth or Consequences, New Mexico, struck him as one of the weirdest.

They were back on the road and still carrying that unusual pair of hitchhikers in the back. It was awful quiet in the cab. Back at Mexican Hat, the old-timer said he'd be pleased to ride with them just a little farther. Mike couldn't refuse him, but now he was even grouchier than before. Mike finally broke the silence, grumbling, "He said all he wanted was a ride to Mexican Hat."

A flat tire fit right into the way things were going. As Mike leaned all his weight into the tire iron, Clay reported, "We're almost back into Arizona." Mike didn't have a hat on. His forehead was burning up and dropping sweat into his eyes. "Lemme help," Clay suggested.

"Lug nuts are too tight," his brother grunted, meaning "too tight for you, but not for me," which may have been the case, but maybe not. Clay was tall, nearly as tall as Mike, and almost as strong. He could see drops of blood squeezing out of a couple of Mike's dried-out fingers. Mentioning it wouldn't change anything. Sometimes Mike just liked to suffer. Feeling worse made him feel better.

"Lucky you've gotten this far with this truck," Willie chimed in from the back of the pickup as he hovered over Pal, ready to keep the burro from standing up.

For once Mike saw things the old-timer's way. "We've got a dead dog for a motor. We might have a better chance of getting back home with your burro."

"Want to swap?" Clay suggested playfully. Then, looking around at the tall buttes and slender towers of red sandstone showing up in the desert ahead, he mused, "It feels like I've been here before."

He surveyed again the expanses of red desert studded with stranded buttes and mesas, pinnacles, towers of solid rock. "I know I've been here before," Clay said aloud, "but that can't be."

"Nope," Mike grunted, lifting the spare onto the bolts, "can't be."

"Monument Valley!" Clay declared. "It's Monument Valley."

"Last time anybody checked," Hubcap Willie agreed.

"Oh, man! *Stagecoach, Fort Apache, She Wore a Yellow Ribbon, The Searchers* . . . John Wayne country!"

"Maybe you'll get into a movie," Mike groused. He pitched the flat tire onto the burro's pack boxes and turned to inspecting his fingertips again. Clay climbed back in the cab. He wished Mike didn't feel so bad.

"No clues," Mike said as they got under way again. He was biting on his bottom lip, and that was never a good sign.

"How do you mean?"

"Uncle Clay. No leads, and you haven't located Restaurant Hay. So what are we doing out here in the middle of nowhere?"

"Just looking around I guess. Somebody will have seen him. Maybe in Monument Valley. Can you believe this! It's even more spectacular than in the movies!"

"We'll ask in Monument Valley. But you know, he really *could* be in Canada. I'm not sure you're being very realistic."

"But we have to try, Mike. We'll find him. I know we will."

"Our money's not holding out too good, you know."

"Mine is. I've got one hundred and seventy-six dollars. I could start paying for the gas—why don't you let me?"

"Yeah, and that's your life savings. I doubt if Mom would be too happy about you spending it all. And I should be making some money this summer, not spending it, even if I do have a scholarship."

"We could get jobs. Work for a while, travel for a while . . ."

Mike was working his lower lip again, even pulling on his left earlobe, the one their mother always said he was going to pull off as he was solving his most difficult math problems. "We don't know much, Clay. Maybe that wasn't even right, about him being seen in Mexican Hat."

"Sounded right to me."

"I mean, what's he to us, really. Why are we even looking for him."

Clay couldn't believe Mike had said something like that. His breath caught in his throat. Suddenly he felt like he had a fever.

"Now don't get upset," Mike said. "I want you to think about it. Let's look at the facts. How often does he call or write?"

"You know Mom says that doesn't mean anything. He just doesn't like to write letters. He's not that kind of person."

"What kind of person is he? Do we even know? Look, Clay, I don't think you see him the way he really is. How could you? You haven't even seen him since you were eleven."

"I was twelve. He took me out salmon fishing three days straight. I spent a lot of time with him—at least I used to."

"It's because you're named after him, isn't it?" Mike said. "That's what it's all about. You've built him into this larger-than-life—"

"That's not true," Clay interrupted. Why was Mike doing this? What good was it going to do?

"Maybe he's more of a misfit than a hero. Just because he was a rodeo star. . . . You know he never made much money."

"Money isn't everything. He *is* something special, Mike. I've always known it. Mom knows it. You used to."

"What I'm talking about is you and your heroes. John Wayne, for example. Life isn't a Western, Clay, with good guys and bad guys."

"Isn't it?"

"Maybe when you're fourteen."

"Yeah, well I'll be fifteen in December. And I like Westerns just as much because of the adventure, and the places—like Monument Valley here."

"Maybe it's because you can't remember our father. Uncle Clay isn't our father, you know. He's not even like him."

Clay's head swam. What was Mike getting at? "I've tried to remember him. How could I? I was only three when he got killed."

"He's your original hero. Shot down trying to cover some foot soldiers in a war . . ."

"I know all that. You've got people you look up to too, Mike, like President Kennedy and the astronauts—Alan Shepard, John Glenn, Gus Grissom . . . you think our father was a hero. I know you do. So what are you saying?"

"Oh, I don't know, Clay. It seemed like I had a point there somewhere. I think you're fine. I don't think you're . . . well, you're just kind of starry-eyed I guess, but that's all right. We didn't grow up like everybody else, that's all, with both a mother and a father. . . ."

Clay broke into a grin. He didn't know why, but he felt better than he thought he might, the way things were going. "For being so smart you can be kinda dumb yourself, Mike. Sure I'd like to have a father, but I wasn't going to nominate Mom's brother."

"Maybe you're right. Maybe it's a good idea to have heroes. Like President Kennedy, like John Wayne . . ."

"Like Marilyn Monroe," Clay said, and laughed. It felt good to be laughing.

Clay lingered at one of the many empty tables in the dining room at Goulding's Trading Post and looked out the windows and across to Monument Valley. The late light was bathing the monuments in a glowing golden aura like the world was ending. He was writing a letter to his mother.

There was only Mrs. Whitmore to clean up all the mess the tourists had left behind, and he sure felt sorry for her. She had a long way to go. "Mind if I write a few letters here?" he asked. About his mother's age, Mrs. Whitmore wore her hair tied back under a blue bandanna. "Sure," she told him. "Make yourself at home."

He could see Hubcap Willie down by the big cottonwood where Mike had parked the truck. The old-timer had a little campfire going down there, probably was cooking supper. The burro was standing by waiting for whatever came next.

Clay was telling his mother about the trading post, how different it was from the tourist traps on Route 66. How it must be a hundred years old, built out of rocks shaped one at a time into blocks—you could still see the chisel marks in them. How the ceilings were made out of logs crisscrossed by hundreds of sticks, how this very room he was writing in was where the casts of the John Ford Westerns ate their dinner every night while they were shooting the movies.

> The walls of this dining room are covered with photographs from the movies they filmed here. I'm writing under the eyes of John Wayne and Henry Fonda and Indian chiefs. I'm seeing some Navajos around the trading post. They don't look like Indians in the movies— no feathers! The men wear the same kind of stuff as Uncle Clay—it's the women who are really striking. Full skirts, long-sleeved blouses of shiny green or blue velvet, silver and turquoise jewelry all over—rings, bracelets, silver squash blossom necklaces . . ."

He set aside his pen. It didn't feel right to be writing letters when this woman was working all by herself. He was going to write to Marilyn next and send along the shark's tooth, but he could do that in the morning.

37

"Thanks," Mrs. Whitmore said, "I could really use the help."

He bused the dishes while she loaded the dishwasher and cleaned up in the kitchen. He'd cleaned the tables and had that letter started for Marilyn when Mrs. Whitmore came out of the kitchen offering a bowl of ice cream topped with chocolate sauce. "Never heard of a kid who didn't like ice cream," she said, and sat down across from him.

Like her husband in the trading post store, Mrs. Whitmore didn't know anything about Uncle Clay. "So you're going to travel and work your way around the West," she said, after he'd told her his whole story. She paused and said, "How'd you like to work for a while right here? We're shorthanded."

"At the trading post?"

"Right here in the dining room. Three meals a day. I already know you'll do a good job."

Clay took another look around the walls, at the photographs. Right here in this room! "What about my brother?" he asked quickly.

"We need a hand at the gas station. Fifty cents an hour for you, a dollar him. Not much, but room and board won't cost you anything."

He found Mike at the truck, gathering up their bedrolls and ground cloth. To Clay's surprise Hubcap Willie was lying down inside the cab. "I was listening to the radio and cleaning up the bed of the truck," Mike said. "He just kind of moved in to the cab. He said it was the closest thing to a bed he'd seen in a long time."

"You're going to let him sleep in there tonight? Inside the truck?"

"Yeah, I guess. He'll turn off the radio after a little while—he said he wouldn't run the battery down."

Clay smirked but he didn't say anything. His brother wasn't such a tough guy after all.

There weren't many good sleeping spots. They found one about a hundred yards away under some box elder trees and away from the glare of the trading post's night-light. Clay thought he'd kept his big news to himself about as long as he could, and spilled it. Mike wasn't as excited as he should have been. "Well, I can see you're all fired up about staying here," he said slowly, and he thought about it a long while.

"I'll try it a few days," Mike concluded guardedly. "Make back a few bucks."

Clay woke with the first desert light. He liked the time between first light and sunrise, and besides, he was too excited to go back to sleep.

A coyote trotting by with its long tail hung low stopped to look at him, cocked its head as if to wonder at him being up so early, and trotted off among the yuccas. The first streams of the sun were lighting up the monuments of Monument Valley, and the towers looked more orange than red in that early light.

Mike would sleep awhile. Clay dressed quietly and slipped away, down to the cottonwood at the edge of the arroyo where they'd left the truck and Hubcap Willie. Pal always seemed to be on her feet, and he'd been wondering if burros slept lying down or standing up. Maybe he'd find out.

It took a moment for Clay to realize as the cottonwood tree came into sight that something was missing. The burro was still there, tied to the tree and standing up. It was the rusty Studebaker that was gone. Their backpacks and their other things lay heaped in a pile, but the pickup was gone.

Hubcap Willie had left behind, for them apparently,

every bit of his gear that went with the burro. Clay found the note on Pal's pack saddle:

Dear Boys,

Hubcap Willie decided to take you up on your offer and has hereby swapped his faithful burro Pal and all of Pal's gear for your Studebaker which is ailing. Hubcap is sure you boys have got the better of the bargain but will not complain. You'll have need of hoofs to find your uncle if he really is a prospector, and Hubcap Willie will have need of wheels where he's headed. Your search for your lost uncle has reminded him of a loved one who lives far away that he has not seen for many years. Don't be concerned that you have sold an old man a bum motor because he is a crack mechanic among other things and knows his way around a wrecking yard. Be good to Pal and she will be good to you, and by all means never strike her for she is a noble soul.

Truly,
"Hubcap"

P.S. This is hereby considered a lawful bill of sale.

Clay looked around to share his amazement with someone, but there was only the burro switching her tail and looking at him with those huge, liquid brown eyes. The burro wrinkled her nose, bared her teeth, and began to bray like a lonesome freight.

"Hee-haw to you too, Pal," Clay said, and ran back with the note in his hand to tell his brother.

40

7

Clay waited anxiously as Mike read the note from Hubcap Willie. His brother almost seemed relieved when he finished it. Mike looked up and said, "Let's go home, Clay. Let's just go home."

"But Mike," Clay shot back, "that's not a legal bill of sale. We can show it to the police. They can stop him and we can get the truck back. Let's hurry!"

Mike was shaking his head. "It's about to break down anyway. Let Hubcap Willie buy the oil and keep it running. He says he's a crack mechanic."

"But—"

"C'mon, Clay, you said we'd swap him the truck for the burro. It's a perfect joke on us, it'll make a great story. Anyway, I'd rather go back on the train. I was thinking, we can take a bus down to Route sixty-six and then catch the train at Flagstaff. Don't you think that would be great, riding up high in that Vista Cruiser with all the windows? Great views . . ."

"What about Uncle Clay?"

"We've got absolutely nothing to go on."

"What about our jobs? What about Monument Valley?

Mike, it's only the twenty-second of June! We've only been gone a couple of weeks!"

"Two of the longest weeks of my life, I'm afraid. . . ."

Here it comes, Clay thought. *Sheila. Don't say it, Mike.*

"I miss Sheila something awful, Clay."

He knew Mike was looking at him, but Clay kept his eyes on the ground. "I thought you broke up with her."

"You know I've been talking to her. We talked again last night, a long time."

Clay hesitated. "Are you going to get married?"

Mike laughed. "Not anytime soon, I hope. We both want to go to college first. Look, I just need to get home and get back to normal, get my job back at the station or somewhere else, and start seeing her again."

He couldn't look at his brother. Probably Mike would get married a lot sooner than he said. It was too awful to think about. The next thing you knew, his brother would have kids and Mike would be somebody else and not very much his brother. It was happening right this moment— his brother was changing and leaving and it had always been the two of them.

Mike took him by the shoulders and said with a little laugh, "It's going to happen to you someday too, mark my words. Some Marilyn will come along—"

Clay laughed, but he was fighting to keep his eyes dry.

"Tell you what, Clay. Let's stay around here for a few days at least, so you can see Monument Valley and get your fill of busing dishes."

But he didn't get his fill of busing dishes. How could you, with those scenes from the movies all around you as you worked? Indians all lined up on a ridge with their battle lances, a cavalry column marching through Monument Valley, and all the while the eyes of John Wayne following you around the room . . .

Outdoors on your own time, how could you ever get your fill of Monument Valley itself or get tired of living right under those sheer red walls hundreds and hundreds of feet high? He liked everything about the place: the red soil, the twisted junipers, the prickly pear cactus, hawks sailing, ravens thrashing the air with their ragged wings. . . . He liked visiting that burro down under the cottonwood, and he liked the way Pal would snort and shake her head with her ears flapping. The ears were always going, like radar dishes swiveling around.

He bought a bale of hay for the burro, carried buckets of clean water. He talked to her and scratched her ears and thought about how strange and a little wonderful it was if even for a few days to have a burro just like his uncle had a burro.

Clay went through the gear Hubcap Willie had left behind. Mike had no interest in it, but Clay liked it because it spoke of the faraway places. Tins with traces of oats, flour, cornmeal, and rice, a couple of two-quart canteens, pots and pans and utensils, a saddle blanket, pack boxes, a tarp, even a harmonica with a fancy engraving of a steam train under the words "The Midnight Flyer."

He liked to wander among the formations early when it was cool and when the light felt rare and golden. On his third morning walk, he could sense that he was running out of time. Mike was itching to go home.

Clay was walking down a sand dune when it came to him, the inspiration, fully formed and perfect. *No reason to go home just because Mike is.* . . . He even tried it aloud. "No reason to go home just because Mike is!"

When he got to the bottom of the dune, he looked back up at it and at the sheer red cliffs behind. A smile came to his face. It had to be the exact spot from the scene in *The Searchers!* He could almost see Natalie Wood running down the dune toward him with the cruel Comanche named Scar in pursuit. But the thought of taking on Scar didn't seem as appealing as pulling Marilyn Monroe out of the river.

He walked on, deep in thought. His inspiration grew into an idea and then a plan as he pictured being on his own, out here in this country he'd always dreamed about. There'd be nothing much for him at home, nothing new and different certainly. Mike would be with Sheila all the time anyway. He'd be alone in the house all summer, with Mom gone and all. In the fall Mike would be off to college. It was time he started thinking for himself and finding his own way.

"What do you say we head back tomorrow," Mike said one evening as soon as he got back from the gas station.

Clay had been preparing himself for this moment. Not like he was telling and not like he was asking either, Clay answered, "I've been thinking I've got the best summer job I could ever ask for. It's like a summer job and scout camp combined. I don't want to leave, Mike."

Mike was awfully surprised at first. "You mean, just leave you behind all by yourself?"

"That's right," Clay answered. "I'll be okay. I'll do fine."

"I'm supposed to be looking out for you," Mike said. "What would Mom think? I don't know, Clay. . . ."

"Mom would let me," Clay answered, trying his best to sound convincing. "I'm going to be fifteen in December. And besides, I'm not out here alone. The people at the trading post will keep an eye on me."

They talked into the night. Clay could see the tide was turning for him. Mike was beginning to picture it!

Finally Mike said, "I think you're right. I think there's at least a good chance Mom would go along with this, if she could see what a good setup you have here, how nice these people are. It's a great opportunity for you, and she's always been a soft touch where you're concerned."

44

That cinched it! "Probably you'll get homesick after a week or two anyway," Mike added. "Then you can take the bus down to the train, same as I'm doing."

In the morning, shaking hands with his brother, Clay knew this was the biggest day of his life. He couldn't keep a few tears out of his eyes. "I know this means a lot to you, Clay," Mike was saying. "I think it's going to be a good experience for you to be on your own. But seriously, take care of yourself. Don't make me regret this."

"I won't," Clay said. "Thanks, Mike. Thanks again."

"Oh yeah, and when you leave, be sure to trade the burro and the gear for as much cash as you can get."

Then his brother was getting on the bus, waving, and then sitting by the window waving as the bus pulled out. Clay was waving too and fighting back tears. He swallowed hard and watched the bus until it gradually merged with the desert's horizon and finally blinked out. His brother was gone.

Those first few days he wasn't so sure he could make it without Mike, or if he wanted to. At home, days could go by with his brother hardly even being around, but that was different. In the truck they'd been thick as thieves, and now there were thousands of miles between them and not even a trace left behind to show they'd even been on the road together.

He'd never been this far away from home, that was for sure. As he calculated that Mike must be nearing Seattle he could picture himself hopping on a bus and heading back too. Maybe Mike was right, that's what he'd do. And Guatemala seemed even farther away than it had before. Maybe he would head back home. Even if he wouldn't see much of Mike, it would be good to have him close by.

But Clay held on into the fourth day and the fifth and the sixth. He kept badgering himself to keep believing he could stay on here by himself. Maybe it was stubbornness that kept him going. He didn't want his brother to think he couldn't make it on his own.

When he felt lonely he thought of Uncle Clay leaving home at fourteen. Uncle Clay must have felt lonely too. Even when Uncle Clay got older he still felt lonely—you could see it in his eyes when he'd come to visit now and again. But you could see as well in his grin and in the way those eyes would shine as he spoke of the mountains and the deserts, that he knew life was lived best as an adventure, and he wouldn't trade his wandering, lonely way of life for any other.

Even in the clatter and commotion of mealtimes, with thirty or forty tourists all chattering at once, he'd keep glancing at the photos on the walls and lose himself in those big empty places. I still think Uncle Clay is out there, he kept telling himself. He's not in Canada. He's *out there*.

Right on Mr. Whitmore's cash register in the trading post, he posted the photograph of his uncle with the notice underneath: HAVE YOU SEEN THIS MAN? IF SO, CONTACT CLAY IN THE DINING ROOM.

A few tourists just wanted to know who the man with the burro was and all, but nobody had seen him.

With each day that he stayed Clay felt himself growing stronger. Maybe he wouldn't hop on that bus anytime soon. Maybe he could stay the whole summer as he'd thought. Maybe he would, and maybe he should.

He'd always been a hiker. When his days off came he took Pal out on long hikes through Monument Valley. No pack, just the halter and lead rope. He discovered that Pal didn't take kindly to being led; she'd plant her front feet and make you tow her like a ship on dry land. But if you walked alongside she liked it just fine. She wants to feel like we're in this together, Clay thought. More of a partner.

Clay wrote letters: to his mother, to Mike, to Marilyn. Marilyn was becoming more important to him all the time.

46

He found he could tell her things the way he wouldn't tell them to anyone else. He could let her know his heart, his innermost feelings. Well, not everything, but the way he felt about the desert, the red cliffs, the sunsets. And he was beginning to explain how he felt about her too. "Write me care of Goulding's Trading Post," he wrote. "I'm really looking forward to hearing from you and finding out what you thought of that shark's tooth. I've been thinking maybe a jeweler could drill a tiny hole in it and hang it on a delicate gold chain. Then you could wear it around your neck."

Along about the ninth of July, he got a new offer from Mrs. Whitmore. Would he like to go over and help out at the other, smaller trading post at Oljeto twelve miles to the west, where they needed him even more? For a week at least and maybe longer if he liked it? "It's around the back side of the mesa," she explained. "A few tourists wander through now and then, but it's the real thing, strictly trading with the Navajos. You'll be doing some of everything as opposed to just working in the dining hall here. You could learn a lot from old Weston, maybe even ride the horses."

Clay thought about it. He thought hard. It was fun being around the tourists and all the activity, but working at a remote trading post, that would be something to tell Mike about and Marilyn too. "Can I take my burro?" he asked Mrs. Whitmore.

"I don't see why not."

She found him an old Navajo man to teach him how to pack Pal right. Clay couldn't tell if Charlie Dilatsi didn't speak English or just didn't talk, but he watched closely as Charlie cinched Pal's forward and back belly cinches and adjusted the neck strap and the tail strap. When the pack boxes were packed—"panniers," Hubcap Willie had called them—the Navajo tarped Pal's load and secured it with a diamond hitch, which Clay more or less remembered from scouts.

When he was all ready he mailed a postcard to Mike, telling him he'd be over at the other trading post where there was no phone and not to worry. He could still send mail. Clay bought himself a new pair of jeans, a long-sleeved plaid shirt, and a black Stetson that he immediately creased down the middle. He looked over the cowboy boots but Mr. Whitmore said he'd probably be more comfortable in his own broken-in hiking boots. "One more thing," Clay said, and picked himself out a fancy silk neckerchief, a blue one.

"Well, you sure enough favor him," Mr. Whitmore said, with a nod to indicate the photo on the cash register.

Clay peeled loose his uncle's photograph and stuck it in his pocket. "I surely hope to," he said. He paid his money and walked out onto the porch. He felt like a new man.

All that was left to do was fill his canteens and tie his backpack to Pal's load. When he'd done that he clucked, "C'mon, Pal," and steered down the dirt road that skirts the cliffs of the big island in the sky that lay between Goulding's and Oljeto. Clay looked back, hoping there was someone to wave to. Charlie Dilatsi gave him a tiny wave, and now he could see Mrs. Whitmore up there by the dining hall waving vigorously under her blue bandanna.

It seemed as if Pal and he had been together for years. The burro seemed content to take up once more the job she was born for, and Clay spent the day feeling exactly like his uncle and picturing Uncle Clay approaching from the distance, leading his burro. He wouldn't say anything; he wouldn't shout, "It's me, Uncle Clay!" He'd let the realization come slowly into his uncle's eyes and watch that trademark grin light up his uncle's face.

A man and his wife who'd wandered away from Goulding's slowed their sedan, then stopped and asked if they could take his picture. "Don't mind a bit," he said cordially, and when they took his picture he realized it was a Polaroid camera they were using. "Could I have one of those pictures?" he asked on the spur of the moment. For Marilyn! was his next thought. This is going to be perfect!

The couple was so pleased to oblige they stopped the car and got out, and as the man tore back the cover sheet Clay was able to see himself and the burro materializing right before his eyes. Just as they took the second picture, he wished he'd been tipping his hat. That would have made it even more perfect. He knew what he'd write for Marilyn on the border at the bottom of the picture: "The Lonesome Trail."

Crumbling stone buildings gave Oljeto Trading Post the appearance of a ruin. Clay liked how it was tucked against the cliffs and commanded a view out to the west as big as the country. You looked out across the broad flats of Oljeto Wash to buttes and high mesas with open sky between them, and towering over everything, the dark sloping mass of a mountain rising high and alone into the sky like a breaching whale.

Two sheep were browsing among hulks of old cars and trucks, rusted-out cookstoves and heaps of tires. Chickens were pecking along the margin of a little garden fenced with wire, poles, and rusted bedsprings. A few of them were starting into the open gravel in front of the trading post. The leaders paused as if for cover at the base of an old-fashioned gas pump, the kind with the skinny glass top Clay liked because you could actually see the gasoline and the bright-colored balls that swirled around and around with the gas moving through.

Clay paused before walking up closer and looked back across Oljeto Wash once again. At the foot of the mesa, surely, that was one of the Navajos' homes called hogans.

49

From this distance it looked simply like a mound of red earth.

"If this place isn't the real thing," Clay said to himself, "then the real thing doesn't exist. No billboards and baby rattlers out here, Mike."

He heard a sudden sound something like a burst of air through a tire valve, and just as quickly those chickens ran flapping and squawking back toward the garden. Clay looked up from one especially indignant hen with a stain of brown juice on her feathers, and saw for the first time an old man rocking back and forth behind the shade line on the porch.

8

Weston could spit prodigiously. Clay came to think that the old man had developed spitting into an art form. A thin old man under a straw hat with more veins on one face than Clay had ever seen, Weston spent most of the day rocking and chewing out on the porch. Every so often on the forward stroke he would spit tobacco juice in the direction of the mesa, "Hoskininni Mesa" he called it. Sometimes it seemed Weston might be trying for the mesa itself, and Clay chuckled thinking maybe he'd hit it a few times in his younger days.

Whether or not Weston had two names Clay never found out. Weston's daughter and son-in-law normally ran the place, but they had gone somewhere and Weston was minding the store more or less.

Clay settled into the chores around the place. He brought in the eggs in the mornings, tended the garden, fed the two sorrel horses, swept the store and the porch, cleaned the bathroom, cooked eggs and hamburgers for him and Weston, made change for the Navajos. Right away he posted his uncle's photograph with the caption HAVE YOU SEEN THIS MAN? on the glass countertop where people couldn't miss it.

Weston did all the dealing when it came to the Navajos' pawn. The people would come to the trading post to have their jewelry set aside for a line of credit so they could buy groceries, cloth, and hard goods, everything from nails to shovels. It seemed an awful shame to see the Navajo women take the rings right off their fingers and give them up across the counter. Even their silver squash blossom necklaces.

The good thing about Weston, you could pester him with questions and he'd never tire of elaborating on an answer. Also he'd say yes in one form or another to any question you asked him, which seemed unusual and interesting.

Maybe Weston just liked having someone around to talk to, Clay decided. The Navajos spoke barely enough English to trade, and the trader seemed to speak no Navajo at all. Quite a bit of the bartering was carried on with fingers raised for numbers. "Do they ever get their pawn back?" Clay asked.

"Of course. You can't sell it off within the time limit you agreed on, or they'd never do business with you again. If they pay what they owe by the time it's due they get their jewelry back. If not, it's gone, usually over to Goulding's."

Clay loved to ask questions about the area, especially about where the Navajos lived. "Is Hoskininni Mesa named after a person?"

"Sure is. He was the chief whose band hid out during the 1860s in that country out there—" Weston spat toward the mountain Clay had thought of as a rising whale, hitting an old galvanized bucket which gave off a convincing ring. "Kit Carson, you ever hear of him?"

"Sure."

"Kit Carson scoured the reservation at the head of the U.S. Cavalry, rounded up the Navajos, and made 'em walk to Fort Sumner, New Mexico, hundreds of miles away for most. 'The Long Walk,' they still call it today. Destroyed

52

their cornfields and killed their stock and cut down their peach trees. Starved 'em out. Anyway, Hoskininni's band hid out in this remote country between here and Navajo Mountain and managed to live free during the years the Diné were in exile. 'Diné' is what they call themselves—it means 'the People.' ' "

"I never knew any of that."

"Yessir. As for Kit Carson, he wouldn't talk of that campaign in his later days, so the story goes."

"They should make a movie of the true story of Kit Carson and the Navajos and Hoskininni. It sounds better than anything you could make up."

The trader spat. "Well, they should. You know, these Navajos have dressed up to play Apaches, Cheyenne, Comanches, you name it—everything but themselves."

"What does 'Oljeto' mean, Weston?"

" 'Moonlight on Water,' I heard once."

"Where's the water?"

"Where you find it, I guess."

"Do you speak any Navajo, Weston?"

"Too lazy. Heard it's as different from our language as Chinese. That about scared me off."

"You know, I always wanted to know how to ride a horse."

"Like your uncle you were telling me all about."

"I'd never be that good, I just want to be able to ride. He and my mom grew up on horseback, she always says. I never got a chance, living in Seattle. So what I was wondering, could I ride those horses over there? Would you teach me how to saddle 'em and ride 'em and everything?"

"Naturally."

"I've got a pair of cowboy boots picked out in the store. Would you take them out of my wages?"

"Prices are high way out here. Forty-nine bucks. You'll have to stay around a while to work those off."

Forty-nine dollars! Clay thought to himself. That's over half what Mike paid for the truck!

Still, he wanted those boots.

He rode a couple hours a day, around the buttes and across the arroyos and onto the mesas, wishing his uncle could see him like this, tugging on his Stetson and riding with the rhythm of that big animal underneath him. At first he'd beaten his behind raw going against the motion of the horse, but the soreness was passing now. Where a horse couldn't take him Clay scrambled on his feet. He climbed up and into three of the ruins of the Ancient Ones, the cliff dwellers Weston said had lived here long, long before the Navajos.

He wouldn't have a complaint in the world if only he'd get a letter from Marilyn. Every day he was more sure than the last he'd get a letter or two or three forwarded from Goulding's as Mrs. Whitmore had promised.

Finally a letter came, but it was from Mike. Anyway it was a fat one. All full of expectation, Clay settled into the other rocker on the porch and broke the seal. Even if it wasn't from Marilyn, somebody out there knew he was alive.

Inside he found two letters, one from Mike and one from his mother. He read hers as fast as he could. It described all about her long automobile trip through Mexico with the other volunteers on the way to Guatemala, and it was mailed before she even got to Guatemala. "Maybe you won't even hear from me once I'm in the interior. I'll try to get mail out but the mail is notoriously slow from Latin America to the States. Take care, you guys. Make me proud."

You'd be proud of me, Mom, Clay thought. If you could only see me now!

Mike had nothing new to say. "Guess you like it out there. Nothing much going on here, same old stuff." Then it got more interesting when Mike talked about the old truck. He said how much he'd enjoyed the trip in the Studebaker, all their crazy adventures, and especially all the time they'd had to be together.

Dummy! Clay wanted to shout. We could have had all summer together!

Nothing at all about Sheila, Clay noticed, folding the letter and putting it away. But then, Mike never really told him much about her.

It sure was exciting to get mail.

"Mind if I try some chewing tobacco?" he asked Weston.

"Up to you."

With his eyes on Hoskininni Mesa, he chewed and rocked. The mesa helped get his mind off the sweet foul taste of the tobacco, especially if he kept his eyes right on that hogan at the base of the cliffs over there.

He was doing all right until he made the mistake of burping. Some of the wad slid straight down to his stomach. It wasn't long coming back up, along with breakfast. He felt sick to his stomach for the next twenty-four hours.

"I'm cured for life before I even started," he told Weston the next day.

"Yessir," the old man said. "Nasty habit."

He wrote to his brother and mother and Marilyn all about Oljeto, trading with the Navajos, learning to ride horses and all, but he left out about the chewing tobacco.

He'd been at Oljeto long enough for his earnings to pay off a boot and a half when an old Navajo couple came in early one evening and bought some groceries, mostly canned goods. The old man wore his gray hair tied up behind his head in white cotton string like his wife's. Their dark faces and hands were deeply lined, from years out in the weather, Clay guessed. Other than that he wouldn't have long remembered them; they spoke little to each other and not at all to him until they were just about leaving. The old woman had come back up to the counter to get some hard candy when her head kind of dropped down toward the countertop and all he could see was the neat way she had her hair tied up. Next thing, she'd called her husband back in and the pair of them erupted in a lively exchange. That's when Clay saw the old woman pointing to Uncle Clay's face in the picture.

Clay looked again. Her finger went from Uncle Clay's face to her own front tooth, which she now tapped a couple of times before returning her finger to the countertop and Uncle Clay's face.

"You've seen this man?" Clay asked incredulously. "That's my uncle—that's right, he's got a chipped tooth! Did you see him? Where'd you see him?"

"Yes," the old man said, happy to agree.

Weston had come inside to see what the commotion was all about. "Weston, they saw him!"

The old couple was nodding agreeably. Clay shouted, "They've seen my uncle! Find out where, when!"

The Navajos were looking from him to Weston and back, ready to be helpful if only they knew how. "They don't speak English," Weston explained.

"They said 'yes'!"

"That'll be about it. I know these people."

"Horses," the old woman said helpfully. "Horses."

"Horses!" Clay declared. "Something about horses!"

"Paiute," her husband added helpfully.

"Paiutes! That's an Indian tribe—I've heard of them. Paiute horses. My uncle must be riding Paiute horses. . . ."

The old people couldn't keep this up. They would smile apologetically and look at the floor, and then look away. Almost like they'd been cornered and had to get free, they turned and went. Clay tried to hold on to them. He ran after them keeping up a stream of questions as they stepped briskly now for their old truck. His manner only seemed to hasten their departure. He couldn't believe it, but he had to watch their truck disappear in the dust.

Clay looked back to Weston still standing on the porch. Weston hadn't seemed to be of much use at all. "You let them go!" Clay cried, all exasperated. "They know about my uncle! They've seen my uncle!"

"Now that's really something," Weston said, settling back in his rocking chair.

"You know these people? You know where they came from?"

"Why sure. Pull up a seat and I'll tell you all about it. Their name's Yazzie. They don't trade as much here as they do over at Navajo Mountain Trading Post, but I see 'em from time to time. Their grandson about your age speaks good English, and so does his dad. Too bad they weren't with the old people today."

"She said 'horses.' What did she mean?"

"She seemed to connect your uncle and horses. . . . Maybe they knew about him being in the rodeo. Can't say. But I can tell you what they meant by 'Paiute.' They were telling you where they saw him—at Paiute Creek. That's these people's sheep camp where their family spends the summer. They weren't leaving you high and dry. They wouldn't have said 'Paiute' just to say where they're from, because they know full well I already know that. They told you where they knew your uncle from, I'm sure of it."

"Then he's there now!"

"Could be, or else he passed through there some time ago."

"He's there now! Why else would they mention it! And 'horses'—maybe he has a horse now instead of only the burro. Maybe that's what they meant. So where is it, their sheep camp?"

"A little over halfway between here and Navajo Mountain. As the raven flies, maybe thirty miles."

57

"Can I call right now? Go over to Goulding's and call? I could talk to that boy who speaks English, or his father."

Weston laughed out loud. "That'll be the day. Not only is this the Navajo Reservation we're talking about, it's the most remote part of the reservation. Call 'em up—that's a good one."

"How close can I get on a road?"

"About right here. A couple miles closer if you went way clear around to Navajo Mountain Trading Post. I'm not sure you get the picture, son. That country's too rugged for roads—it's all up-and-down and every-which-way. People around here call all that country 'the Back of Beyond.' Nobody even lives out there year-round, only in summer. Sure makes me wonder what your uncle's doing out there. . . . Every decade or two a white man will drift in there looking for Hoskininni's lost silver mine, the one they call Pish-la-ki."

"Maybe he's found their silver and they're . . . hostile."

"*Hostile!* On the warpath you mean? That's another good one!"

"Well, where's the closest phone to their camp?"

"Navajo Mountain Trading Post."

"Then that must be where my uncle called me and my brother from, back when he called us in Seattle. But it doesn't sound anything like 'Restaurant Hay.' "

"Come again?"

"That's all right. Never mind. How long would it take me to get to Paiute Creek . . . to the sheep camp . . . if I walked and led the burro. . . . I'm a good hiker."

"You're thinking so fast your brain's going to burn up. I rode a horse, led a packhorse from here all the way to Navajo Mountain when I wasn't much older than you. . . . I suppose it would take you three or four days on foot."

"I could do it! I can read maps and all that—couldn't I do it?"

58

"I imagine you could, but doing it alone's the risky part. Nobody to help if you get into any trouble, you know what I'm talking about? What if you slipped and fell or something?"

"But you did it yourself—you've crossed through there, other people have crossed through there alone. My uncle did."

"True enough," Weston said, his gaze drifting off toward the canyons. "True enough. And I could help you get ready. Now why don't we think about something else for a while here, like fixing something to eat? We can work on this tomorrow."

It had gotten late by the time they finished supper. Looming to the west in the twilight, Navajo Mountain beckoned. Clay couldn't sleep. How could he with so many plans to make. Nothing could stop him now, he could see that. Weston would help him, he said he would.

He would have to make a plan, a way for Weston to know he had made it safely. When he got to the trading post at Navajo Mountain he could call back over to Goulding's. They could get word to Weston that he was okay. He thought about how much time to allow. If they didn't hear from him in eight days, he decided, that's when someone should come looking for him. From what Weston had said, eight days would give him time to find his uncle and to ride on in to the trading post, plenty of time. It would work out perfect.

He'd buy another two-quart canteen and that would make three. He'd take the backpack along in case the burro went lame or something. In the empty backpack he had his scout survival kit. He'd buy all the supplies he needed right here in the trading post, he'd pack that burro and throw the slickest diamond hitch this country has ever seen.

Mike, he thought. Do I tell Mike? Maybe I should go

to Goulding's in the morning, maybe I should go tonight and be there at the phone in the morning to catch him before he goes to work. I can tell him I know where Uncle Clay is and tell him to get back out here and join me.

But he won't. He won't leave Sheila, he wouldn't come all the way back out here. And then he wouldn't like the idea of me taking off by myself. Better not to tell him. If I wait I'll be able to call him from Navajo Mountain Trading Post, say hello, and then put Uncle Clay on the line. That's the way to do it. I wish I could see the look on his face!

But I can tell Marilyn. I can tell her everything.

He wrote into the night. Finally his weariness caught up with him and he brought his letter to a close:

> In a few days I'll find my uncle. It's going to be a great moment when I come walking into that sheep camp. Please write me directly at Navajo Mountain Trading Post, Navajo Mountain, Arizona. I can't imagine what's happened to your other letters—I've been wondering if you received my picture alongside Pal. I'm going to ask Weston to forward my mail to Navajo Mountain as soon as anything arrives. I'll be thinking of you. Do you know that song, "Cast Your Fate to the Wind"? Think of me out there in the Back of Beyond, Marilyn. I'll be thinking of you. The Big Wander continues!
>
> Lovingly,
> Clay

9

Clay woke with a start, wakened out of his fitful sleep when the back of his mind told him he wasn't just dreaming about monsters, that one was actually right next to him in the dark breathing down his neck with a wheeze and a rattle and a roar. He had no idea where he was or what was happening. It was pitch-black and something very large and not human and very much alive was right there next to him. He tore his way out of his sleeping bag, and seeing the dim form of a doorway in the darkness he scrambled for it, remembering that he was alone in the wilderness and had gone to sleep inside a long-deserted hogan.

Outside, he didn't go far. A sudden pain in his foot stopped him and reminded him he was barefoot. In the light of the crescent moon he could make out that some small something had attached itself to his foot. A cactus.

He turned around to look at the hogan's doorway and saw the silhouette of a burro's face and long ears looking out at him. "Oh, it's only you, Pal," he said into the night. "Good grief. Don't scare me like that."

He'd forgotten he even had a burro, or left her on a rope long enough so she could come inside. Well, now he knew they sometimes do sleep lying down. Clay laughed at himself out loud, but the sound of his own voice being extinguished by the darkness and evoking no reply hardly reassured him. He shivered all the way through his spine. Was it the desert's night air or his own fear? He'd never felt like this when he was out with Mike.

Mike. His brother had no idea he was out here. "You'll be safe here," he remembered his brother saying when he agreed to let him stay behind at Goulding's. "Don't make me regret this."

The burro came outside the hogan and Clay ducked back in and fumbled for his flashlight. Carefully he pulled the cactus segment free of his toe. Now it was stuck to his finger. He shook it loose and it stuck to one of the poles in the hogan's cribwork roof.

Clay got back in the mummy bag and zipped it all the way up. He could turn back, he considered. It had taken so long to get packed he'd only made it around the north end of Hoskininni Mesa. He could be back at Oljeto by afternoon. He could go back to work there or even back at Goulding's, and have word sent somehow to his uncle to come visit him.

What would Weston think about him quitting? The old man had even worked on Pal's feet, which hadn't made the burro happy. Weston hadn't been sure Pal's shoes would stay on, and he said there'd be a world of bare sandstone to cross. . . .

He tried his belly, his side, his back. His wadded-up jacket felt more like a stone than a pillow.

The night air in the desert had a bite to it. Still, the cold didn't compare with the North Cascades, or even the damp woods along the coast. He had to smile thinking about all those freezing nights when he was out with Mike in the old days. Mike had told him that he'd heard you slept a lot warmer in a sleeping bag if you slept with no clothes on at all. It was hard to follow, but Mike had some explanation for the science of it. So he'd followed Mike's lead, and he'd shivered all night long—for years. He never slept at all unless in fits. It was Mike who eventually experimented with sleeping with his clothes on, and suddenly the old science was overthrown.

For a long time after that, Clay remembered, he'd slept in every layer he had until he was so bulky he couldn't roll over, until he was so warm he thought he'd roast.

Pish-la-ki, Clay thought. The name popped into his head like a magic word. Abra-ca-dabra, pish-la-ki. The lost silver mine of none other than the legendary Hoskininni. He could picture his uncle digging with a pick deep inside the mine, working only at night and by the feeble light of a headlamp. Uncle Clay might do that; treasure would appeal to him. Or perhaps the silver was already melted into bullion, and Uncle Clay had discovered its hiding place, and the Navajos have caught him with all those silver bars. Weston had laughed, but the Navajos might not think it was so funny. Maybe they had him locked up in a cage in their sheep camp . . . but then why would the old Navajos have drawn attention to his picture at Oljeto . . . that still didn't explain about horses or Restaurant Hay. . . .

Clay had almost drifted off to sleep when he heard the scampering of little feet on the dry leaves that had blown into the hogan. His flashlight revealed a cactus mouse with its outsized hind legs hopping around the dusty floor. He ushered it outside and was almost asleep again when sudden barks shattered the stillness not far away at all. He bolted upright. It wasn't but a second until the barks became yips and the yipping shifted into quavering sirens climbing higher and higher in pitch, as maybe a half-dozen coyotes harmonized like a band of lunatics and brought the hair rising on the back of his neck. Barks, yips, howls, and then only the quavering sirens wailing in the night, reminding him just how alone he was and how little he knew.

As suddenly as it had begun, their singing ended. Clay reassured himself that the coyotes wouldn't come after him. It was a good thing they thought he was so powerful. He wasn't going to tell them any different.

Almost asleep again, he thought he heard a faint whimpering outside. No, he thought, lifting his head. Just my imagination.

But as soon as he put his head back down he heard it again. This time louder, at the doorway.

A patch of white. A little ball of white. Clay flicked his flashlight on, and its beam fell on a tiny dog trembling and wanting to come in. A tiny curly-haired white dog with brown ears and brown patches over his eyes like question marks. "Come on in, little guy," he said reassuringly. "Did those coyotes scare you too? You can come in."

The little dog came in with his head almost on the ground and wagging his long tail hopefully.

Clay went to the door. No sign of any people, just the night and the stars. "Where did you come from, little guy? Did someone leave you alone out here?"

Clay stayed up talking to the dog and petting him, and listening to his whistling breath as the dog fell happily asleep. "Curly," Clay said aloud. "I'll call him Curly." He fell asleep with the dog's paw on his hand, and he woke a few hours later looking into the dog's bright black eyes, alert and friendly. Curly's tail was beating out a rhythm on the dusty floor.

He mixed up some powdered milk and made pancakes, plenty of pancakes with canned peaches he diced and added to the batter just for the occasion. Mike would have been impressed. Curly liked the pancakes just fine and ate like he was starving, which he probably was.

Pal came over and joined in, ate two or three before Clay sent her back to browsing for her own breakfast. After grazing on the sort of brush that made Clay's mouth hurt just watching, the portly burro came back over and gingerly removed and chewed up the label from the peach can. Any sort of paper she considered a delicacy.

Clay oriented his map with the biggest landmark around, the broad forested dome of Navajo Mountain rising to the west. "You just joined the Big Wander," Clay told Curly. "Lucky for you, you found me. Lucky for me I found you. You may not believe this, but I was thinking about turning tail."

The dog lay down, ran his tongue up and across his rubbery black upper lip, and placed his two front paws barely on the map.

"What do you think, Curly? Across the head of Copper Canyon—doesn't look too steep—up and through the gap between No Man's Mesa and Nakai Mesa, down into Nakai Canyon, up onto Paiute Mesa, and down into Paiute Creek to find the sheep camp. That's how Weston said to go. And that's where we meet up with Uncle Clay. Big black hat, on horseback or leading a burro. Chipped tooth . . . no, not the burro, the man. You ought to have a conversation with Hubcap Willie if you think I'm confusing. Hubcap was an old desert rat I met. Maybe that's what I'm turning into, a desert rat. What do you say, Curly? We can do it!"

The little dog barked sharply in reply.

"That's it, Curly. You and me, pardner."

10

Half an hour down the bare slopes into upper Copper Canyon, Pal's load shifted and pitched over on one side. A few more steps, and one pannier ended up practically underneath the burro. Clay's empty backpack was dragging the ground.

The burro was looking at him with undisguised disdain.

"Sorry Pal," Clay apologized. "I thought I had those belly cinches tight. I'll never do it again."

There was nothing to do but unpack and start over, and it wasn't much fun. As early as it was, the day was scorching already. Being pinned in one spot sure didn't help.

A minute after they'd started up again, Pal lay down. She was obviously having second thoughts about this expedition.

It took some mighty pulling to bring her to her feet.

A little ways farther, she lay down again.

Clay looked for something to hit her with, to make her get back up, when he remembered, "Never strike her for she is a noble soul."

"Rise, noble donkey!" Clay commanded, pulling with all his strength on the halter and lead rope. "Help me, Curly!"

The dog's high-pitched barking did seem to help. As Pal rose to her feet, the burro's lustrous eyes and droll mouth seemed to say, "Sure you know what you're doing?"

Clay pressed into the barrenlands hoping the day would produce a rain shower, but it hadn't rained since he arrived at Monument Valley and this day was starting out like all the others with the sky nothing but blue. And he'd started on the last of his two-quart canteens already. Back in Oljeto he'd thought a gallon and a half was plenty of water. In the Cascades he and Mike had carried only a quart each.

"This isn't the Cascades," he observed aloud, surveying the gravelly redlands around him and the slickrock monuments scattered here and there to the north and back to the east. "And this isn't the movies either. We'd better find some water. Nobody's going to come looking for us for seven more days."

It felt like the moisture was being sucked out of him by the minute. Now that he'd started thinking about being thirsty, his throat felt more and more parched. In the wide wastes of Copper Canyon, Clay found no water along the bottoms of the gullies. Thank goodness for my long sleeves and my hat and my trousers, he thought. You wouldn't have a chance out here without them.

"We could stand to find water anytime now, guys," he told his companions.

He wandered ahead into the heat of midday until he knew he didn't have any choice, he had to get out of the sun. At last he found a bit of an outcrop with just enough shade for him and the dog.

Clay crouched there all afternoon, moving by fractions of inches with the small piece of shade, and watched the moon set. Too bad the moon's not up in the evenings and brighter, he thought. I should be traveling when it's cool. Curly had his tongue out and was panting heavily. It was alarming to see how steadily the beads of water dropped

67

from his tongue. The burro stood in the open with eyelids at half-mast.

When he started up again in the late afternoon, Clay thought he'd try saving Curly all those thousands of steps, and set him in the little hollow in the tarp atop Pal's load. Curly could see the advantages right away. He never even thought about jumping off.

Clay walked on as the late light erased the midday glare and brought out the true and vivid colors of Copper Canyon: blue-green, gray-blue, purple even, with a brilliant scarlet red glowing in the highest formations. "Vermilion" he'd once heard that shade of red called. He passed through the gap between No Man's Mesa and Nakai Mesa and started down into Nakai Canyon in the dusk, searching the bottoms of the gullies for water. The July day held on and the dusk lingered, but he found no water. The canyon was dry.

When darkness all but caught him he had to quit the search. "Dry camp," he announced to his companions. "The good part is, we're almost halfway to Paiute Creek. We're making good time."

Clay lifted Curly down from the burro. Faster than Clay could even register on what was happening and reach for the lead rope, Pal took off clattering down the canyon.

"No!" Clay yelled after the burro. "Pal, no, what are you doing?"

He was so angry at the burro. He scrambled after her as fast as he could. Panic ripped him as he realized how fast Pal was disappearing into the night. Pal had everything! The last bit of water, all the food, the map, the survival kit inside the backpack—everything.

"Pal!" he called as he ran. "Pal, come back!" He was running blindly toward the sound of her hoofs. Suddenly, his shin struck a rock and he was lying in pain on the hard, dry creek bottom.

It took long minutes before the pain would clear. That ball of white was licking his face. "I just hope I haven't broken my leg," he told the dog. "What if I've broken my leg?"

He was breathing hard and shaking through and through. He thought of his brother, but he'd put himself beyond Mike's help and beyond all help.

He knew the night couldn't be this cold. He was going to scare himself to death. "Calm down," he told himself. "Just calm down."

At last he could try the leg. It was going to be okay.

I'm still in bad trouble, he thought. Why'd you get so angry? Why'd you act so stupid? Settle down. Don't panic and do something even worse. What were you doing running around in the dark?

Think about the morning. Think about what you're going to do if you can't find the burro. How long can you last without water?

He sat back down and the dog nestled into his lap.

You're going to have to find water, Clay told himself. Where can you find it for sure? Think of the map. You studied it enough you should know it by heart.

The San Juan River. All these canyons between Oljeto and Navajo Mountain flow north into the San Juan River, on its way to join the Colorado River. The San Juan's the river you and Mike crossed upstream on that suspension bridge at Mexican Hat.

If only Hubcap Willie had got off at Mexican Hat the way he was supposed to, he never would have ended up taking the truck. None of this would have happened.

Why didn't I just go home with Mike?

What if I can't find the burro?

Clay had all night to try to fight back his fear, to regret and shiver and think. If the days are long the nights have to be short, he kept telling himself. I'll drink my fill at the river, then head back for Oljeto when the sun's starting down. Jog in the dusk, go slowly by starlight if possible. Jog through dawn into the morning.

He couldn't sleep for shivering, and he couldn't talk the fear out of his bones. The night went on and on and on.

At first light Clay started moving down the bottom of the canyon. At least he was moving. He scanned the slopes on the sides so he wouldn't pass by Pal accidentally.

All slickrock, the canyon bottom showed no hoofprints. He could only hope Pal had come this way, hadn't somehow doubled back. At any rate he was closing some of the distance between himself and the San Juan River before the sun started broiling again. Why hadn't he thought more about how hot it would be? It had all seemed so simple back in Oljeto.

He stopped to look at a curious structure on the left-hand side, a stairway of sorts leading from the canyon bottom up to the first ledge. It was made of piled-up rocks and a couple of bleached juniper logs. It hadn't been used in some time, but he thought it must have been built for burros or mules or horses.

He walked briskly now. He had to get to the river as soon as he could. How many miles?

Down the canyon, droppings. A pile of droppings on the slickrock. Pal droppings, fresh ones! A pile of dung never looked so beautiful.

At first he thought he'd heard a raven, but he listened again. A frog croaking, wasn't it? The brown question marks above Curly's eyes rose as he listened also, to the intermittent and eerily amplified croaking of a single frog. Clay broke into a run. Two bends down the canyon he spied a long line of greenery on the left side, about man-high on a ledge. Grasses and ferns grew above the water-stained slickrock. "Water!" he yelled to Curly.

The seam dripped water all along that ledge. He could drink it one drop at a time if he had to. Along the canyon's slickrock floor it didn't run deep enough that you could collect it.

Still running, he turned a corner and found his burro, fully packed, standing beside a pothole the size of a bathtub with water flowing in and out of it. Pal was browsing on a patch of grass that grew in a sandy spot, and she had a long red wildflower between her lips. Her tail was switching and her long ears swiveling. Those lustrous brown eyes and white eyebrows seemed to be saying, "Welcome to paradise. Where have you been?"

Clay grabbed her lead rope, then threw himself down on the slickrock and began to drink. Looking into the pothole, he could see diving beetles, the kind with one oar on either side. They were stroking their way down toward the bottom. Pal's face was reflected in the water—a beautiful sight. He felt so thankful. The water sure tasted good. Curly was lapping away right next to him.

Clay took an extra wrap on that lead rope as he stood up. From here on out he would never let it go unless Pal was tied or hobbled. He began to scratch the insides of the burro's ears the way she liked. "So you lost confidence in me, is that what happened? Well thanks for finding the water, Pal."

He found an alcove for the heat of the day, a room-size shady spot under a roof of stone. He unpacked the burro and opened some Vienna sausages, broke out some crackers. "Turn back or go ahead?" he asked the dog. Then he spread out the map again. He already knew the answer.

11

It was starting to cloud up, and Clay was free to come out into the open. He began to think he might be able to climb out of Nakai Canyon this day. He returned to the spring and drank again, then filled his canteens. Barely breaking the surface, Pal put her lips to the water and drank. Clay had never seen such a dainty drinker. "Let's take a bath before we go," he told his companions.

"Mighty nice," he said, settling into the cool water. "All the comforts of home." He inspected the shin with the bad bruise. It was sure enough ugly, but the swelling was going down.

Curly came close, and Clay reached out for him. The tiny dog's nails dug for traction on the rock. "Come on in, Curly. Hey, you hardly weigh anything. C'mon, you could use a cool-down."

He placed Curly in a shallow spot like a shelf in the tub. Curly stood still, wet up to his neck, and the brown patches above his eyes seemed to be asking forlornly, "Why are you doing this to me?" Clay scratched him behind his ears and along his back, then lifted him back onto the slickrock. With his white fur plastered against his sides and his tail so long and skinny, he looked more like a rat than anything. Clay couldn't help laughing. "I guessed you were some kind of a poodle-cross. Now I know, what with!"

It wasn't hard to see he'd robbed the little dog's self-respect, and as soon as Curly was done shaking himself out, Clay apologized. It took some coaxing but at last the dog came to the edge of the pool and give Clay's face a few licks. The heat of the desert quickly restored his curls and his dignity.

In an hour's time Clay was standing once again at the horse ladder he'd discovered in the morning. Scanning the cliffs, he traced a route up through the ledges and onto Paiute Mesa. He hauled rocks and stacked them to make the ramp passable once again. Before he started up he thought to fold up his map and stick it in his shirt pocket along with his compass. Clay fished his survival kit out of the backpack and stuck it in his other shirt pocket. "Just in case," he said aloud. After he'd slung one of his canteens around his neck, he was ready. "And Curly, I don't think you should ride until we get to the top. I don't want you to slide off—there's a lot of cliffs up there."

Pal scaled the horse ladder without hesitation and it was a marvelous thing to see. Then the burro began clawing her way up through the ledges with the confidence of a mountain goat.

Here and there they paused to rest. The clouds were boiling up right out of the turquoise sky, monumentally tall, and were starting to turn dark. "They might mean business," Clay said. "I'm glad we aren't way down there on the bottom of the canyon."

Thunder began to rumble inside the clouds and the wind began to blow. After all the relentlessly hot days he'd seen since he first came to Monument Valley, it was pleasant to feel the wind on his cheek and to listen to thunder, to enjoy shade out in the open and watch the clouds begin to spill rain in tall columns. Even if the rain did separate into streamers and dry up before it hit the ground, it made a welcome sight and he'd take dry rain any day he could get it.

When at last Clay reached the top and the flat expanse of Paiute Mesa, he was pleased to find it grassy and sprinkled with piñon pines and junipers. Closer than ever, Navajo Mountain commanded a good piece of the sky, close enough he could make out individual trees along its skyline. Tall timber grew up there, and he could see why: the rain up there was falling wet instead of dry.

Pal deserved all the grazing she wanted, and it looked for now like she intended to eat up the whole mesa top. He fastened her hobbles exactly the way Weston had shown him, and let her graze. She couldn't go far. Then he threw himself down on the rimrock and took a good rest with Curly by his side.

I'm getting close now, he thought. All I have to do is cross the mesa and drop into Paiute Creek. I'm a long way from Seattle, that's for sure, and practically shouting distance from Uncle Clay. "Make me proud," his mother had written. That's exactly what I'm going to do, he thought.

When he woke from his nap the sun was dropping low and casting glory all around. On the far side of Nakai Canyon and tucked under the rimrock, a golden two-room ruin of the Ancient Ones caught his eye. In the eastern sky, like colossal Portuguese-men-of-war, boiling white and black thunderheads trailed streamers of evaporating rain lit up in pinks and oranges and reds, golds and lavenders and violets. Shafts of light pierced the lowest layers and illuminated the domes and towers of the redlands below. The mesas were glowing vividly purple.

The whole world seemed to drop off in front of him. He could see in the distance the shadow-casting buttes of Monument Valley and far, far beyond, a dark mountain range to the southeast. To the northeast the San Juan River ran in a winding green strip toward Mexican Hat. Set back from the river above a bulwark of tall cliffs, a forested plateau rose above the canyon of the San Juan and pitched up to mountains so high that a patch of snow still lingered above timberline.

All of it glowing and shifting and changing in a bath of colors—no two moments were the same and each, it seemed, would make a memory for a lifetime. This is why I've come, he thought. More than anything else, this is why.

If only I had someone to share it with.

Under way, walking into the evening, he let his mind drift. Pal stopped to graze where she found it to her liking and Clay didn't care to hurry her along, although he did keep a death grip on her lead rope. He was thinking of all the things he had saved up to tell Marilyn the next time he wrote. As he walked into the gathering dusk he could almost see her. Well, he couldn't remember her face exactly, only her hair. In fact he couldn't remember her face at all and that bothered him. If he tried harder it would come back.

Suddenly though, he recalled her perfume. He could smell those intoxicating flowers as vividly as if she were walking alongside him. It was easy to picture himself taking her in his arms. As he walked alongside the burro, he saw himself doing just that. He would take her in his arms and then he would kiss her. How perfect everything would be if Marilyn were with him right now.

A great horned owl hooted in the moonlight two, three, four times, and then after a pause, four times again. Clay asked the little dog, riding the pack and bobbing at eye-level alongside, "What's he saying, Curly? You can almost make it out. There, I've got it. 'You, you-oo, you, you . . . Love you, you-oo, you, you.' "

He found himself crossing slickrock terraces rolling like ocean waves. Before long the slickrock was cratered with deep potholes, and in the deeper ones he found several feet of standing water. Not far away stood an old shelter made of poles and roofed with tree branches. A sheep camp! Surely, a sign of the main camp! He must be getting close!

Next to the shelter Clay found a small corral made of poles and he dragged Pal in there, very much against her wishes. Then he cooked up a big can of pork and beans and fried up some biscuits. Tomorrow would be the day! After supper he visited the corral and Pal swiveled one ear forward, then the other to have them scratched. While he scratched an ear, Clay was trying to pick out a tune on the Midnight Flyer—"Cast Your Fate to the Wind."

Evidently Pal didn't think the performance up to her standards. Hubcap Willie had probably been a virtuoso harmonica player "among other things." The burro took Clay's neckerchief by her teeth and took a step back. Clay felt himself losing his balance and took the harmonica in his mouth, bracing himself with both hands against the fence. He was eyeball-to-eyeball with Pal, and he thought he saw a glint in the burro's eye. "Okay, Pal," he said, the words turning into notes through the harmonica, "you can turn me loose now."

The burro tugged a degree harder, and for the longest time Clay was suspended there, with one leg back in the air for balance like a ballet dancer. Finally Pal tugged a fraction more, and Clay felt the corral giving, and then giving way altogether as he fell down in a clatter of falling poles. The whole side of the corral was on the ground. "Okay, Pal, you win," he said, as he dusted himself off. "Let's not keep you in here tonight after all."

* * *

76

Bound for Paiute Creek in the morning, Clay could feel his strength and his confidence in his muscles and his bones. It felt like he was taking ten-foot strides.

At the bottom of the creek he was faced with a decision. Turn up the canyon toward the plateau where it originated, or turn down the canyon toward the San Juan? Weston hadn't known where exactly to find the camp; he hadn't been in Paiute Creek for over fifty years.

To the river, Clay decided at last. The sheep must need water. The creekbed was dry. So where could you water sheep better than at a river?

The canyon soon widened out to a half mile or more, and here and there the water popped up from underground and flowed awhile on the streambed before disappearing in the gravels again. He sighted four hogans up ahead in the sandy flats below the cliffs and his heart began to drum wildly. For some reason he started singing "The Loco-Motion." That didn't seem right after a minute, and so he switched to "The Man Who Shot Liberty Valance."

Unfortunately the hogans were abandoned, and seemingly long ago. A shade-break no longer provided shade, and a few logs on the ground in a ring barely resembled a corral.

He could hear the river before he could see it, and he knew he must be approaching the sheep camp and the big moment with Uncle Clay.

Every step brought him closer to . . . disappointment, as it turned out. No sheep camp, no uncle, only a boulder field where the canyon dumped into the river, and the rapid roaring where the river spilled over the boulders.

"Well, guys," Clay announced. "Nobody here. Stick with me, Wrong Turn Lancaster."

He tied Pal up to a driftwood log, then unpacked her. Close to the river would be a good place to camp for the night. When he was done with the work, he stripped and walked out onto the sand beach. His toes felt good in the sand. Then he waded out into the river and swam with powerful strokes, playing in the sandy brown San Juan like an otter. Curly was barking all the while on the beach. "Perfect temperature!" Clay shouted. "Come on in, Curly!"

As Clay pulled on his clothes it occurred to him that there just might be fish in those sandy waters. Catfish maybe. "Fresh dinner tonight!" he shouted. "I'm a pretty good fisherman," he confided to the dog and the burro. "Well, not *pretty* good, I mean *awfully* good. You should see the salmon and steelhead I've caught in my day.

"You may be wondering where I've been keeping my fishing pole. Well, an ace fisherman like me doesn't need one. I'm pretty handy with a hand line, and I just happen to have some fifteen-pound-test, hooks, and sinkers in my survival kit right here in my pocket.

"I'm sure you won't mind waiting a few minutes, Pal, while I catch us some supper. No comment? I bet you can't even hear me over that rapid. We're not talking about a can of beans, guys, we're talking about fresh fish. Doesn't that sound good?"

The dog seemed enthusiastic but the burro was baffled.

"Come to think of it, Pal, you don't look like a big fish eater."

From his supplies Clay broke out a long, rock-hard hunk of wine-soaked salami and sawed off a piece. It was his mother's ceremonial gift to him and Mike, for their big trip, as she left for Guatemala. She'd presented them with one as they set out on backpack trips for as long as he could remember, and they'd always joked over who was going to have to carry the thing, it was so heavy. "Bait," he explained to Curly, and sawed off a second hunk for himself, a third for Curly. "Don't want to eat too much of this stuff, now—you might get drunk on it."

For a long time Clay waited on the alert for a strike, but as the tall canyon walls started to provide shade, he thought he deserved a nap and he lay down on the beach. He thought it might be fun—he'd never tried it before—to tie the line off to a big toe, and then just make himself comfortable and doze off, letting his big toe warn him if the salami found any takers. He was thinking about what a great fisherman his uncle was, and what a strong swimmer too. They were fishing from a canoe once out at Goose Lake when his uncle suddenly stripped down to his skivvies. "What're you doing?" he'd asked his uncle.

"I want to see if I can nab that big turtle over there basking on that log," Uncle Clay had said.

"How come?"

"I just thought it might be interesting."

"You won't get within fifty feet before he slides into the water, and they're great swimmers. You know how they are."

"I know," his uncle had said as he lowered himself over the side of the canoe. "That's what'll make it interesting."

Clay started to doze off. The sand sure felt good. He hadn't known his body was so sore. The roar of the rapid seemed so restful as his memory drifted him back to Goose Lake. He could remember his uncle swimming so slowly toward that log, with only his nostrils stuck up into the air like a turtle himself, he'd begun to wonder if Uncle Clay had a chance. Maybe he'd get within thirty feet. . . . And now he pictured his uncle submerging with fifty feet anyway yet to swim before the log, and then he didn't surface for what seemed too long a time, until finally Uncle Clay burst out of the water like a dolphin with arms. The turtle splashed into the water out of his reach and then Uncle Clay kicked and dived after it. He stayed under until he surfaced with a victory cry and held up that big turtle with both hands. The way that shout exploded from his lungs, you could have heard it from clear across the lake. . . .

It was late afternoon when the alarm on his toe—something tugging hard—brought him out of a dream, a sweet dream in which Marilyn was trying on his Stetson just for fun. What a combination the black hat made with her blond hair. For a second as he woke up, he could almost remember her face but then it slipped away.

Anyway he had a fish on the line and there's nothing in the world quite like having a fish on the line. There's a current running through the line that connects you in that moment to everything that's beautiful and mysterious and wonderful. In this case the current was running into him through his toe.

Clay took the line in his hand and gave it a couple of wraps. No time now to free his toe—he had a *big* fish on. Up and down the beach and out onto a sandbar he fought it, trying his best to ignore the fact that he had a piece of fishing line connecting his hand and his toe.

Working the fish up and down the sandbar, he was having a hard time trying to stay on his feet. That piece of line kept tripping him up, and twice he fell down in the water. But he'd seen the prize: a big silvery fish almost like a salmon, but with a smaller head and the fins different. Once he was onto a big fish, there was nothing in the world but him and the fish and victory or defeat. Clay could feel the world blurring away at the edges. There was only him and the fish in all the world and the current of the world was running through him.

Behind him, Curly was barking. Curly must be pretty excited about the fish too, Clay thought. Pal was snorting loudly. Even Pal was inspired by the battle. It isn't easy to give and retrieve line when your hand is the fishing reel and the line's cramping your palm and cutting your fingers.

Now's the most critical time, he thought. He's in the shallows and I haven't got a net.

Twice Clay tried to wade in after the big fish to get close enough to grab it. But when the fish saw him coming it was off to the races. At last Clay saw no other way than to pull on the line hard enough to drag the fish into shallow water, and so that's what he did. The big fish was coming onto the shallows. Clay thought he'd won the day when he heard that sickening *ping*, the distinctive sound he'd heard too many times in his life before with salmon or steelies on the line, the distinctive sound of fishing line under high tension snapping.

Seeing his long-fought prize heading for deeper water, Clay splashed in after it hoping to grab the fish somehow. But he forgot all about the length of line connecting his hand and his toe. He fell flat on his face in the river.

As he sat up, he replaced his hat on his head and turned around toward the shore. That's when he discovered two Navajos, a man and a boy, dark-skinned and dark-eyed, mounted on spotted horses right there on the shore and just looking at him. No expression at all, unless there was a trace of amusement around their lips and eyes; it was hard to tell.

Curly was looking from Clay to the Navajos and back, and wagging his tail ever so faintly.

Clay was sitting in the river with only his head and shoulders out of the water. He knew somehow that they had been watching him for a long time. The man was big and barrel-chested, his face broad and heavily lined under a flat-brimmed, tall black Stetson. Hammered nickels ringed his hat and large silver conchos belted his waist, prominent against his vermilion shirt with the tails worn long. Large silver bracelets studded with turquoise adorned both wrists.

Clay couldn't believe he'd had an audience for the worst fishing episode in his entire life.

Everything in the man's appearance and demeanor spoke authority, and for an instant Clay was afraid that the man was hostile. But the glint of humor in the man now grew and spread across the broad face as the man said in English, "You horsed him."

Now father and son, as he took them to be, broke out laughing, and Clay was laughing with them. He stood up and water streamed from his clothing.

Hatless, the Navajo boy wore a red headband and a string of red coral beads around his neck. His shaggy hair spilled over the back of his collar. The boy's smile flashed as he said, "We were wondering why you have your fishing line tied from your hand to your toe."

Clay shrugged and smiled back, and said, "Oh, just to make it interesting."

Suddenly the boy became greatly animated. He pointed in Clay's direction with his lips, then spoke rapidly to his father in Navajo. Among the boy's words, Clay picked out these two: "Hosteen Clay."

12

" 'Hosteen Clay'?" Clay's heart was pounding fast. "Did you say 'Clay'? I've come a long way, and I'm looking for my uncle—Clay Jenkins."

He walked up onto the sand and reached to pat Curly, whose tail spoke happiness at having Clay back on solid ground.

"We know your uncle," the boy said proudly. "You sort of talk like him, same neckerchief, same hat. You're Clay Lancaster."

"You know my name?"

"Your uncle spoke of you often," the man said. "And you have a brother Mike."

"Yes, but he's not with me, he went back home. . . ."

For a moment both Clay and the two Navajos fell silent, each trying to put together the pieces.

"Are you from the Yazzie family? I met an old couple in Oljeto. . . ."

"My grandparents went there," the boy acknowledged. "They aren't back yet. My name is Russell, my father's name is Sam."

Clay noticed the silver work in the horses' bridles. He'd never seen the like of it or of the splendid spotted horses.

83

"Your horses are really something. I've never seen such beautiful horses."

"Yes," the boy said. "*Hozhoni*—beautiful. They're gifts of your uncle."

"Really? Your grandparents were trying to tell me something about Uncle Clay and horses!"

"There's much to tell," Sam Yazzie said with great seriousness, and even a touch of what may have been sadness.

"Is my uncle's with you right now? I mean, back at your camp? I want to see him as soon as I can."

"No, he's no longer at our camp. He's across two rivers," Sam Yazzie replied.

"He's all right?"

"We see him again on the twenty-seventh of July."

"Nine more days," Russell Yazzie said. "I've been counting."

"Why the twenty-seventh? Where's he coming from? Where will you see him?"

"Let's make a camp here," Sam Yazzie said. "It's too far to return tonight. And there's some things you should know before you meet your uncle."

"Can I go with you when you go to meet him?"

"That would be a good thing."

It didn't concern the Navajos that they had no overnight gear. They would stay close to the fire, Russell said. They'd spent nights out before, it wouldn't bother them.

Clay wondered what was troubling Sam Yazzie, if there was something bad he wasn't telling. Russell's father had left them after briefly speaking to his son in Navajo, and his face seemed clouded with concern. Clay began laying out his stores, thinking about what he might offer his guests to eat. "Chili con carne . . ." he was thinking aloud. Suddenly there was a big commotion and Clay looked up to see

Pal crow-hopping around and making a big spectacle of herself.

"What's she doing?" Clay exclaimed, all alarmed. He jumped up, ran over and grabbed the tie rope, freeing one of her legs which was caught.

"Oh, I've seen that happen before," Russell said with a smile. "She was scratching her chin with one of her hind feet and it got caught in the rope."

Clay hobbled Pal so she could get around a little and graze. Sam Yazzie was down by the river assembling three long forked sticks, green willows he'd cut along the river, into a conical frame.

Clay asked, "What's he doing?"

"Building a sweat hogan," Russell replied. "He wants to . . . to purify himself before he tells you the things he needs to tell you."

"Is it that bad?"

Now the boy's face clouded. "It's very difficult for Navajo people to talk of certain things . . . to talk of people who have . . . but my father believes you need to know these things. If he prepares himself in the right way, it will be all right."

"Uncle Clay's okay, isn't he? What's happened to him?"

"He's all right. My father will explain everything. He won't eat tonight, and we won't speak to him until he's all finished with the sweat hogan."

As Clay and Russell were collecting firewood and getting the fire started, Clay watched Sam Yazzie lean upright sticks against his frame and then slabs of juniper bark. He was leaving a doorway facing upriver, to the east, chanting as he worked.

Clay might not have been able to hear the chanting over the roar of the rapid, but the wind would shift and carry the man's high-pitched singing their way, riding on a rhythm so regular and monotonous the song would have seemed to be sung to the accompaniment of a drum. Clay had never heard anything like this singing. It reminded him a little of the coyote sounds he had heard in the night.

Russell was mixing up some cornmeal for corn bread. "Wait until you get to the summer hogan," he said. "We'll have lots of frybread."

"I'd like that. I haven't had any bread since Oljeto except some biscuits I fried up."

Russell added a little more water. "This corn bread isn't as good as frybread, but it'll be good with your chili."

"A trader told me I should have some cornmeal, but I didn't know what to do with it." Clay was happy to have someone to talk to who talked back.

Russell greased Clay's deep frying pan and set it on the coals to heat up. "I'm glad you're going to stay with us. Everyone back at the summer hogan is going to be excited to see you. We'll have plenty to eat. . . . Everyone will be happy to see the second Clay. Everyone will want to hear the story of how you came searching for your uncle."

Russell spooned the batter into the pan and covered it with a metal pie plate. He spread most of the coals out of the way with a stick, then started the corn bread baking on the thin layer that remained. Picking up a coal at a time, he used two twigs like chopsticks to cover the lid with coals.

"Did my uncle live with you at your sheep camp? When?"

"Last summer . . . it was a happy time for everyone."

"But not this summer? He doesn't live with you anymore?"

Russell didn't say.

It wasn't long before Clay could smell the corn bread. He rummaged for his honey. The bread was done and so was the chili.

"What's it about, what your father is singing?" he asked Russell as they ate. "Is it a ceremony or something?"

"It's not really a ceremony," Russell answered. "It's his own way of preparing himself. What he's singing right now, it's about *Bik'é hozhoni*, the trail of beauty. This is what he's saying:

Beauty before me, with it I wander.
Beauty behind me, with it I wander.
Beauty below me, with it I wander.
Beauty above me, with it I wander.
Beauty all around me, with it I wander.
On the beautiful trail I am, with it I wander."

"That's what I feel like, Russell," Clay said, "being out in these canyons."

"Then it's your song too."

"Do you like peaches?" Clay asked him.

"I love peaches."

"Then let's open two cans for dessert. Hey, I'm sure lucky I found you. I mean, I'm sure lucky you found me. And that you speak such good English too. I couldn't talk to your grandparents at all. I mean, I don't know any Navajo. . . ."

"Oh, I go to a boarding school. . . . They only let you speak English there. At home everybody speaks in our own language. When Hosteen Clay was here my father got to use his English again. My father was in the marines in World War Two—he spoke English all the time then, except when he was a code talker."

"What does that mean—a code talker?"

"There were about four hundred of them," Russell said proudly. "All over the Pacific. The Navajo code talkers. If the enemy ever cracks your code, they know all about

87

your biggest secrets for all the landings and battles and everything. But no matter how hard the Japanese tried, they could never crack the code made from the Navajo language."

"I never heard about that before! That's really something, that your dad was one of them."

"He was at Iwo Jima and Guadalcanal, lots of different battles."

"Uncle Clay was in the Pacific too, and so was President Kennedy."

"I know. *PT 109!* The Japanese sank his PT boat and he had to swim through the flames."

"Maybe Uncle Clay and your dad and President Kennedy all met each other in the war, only they didn't even know it. . . . What does that word mean, *Hosteen?*"

"Like 'honored.' It's usually for older men like grandfathers."

"Where is your school?"

"Oh, about a hundred miles from our winter home near Navajo Mountain."

"You're kidding! How do you get home?"

"We don't, me and my brothers and sisters. Only at Christmas, and a week in the spring. We live at the school. That's what a boarding school is," he explained. "You live there."

"That's terrible! That must be really hard!"

Russell shrugged. "Sometimes it is hard, especially at first, especially for the little kids. But that's the way it is. Summer's a lot better," he said, indicating the canyon walls or the river or all of it with a twist of his lips.

They built up the fire. In the outwash of the canyon, where the dry creek met the rapid, they gathered stones to be heated in the fire. Russell wanted round river rocks for his father's sweat hogan. Sandstone explodes suddenly and can throw little slivers like razors, he explained.

It was getting dark, but Clay could see that Sam Yazzie was packing the outside of the sweat lodge with mud now and sealing up the cracks.

Back at the campfire, they dropped the rocks in the fire and added still more fuel. Sparks were flying into the night and joining the stars.

His new friend was squatting comfortably back on his haunches but not quite touching the ground. Only his feet touched the ground. Clay could do that too, and now both of them sat that way with their hands on top of their knees.

"What are the two rivers?" Clay asked. "Uncle Clay's across two rivers, your father said."

"The San Juan here—we call it Old Age River—and the Colorado. We'll meet him where the Escalante River joins the Colorado, and help him move the horses across."

"Horses?"

"He's going to be bringing some more wild horses out of the Escalante country and across the river like he's done before."

"Wild horses! Is that what your grandparents meant by 'horses'?"

Russell nodded. "My horse and my father's—they were wild horses. Mustangs. Hosteen Clay brought them across late last summer. My father will tell you how all those things happened."

Something was turning in the back of Clay's mind, demanding to be remembered. "Es-ca-lan-te," he repeated. "You said Es-ca-lan-te."

"It's the name of the river and also the town where the Mormons live, up the river somewhere, in Utah."

"That's it! Restaurant Hay! Escalante! My uncle called us from there, and I got the name all mixed up!"

Russell laughed hard at that. "You thought the name of the town was Restaurant Hay? That's a good one. We'll have to tell that to my father."

The stones were glowing red in the fire. "They're ready," Russell announced. Carrying the glowing red stones on two poles they held together between them, Clay and Russell walked in the darkness to the sweat hogan. Then the boys poked and pushed the hot rocks into the hole Russell's father had made in the wet sand in the floor's center.

They returned to the campfire and let it burn low now. The night air was pleasant and they didn't really need the fire for heat. After a time Clay realized he was hearing the muffled sound of chanting from inside the hogan. His eyes must have asked the question because Russell began to explain. "He's singing the Sweat Bath Song now. It's an old story. It tells how First Man put down the first sweat hogan at the edge of the hole where the people came up from the world before this one. 'Everlasting and peaceful, he put it down there, the Son of the She-Dark.' That's what the sweat hogan's called—it's really dark in there too."

A little later Clay heard a sound like a stone plunging into the river. "What was that?"

"My father. Now he's bathing in the river. It's so hot in there, it feels really good when you jump in the river."

"Have you done it before?"

"Sure. Hosteen Clay liked it a lot. If you want, we can go in there. My father is finished."

"I will if Uncle Clay did."

Clay peeled off his clothes and followed Russell inside. The stones were still glowing faintly. "You were right about how dark it is in here," Clay whispered. Russell reached out and closed the door tight. "Still pretty hot too," he whispered.

"It must have been really hot when your father came in here at first."

Clay heard the hiss of steam as Russell sprinkled water from a canteen onto the stones. Instantly, a blast engulfed both of them and he ducked his head to avoid it. "Wow," he said. "That's really hot."

"You like it okay?"

Moisture was gathering all over Clay's arms, his legs, his hair—all over. He didn't know if it was steam or sweat or both. "I like it," he said.

Russell sprinkled some more water on the stones, and another blast washed over them.

Just when Clay thought he couldn't stand it anymore, Russell parted the flap and they both went outside. The moon hadn't risen over the canyon of the San Juan yet, but he could see his friend's profile by starlight. He waded knee-deep after Russell, then plunged in alongside him.

It felt cool and cleansing and . . . purifying. Clay got out and stood on the shore. He felt lighter than air. Suddenly dizzy, he sat down in the sand. The dizziness passed as quickly as it had come. He thought he had never felt better than he did right now.

Clay could feel Curly's wet nose on his arm, and he reached out to hug the little dog close. Now it was time to dress and to rejoin Russell's father by the campfire. Now it was time to learn what it was Sam Yazzie was so reluctant to tell.

13

"Three of our horses ran off the year before . . ." Russell's father began. The big Navajo man looked only into the fire. He cleared his throat, then continued.

"We knew they'd be spooky and it would be hard to catch them. It was early in the summer, just after we'd come to the summer hogan with the sheep. The yucca was still blooming. Three of us, we searched for four days in all these canyons. We were about to give up. Then we came across your uncle. He rode an Appaloosa horse with two burros behind.

"We were surprised to find a *biligaana*—a white man— in such a place. One of us joked that he must be looking for Pish-la-ki, a silver mine only white men believe in. He had no digging tools, we found out later, only things a man needs to live.

"I asked if he had seen any horses. He knew where they were, he had seen them. He led us to them. That's when we found out how much he knew about handling horses. The People are good horse wranglers from way back. Navajo people raided for horses a long time ago, we traded for horses, horses are in our blood as you say. But your uncle had his own way of gathering up horses. No one had seen anything like it.

"We invited him to come to the summer hogan and he came along with us. We only found out much later that he was a big rodeo star. Some people at the trading post recognized him and told us he used to be in all the big rodeos, that he was 'All-Around Cowboy.' Hosteen Clay had never told us that himself, and he lived with us the whole summer.

"All the kids liked him and would follow him around in a pack. The old people liked him, everyone liked him. The first time my sister—"

Sam Yazzie paused and looked straight down at the ground. It seemed to Clay almost as if Russell's father had seen something. Quickly the man looked back into the fire and continued, by force of will it seemed. "The first time my sister saw him, she liked him. I saw it, I was there. I knew her feelings. She hadn't married—no one could arrange a husband for her. She was a strong woman. But when she first saw this man it was different.

"Everyone could see that Hosteen Clay had deep feelings for her the first time he saw her. He didn't speak to her for three days, he was so shy.

"I told my mother not to speak to him again because he would be her son-in-law. She said she didn't need to be told, she already knew it.

"He hoed with us in the cornfield and in the bean field. He rode out with the sheep and kept them company every day. He worked on the stone corral where the stones had fallen down. He wanted to learn how to make silver, and I began to teach him. He wanted to know the Navajo words too. He wanted to learn everything, but quietly.

"Often we would talk about horses. He learned that we like the spotted ponies the best, the pintos. We told him that the best horses were the old mustangs, the wild ponies. They weren't big but they could run all day and never slipped and fell even in country like this. From way back, Indian people especially liked to catch the painted mustangs and breed them for their colors.

"Hosteen Clay wondered if there were any mustangs left on the reservation. We said no, just broomtails like ours that ran off. Maybe there are still mustangs in the Escalante Mountains in Utah, we said. Across the San Juan River and across the Colorado. We told him that the People used to trade with the Mormons in that country ever since way back. Jewelry and blankets for sheep and horses. Sometimes the People traded for those mustangs. But nobody had been over there since before the war.

"About this same time he was asking me about how Navajo people are married. I knew his heart before he told me that he wished to marry my sister, of course. He told me he had never married, he had no children. Now he wanted to be married to my sister for the rest of his life—how should he go about it properly?

"I asked him if he wanted to take her away and marry her in a church. He said no, he wanted to marry her here, in the Navajo way if that was possible. I told him that he would need someone to speak for him who was not of her family, a friend or relation of his. The go-between would suggest the marriage and propose the dowry, jewelry or horses usually.

"Pretty soon he asked me how to find the crossings on the San Juan and the Colorado. I knew what he wanted to do. 'There might not be any mustangs left over there,' I told him. 'There's only one way to find out,' he answered. I let him go. It was the kind of idea that made him happy. Before he left my sister saw him stacking rocks up high in the corral, higher than they'd ever been before. She kidded him about if he thought we had flying sheep, to make a pen that high. I never told her, but I think when he left the next day and said he would be back, she knew he'd be bringing horses for her father.

"Two weeks later he returned with these two horses you've seen today. No one had seen ponies as beautiful as these. He ran them right into the corral. No one pointed out that he had delivered the dowry before the go-between asked if it might be accepted.

"Along with the horses he also brought his go-between, a cowboy who helped him wrangle the horses across the rivers. The cowboy suggested the match to my father, who accepted the horses and set the date for seventeen days later, the first of September. The cowboy returned to the Escalante country.

"We built a new hogan for Hosteen Clay and my sister to be married in and to live in. I asked my sister if she thought her new husband would stay and live among us, or if they would leave sometime and go somewhere else. She said he was happy here and had said he didn't care to live anywhere else, but if he changed his mind one day it wouldn't matter to her.

"It troubled him that he couldn't help build the hogan. We laughed and told him to go out and watch the sheep. It was only a summer hogan anyway—a brush shelter. He could help when it came time to build a hogan of wood and earth at the winter place near Navajo Mountain.

"When the day came he was married in the Navajo way. He entered the hogan first, passed around the south side, and seated himself at the rear of the hogan facing the door which is east. Bringing the basket of boiled cornmeal, the bride entered with her family and took her place next to him on his right. I myself was the master of ceremonies and it was a happy day for me. The groom was my friend and the bride was my sister. Everyone could tell they would be together from that day into old age. I put the water jug in front of my sister and handed her the gourd ladle. I poured water into it and asked her to pour the water onto his hands. When he had washed his hands, he then poured the water onto hers.

"I brought out my bag of corn pollen and sprinkled pollen over the basket from east to west, and from north to south. I proceeded to do everything as it should have been done. The bride and the groom ate from the boiled cornmeal and the pollen in the correct places, in the correct order. When they were finished I instructed everyone to begin eating the wedding feast.

"They stayed in their hogan for four nights and four days, as is expected.

"For a month all was beautiful and peaceful. Then Hosteen Clay suggested that he and his wife would return to Escalante to buy several more mustangs for themselves, from the man Barlow who had sold him the others. I told him I would go along, my son as well, so that both of us could cross the Colorado and see that Escalante country as my father had, and trade with the Mormons as he and his father had. I made new silver—rings, bracelets—and brought some of my old silver too.

"We forded the rivers. It was autumn and they were low, but not so low the horses didn't have to swim. We climbed up through the tall Hole-in-the-Rock where the Mormons had made their wagon road down to the Colorado long ago. I had heard of these places but never seen them. On top it was beautiful, all rock up there.

"My sister was feeling sick, but we didn't know it until we'd ridden half the way from the river to Escalante. She had a bad pain in her stomach, and it kept getting worse. It was so far back home we knew we had to keep riding toward Escalante because it was closer.

"We got to the corral at the head of Coyote Canyon where Hosteen Clay had bought the mustangs before from the man named Barlow. This time there weren't only two in the corral, there were thirty or more. They were being loaded into cattle trailers, all crazy, fighting, screaming, breaking everything including their own bones. Two of them were destroyed right there.

"That's when we learned what was going on, from one of the cowboys. This man Barlow was bringing the horses out of the mountains and keeping them for a while at his corral at Coyote Canyon until the slaughterhouse sent trucks for them. We learned that the horses were being made into food for dogs and chickens, and turned into fertilizer. This man Barlow held back only the spotted ones because he knew people would pay well for them.

"Hosteen Clay kept his anger over these horses inside. He was concerned for his wife, to get her to a doctor as fast as he could. The cattle trucks left with the wild horses. Three pintos were left behind in the corral. We weren't going to buy or trade for them now—my sister was in bad pain. Barlow's cowboys were driving off fast with their pickup trucks and horse trailers. Hosteen Clay told Barlow he had to have a ride for his wife to get to the doctor. Barlow was the only one left. I could see he didn't like one of his kind being with us, worse that he was married to one of us.

"Hosteen Clay said he was afraid his wife might have appendicitis. Barlow laughed and said she probably had indigestion from eating too much frybread. He said he wasn't taking any squaw to the doctor. He just drove off and left us.

"We tried to ride on to Escalante. No more trucks came. It was too great a distance. My sister died in the night. Hosteen Clay took her away in the morning and buried her himself. When he came back he said he had buried his heart. He returned with us to *Diné Bikéyah*—Navajoland— but it wasn't long before he went away again.

"We didn't hear from him all winter. In the spring he wrote a letter and said he wasn't going to let Barlow take the last horses out of the mountains to be slaughtered.

"He rounded them up himself. He ran them down the canyons of the Escalante River, pushed them all the way down to the Colorado as he had hoped. We were there to help him swim them across the Grey Mesa where no one lives and where Barlow would never get them. We brought a few across the San Juan for ourselves.

"Nine days from now he'll run another bunch down the canyons of the Escalante. They could be the last mustangs in all that country. We'll be there to meet him. He won't know his nephew will be with us. That should bring some joy once again into his heart.

"That is all," Sam Yazzie concluded.

Clay saw the man glance in his direction, then look away. "Life is for the living," Sam Yazzie said. "Let's speak no more of the dead."

14

They feasted him. Clay squatted on the hard-packed dirt floor inside one of the shelters topped and sided with cut branches, and he feasted on frybread and mutton ribs and coffee. He'd never liked coffee before. He'd always said to his mother, "Who'd want to drink bean juice?" But when Russell's gray-haired grandmother, the old woman he'd encountered at Oljeto, made a pouring motion with the pot and glanced his way hopefully, he nodded "Yes, please."

The coffee was good. Maybe because it was brewed on an open fire, he thought. Russell's mother forked a new piece of frybread from the hot oil and gave it to him, smiling. The frybread tasted especially delicious with the coffee. They were pleased with his appetite. The kids wanted to make sure he was getting enough ribs. Yes, please, I'll have some more.

Clay's eye was drawn to the weaving on the loom behind Russell's mother. A blanket of dazzling color and complexity was nearing completion. How could she make that design, and make it right out of her head? And they thought he was something special. What had he ever done?

He was welcome here. He could feel it in all their faces, from the smallest kids to the old people. But who were all these people? Relatives, somehow. Russell tried to explain but it was hard to follow. They didn't call each other by their names. It was always something like, "My brother who is the son of my mother's youngest sister." They were two families of all the generations joined together, he'd figured out that much.

Many of them couldn't speak English, including Russell's mother. It didn't matter. They made him feel welcome. He was their second Clay. Everyone knew his sadness on learning of his uncle's great loss. It was theirs as well. No one mentioned his uncle or the woman from among them who'd fallen in love, married, and died.

In the evening Curly was attempting to help the sheep-dogs keep the flock in line as they blatted and funneled their way into the stone corral for the night. The children were all laughing at Curly's shrill barking, the way he ran back and forth not really knowing what to do but looking back to Clay all the while for approval. "What kind of sheep are those?" Clay asked his friend, as he pointed out one cluster with horns and especially long fur.

Russell laughed. "Those kind of sheep are called goats." The other kids were laughing too, and it didn't take a minute before the story was on its way to everyone in camp.

Clay went to sleep happy. He felt a great contentment. And tomorrow was all arranged. Russell would make the trip to the trading post with him, one day there and one day back. They'd go on horseback and take Pal to carry their supplies. He was looking forward to pulling on his cowboy boots again. He'd make his phone calls; his brother would be astonished at all the news. And Weston would be glad to hear he didn't have to come looking for him. Even better, he'd get his mail. He could see it now, a stack of letters from Marilyn. How many? Six? Eight? He could almost make out her handwriting, he could almost make out her face. . . .

"Got two," the trader said. The man wore red suspenders and had an oversized face, puffy like dough.

"There must be more than that."

"No, there's only two. One from a Mike Lancaster and one from a Marilyn Blanchford."

Thank goodness, Clay thought. At least there's *one* from her. A letter from Marilyn!

"This one here sure smells good," the trader teased, holding up a pink envelope. "This one from the Marilyn . . ."

Indeed it did. Clay could smell her perfume just as plain as if she were present.

The trader handed the letters over slowly, just to tantalize him.

Clay was blushing, he knew it. He wanted to get out of there and he wanted to read her letter as fast as he could. Russell was waiting outside on the bench. His eyes seemed to ask if Clay had good news. Clay didn't know yet. He sat down on the far end of the bench and tore open the envelope. The shark's tooth fell out of the envelope into his hand.

The blood pounded in his temples. He could barely breathe.

Dear Clay,

When I gave you my address in Red River, I thought you were going to send me a postcard. I hardly even know you, and here you're writing me these long letters.

Clay had a bad feeling in the pit of his stomach. Suddenly he felt weak all over.

Russell left the porch, taking a polite walk over to the horses.

You think about a lot of things, that's kind of interesting. But you get carried away. Boy do you get carried

101

away. "I think of you under these same stars," and all that—"Love," "Lovingly," and so on—it's really embarrassing. You obviously don't care about making a big fool of yourself. My parents are kind of worried about this and my mother thinks you're some kind of weirdo. And that shark's tooth! There are lots of things I'd rather wear around my neck than a shark's tooth. So while you're out there in the "Back of Beyond," GET LOST! And don't write me any more letters, please.

Sincerely,
Marilyn Blanchford

Now he was suffocating. Yes, what a fool he was, what a complete fool! All those things he'd said to her. He'd told her everything! "I think of you under these same stars. . . ." He'd said that! He'd said a lot of things. He'd never felt this awful. He'd never felt this stupid. He'd never felt this . . .

Clay called Goulding's with the message for Weston, and then he called home. Of course Mike wasn't there. Mike would be at the gas station. He called information, he dialed the station number, Mike answered. His brother was on the line. It seemed so strange, and didn't feel anything like he'd expected.

"Mike," he said, "this is Clay. I'm calling from the Navajo Mountain Trading Post."

"You're at some other trading post again? I thought you were at Oljeto."

"Well I'm here now."

"Did you get my letter?"

"Yeah. . . . They sent it over here. I forgot to open it."

"Whaddaya mean, 'forgot'?"

"I mean, I'll read it in a minute. I just got it. Any big news?"

"Well, no, but—"

"Look, Mike, I'm living with some Navajos that Uncle Clay lived with last summer, in fact he got married to a Navajo last summer and she died and we're going to be riding across the San Juan and the Colorado soon to meet him—he's bringing some wild horses across—and if you hurry you can get here in time to join us."

"Hey, slow down there, Clay, let's take it from the top."

Clay almost ran short of quarters trying to explain it all. Mike was having a hard time taking it all in, he seemed so far away. He was sorry about their uncle, but after it was all hashed out Mike couldn't come out to meet up with him. His job, and wanting to be with Sheila: nothing had changed. In fact he tried to talk Clay into coming home. Mike didn't really understand at all. "You can always meet him later, now that you know he's okay."

"No chance, Mike," Clay said. "Not when I'm this close."

"You sure are a persistent cuss," Mike said slowly. "I'll give you that. I don't like the part about how you took off on your own between these two trading posts. I still think you should come home. At least promise me you won't do anything else stupid, you hear?"

"Sure, Mike."

"So when are you coming home? It's already the twenty-first of July."

"After I've spent some time with Uncle Clay, Mike." Remembering it wasn't his brother he wanted to kick, he added, "Think of us on the twenty-seventh—that's when we're going to meet up. He doesn't know I'll be there."

"Still got the burro?"

"Sure, I've got her right here. I have a little dog too. His name's Curly—I'm going to bring him home with me."

"Just so you don't show up with Pal. I wrote Mom about what's going on but of course I don't know if she got the letter. Still haven't got any more letters from her. Hey, I saw *The Man Who Shot Liberty Valance*—have you seen it? It's good, real good."

"I haven't thought much about the movies lately."

"Hey, have you heard anything from that Marilyn you met in Red River?"

He hated lying. It made him feel awful. "Nah. . . ," he said.

Well, how could he feel any more awful?

He got out of there as fast as he could. Away from that trading post and back on toward the sheep camp. He rode alongside Russell without speaking. With a flick of the wrist he tossed the shark's tooth aside. His mind was on fire, it was burning up. How could she do that? How could he have written those things? What was he thinking? What did he know? About girls, nothing. It was hopeless.

They made a camp while it was still a little light. Pal proceeded to roll around on her back and take a dust bath.

Curly came and licked his face. He pushed the dog away.

Pal stepped in a tin can and got her hoof caught. Now she was hopping around on three legs again. Russell smiled, but Clay didn't see what was funny.

"The moon's starting to grow," Russell said meaningfully. "We meet him when it's half full. Not too many days now."

Clay knew what Russell was getting at, a much happier day was coming. But he said, "I don't see why they want to go to the moon anyway. There's no air up there, there's not even much gravity. You couldn't even stay attached to the ground without big old weights in your boots, and you'd have to wear a big old suit with tubes and stuff like a scuba diver."

"I guess so," Russell said.

"It's just to beat the Russians anyway. On the moon by the end of the decade and all that stuff. Maybe we won't even be alive by 1970—that's eight years off. Maybe we'll all get blown up with atomic bombs. Do you ever think of that?"

"Not much . . ."

"My brother says the Russians and us came this close last summer when the East Germans were building the Berlin Wall."

Clay realized that the thumb and first finger he'd held up were touching. He was getting carried away. His friend had his head down and was digging a little hole with his boot heel. Why was he making Russell feel bad?

"I used to worry about it a lot," Clay continued, trying to explain himself, and much more softly now. "They're always talking about whether you should have a bomb shelter. Some people have them. This one family on our block has one. Do Navajos have bomb shelters?"

"Not that I ever heard of."

"I don't think we're really going to have an atomic war. But it's scary."

"I know. We learned about it at school. We practiced getting under our desks in case there was an air raid."

"We did that too. Didn't you wonder what good that was going to do? I got my hair stuck once in some gum under there."

Russell chuckled, and then he said, "I remember once, everybody was real quiet and I couldn't help it, I said *Ka-Boom!* real loud. But the teacher didn't appreciate it."

105

Then they both were laughing. It felt good to be laughing again.

Clay was glad to be back in the sheep camp, glad he wasn't alone right now. Working alongside Russell, he hoed in those corn and bean fields with a vengeance. He helped to harvest squash and melons, and he rode with Russell every day on horseback to accompany the sheep. They were being called twins, to everyone's amusement. When had he ever had a better friend?

Each day it seemed they were giving him something. He'd admired Sam Yazzie's hatband of nickels, and now his Stetson was decked out the same way, with buffalo nickels he'd seen Russell's father shape over a conical mould. The silver parade of buffaloes looked sharp against the black felt. At his wrist he wore a bracelet Sam Yazzie had made, with three large turquoise stones set in silver. Around his neck he wore a strand of red coral just like Russell's. "I can't take all this," he said each time, yet each time he could see how pleased his friends were in the giving.

One evening the kids made a campfire and he played the scratchiest "Oh Susannah" imaginable on the Midnight Flyer. Then Russell tried the harmonica and taught all the dogs to sing along to certain chords that would set them off. The kids laughed especially hard when Clay's tiny white dog laid his brown ears back and sang. "Elvis," suggested one of the kids, and that's what they called Curly after that.

The next night everyone in the camp came together around the campfire. Russell's grandfather was drumming monotonously, and he and the men were singing their wild and eerie songs. Many of the boys were chanting too and dancing in the firelight. Russell was among them, shaking a gourd rattle to the beat of the drum. Thinking he'd add another instrument, Clay joined in and produced some unusual notes on the Midnight Flyer. Then he tried to chant along with the singers, which the Navajos found the funniest thing in the world with the possible exception of his dancing. Whenever he'd fall out of rhythm, or stumble as he did a number of times, the Navajos had to hold their sides they were laughing so hard. Tears were falling from the women's and the old people's eyes.

He was beginning to heal. The hurt would stay, but the scar was forming over the wound. Maybe he would always be this way. Maybe he would never be able to make his heart known to a girl. For him it was different than it was for Mike, and much harder. He'd always known it was going to be hard. It would have to be a miracle, like saving a girl from a raging river and her falling in love with you.

Then came the morning for him to leave with Russell and the men and to cross those two rivers. Pal was all packed. Curly was already settled in his perch and ready to go. Sam Yazzie had said that Pal wouldn't be too happy about crossing any rivers. Burros hate any water that's more than ankle deep, he said. But when he saw how much it meant to Clay, he said, "She'll swim when we don't give her any choice."

"Besides," Clay added. "I might need to go on to Escalante with Uncle Clay. He might be going back there."

Here was Russell, all ready for the journey, dark eyes shining as ever. He was mounted on a chestnut mare and trailing a packhorse. "Where's that painted pony of yours?" Clay asked him.

Russell's mother appeared in all her quiet beauty. Her full skirt was a deep blue, with a braid stitched near the bottom to match her shining green blouse. Around her shoulders she wore a colorful fringed blanket, and from her neck hung many strands of fine turquoise beads. She was leading Russell's spotted pony, adorned as always with the silver bridle but displaying this morning a bright new saddle blanket with distinctive geometric patterns and bright colors.

Russell dismounted, and his mother handed the reins of the spotted horse to Russell. Clay would never cease to marvel at this horse's beauty. Mostly white, it had a golden mane and reddish brown spots along its spine, red stockings, red marks too on the front of its face and chest.

"This kind of horse is called a Medicine Hat," Russell said almost bashfully. Clay could see Russell's grandparents looking on from a little break between the stunted junipers. "Good war horse," Russell added with a laugh. "Some tribes say these markings are good luck because they look like a war bonnet and shield."

Clay didn't understand why Russell was telling him these things right now. The little kids were quiet, and looking back and forth between their brother and his friend.

Russell transferred the reins to Clay's hand. He glanced ever so slightly at Clay, and then he looked away as he said, "This horse is one of the two your uncle first brought from across the Colorado, to arrange his marriage. You'll look good on this horse going to meet your uncle. I want you to keep this horse."

Clay wanted to say right out, This is too great a gift. Almost twenty pairs of dark eyes were waiting now, looking away in their fashion but watching him still. He knew it was their custom also not to say "thank you" at every turn. Their dignity and pride did not allow it. But for great occasions and with great humility the word could be used. "*Kehey*," Clay said, his voice breaking with the depth of his feelings.

His time at the summer hogan had come to an end. It was time to leave the sheep camp and to cross two rivers.

15

They waited on the banks of the Colorado. On the designated day, the twenty-seventh of July, they waited, gazing all the while across the river at the narrow canyon mouth of the Escalante, watching for Clay Jenkins and wild horses.

Clay waited with Russell and his father and four others as the half-moon rode across the daytime sky. He waited with them into the night until the moon set behind the canyon walls and darkness fell, obscuring the mouth of the Escalante River.

Clay hoped they wouldn't give up and leave. Maybe something had held Uncle Clay up, maybe he was just late.

He needn't have worried about the Navajos giving up. They were much better at waiting than he was. Together they watched through the next day, through the heat and the endless minutes and hours. It seemed his companions didn't even need to talk to pass the time. The river rolled by and lapped gently at the sandstone. The swallows over the river twisted, dipped, and climbed endlessly, those violet-green acrobats. Sometimes they skimmed the surface—for bugs or a drink of water? He kept wondering what had happened to his uncle, and worrying.

It occurred to him, he'd never once heard the name of

Sam Yazzie's sister, the woman his uncle had married. When he asked Russell, it was obvious how uncomfortable he'd made his friend. "It's not good to speak the name of someone who's dead," Russell whispered.

They waited a second night and he watched the slow passage of the waxing moon with his friend. No figure appeared at the mouth of the Escalante other than a coyote who came to the riverbank, then turned around and splashed back into the shadows up the shallow bed of the river. "It's good we've come to see this place again," Sam Yazzie said. "Next year there'll be no coyote here and no crossing."

"But why not?" Clay asked. "Why wouldn't there be a crossing?"

"Didn't you know? They've been building a big dam down the Colorado for years now. It's almost done. Next spring, they say, the water will back up into all these canyons. All these hundreds of tall canyons of the Colorado and the San Juan too. Even Paiute Creek—it's all going to be underwater."

"How far up these cliffs right here?"

Russell's father pointed almost straight up. "Way up there, they say. Only the tops of these canyons will be left. They say they're going to call it Lake Powell."

In the morning, after they had waited as long as they could, Clay knew what he would do. When Sam Yazzie said it was time to return to the sheep camp, Clay said, "I'm going on to Escalante, if I can get across. I came this far."

They transferred Pal's boxes to a packhorse, as they had for the crossing of the San Juan. It would be hard enough for the burro. They didn't want her loaded down with gear.

Russell's mother's brother led the way across, trailing the packhorse.

Sam Yazzie followed with Pal's lead rope snubbed around

his saddle horn. Clay and Russell and two others pushed forward in a tight ring and forced the burro into the coffee-and-cream-colored Colorado.

It was shallow at first, and the burro tolerated being driven. She had no choice. Then Sam Yazzie's horse was swimming. Clay saw the whites of Pal's eyes roll as the burro brayed in terror—her legs had suddenly lost the bottom too.

Clay's own spotted horse was swimming now. Curly's little head and ears were poking out of Clay's shirt, and his black eyes were looking all around. One of Clay's feet lost a stirrup but he clung tight with his legs, and clutched the mustang's flaxen mane with one hand.

Once on the far shore, Clay set to repacking the burro. Taking his leave wasn't going to be easy. He stowed everything away but the harmonica.

"The third canyon on the left side leads up to the top," Sam Yazzie said. "I remember it's got a cliff ruin in it. Maybe you won't want to go all the way up the river to get to Escalante. You could go out a side canyon."

"Just think, I'll be with Uncle Clay in a couple days!" Clay said.

Everyone stood around nodding their agreement, but it seemed none of them would speak now that the parting was so close. He brought the harmonica out of his back pocket and gave it to Russell. "I hope you can learn how to play this thing," he said. "I'm sure I was never going to."

"*Kehey*," Russell said.

"You teach those dogs of yours to sing a tune."

Clay mounted the spotted pony and snubbed Pal's lead rope around his saddle horn. "On a beautiful horse I wander," he said. "With my dog Curly I wander. Toward my uncle I wander. Saying good-bye to my friends I wander."

"Your horse's ears are made of round corn," Sam Yazzi answered, speaking in a chanting rhythm.

"Your horse's ears are made of stars.
Your horse's head is made of mixed waters.
Your horse's teeth are made of white shell.
The long rainbow is in his mouth for a bridle.
With it you guide him."

"Come back one day," Russell called as Clay rode away.

"I promise," Clay said over his shoulder.

He wound his way up the canyon of the Escalante at the feet of its overtowering red cliffs, up its gentle streambed of sand between the swath of bright green willows on its banks. Pal didn't mind the water now, it was so shallow. And it ran delightfully clear.

It was cool in the morning shadows. It was peaceful. Never in his life had Clay seen the like of these sheer red walls cut as if with a knife. He realized with a pang, he would never have the chance to share them with Mike. Next spring, water would be rising up these walls.

On some of the banks there were bright patches of clover. At every bend in the canyon, he let the mustang and the burro browse to relieve their hunger.

The canyon walls allowed him only a slice of the sky. All through the morning the slice remained a hard, bright blue. When the sun cleared the canyon rim high above, it didn't shine for long. Tall thunderheads were boiling up in what little of the sky he could see, and they were turning dark.

Faster than he would have thought possible, the wind was blowing hard and those clouds were growing positively black.

Clay urged the horse forward and felt the resistance from Pal as the rope went taut. "Let's get a move on, Pal," he said anxiously. "You remember what Weston said about being caught in the bottom of a canyon at a time like this."

He started eyeing the sides of the canyons for refuge. Nothing as far as he could see. He couldn't remember a safe place behind him. Fifty miles of this canyon lay in front of him with side canyons coming in left and right. It came to mind how Sam Yazzie had described the world on top that these canyons drained: solid rock. This isn't the Northwest, he told himself. No forest, no soil to hold the water back like a sponge. What would a flash flood look like roaring down this canyon?

Instantly, he could imagine one. Hung up high on a talus slope that fanned out from the base of the cliffs, a long white log was perched. Formerly a cottonwood tree, he realized, stripped of its branches and bleached out by the sun. Left there by ebbing floodwater. At exactly the same level, on the other side of the canyon and ahead, other logs testified to the same conclusion: this canyon could rage in a flash flood, and when it did, anything walking up its bed would be flushed out into the Colorado on a high-speed jet.

Clay passed the second canyon on his left. It might lead him up and out, but probably not. These canyons were so monumentally deep and narrow, most of them would likely cascade down to the Escalante in a series of pour-offs.

The wind blew harder still. The burro's ears were swiveling faster than Clay had ever seen them, and Curly there in the little hollow on top of the load was yawning with anxiety.

"Let's keep movin'," Clay said. "Nothing else we can do. Getting scared won't help. Try to think about something else."

I haven't named this horse yet, he thought. Russell said he'd never named him either, that I could give him whatever name I wanted. "Starbuck," Clay said aloud. "After the little town where my mother and my uncle grew up. Steer us out of here, Starbuck. Take us up high where you

113

came from, to the Escalante Mountains. But hurry if you please."

The drops began to fall. They splashed sporadically in the shallow river with unlikely force, as if stones were being cast into the water. Several hit Clay's hat, and one his face. That was a raindrop? It seemed about like a liquid baseball!

Lightning tore down between the walls with a whine like an incoming artillery shell in a war movie and he heard a *Craack!* that sounded like it should have been produced by the canyon wall itself splitting open. This is no movie, he told himself. This is not a movie.

Curly was running around under Starbuck's feet, splashing in the shallow stream. The thunder must have rumbled him right off his perch. Clay dismounted and swept Curly up, got back on the horse with Curly in his lap.

There was the narrow opening of the third canyon, up ahead on the left. He knew it would lead him up onto the top. But how quickly? Should I take it or should I stay with the Escalante?

As yet the storm hadn't broken. Keep scouring the sides of the Escalante for places to get up. Where? Where?

Now he stood at the mouth of the third canyon. It had a dirt bottom and a tiny creek flowing out of it. Box elder trees and cottonwoods. Didn't he have to try it? How many side canyons could dump into the Escalante in fifty miles? All their waters would be combined this close to the Colorado. Wouldn't he have a better chance in one smaller canyon, especially if he could go fast and get up and out? Sam Yazzie mentioned a cliff ruin up this canyon. How far? Could he climb to it? Could he reach it in time? Could the burro and the horse?

Don't think anymore. Thunder's rumbling, lightning's snapping. Go. Go as fast as you can.

The rope back to Pal tightened. Pal was planting her

feet. Now's not the time! He kicked the mustang forward and dragged the burro on.

Pal wasn't breathing right. She was wheezing and her sides were bellowing in and out. What could be wrong?

A half mile up the canyon, the sky broke loose with heavy, stabbing rain and the cliffs spouted waterfalls within a minute. The bottom of this narrow, narrow canyon was running a rich, muddy red.

Wrong choice, Clay realized. You don't leave a wider canyon for a narrower one. The water's going to come through here deep and fast real quick, and I don't have time to get back to the river, or do I?

He turned them around, and that's when he saw it through sheets of rain. The cliff dwelling hadn't been visible from downcanyon. Safe haven if he could reach it! His eyes traced a possible route up through the ledges to the delicate cluster of cliff houses nested under an arching stone roof.

He heard a roar and saw a surging wall of water coming their way. Starbuck was already climbing.

With agility to rival the burro's, the mustang scrambled and clawed his way up and out of reach of the floodwater now raging below them.

Up, up, up. At last they gained the safe, dry, chalky floor of the alcove. Trembling, Clay got off his horse and set the tiny dog down. Curly shook himself out and looked around. Clay spun as he realized Pal was lying down with her pack fully loaded. She'd hadn't done that since the second day. "What's wrong, Pal? We won't go any farther today, okay? We should be safe here."

The creek was racing, flooding, rising. Walls of red water overtook previous walls of red water. This was the sort of rain that carves these canyons, Clay realized. Higher and closer toward them the red waters rose. He pulled Pal back to her feet and unloaded her. The canyon walls reverberated with thunder and the rain slashed at the wall across from them for another half hour. It was strange to see the bright foliage of trees in the red torrent. Every few minutes entire trees would come floating by, and underneath them you could hear an ominous grinding as boulders walked their way down down to the Escalante. Even though his mind told him they were safe where they were, his heart pounded with terror and excitement.

The rain quit suddenly. Still, the waters rose until finally they crested safely below the ruin. For a thousand years this place had remained intact. A thousand years and an afternoon. Thank you, Ancient Ones.

He could breathe easily now, he could look around.

Clay crawled into the little rooms and looked out the keyhole-shaped doorways to the flooding creek. Suddenly he felt himself back in time, and a chill ran through him. Others had sheltered in this same place a thousand years before and survived floods like the one he'd just witnessed.

At the rear of the alcove he found pictures left by those long-vanished cliff dwellers painted in white pigment on the rock. Handprints, trapezoidal human figures with antennas like spacemen, animal drawings that looked like deer or maybe sheep. He found spirals chipped into the stone.

Pal was lying down again. She was breathing heavily, panting. Obviously she was sick—it must have been all that clover she ate. She'd always seemed fat, but now she looked bloated like those cows you hear about that get into feed that's too rich and then bloat up with gas until they burst and die. The only thing you could do was lance them with a knife, if you knew how, and let the gas out. But he wouldn't know where to begin!

Curly was sniffing around Pal's backside, and now Clay could see that Pal had one of those back legs up in the air and was kicking the air with it. Her sides were heaving and she was breathing harder, groaning. She was going to die

116

in a minute! He pulled out his pocket knife—what was he going to do?

Curly seemed awful excited there, by Pal's tail, and Clay took a look.

"Holy cow," he whispered. A little burro face and two little hoofs were coming his way out Pal's backside, all wrapped up in a filmy sack, alive and wide-eyed.

16

By morning the baby burro was on its feet frisking around. He would leap suddenly into the air, then come down in a whole other direction and gallop off. Clay grabbed him to keep him from prancing over the edge. His long ears and huge head seemed all out of proportion to his body and gave him a comical appearance. Mike, have I got some news for you, Clay was telling himself. Guess what Hubcap Willie didn't tell us about Pal, maybe didn't even know. There can't be a cuter baby animal in all of creation. You should see the white rings around his eyes, his white mouth, his little hoofs.

Curly was licking the baby burro's face, freshly wet with milk.

"I just had an idea," Clay announced. "*Ito* means 'little one' in Spanish. Let's call you Burrito! Little burro!"

Below, the creek still ran red, but had subsided nearly to its normal trickle. But the going would be more difficult now. Not all of the rubble had been swept downcanyon. He wanted to find his way out of this canyon and up onto that open country above. That wasn't going to be easy, especially with the baby burro. Burrito didn't seem to be able to predict which way his legs were going to go.

The backpack! I'll bet he'd fit in the backpack!

When Clay was all set to go, he tried it. Sure enough, Burrito made a perfect fit. Clay shouldered the pack; it was quite a sensation to look out of the corner of your eye and see that face and those ears. Burrito's legs were held so snugly, he didn't even bother to kick.

Less than a mile up the canyon, where the top of a talus slope met the slickrock, Clay found a horse ladder angling up to a trail that clearly led out of the canyon. He walked his string of horse and burro up it, and within an hour he found himself on a sea of rolling white slickrock on top of the canyons.

When the footing was good, Clay could give Burrito his legs and let him frolic his way toward Escalante, nursing along the way. The first day, the baby burro tired easily, and Clay mostly carried him in the backpack. The second day Clay was able to ride his pony half the time while Burrito walked, and by the third day, when they had to be nearing Escalante at last, Burrito had complete command of his legs and had no trouble keeping up. As if for his own pride, and just to be with the little burro, Curly had taken to his feet as well.

The whole while Clay had been paralleling the road that led from Escalante down to the Hole-in-the Rock crossing, where Sam Yazzie had told about the Mormons lowering wagons down to the river a long time ago. Occasionally he could see the plumes of dust from the pickups. But he didn't want to follow a dusty road into Escalante. He wanted to come into town reading the contours of the land.

He was following a wash upstream that was leading him out of the slickrock country and into the grassy valley he had glimpsed ahead at the foot of the mountains. A couple of big-eyed yearling cows watched him go by, then clattered downstream.

Clay's spirits soared as he imagined himself meeting his

uncle after all this time. He sat up a little straighter in the saddle and tugged at his worn black hat. Funny, he'd even forgotten about it. The hat had become a part of him. Now it was ringed with the hammered nickels, the silver buffaloes. At his neck, the red coral; on his wrist, the beautiful bracelet. Riding toward Escalante on his painted pony with the many-colored saddle blanket and the silver bridle, he felt like he was riding on clouds. *"Bik'é hozhoni,"* he said aloud.

After all the miles he'd come, and all the turns in all the canyons, nothing could have prepared him for the suddenness, the shock of turning a bend in the wash and meeting, right there, a girl on horseback.

Clay reined in Starbuck. Curly too stopped in his tracks, just as dumbfounded. Right in front of him, a girl on a palomino horse. Under a gray Stetson, a girl with a single long braid down her back. A girl in a western shirt and jeans with an open, pretty face and brown eyes, and a smile on that face quickly replacing her surprise.

Suddenly three black-and-white Border collies came racing down the wash from behind her, barking protectively and enthusiastically as if to make up for having been off chasing a rabbit when they should have been out in front. She called them off and they went about the business of getting acquainted with Curly, who being no fool, had quickly shown his belly in the presence of a superior force. Along Burrito's spine, the hairs were all standing straight on end.

The girl's eyes took in the painted pony underneath him, the packed burro, the baby burro, and looked back at him inquisitively.

"Where you headed?" she asked, and let her horse take a few steps closer, until there was almost no distance between them.

"Esca—" He tried to say *Escalante,* but the word tripped

120

over itself in his dry throat and fell short. "Escalante," Clay said, clearing his throat. He glimpsed her face again, those eyes, and he saw clouds and mesas, stars, the desert fresh after a rain, a girl riding a rainbow over all of it. . . . His heart was beating madly in his chest, and he knew if he tried to speak again he wouldn't be able to speak at all. He couldn't stand it. If only he'd had a little warning. Anything he was going to say would be wrong, he knew it. Alarms were sounding in his head: you're about to make a fool of yourself, you're about to make a fool of yourself, you're about to make a fool of yourself. . . .

She sensed his extreme reticence, and her eyes went back to the packed burro and the baby burro.

Clay was grasping at straws, and it suddenly occurred to him that his best chance of survival was in playing a man of few words.

"You've come a long way?" she asked.

"Yep."

"I guess you've already told me where you're heading." She seemed to be saying she knew the code, you don't ask a man of few words much when you meet him by chance on the trail.

Her dogs were looking up at her, wondering what next.

"You haven't by any chance seen some steers?" she asked him.

"Yep," he said. "Two." If he would have thought of it he could have said where, but he was responding so cautiously it was hard to get that many words out without checking each one first to see if wasn't going to turn on him.

Her eyebrows lifted under that gray Stetson. Dark eyebrows, dark crescent moons lying down. "We're missing two. I've been searching all morning—I've been searching for a couple of days."

Clay swallowed, and guessed he could manage a few words. "Two's what I seen."

He'd surprised himself with "I seen." He never talked like that. Now she was looking at him again. He shouldn't have said anything. He should've held up two fingers.

She seemed to be waiting for him to speak again, and so did Curly, who was looking at him oddly as well, curious perhaps about his grammar. Suddenly it hit him that she was waiting for more about the steers, and he hiked his thumb back over his shoulder. "Down this wash," he managed. "Just a few minutes ago."

Her eyes lingered. It felt like she was looking at his hatband and the Navajo bracelet on his wrist. He couldn't tell. Barely a glimpse of her and he was lost in clouds and mesas and canyons.

"Much obliged," she said, and with a hand signal to her dogs that sent them running on the scout downstream, she gave him a smile and clucked to her horse, and was passing him by.

"Same here," Clay replied, then as soon as he said it, he knew it sounded stupid. What was he obliged for? As he clucked to his own horse, he thought, I don't even cluck right. I sounded like I'm calling a chicken, and I only hope she didn't hear that. When he thought he might be safely out of sight he held up and glanced back, and sure enough she was gone. Now he knew what he was obliged for. He was obliged for the opportunity to make a fool of himself, which he'd managed despite all odds. How difficult would it have been to have a simple conversation with her?

Clay rode along not even noticing that the wash was giving way to open lands and ranch houses here and there, corrals and barns, or even that he was following a dirt road now. He could have asked her name for starters. When she asked if he'd come a long way, he could have answered "Monument Valley" and it would have been a whole lot to say in just two words. Then she would have started to ask him about his trip and he could have told her some. He could have told her about Burrito being born, she would have liked that.

Then he remembered the first thing he should have asked her. He needn't have worried about talking about himself. He should have asked about his uncle. Probably she'd heard of him. She lived around here!

Where she lived, he'd never know. He didn't even know her name. Mike would have learned her name. Mike would have had a conversation with her. If Mike had seen what had just happened, Mike would have razzed him no end. Well, Mike wasn't here. Good thing.

When Escalante came into sight, his heart soared despite himself. Forget her! What about Uncle Clay? The very idea, after all the places he'd been, that Uncle Clay might be right here, right now . . . He could feel his uncle's presence.

Probably he couldn't even remember her face. No, there it was, clear as a bell. Tanned from being out in the sun, bright smile, brown eyes tinged with yellow, dark eyebrows almost black.

Forget her! Think about Uncle Clay! Well, maybe she hadn't thought he was a complete fool. What had he actually said? Very little . . . He smiled to himself, and then his smile turned into a grimace as he heard himself saying "Yep . . . Yep . . . Yep . . ."

As he entered the town through back streets, Clay had the feeling something about it was different from any town he'd seen before. What was it? It had the look of an old town, lots of old brick, two-story houses, but that wasn't it. The streets looked much wider than regular city streets. It was the width of the streets and the size of the lots. That was it, and the huge gardens and chicken coops in the backyards. You couldn't really call them yards. Each lot was more like a miniature farm. Goats here, a milk cow there, rabbits in cages, sheds everywhere with lumber and hay and coils of wire fencing and all kinds of who-knows-what. There were lots of little kids around, and some of them stopped playing to watch him and his animals go by.

When he reached the last house before the paved street that ran through town, he asked a pair of legs that were sticking out from under the front end of an old truck if he might get some directions.

A bald head streaked with engine grease swung out by a wheel, and said "Shoot."

Clay said, "I'm lookin' for a man name of Clay Jenkins. Can you tell me where he is?"

A funny expression came over the man's face, and he said, "Clay Jenkins, rodeo star?"

"That's the man."

For some reason, the man thought this was amusing. He had a stupid grin on his face as he got up from under the truck and wiped his hands on his overalls. "See that big building over yonder?"

"On the main street?"

"No, the biggest one in town, two streets back. That's where he lives." As he spoke, he looked Burrito over, and the packed burro and Curly, and he thought something was terribly amusing.

"Do you know if he's there now?"

"Yes sir, I believe he is."

"Much obliged," Clay said abruptly, and left the man standing there enjoying his chuckle.

Clay crossed the main street and followed the dirt streets on the other side toward the tall building made of large blocks of stone. He was surprised to learn that his uncle was living inside a building at all. He'd pictured him living out in a canyon nearby and cooking over a campfire. You wouldn't think he'd be rounding up wild horses from a house in town, like a boardinghouse or something.

Clay could feel the goose bumps rising on his arms, on his neck, as he approached the big building. He was surprised to find that it was a public building. In fact it was the courthouse.

He tied Starbuck and Pal to a bench in the park across the street, and then he retied his neckerchief and straightened his hat. Burrito went to nursing; he was always hungry. The man under the truck had to be wrong, but he'd go inside and find out. Someone in there would know.

Clay walked up the broad steps, Curly right beside him, and he walked inside and down the hallway. It felt strange to be walking on a floor. He asked at the first office, the county clerk's. The woman there looked at him and looked at the little dog at his feet, and said, "You better go back outside and ask at the office at the back of the building."

People sure were different in Escalante, he thought. Maybe they don't see many folks from the outside.

He led Starbuck, Pal, and Burrito around the back, and discovered it was the sheriff's office. These people really were confused. On the other hand, it made sense that the sheriff would know where everybody was. He tied his animals to another bench, on the grass to the side of the building.

Inside, Clay stood at the counter and waited a long time for someone to show up. There wasn't a bell or anything. At last a big lady walked in, kind of old but not real old, with a beehive of silver hair. She had a mop and a bucket in her hand. "Sheriff's out for the day, dispatcher's out for lunch—what can I do for you?"

He took off his hat and he picked Curly up. "I'm looking for Clay Jenkins," he said.

The old lady kind of squinted, and said a little suspiciously, "And what's your business?"

125

"I'm trying to find out where he lives. They told me to ask here."

"Well he lives here, in a manner of speaking."

"You hear that, Curly? Whereabouts, Ma'am?"

She put a few fingers to her chin. "What are you to him?"

"I'm his nephew. I'm Clay Lancaster. He's my mother's brother."

Her face lit up and all the wrinkles in her face sang a different tune. "Why didn't you say so? How far have you come to see him?"

"From Seattle, Ma'am."

"Seattle, Washington?"

"Yes, Ma'am."

"My, my . . . call me Aunt Violet, everyone else does."

She opened the swinging half door for him and gestured with her head toward a set of wide stairs leading down. She took a small ring of keys out of her dress pocket and said, "Never said anything about relatives coming to visit."

Clay followed her down the stairs. Just as soon as he turned the corner and met a fence of bars across the wide hall and could see into a basement full of cells, it occurred to him that his uncle was in jail.

17

Clay held his breath. Curly's toenails clicked on the concrete floor as the old lady led them past the empty cells. All of them were empty. His heart was pounding. He didn't know what to think. His uncle was in jail! The long walk ended as the woman called eagerly, just before they reached the last cell on the right, "Visitor to see you, Clay!"

The man had just risen to his feet and put down a paperback book.

He recognized his uncle at once through the bars and under that black hat, even though it had been a long time. Here he was at last, the lanky man with the angular face and dark eyes, those crow's-feet around his eyes smiling even when he wasn't smiling. And the dark, three-day beard. Still there, the faraway look in his eyes. But where was his All-Around Cowboy belt buckle, the big silver belt buckle?

His uncle was looking him up and down, looking at the jewelry, returning to his face. Then he broke into that beautiful smile with that chipped tooth. "If I live to be a hundred . . ." Uncle Clay marveled. "Look who's all grown-up."

"I'm workin' on it," Clay said with a grin.

"Well you're nearly as tall as I am."

"I grew about six inches just the last year."

"If you aren't a pair," Aunt Violet said. "Two peas in a pod."

Curly barked suddenly, wanting to be included.

"My dog, Curly," Clay announced.

"I'm going to leave you boys," the old woman said. "I've got some cooking to attend to."

"I take it you've met Aunt Violet," Uncle Clay said. "Best cook in the county, maybe the state."

"I'm going to give you boys the run of the downstairs," she said as she jingled her keys and opened the cell door. "Be back in a bit."

Uncle Clay stepped out and shook Clay's hand, firm and long. "Man is it good to see you. Where's Mike? How's your mother?"

"Mom'll be back at the end of the month—she's in Guatemala."

"You were telling me she'd gone down there for the summer. Good for her—I was real happy to hear it."

"Mike's in Seattle. When you called, we had a really bad connection. I couldn't tell anything you were saying."

"I know. But at least you heard I was in Escalante."

"I didn't even hear that! What I heard didn't make any sense to me. But what are you doing in jail here?"

"Oh, well, I shouldn't be in here for long. I got into some trouble over some horses. I should be out soon. Here, let's pull up a chair—" His uncle spun and pulled the chair out of his cell, then went for a second from another cell. Clay stared into his uncle's cell, at the toilet, the bunk, the barred window that looked up to the outside. He still couldn't believe his uncle was in jail.

"I like the hat," his uncle said with a grin. "I like the Navajo jewelry. So tell me, you've got me stumped. How in the world did you find me?"

"That's a long story. . . ." Clay said. "Take a look out one of those windows on this side. I've got three friends out there, and you might recognize one of them."

His uncle stepped onto a bunk in one of the open cells. "Three friends . . . now who could that be . . ." He looked out, then looked again. "Lord, Lord." His uncle's voice was suddenly overcome with emotion. "Yes, I know that horse. It's one of the first two."

Stepping down from the bunk, his uncle said, "Sam Yazzie's who made your bracelet!"

Clay nodded. "I've come a long way," he said quietly. "I started out in Monument Valley—I came across Russell's grandparents there."

Tears were gathering in his uncle's eyes. "To find me? You came all this way to find me?"

Clay shrugged. "It's so different from back home out here . . . I really like it, and I thought it would be an adventure. I thought it was the kind of thing . . . that you would do."

His uncle took his handkerchief out of his pocket and wiped his eyes, then blew his nose once, twice.

Uncle Clay was laughing through his tears. "Look at me. Bawling like a baby and honking like a goose. And here I thought I was pretty much alone in the world."

"I know about what happened. That you were married, that you lost your wife."

The man looked up, and then away. Clay had never seen desolation in his uncle's eyes before. "It was hard, Clay, so hard I thought I'd just die from the grief. I've been alone my whole life, until Lily. When I met her, I could see the rest of my life in front of me. I loved her. . . . I'm awful sorry I didn't write, Clay. I've been trying to work up to it, and that's why I called finally."

"I'm just sorry about what happened. I'm really sorry, Uncle Clay."

"They say 'don't look back,' but I'll remember those days with her and her family as long as I draw breath. They were the best of my life. It pleases me so much, that you've just come from the Yazzies. You and I've got a lot to catch up on."

"We waited at the Colorado on the twenty-seventh for you to bring the horses down. What happened?"

His uncle flashed that broken-tooth smile. "Got caught!" Then he winked and said, "I know Aunt Violet's uncommon nice, but this isn't a hotel she's running, you know."

"What happened to the horses?"

"It's a real shame—that bunch is off to the slaughter-house, and now the same thing will happen to the last band up there."

"There's still some up there then?"

His uncle's face lit up. "A buckskin stallion with a black stripe down his back and rings on his lower legs, a lead mare as blue as a mountain bluebird, and about a dozen other mares, mostly with colts. They're the last ones. After that last bunch I was going to head for Seattle and look you and Mike and your mother up. Do some fishing with you, maybe even go back to working on the salmon boats."

"How soon can you get out?"

"Soon I think. A lot of people around here don't think all that highly of Barlow and what he's doing."

I've heard that name, Clay thought. Yes, from Sam Yazzie. "Isn't he the one that's selling the wild horses? The one that wouldn't take your wife to the doctor?"

"The same. But let's not talk about him. I want to hear all about your journey with Curly here and those long-eared rascals outside. Don't you just love 'em?"

Aunt Violet was wheeling in a cart. She sang out, "You boys hungry for fried chicken?"

"This fellow's come all the way from Monument

130

Valley, Aunt Violet. Bound to be hungry. He's a regular vagabond."

"And they say they don't make 'em like they used to. I've been thinking, it's such a nice day, why don't you boys take your trays outside—you could see your nephew's animals up close, Clay."

"I don't see why not," his uncle said with a wink. "We'll be good."

"I know you will. Sheriff Darling won't mind. Behind the building you won't raise much notice. No one'll mind."

"C'mon, Curly," his uncle said. "We're moving it outdoors. I've got a lot of catching up to do with your buddy here."

"What did they do with your horse? Was it one of the wild horses once?"

"No, me and Loosa have been together a good while. She's in the sheriff's corral in the next block over here. She's fine, they're taking good care of her."

"That reminds me—where's your All-Around Cowboy buckle? You always wore that buckle."

His uncle shrugged and said quietly, "I . . . I left it behind."

Clay bought a few groceries at the general store in Escalante and then he headed out of town to find himself a place to camp. He felt drawn by the cliffs above a valley a few miles beyond town, and he steered that way. It looked inviting when he reached it: good grass and tall pines and a clear stream that ran steady if only a few inches deep. Above the valley, sheer red walls towered on both sides with fir trees clinging to the high ledges.

A road led up the valley, probably a logging road leading into the mountains. But he preferred to stick to the creek bottom.

The spot didn't look different to him than any other

131

spot on the sandy creekbed. Shallow water was rippling its way downstream in undulating waves over miniature sand hills. Not enough water to concern a burro.

He wasn't watching that closely. He was walking in front of Starbuck, leading him because the pony had started to favor his left front leg as they left Escalante. There might have been something to see at that spot in the creekbed but he wasn't looking all that closely. He was on the deck of a salmon boat with his uncle, and they were catching salmon until their arms were about to fall off. They were heading up the Inside Passage toward Ketchikan, Alaska, with the steep, dark mountains wrapped in mist rising straight out of the sea. He'd always liked that name, Ketchikan, and thought he might get there one day. . . .

Suddenly Clay was chest-deep in the creekbed. Quicksand! He tried to kick his way out, but succeeded only in kicking his way out of his cowboy boots and worsening his predicament. Now only his head and shoulders were free. He thought he'd better quit struggling and breathe easy with his arms out as wide as he could keep them, and see if it would give him time to think.

Curly stood wisely back from the soft spot and eyed him one way, then the other, finding it unusual that his companion had only a head and arms and a hat.

"Throw me a rope, Curly," Clay joked desperately, trying as fast as he could to think of only one of the dozens of ways he'd seen dogs rescue kids in quicksand in shows like "Lassie" and "Rin Tin Tin." He couldn't think of even one. Apparently Curly couldn't either.

Curly reacted by barking in his high-pitched voice while Pal and Starbuck waited patiently for him to extricate himself. It crossed Clay's mind, even at a time he couldn't afford distractions, that Pal had been right about not trusting water. Her big eyes, ringed with white, seemed to be saying, "You didn't listen" as she nudged Burrito away from the danger.

At least he wasn't sinking any further. Curly continued to bark, and the minutes went by. Days it seemed like. The quicksand had him locked up but good. At least it's cool, he thought. What a way to beat the heat. If I'd thought to wear a whistle around my neck, I'd sure blow on it about now.

Then he heard barking, not Curly's but deeper barks from bigger dogs, and suddenly those black-and-white dogs he'd met earlier in the day showed up, those Border collies. One of them started toward him to investigate, but stopped and lifted one paw in the air, then wheeled around and returned to the bank. In a minute Clay was looking at the girl riding up, the dark-haired girl of the clouds and mesas and rainbows, the girl with the gray Stetson and the long braid down her back, the one who had taken his breath away. Somewhere close by, those two steers were complaining to the afternoon.

"We meet again," she said with a smile. All he could think of was to be polite, and so he lifted his hat from his head, and greeted her with a gentlemanly nod.

18

"Stay still," she said.

"Okay," he replied. "I won't go anywhere."

The girl with the long braid smiled as she reached for her lariat, and she dismounted in a smooth motion. Whirling the lasso around her head, she took a few steps closer. He looked up into her face, all concentration. She wasn't laughing at him, at least.

This isn't the way it's supposed to be, Clay thought. I should be saving *her*.

One thing he was glad of: his brother wasn't here to see this.

She roped him on her first try. As she mounted her horse she said, "We're going to pull you downstream so you can come out on your back with your face up. Try to backstroke if you can help us. Just like you're swimming."

Her palomino horse responded as if he were trained for the occasion. It all worked like she said. He flopped around like a fish, but at last he found himself on solid ground. Clay picked himself up, freed himself from the rope, and said quietly, "Thanks. Thanks for pulling me out."

"It wasn't anything," she said with a shy smile. "Roping a calf is a lot harder."

There he was, standing in front of her in his bare feet. He couldn't have looked more ridiculous. He knew he'd never see those expensive cowboy boots again.

"I like the baby burro, and its mother, and your little dog."

"Thanks," Clay said dispiritedly. It had taken a lot out of him, making a fool of himself twice in one day with the same girl.

"And your horse—I think that's the most beautiful horse I've seen in my life."

"Thanks. Something's wrong with his foot, the front left one."

"Really? I'll take a look."

Clay went to unrigging Pal's diamond hitch to get at his hiking boots.

"You sure surprised me this morning," she said, as she took her time to get acquainted with his horse. "Where in the world did you come from? I've never seen you around here before."

"Monument Valley." He felt a small surge of pride saying it. Maybe he could talk to her, even if he had made a fool of himself—twice. Maybe that would even help. He'd gotten it over with.

"Really? No kidding—you came from Monument Valley? I've always wanted to go there."

"That's where I started," he said, taking his first deep breath since the creekbed had squeezed the starch out of him.

"You out here on your own?"

"Pretty much."

"That's amazing. Here's the problem, he had a big pebble in his frog."

"Frog?"

"The soft spot in the center of his hoof. Funny name, eh?"

135

Clay laughed. This girl made you feel good. It was easy to be with her, even if she was so pretty.

"I like your bracelet, and your hatband."

"Thanks." He was lacing up his boots. "I've seen a lot of places since I started out, but this valley's special. It's got the red cliffs and the big trees at the same time."

She seemed so pleased. "Really?"

"Sure."

"I live here—just a couple miles up. My family's is the only place in the valley."

With an occasional hand signal and not a word spoken, she sent the dogs to outflank the steers whenever they strayed. As they rode up the valley side by side, they were looking for a good place for him to camp. But they got so busy talking they weren't looking for campsites anymore. Her name was Sarah and it was the easiest thing in the world to talk with her. It didn't matter that he loved her—and that it was hopeless. He could set that aside. He could talk to her about the country he had seen. She had that look in her eyes. She loved the wild places the way he did.

Clay tried not to talk too much, to make big of himself. He didn't want to hear himself talking that way. He wanted to set himself aside and tell her what it was like, just being out there.

But she wanted to know more and more and more. By the time they reached the end of the valley, he'd told her all about his search for Uncle Clay. He'd even told her that the horse he was riding was born in the Escalante Mountains, that his uncle was in the Escalante jail.

"Clay Jenkins, the rodeo star!"

"That's him."

"Lots of people think he's right to try to save those horses—I sure do! So he's your uncle."

When Clay saw the ranch nestled in that green valley

under those red walls, with its fenced pastures, orchard, barn, and the creek running right by a two-story log house, he said, "Sarah, you live in heaven."

"My dad built our house," she said fondly. "He brought the logs out of the mountains. That's him coming this way."

Her father came riding up on a sorrel horse, his eyes asking unspoken questions about what his daughter had dragged home, this muddy fellow with the unusual entourage. "Sarah, you found those steers!"

"Dad, this is Clay Lancaster. He's from Seattle, and he walked and rode all the way from Monument Valley. He came to find his uncle, who's Clay Jenkins."

The smile playing in the tall man's eyes spread to the rest of his face. He said, "Well, I'll be."

"I think he could use a place to stay for a little while."

"He's got it," her father said, reaching over to shake Clay's hand. "Bud Darling."

"I'm glad to meet you, Mr. Darling."

"Please," he said with a laugh that his daughter echoed, "anything but that. If you had my name, you'd much prefer people just left it at 'Bud.' "

"Thanks for the hospitality, Bud." Still, Clay thought, it doesn't feel right to call him by his first name.

"My wife likes 'Mrs. Darling' just fine. Somehow it suits her better than me. Yours must be quite a story and she'll want to hear it. Libby and Nora will too, and I haven't even heard it yet myself. You're quite welcome here, Clay. You take care of him Sarah, I'll look after these steers."

As they rode in, two girls flew out of the house onto the porch all excited and big-eyed at the sight of Clay, the packed burro with the little dog nestled on top, and especially the baby burro frisking alongside. Unlike their sister Sarah in jeans, both of these girls wore long dresses. Like homemade, Clay thought. The older of the two had a long ponytail that swung from side to side as she ran.

137

"Libby's ten and Nora's five," Sarah said.

Mrs. Darling, also in a long dress, appeared right behind them as Nora made a beeline for Burrito and hugged him around the neck. The little girl in pigtails looked up at Clay and said, "This boy sure is muddy."

"Where'd you find him, Sarah?" asked her sister Libby.

"She fished me out of the creek," Clay explained.

Sarah laughed. "Biggest fish I ever caught."

As Clay soaked in the tub, he could see Mrs. Darling down by the creek rinsing the mud off his jeans and his shirt. He'd tried to save that chore for himself and thought he'd won, but there she was. She had all of his clothes, and she'd slipped him some of Mr. Darling's through the bathroom door. It was embarrassing. He hadn't exactly been looking after clothes washing on his travels. Now and again he'd rinsed his clothes and lay them out on the rocks to dry, but he'd never picked up any laundry soap and he hadn't thought to use his bar soap on his clothes.

Libby and Nora were playing outside. Nora was shrieking with joy and Libby was yelling "Look at him go! Look at him go!"

The little spot in the window he could see through showed Burrito galloping across the yard with Curly in ear-flapping pursuit. The little burro suddenly snorted and leaped into the air, pirouetted, and raced off around the house.

For the first time, Clay tried out her first name with her last. Sarah Darling. Sarah Darling. Sarah Darling. Her name shook him up so badly when he heard himself repeating it, he thought he'd better not think about it for a while.

Suppertime. He felt so grateful and so . . . clean. He'd scrubbed himself raw to try to present himself suitably.

Sarah's father was saying the grace, and he was having a lot to say. Dark-haired like Sarah, he had a bit of gray showing in his sideburns. The roast beef was steaming on the platter and it sure looked good. They'd raised everything on the table themselves: the beef, the potatoes, the carrots, the salad greens. He felt a little funny in her father's clothes. The shirt felt like it was starched. He sneaked a glimpse of Sarah. She'd changed from her jeans into a long homemade dress like her mother's and her sisters'. Sarah Darling, Sarah Darling, Sarah Darling . . . Libby was watching him take that glance at Sarah, and then she was watching her big sister. Libby had a curious little smile on her face. "Amen," Mr. Darling concluded, and Clay whispered "Amen" along with the rest of the family.

"Did you get through to your brother Mike?" Mrs. Darling asked as she passed him the gravy.

"Yes, Ma'am, he was pretty excited about me finding Uncle Clay. Awful surprised to find out he was in jail. And he read me a letter from my mother. It's the first one that's gotten through since she was actually in Guatemala."

"And how's she doing?"

"Perfect. The people are really poor I guess, but really nice. She likes being down there as much as she thought she would."

"It's quite brave," Mrs. Darling commented, though she looked a little skeptical. "Did you and Mike talk about how you'll get home?"

"Yes, Ma'am—with Uncle Clay on the train, closest we can catch one."

Libby said wistfully, "I'd like to ride on a train one day."

"Come out and see us sometime!" Clay proposed. "You could stay with us while you're there. Uncle Clay and I are going to go out on a salmon boat. He might take up fishing for a living. Do you like fishing, Mr.—Bud?"

139

"Mr. Bud!" little Nora giggled.

At the mention of fishing, a profound look of happiness had come over Mr. Darling's face.

"Does he ever," Mrs. Darling explained. "Sarah too."

"Fishing for a living . . ." Mr. Darling rhapsodized. His deep green eyes reminded Clay of the depths of his favorite mountain lake in the Cascades. "That wouldn't bother me one bit."

"It's different out there," Clay said. "I hope you'll like it. It's pretty and everything, but where we live, it's not like this. We live on a regular street, you know, with houses close together on both sides."

Clay could see Sarah and her sisters trying to imagine it.

"Like in town in Escalante?" Libby suggested.

"Oh, they're a lot closer than that. Uncle Clay probably wouldn't live with us or anything—he'd feel too cooped up. He'll probably live in one of the little fishing towns. Or maybe he'll live on a boat."

"Your uncle is much admired around here, by some, that is," Mrs. Darling observed. "Some people even think of him as a sort of Robin Hood for the wild horses. I know Sarah does."

A serious expression came over Mr. Darling's face. "It's really pretty extraordinary, Clay, what's happened here since your uncle came along. People are starting to wonder if it's right, what's happening to these horses. You see, this is cattle country, and it's hard enough making a living around here as it is. Most of the cattle grazing is on government land that the ranchers lease. It's true that the wild horses forage for the same graze that we need for our cattle. Except for the mountains, people call this land around here 'ten-thirty country.' You explain it, Sarah," he asked with a wink in her direction.

140

"Sarah's as good a cowboy as Daddy," volunteered little Nora, eager to get in on the conversation.

Sarah blushed. " 'Ten-thirty country' means your cow has to have a mouth ten feet across, and has to be able to run thirty miles an hour to find enough grass around here to stay alive. You've seen the country around here, Clay, not much for a cow or a horse to eat."

"The country won't be so big or beautiful without the wild horses," Mr. Darling said. "But there's nothing to protect them—in fact, the law's all on the other side. Barlow has a legal contract with the government to take out every last one, and people here do believe in obeying the law."

"The horses should come before a piece of paper," Sarah said with emotion. "No one asked the horses."

Nora whispered, "They're making them into *chicken food.*"

"We hope they won't deal with your uncle too severely," Mrs. Darling said. "We hope he can just get on that train with you, wherever you're going to catch it, and that'll be the end of it. It's not like he hurt anybody."

Libby said importantly, "Daddy's brother's the sheriff."

Clay's eyes found Mr. Darling's. "How soon does he think Uncle Clay will get out?"

"The sheriff is hoping your uncle will be able to pay a fine and agree not to come back around here again."

"Let's not talk about that anymore," said Mrs. Darling. "Let's have some peach pie and ice cream and think about what you kids are going to do tomorrow."

"There's a John Wayne movie that just came to town," Libby said.

Clay almost jumped. "What is it? I like John Wayne movies."

Libby ran into the living room for the newspaper. "*The Man Who Shot Liberty Valance,*" she called.

141

"That's the one I've been looking for!" Clay declared. "I'd give anything to see that movie."

Mr. Darling laughed. "Fifty cents ought to do it. Sarah likes John Wayne too. Sarah, your mother and I were going into town tomorrow night anyway, to meet with the other people planning the county fair—why don't we drop the four of you off at the movies on the way?"

Clay and Sarah nodded in agreement.

"Let's get these dishes done," Mrs. Darling said. "It's getting late, and we've all had a big day, especially Clay here."

Everyone got up from the table. Clay helped Sarah with the dishes. Her sisters went off giggling to their room upstairs. Sarah's mother was finding some bedding for Clay to take out to the bunkhouse.

Sarah disappeared as he was drying the last few pans. When she came back a few minutes later she said, "I've been talking to my father. If you and I got up really early tomorrow morning, I could take you fishing up at Cyclone Lake—we could ride our horses. We'd still be back in time for the movie. Do you think you'd like that?"

19

They climbed all morning into the big pines and firs, until it started to feel almost like the Northwest, Clay thought. Starbuck seemed to be enjoying the work more than in the lower country, and as the air cooled and thinned and they entered groves of aspen and spruce, the formerly wild horse became more animated than Clay had ever seen him. "Look at him, Sarah, he's acting like a colt."

"He's back in his summer range."

"How high is Cyclone Lake?"

"It's over ten thousand feet. I'm glad we brought the dogs with us—they're having a great time. And look at Curly! Look at those little feet go! He isn't having any trouble keeping up with my dogs."

They paused on an outcrop that gave them a view of the lower country below them: the town of Escalante at the foot of the mountains, marked by the smoking tepee burner at the sawmill, and beyond the town, a world of slickrock and canyons as far as the eye could see.

"That long, narrow canyon between us and the Colorado River," Sarah said pointing, "that's Escalante Canyon, where your uncle ran the horses down. It was such a beautiful idea. It's so narrow the horses had nowhere to go but straight ahead. It's so great to think one man was able to do that by himself."

"The side canyon I climbed out of? What's it called?"

"I'm sure it was Davis Canyon. Third one up from the river, and it has a horse ladder."

"You know all this country."

"Look how much there is! Some of those canyons are so narrow you can touch both walls with your hands, and they're hundreds and hundreds of feet deep. There are so many out there, probably no one's seen them all. Sometimes the cows get down in those canyons and it takes a lot of searching to find them out."

I'd help you search for those cows, Clay thought. I wouldn't care if we never found them.

"Between us and the beginning of Escalante Canyon there's a box canyon called Death Hollow. That's where your uncle had the horses stashed before he started them down the Escalante."

"Look, Sarah—there's Navajo Mountain, all by itself over there across the Colorado. I was right up close to it."

They spread out a checkered tablecloth on the grassy bank of Cyclone Lake, and brought out their sandwiches. Nothing could be more perfect than this green grass and the music of her voice, watching the clouds go by and sharing a picnic lunch. There could never be another day like this one. There could never be another girl like this one.

Curly showed up and licked him on the face. He wished it were so easy to kiss Sarah, just like that. Well, not just *like* that.

Clay looked at her long, and she looked back at him, and his heart was beating like thunder. He felt like he was about to kiss her, but it felt like being about to step over a cliff. It was the scariest moment he'd faced in his life.

"The dogs," Sarah said suddenly. Her dogs were standing frozen like Border collie statues, and even Curly was standing still like a statue.

Clay looked in the direction the dogs were looking. Way down near the end of the lake and on the other side, horses were coming down to the water.

"Wild horses," Sarah whispered. "Keep low!"

The dogs knew not to bark. Even Curly kept quiet.

"Look," Sarah whispered. "That's the lead mare bringing them down to the lake. She looks blue even from here."

" 'Blue as a mountain bluebird,' " Clay said thoughtfully. "Sarah, these must be the ones Uncle Clay had his eye on. This must be that last band he told me about. The stallion's a buckskin with . . . lemme think . . . a black stripe down his back and rings on his legs. A dozen or so mares with their colts, he said."

"That's about what I count. Look, there's the stallion standing guard. With markings like those, he'd be a real throwback. You know, there's only about twenty thousand mustangs left in the whole country. The lead mare's drinking now, then the next in rank and so on. If the stallion tries to drink before all the rest are finished, the mares will run him off. I saw it once."

"I count eighteen."

"They'll be dead soon, and Barlow will make his five cents a pound. Aren't they beautiful? They probably are the last ones. Let's see how close we can get to them, Clay."

Silently they crept back into the trees, where they had left their horses, and circled the lake in the spruce. The dogs understood the need for stealth. Though Curly didn't understand Sarah's hand signals, he was taking his cues from the other dogs and he was learning fast.

Clay watched her give the hand signals too, watched how quietly her palomino moved in the woods, careful not to break a stick.

145

At the edge of the woods, Sarah let Clay draw alongside, and they watched the wild horses at lakeside through an opening in the woods. The stallion was drinking now. Most of the mares and colts were rolling in the mud at the edge of the lake.

"Look at that," Clay whispered.

"To protect themselves from the flies. The mud dries and gives them a thicker skin."

Suddenly a new horse galloped up, all black with a white blaze on his forehead and white stockings, and before Clay could even see how he'd done it the black had cut out the two mares and their colts who weren't in the mud, and he was herding them away as fast as he could.

The big buckskin took off in hot pursuit, and before the black could herd his prizes into the woods, the buckskin cut him off and the two stood in full display, their necks arched and their front legs pawing the ground and then pawing the air.

"I've always wanted to see this," Sarah whispered.

Clay strained to get a better look, expecting to see a big battle. Yet with no blood drawn, it wasn't but half a minute until the buckskin was racing back to the rest behind the four that had been kidnapped, nipping the trailing colt to make him go faster. "What happened?" Clay asked. "I didn't even see what happened."

"The black's probably a much younger stallion," Sarah explained. "He knew he wasn't the buckskin's match yet, so he backed down. You know what I'm thinking, Clay. . . ."

She had the most wonderful grin on her face.

"If we could possibly do it, we could hide them away and no one would ever suspect that they've been stashed away because your uncle is in jail! And then, as soon as he gets out, he can run them down the Escalante! They'd be across the Colorado and so would he, before anyone could say Jack Robinson!"

Clay's mouth dropped. "Could we do it?"

For no apparent reason, a couple of the mares nickered, and there was a distinct note of alarm in their voices.

"Maybe they smell us," Sarah whispered. "We have to make our move fast. Follow me, and hang on to your hat!"

With that she exploded out of the woods, giving signals to the dogs, and the wild horses exploded into flight as well.

"Death Hollow!" Sarah shouted.

With a grin spreading across his own face, Clay galloped to catch up as she raced to keep the stampeding horses between her and the lake. What a sight Sarah was! The mustangs tried to make a break out and toward the woods. They ran at full speed with their manes and tails flying, but her dogs headed them around the end of the lake and down into the beginning of a draw that fed off the mountain.

And then it was all pleasure, just trying to keep up with Sarah, with his heart in his throat and his legs slapping Starbuck's side and his eyes on that long dark braid that seemed to have a life of its own. Down the mountain he flew through the tall spruce and into the aspen breaks and down into the pines, enjoying an occasional glimpse over his shoulder of a small blur of white and hearing Curly's high-pitched battle cry.

It was all pleasure except for one thing. He was having the hardest time trying to keep the blocky toes of those hiking books in the stirrups. If I live through this, Clay thought, I'll get me a new pair of cowboy boots in the morning!

Rock formations started to show up, then cliffs and domes and spires of rock with the tall trees growing in niches, and the chase was dropping through sandstone formations now and into the beginnings of a canyon.

He caught up with Sarah, who'd slowed to a walk. At last they could hold up and rest. The wild horses couldn't get up the sides of the canyon unless they could fly.

147

"Is this it?" Clay asked, all winded. "Death Hollow?" Now Curly caught up, panting and proud.

"Not yet," she replied. "They could work their way back up to the lake from here. I know a way into Death Hollow a few miles down. That's where we'll take them."

And that's what Sarah did. She knew a place where only two horses at a time could squeeze between the rocks, and she and her dogs funneled them through the crack, all eighteen of them, and into Death Hollow. Clay helped her drag logs and brush until they'd plugged the gap behind them.

Through a world of bizarre rock formations they rode into the afternoon. They drove the horses into the bottom of Death Hollow where sufficient grass and a flowing creek would provide a sanctuary. Sarah flanked them, pushing them back upstream a ways, and then she said, "Let's go fix the fence."

Clay took a last glimpse at the horses and started down the canyon. They soon came upon an old homestead by the creek, long abandoned. Where the canyon walls narrowed to a gap a half-mile farther, they stopped to repair the high pole fence that was down in two places. "Your uncle sure put a lot of work into this," Sarah said as they lifted the first pole into position.

It didn't take long to put the fence back to rights. "Those horses aren't getting out this way," Clay commented as they stood back to admire the fence, intact once again. He lifted his hat and wiped his shirtsleeve across his forehead. "They'll be waiting right here for Uncle Clay. On to *The Man Who Shot Liberty Valance!*"

As they rode into the ranch, they felt like they were still ten thousand feet up. It was a good feeling, exchanging glances as they approached the house, having a secret between them.

148

Her mother was working at the sink. She was wearing rubber gloves and lifting jars of bright red tomatoes out of a steaming enamel pot. The radio was on; she'd been listening as she worked. Her apron showed she'd been through something. "How was it?" she asked Sarah brightly. Suddenly aware of his hat, Clay doffed it and held it by his side. "How was the fishing?" her mother asked.

"We forgot all about it!" Sarah replied.

Clay added, "It sure is beautiful up there, Mrs. Darling."

"I'm glad you liked it, Clay. It doesn't seem like the fishing's ever that good late in the summer anyway. Sarah, I haven't heard a peep out of Libby and Nora, and you know that's not a good sign. Would you check on them? We have to keep moving if we're going to get you to the movies on time. Your dad's got the charcoal going. We're just going to have some hamburgers and potato salad. They were up in their room getting ready for the fair."

"County fair starts this weekend," Sarah explained. "It starts the day after tomorrow, actually tomorrow night with the dance out at Dance Hall Rock."

"We hope you'll be staying through the fair, Clay. Have you ever been to a county fair?"

"No, Ma'am, but I'd sure like to. I guess they have them out there. But not where we live. I'm pretty much of a city kid, I guess. Well, not really a city kid—I guess I'm a kid from the suburbs."

"After the summer you've had I'd say you'd pass for a cowboy."

Clay smiled. "I feel like I'm from out here. They say in the Northwest, you can tell the natives because they have moss growing on their north side, but I feel like all mine must've burned off by now."

He followed Sarah into the living room. They heard something, and then they listened again. They glanced at

149

each other. Could it be? Yes it was. The unmistakable sound of small hoofs galloping.

"Uh-oh," Sarah said, and went flying upstairs.

She disappeared. Still more galloping.

Clay hesitated, then climbed the stairs. He'd better catch that rascal before he broke something of the Darlings'.

At the top of the landing he saw Burrito streak from one room into another with the girls on his heels. What in the world? Did he see what he thought he'd seen?

Clay poked his head in the doorway.

Yes indeed. Burrito was dressed to kill in a blue vest and matching blue bonnet that fit down over his ears. The baby burro was standing in the middle of a large bed, on a fancy lace bedspread, snorting loudly and all cocked for mischief. With a glance Clay realized this was the parents' bedroom. Porcelain knickknacks on low nightstands were poised delicately just waiting to crash.

"You guys . . ." Sarah was saying ominously. She was on one side of the bed, her sisters on the other.

"We've got him surrounded," Libby said.

That's when Burrito bolted, and Clay tried to grab for him. The burro galloped as if to one side, then swerved and shot right between his legs.

"Get him!" the girls were yelling, and little Nora was shrieking for joy as she and her flying pigtails chased the burro down the hallway.

"What's going on up there?" their mother was calling. "You girls should be getting ready for supper and the movies."

"Nothing, Mom," Libby called back. "We're getting ready."

Past a brightly colored room with two beds, Burrito raced into the one at the end of the hall. When they caught up with him Burrito was standing in a white wicker rocking chair and bracing himself against its motion. His ears swiveled around one at a time and pointed at them, and he snorted explosively.

"I've heard of a rocking horse before," Libby said, "but never a rocking burro."

"And look what he's standing on," Sarah said less than enthusiastically.

Nora put her little hand over her mouth. "Your dress, Sarah! Your dress for the dance!"

"I'll get him," Libby said confidently, edging closer.

And she did. When Burrito leaped from the rocker, Libby caught him in midair. Suddenly the burro was still, but he was breathing heavily. "You little devil," Libby said affectionately, and kissed him on the nose.

Sarah was arranging her dress over the top of the rocker. It was a beautiful rose color, with a neckline of embroidered flowers and the bottom circled with layers of pink and white ruffles.

"Sarah made it herself," Nora explained importantly. "Especially for the dance. This is Sarah's room."

Clay could already tell that. There was one entire shelf dedicated to figurines of horses. There must have been two dozen of them.

"Burrito's outfit is awful cute," Sarah said, and her sisters beamed. Clay scratched the inside of one of the burro's ears and explained to Libby, "He likes that."

"We're entering him in the county fair!" exclaimed Nora. "In the pets division!"

"If he wins a blue ribbon, it won't be for Best Behaved," Sarah replied.

Her sisters left to see if it might still be possible to sneak Burrito out of the house. Clay was looking around the room.

"It's a mess," Sarah said, blushing.

"No, it's not, it's just the opposite. You should see my room if you want to see a mess. I like your dress. You really made it all by yourself?"

"Sure."

It seemed amazing to be in her room. Right where she lives. In the heart of where she lives. His eyes were drawn to a bulletin board about half covered with blue ribbons, and under it photos of her at all different ages with ponies and big horses too. "You won all these ribbons?" he said, as he looked closely at her as a little girl.

"Don't look at those," she said. "I look terrible."

"You look . . . wonderful."

Beside the first, a second bulletin board was covered with photos clipped from movie magazines, of different movie stars and one of Monument Valley!

She wasn't speaking, she seemed bashful and uncertain. Clay's eyes were drawn back to the figurines of horses, some crystal, some porcelain, some wood. "They're beautiful," he said.

The shelf above was full of books. "*Misty of Chincoteague*," he said aloud. "Hey, I remember that book. It's about wild horses! How the Spanish conquistadores first brought them over, and they got away and went wild!"

Clay scanned the titles. "All these books are about horses!" It came to him, something he could do for her when he got back home. He had a wood-carving set he'd gotten for Christmas and never used once. If he could learn to carve well enough to send her a carving that he had made with his own hands, she would keep the horse he'd made right here along with the others.

20

Clay and Sarah were whispering when the lights went down, the big screen lit up, and the music began. They whispered through the opening credits when those words appeared across the screen, *The Man Who Shot Liberty Valance*. "Who do you think shot him?" Clay whispered. "Jimmy Stewart or John Wayne?"

"Shhhhh!" came Libby's voice amid her giggles, from right behind them. Little Nora chimed in, "They're on a date! They're on a date!"

Clay glanced from the screen, where Jimmy Stewart was stepping off the train, to Sarah's face. Her eyebrows were saying, "My sisters are pests, but there's nothing we can do about it."

He didn't mind. He'd enjoyed treating them to popcorn and soda. He was thinking of them more as pets than pests.

Back to the screen. He didn't want to miss a bit of it. What matter that her sisters were giggling behind them? It was dark, it was a movie house, and here was John Wayne bigger than life. This really was all happening to him, all in the town of Escalante, Utah, on a day he'd run wild horses out of the mountains with the girl sitting right beside him, a girl made of the stuff of his own heart.

Liberty Valance swaggered onto the screen, leering and vile, and his whip hand knocked Jimmy Stewart to the ground. "He's awful," Sarah whispered. "He's scum," Clay whispered back.

"Is he going to kiss her?" Nora asked Libby. Then the two were giggling again.

Clay pretended he didn't hear that. The movie heated up. The girls were all caught up in it now too.

When the big moment in the movie came and Clay realized the sacrifice John Wayne was making, that he would give up the girl he loved to Jimmy Stewart, that he would let her and everyone believe that it was the tender-foot with the law books who had shot Liberty Valance, Clay couldn't keep the tears from his eyes and his hand from reaching for Sarah's. The girls were too absorbed to notice and he watched the last minutes of the movie with her hand in his. He felt her gentle grip as the joy and the sadness of the day and the movie ran back and forth between them.

The music swelled and the lights went up, and Clay was blinking away the tears. John Wayne had lived out his life and gone to his grave lonely. Clay felt sure there was nothing as miraculous in life as love. "Great movie," he said.

Sarah squeezed his hand and then their hands parted. Sarah's eyes were misty too. The girls were giggling again. People were standing up and stretching, and moving up the aisles.

"That's him," Sarah said suddenly. "Staring at us. That's Barlow, in the vest."

Clay saw the man there, across the aisle and down to the right, still seated and staring at him. Yes, at him.

Why?

Now the big man raised himself slowly, fitted his hat to his head, staring all the while. Clay could feel the fear

154

coming from the little girls—the man sent a chill through him too.

Barlow lumbered up the aisle, but as he reached their row, he stopped. They were only a few seats in and Barlow was leaning toward them. His face was hard like an anvil, and his eyes squinted with hatred.

"So you're the kid," Barlow said hoarsely. "I heard you were staying with the Darlings."

His voice made everything sound like swearing.

"So you're the big ex-rodeo star's nephew."

"That's right," Clay managed. It felt like there was no air in his lungs to talk with. I'm not going to let him bully me, he thought. "—And proud of it," he added in a louder voice.

Libby and Nora were frozen to their seats. Sarah was tensed and waiting.

The man brought his face closer, and his voice began to rasp even before he spoke. "I bet you think this is all a game, don't you kid? Your uncle stealing my horses, resting up a few days in jail. Just like in the movies, right? We'll see what you think in a few days."

Now Barlow stared at Sarah as well, and then back at Clay. "I'm not surprised you're staying with the Darlings. Well, her father and his brother Sheriff Darling are going to find that things aren't going to turn out quite the way they thought. I'm putting a stop to all this, once and for all."

With that he was gone. The big man strode up the aisle and disappeared.

"Isn't he awful," Libby said. "He thinks he's so big."

"He was worse than Liberty Valance," Nora declared.

Clay looked around. Barlow was gone. Everyone had left the theater but them.

Sarah hadn't spoken but now she did. "Horsekiller," she said between her teeth.

"I wonder what John Wayne would do to him," Libby said. "He'd take care of him."

Clay looked at Sarah. She was just as shaken as he was. "Sarah, what did he mean? What's he going to do?"

Deeply troubled, Clay said good night to the Darlings and collected Curly, then walked over to the bunkhouse in the bright moonlight. He'd sit awhile out on the porch, where he could think. What did Barlow mean? What did he know?

It wasn't but a few minutes until he saw Mr. Darling coming his way. He took a seat on the porch next to Clay.

Clay wondered if Mr. Darling had come over to talk about Barlow. Sarah had told her father all about what happened at the movies, that Barlow had made some kind of bad threat about Uncle Clay. But her father had said little about it, remaining strangely silent.

"We used to have a fair number of mountain lions around here," the rancher began slowly, as if he were talking to the night.

"Once in a while a lion would take a few calves, not many. Now the lions are about gone. We're making the world safe for cows, I guess . . . When I was a kid, younger than you are now, I saw the last wolf in these parts."

"You saw a wolf, around here?"

"Lobo Arch is named after him, down in Coyote Canyon. That wolf was likely the last survivor of a pack in the Arizona Strip, and must've swum the Colorado over to the Escalante side."

The man's voice trailed away, as he seemed to have drifted out of the present. But then he picked up his story as he reached for a pine needle on the railing that he stuck in his teeth like a straw. "That wolf had a habit of nosing through piles of tin cans and garbage out around the line shacks. Finally he put his foot in a trap hidden in one of those piles. He dragged that trap ten miles before he was finally shot."

"You were there?"

"Got there right after he was killed. That wolf was the most bedraggled canine I've seen in my life. Last wolf. It was my father that shot him. And you know, after that he wouldn't even shoot a coyote. Never talked about it, but I could tell killing that wolf had changed him, and I guess it did me too."

Clay didn't know what to say, and wasn't sure why Mr. Darling was telling him these things.

"Clay, we're sure pleased you'll be here to take in the county fair with us. It starts with the dance tomorrow evening out at Dance Hall Rock—it's to commemorate the dances that the pioneers held there back in 1879. They were on their way to Hole-in-the-Rock, to cross the Colorado and start a mission up the San Juan. Anyway, I wanted to ask if you'd help me with the chuck wagon tomorrow afternoon. We'll go out there in the old style and get the barbecue started with some other fellows, and Mrs. Darling and the girls will drive out a little later with the side dishes and all. Would you do that with me?"

Clay didn't understand why Sarah's father was being so formal. "Sure," Clay said. "Happy to."

Mr. Darling didn't say anything for a while, then at last he said, "After that meeting we were at this evening, I had a chance to visit with my brother, the sheriff. I don't know how else to tell you this, but you deserve to know, so I'm just going to have to come out and say it. There's some news about your uncle that isn't so good."

How bad? Clay thought. How bad?

"Barlow has some connections in Salt Lake. He's succeeded in having another court hear your uncle's case rather than ours here, on the grounds that this is a small town and everyone's too worked up on one side or the other. What that means is, your uncle's going to be moved way up to Salt Lake."

"How soon?" Clay asked desperately.

"Day after tomorrow . . . I know you're disappointed, but I'm glad you got to visit him—"

"Can I see him in the morning?"

"I'd sure think so. My brother's disappointed that it's worked out like this. . . . Maybe your mom, as soon as she gets back, can find the best lawyer possible for him."

"How bad is it? How much trouble is he in?"

Mr. Darling looked away, and thought awhile, and then he looked back. "No telling yet, but it doesn't look good. There's a chance he'll have to serve time in the state prison. Make an example out of him, that kind of thing. To tell you the truth, I wish he'd managed to get away last week when they first caught him. If he could have made it back onto the reservation and across the Arizona border . . . This sort of offense they wouldn't bother to extradite a man for. Likely wouldn't be any more trouble if he just stayed out of the state."

21

"Sarah's in the root cellar, Clay," Mrs. Darling said, and pointed across the yard. Her eyes were asking how the early morning visit at the jail had gone, but she knew that's why he wanted to see Sarah. "Clay, would you take that box of jars in the kitchen down to Sarah? Those tomatoes are heavy."

In the shade of an immense cottonwood tree, steps led down to a door at the front of a long mound of earth. Sarah looked up when he came in. Her beautiful smile was mixed with worry.

"Tomato delivery," Clay said as bravely as he could. Really, he wanted to cry. But he'd cried on his own outside the jail, and what was happening was sad enough, he'd better not think about it too much or he'd start crying again.

She was labeling a canning jar filled with some kind of long unsightly vegetables. "What is that stuff?" he asked, and wrinkled his nose.

"Pickled okra. We're going to enter it in the fair."

He picked up a jar of cherries she'd also labeled and set with other jars she'd singled out. "If they need tasters, I'll volunteer for these, but I'll pass on that okra stuff. My mom says I have a rule—if it sounds funny and looks weird, it can't be good to eat."

Remember, Clay told himself. You told your uncle how much you were looking forward to the dance, and you even told him about Sarah's new dress. "This dance tonight is going to be extra special for Sarah," Uncle Clay had said. Don't spoil it for her was what he meant.

He was looking around at the shelves upon shelves of canned fruits and vegetables. It was staggering how much food her family had stored away. "It sure is cool in here," he said absently.

"I like your new boots, Clay. Did your uncle see them?"

"No, I got 'em on the way home."

She was placing the tomatoes on the shelves. "My father told me what's happened," she said. "How is your uncle Clay?"

He had to share his heart with her. His lip was quivering but there wasn't anything he could do about it. If he couldn't tell her how he felt, who would he ever be able to talk to? "My uncle was trying to be brave about it, but I could tell how bad he felt. I just don't think you can lock up somebody like him. You know what he said? 'Freedom's the air I breathe.' "

"I know, I've been thinking what that would be like. There wouldn't be anything more awful."

"I feel so . . . useless."

"You made him happy—you came all this way to find him. I'm sure you lifted his spirits this morning."

Clay's eyes returned to the pen in her hand. "I didn't mean to keep you from labeling those."

"I'm just about done," she said, and wrote "August 1962."

"I can't believe how much food you have down here."

"It's part of being in our church," she explained. "Every family has a year's supply of food stored away. There's flour

160

in those barrels over there, cornmeal, and rice, and in the sawdust bins, apples and potatoes."

"I guess you'll be in good shape if there's an atomic war."

"That's part of it," she agreed. "Here, let me show you what's back here."

At the rear of the root cellar Sarah opened another door. It opened onto another room with four simple beds and a tiny kitchen with a counter, sink, and an old-fashioned cookstove.

"What's all this?"

"Our bomb shelter. Behind the partition there, there's even a little bathroom."

He felt awful. "That's nice," he said uncertainly. "You won't be able to go outside for a half a year or a year or something."

"I know. Even if we're not a target or anything, they say the radiation just falls out of the sky and poisons everything. But I don't think it's really going to happen, Clay."

He looked at the shelter. It said otherwise. He was never going to have the chance to do something great, like one of the people in President Kennedy's book, *Profiles in Courage.* "Seattle's going to get blown to kingdom come," he said.

Sarah said with conviction, "I don't think so."

"Why not, then?"

"It's like last winter when John Glenn's capsule was returning into the atmosphere, and for a few minutes there was no radio contact and they were wondering if the heat shield came off the capsule and he'd burned up. Did you think he was going to be okay or that he'd been killed?"

"I thought he was going to make it. I was praying like anything."

"So was I, and I thought he was going to make it too. If we were always going around afraid . . . We wouldn't even be able to go to Dance Hall Rock this evening. We'd have to stay close to our bomb shelter in case anything happened!"

There she'd done it, she'd made him smile again. That long braid swung as she closed the door and turned toward her canning jars. He wanted to reach out and touch that braid, but he watched it go. "Let's get back to work," Sarah said. "Let's box up these things we're going to enter in the fair so they're ready tomorrow morning. If you think I've got ribbons you ought to see Mom's. If we're lucky, maybe she's made an extra pie while she was baking the ones for the fair."

"Sarah, what will happen to the horses now, the ones we hid in Death Hollow?"

"I don't know, Clay, I just don't know. Maybe I'll have to go back and let them go."

Outside, Libby and Nora were riding Pal, and Burrito was trotting alongside. "Look Sarah," Libby shouted. "Dad's going to let us ride in to the fair tomorrow on Pal if it's okay with Clay!"

"You bet it is," he called.

Clay looked at Sarah. She sure was fond of her sisters. It seemed like the three of them should have a brother.

Wait a minute, he told himself. What am I thinking about! Not in a million years would I begin to feel for Sarah like a *brother*!

It was a goodly distance out to Dance Hall Rock. Clay was riding Starbuck alongside the chuck wagon, an old covered wagon full of the pots and pans and other paraphernalia needed to put on the big feed before the dance. Now and again Mr. Darling would cluck to the team of four horses and give the reins a snap. Like his daughter, that man knew how to cluck to a horse without coming off like a chicken.

A friend of Mr. Darling's was seated on the wagon bench with him so Mr. Darling wasn't lacking for company. In between them stood Curly with his little front feet up on Mr. Darling's legs, commanding a view of the team and the road and panting as if he didn't have that canvas shade over his head. Clay was happy to have the time to himself to think, to just let himself go with the rhythm of the saddle and drift off the way he liked.

He drifted off a couple different directions, but he would never drift very far until he returned to the man in the cell. Tomorrow Uncle Clay would be sent up to Salt Lake City and he'd be put in a jail that wasn't like the Escalante jail at all. There'd be no Aunt Violet there who knew he wasn't the kind who should be in jail and treat him kindly. How long would he be in prison? Pretty long, Mr. Darling had implied. You could see it written all over her father's face. How long? Three years, five years, ten years? Even three would be forever.

In three years I'll be out of high school, Clay thought. That's so far away you can't even begin to picture it.

What about the salmon fishing they were going to do? What about the boat up to Ketchikan, Alaska? When he'd found his uncle it felt like they were just getting started. His uncle had seen he wasn't a little kid anymore.

Or was he a little kid? Growing tall, but still a kid.

There was something that was nagging at the edge of his memory like a raven squawking when you're coming out of a nap in the shade. What was it? Something important. Oh, well.

Dance Hall Rock sits in some pretty country, he thought. Yucca and junipers, red sand, dunes and rolling slickrock, rock outcrops of red and pink and white sandstone. A lot like Monument Valley, really. He wondered if they'd ever made any Westerns here. Well, they should.

It was something Mr. Darling had said, he realized. That's what was nagging at him and demanding to be remembered. When her father had been talking about Uncle

Clay, when he'd been talking about him getting caught—
that was it. "He'd be all right as long as he didn't come
back to the state of Utah." That was it, that's what he'd
said.

Uncle Clay needs to get out of there, Clay thought.
That's what he really needs. He needs a good old-fashioned
escape. All he needs is to ride through these dunes and over
this slickrock and out of this town and this state.

That's what he should really be doing, figuring out how
to bust his uncle out of jail.

But how would you pull it off? Could that even be
possible?

He must have seen a thousand jailbreaks. . . . If he
could only remember, one of them would show him the
way. What would John Wayne do? How about hitching up
Starbuck to the bars in Uncle Clay's cell window, the little
one at ground level in the window well? What if he hitched
up Pal too? What if he used this team of four that Mr.
Darling was driving?

Who was he fooling? He'd seen those bars. The ones
they use for the movies must be hollow or something.

What about dozing deputies? More than any other ploy,
that was the one that seemed to work the most often. Figure
out how to sneak the keys right off a dozing deputy or from
right under their nose. With a broom handle and a little
nail bent at a right angle sticking out of the end of it, he
could lift that big key ring right off the end of the dozing
deputy's sleepy fingers. . . .

Wait a minute! The deputy in this case was Aunt Violet,
and she was never dozing. She was always sweeping or
mopping or cooking or something. Not only that, she didn't
have one of those big old movie key rings with all the giant
keys. She only had an ordinary little key ring with four or
five keys on it, probably her car key and house key and her
jail keys. And she didn't keep them where you could send

Curly after them or snag them with your fishing line and a hook—she always kept them in her dress pocket.

"There it is," Mr. Darling called.

"What?" he replied, half-startled.

"Dance Hall Rock. Say, did you fall asleep on your horse?"

"Just kind of daydreaming," he replied.

To himself, he added: "As usual."

Clay helped unload the chuck wagon, and then he had a chance to inspect the "dance floor." It was easy enough to picture those pioneers at this natural slickrock pavilion, and it was easy to imagine how perfectly the huge sandstone backdrop projected the sounds of the instruments back to the dancers.

In a minute Clay had an ax in his hands and he was helping to make kindling and to lay it into the barbecue pits. Right on cue a pickup pulled in full of seasoned scrub oak and he helped to get the fires going. In another half hour the folding tables and chairs arrived and he went to work setting them up on the slickrock. The men and the boys were dressed in their newest jeans and best shirts, dress boots and go-to-church Stetsons. They were kind of shy about talking to him, but they were happy to have him working alongside. It was good to have something to do, to keep his mind off tomorrow.

Some of the younger boys couldn't keep their eyes off his jewelry. That's what set him apart from them, and the fact he was a stranger of course. Everybody around Escalante knew everybody else. He heard several whisper, "That's Clay Jenkins's nephew."

The meat was brought out soaking in barbecue sauce, in dozens and dozens of deep metal pans.

It was late afternoon now and the whole town was driving in, the whole county. He had a giant pair of gloves

165

on and a huge fork in his hands, and he was helping tend the beef over the red-hot coals. It felt awful good working alongside Mr. Darling. It felt good to see all the women arriving with their colorful dresses and their hair all done up, and going right to work spreading out tablecloths on the tables and laying out more food on the buffet lines that he'd ever seen in one place. There were kids running around, excited as baby burros, hundreds of kids.

He asked Mr. Darling, "How many cows are we cooking up here?"

Before Clay heard an answer, his eye caught Libby and Nora and Mrs. Darling and a fourth with them, a young woman with wavy dark hair all down her back and a flower in her hair. All were wearing long dresses and carrying dishes of food toward the buffet tables. Who was that young woman, or was it a girl, in the rose-colored dress. . . .

Then he realized—Sarah! You fool, it's Sarah, with her hair all combed out down her back. That's Sarah, in the dress she made!

22

They sat down right across the picnic table from one another. At first Clay was so taken with how different Sarah looked, he could barely look at her. All he could do was eat; he was good at that, and he'd heaped his plate high. He was beginning to feel he didn't know her at all, didn't belong here, when Sarah said, "I wish you could see the colors next month up around Cyclone Lake, when the aspens are turning."

What a relief to hear her speak. She was still the same Sarah. She was real, not someone he'd dreamed up. Now he couldn't take his eyes off her, this girl in the rose-colored dress with the embroidered flowers at her neck, this girl with the long wavy dark hair all glistening. He was going to miss her so badly, it hurt already. How much longer could he stay? Another week?

"There's Uncle Dave," Libby said, pointing out the man in the starched uniform returning from seconds at the grill.

The sheriff, Clay realized. He looks so stiff, and so official. It was hard to imagine he'd been sympathetic with Uncle Clay.

"Their family always sits with us," Libby said. "How come they didn't this year?

"The election's coming up soon, and he has to campaign," Mrs. Darling said. "He has to mix with everybody."

"And there's that Mr. Barlow," Nora sang out. "He's worse than Liberty Valance."

"Shush, now," Mrs. Darling said. "Nora, see if your father's got enough help so he can come sit down with us yet."

"Clay, let's get some dessert," Sarah suggested.

The sun had set. The slickrock in the distance, out toward the Colorado, was rimmed with orange. Guitars and fiddles were tuning up, a banjo too.

They ran into Aunt Violet dishing out slices from the homemade pies. She was wearing one of those ruffled dresses and she had her gray hair piled up extra high with a purple ribbon to match the dress. She broke into a big smile when she saw him. This felt like running into somebody you knew from home. "You look great tonight, Aunt Violet," Clay told her.

"I'm going to take some of these back to your uncle," she said. "One of each kind, so he can take his choice and eat as much as he wants. I hope you came to dance, Clay— you're going to see quite a shindig here tonight."

He could tell she was trying to cheer him up. She knew too, what was going to happen in the morning.

The band looked like they were ready, but then they set their instruments aside. "There's going to be a few speeches," Sarah explained.

They drifted away from the speeches toward a nearby rock formation, where they sat and watched quietly. The moon was just about to rise across the Colorado. He reached for her hand as they watched the moon lift huge and orange from those slickrock badlands between the two rivers. The full moon freed itself from the rock ocean and buoyed up enormous and bright and orange into the night sky. She squeezed his hand. They looked at each other, knowing each other's hearts. Curly appeared from the busy rounds he'd been making and jumped up on their laps, offering his moist black nose.

The speeches were short, and the band soon launched into a full-speed-ahead "Orange Blossom Special." Sarah's feet began to tap. It was easy to see she was looking forward to dancing, and Clay guessed it wasn't going to be any sort of dancing he could manage. They walked over closer to the dance floor and watched.

The next number slowed things down some, and the people didn't wait to be invited to commemorate the dances that the pioneers had held on this very spot so many years before. Clay and Sarah stood to the side and watched the men twirl their partners gracefully. The petticoats were flying. A harmonica player joined in and Clay thought of his friend Russell and the Midnight Flyer and the campfire that night when he'd tried to dance their way and only ended up creating his own unique style. This kind of dancing was just as foreign to him as Navajo dancing.

Her parents joined in at the next dance. Aunt Violet was out there too, and she was quite a dancer. To Clay's horror, a boy came up and asked Sarah for the next dance. To his everlasting relief she shook her head, and the boy disappeared. "That was George Winchell," she said, "from school."

"Sarah," he said. "I'm not sure I can do this kind of dancing, but I'll give it a try."

"Let's practice a little right here, first. I'll teach you."

"Really, right here?"

He concentrated hard. With your hands on her hips, or with your fingers entwined, you signaled what you were going to do, and then you just did it. She was making it seem easy. Before long he was twirling her too, and those layers of pink and white ruffles were swirling like a top. Then they joined the other dancers. Her long hair was flying, and she was looking into his eyes. It didn't matter if he lost the beat; he could find it again. It was so crowded, nobody was really watching anybody else and there were collisions besides the ones he caused. It all seemed to be part of the fun. "You're so lucky to live here, Sarah . . . ," he said all out of breath. "Everyone in town must be out here tonight."

"Escalante's deserted," she agreed.

Except for my uncle, he thought. In the basement of the Escalante courthouse. One man down there very much alone.

Aunt Violet swept by with an elderly gentleman a head shorter than she. She was having the time of her life.

Aunt Violet's not at the jail, he thought. Aunt Violet's here. She's your dozing deputy. . . . She's the key. . . . *She's got the keys!*

Clay tried to steer Sarah toward Aunt Violet. He was working on an idea and it was firing him all up inside like a Roman candle. He got a pretty good glimpse of Aunt Violet again, but he couldn't tell for sure what he needed to know. "Sarah," he whispered, "I need to talk to you."

He tugged her away from the dancers, and then he whispered in her ear, "Would Aunt Violet's dress have a pocket, like the ones she wears at work?"

"Mine does." Sarah's hand slipped between folds in the pattern of her dress on the right side, and he could see the white of the lining there. "How come you're wondering?"

Clay's eye was still on Aunt Violet, wheeling there among the dancers. She always kept the keys in her dress pocket. Of course she'd have them with her. That's where she kept them. This dress would have a pocket too. It had to.

The song was ending. It was crazy, but if he was going to try it he better not think about it too long, he better do it now. "Watch," he said. "Stay right here. I'll be back in a few minutes."

Clay squeezed between couples getting their breath. You'll only have one chance, he told himself. I don't think she's left-handed. Her pocket would be on her right side. Try her right side.

Aunt Violet's partner was thanking her for the dance. Clay presented himself. "May I have the next dance?" he asked as gallantly as possible and all out of breath.

She was delighted. She probably thinks I can dance, Clay thought.

It was a pretty fast dance, a "Texas swing dance" as he heard Aunt Violet remark, and he swung himself into it and swung her too, like a whirling dervish. The Navajos would've loved this! Aunt Violet was smiling through it at least. She had a nervous smile you might expect from someone at the top of a carnival ride that's a lot scarier than they expected.

When Clay had things wound up as much as he could wind them, he gave Aunt Violet a huge spin and stuck out the tip of his cowboy boot below her flying dress to catch her ankle, and then he lunged to make sure she would land on him, which is what she was doing. He was enveloped by her skirts and reaching for that pocket even before she went down. To Aunt Violet it might have seemed he was thrashing around trying to escape her considerable weight; to him all the motion was meant to camouflage the job of the one limb he was counting on, his right arm and his right hand.

He had the keys! And yes, his hand was free of her pocket and those keys were tucked in his own jeans before all the confusion came to rest. People close by were standing around, some chuckling. The band was playing on, thank goodness, and he was apologizing all over himself to Aunt Violet who was dusting herself off. "I'm pretty dangerous," he said, snugging his hat back on his head.

"That you are," she agreed.

"This kind of dancing's all new to me. But you should see me do the Twist."

"Another time, Clay," she said, laughing now. "Another time."

That lady wasn't going to let one fall spoil her evening. Her partner was back to save her, and she went right on dancing.

Clay whispered in Sarah's ear, "I want to show you something." A little ways into the moonlight, he took her hand and led her toward the formation where they'd watched the moon rise. A little ball of white joined them. "Curly!" Clay said. "Stick close, now."

Behind the rock formation he pulled the keys out of his pocket. "Sarah," he said. "These are Aunt Violet's keys. The keys to the jail and Uncle Clay's cell."

She gasped.

"Uncle Clay's horse is in the corral right by the jail. We can make it to Arizona. I have to try."

"The sheriff will come after you, and Barlow will too."

"They won't find out until sometime after the dance. I figure it'll be hard to track us if we stay on the slickrock."

"You're right about that. I'm sure they'll come in their trucks, on the road. . . . With the moonlight, you could ride at night and hide in the canyons by day. . . . I think you'd have a chance anyway, Clay."

"Sarah, I have to go fast, I have to get back to town as fast as I can."

He reached out for her. The moon lit up the yellow flecks in her eyes. Clay touched her cheek with one hand, and his other hand found the silkiness of her hair. His lips touched hers, and then their lips met, and it felt like . . . canyons and mesas and rainbows, and the desert fresh after a rain. It felt like the promise of the life that lay before him all shining and ready for him to make something of. "I love you," he whispered. "Sarah Darling, Sarah Darling."

"I love you, Clay. I really love you."

They held hands. "I just got here," he said, and a tear popped out of an eye. "I just met you."

"I know. . . ."

"Say good-bye to your folks for me, and Libby and Nora. They won't mind keeping Pal and Burrito for me, will they?"

"Pal and Burrito will be eating at the table."

"It'll be good to know exactly where those desert canaries are. And I'm going to come back and see them."

"You better," she sniffled. "And take care of yourself, Clay. Remember, there's no one else like you."

"Do you like letters? Long ones?"

"The longer the better."

He took the silver bracelet with the three beautiful stones from his wrist and he put it on hers. "It's a little big," he said.

Sarah slid it up her arm some. "Fits perfect."

He kissed her again, and then their lips parted, and then Clay stood up to leave.

"But I want to see you once more," Sarah was saying. "Maybe there's a chance. I know where you'll be going, I can try to guess how long it might take you. . . . Be sure to look around for me before you cross the Colorado. I just might be there."

Clay tucked Curly to his chest so no one would notice the ball of white. As he walked his horse away from the music echoing out of Dance Hall Rock, he could hear the band singing, "A-way, I'm bound a'way, a-cross the wide Mis-sour-i."

Missouri nothing, Clay thought as he mounted Starbuck and nestled Curly in his left hand against his stomach. Across the Colorado and into the reservation. *Across the Colorado and into Arizona!*

173

23

By night, they rode. Late in the night that first night, they saw the headlights of vehicles prowling around on the slickrock. But it was a big country and none came close enough to cast its lights on them. Occasionally they'd encounter a cluster of cows taking in the moonlight, and Curly would bark under his breath. Clay explained to Uncle Clay that they must be those "10–30" cows.

Whenever their horses left a pile of evidence behind, Uncle Clay brought his gloves out of his saddlebags and buried it in a patch of sand. He was being that careful. "I won't give Barlow much credit, but I'm guessing he knows the difference between cow pies and horse apples. You know, Clay, we're just like two Apaches. On all this slick-rock, they'll never find us."

"I sure hope not," Clay said with a feeling of dread. His uncle was feeling awful good, but was he being realistic?

"Lemme tell you about Apaches," Uncle Clay said, with a wild glint of moonlight in his eye. "They say, out in the middle of the desert with just rocks and sand, and scrub around no taller than your waist, you could turn your back on an Apache and he could disguise himself no farther'n a stone's throw away, disguise himself so well you just plain couldn't find him."

"Is that true?"

"I wouldn't doubt it. There's so much we don't know. . . . Those colors in your saddle blanket, they all come from the plants around here. Those Navajo women know exactly which ones, and whether its the roots or leaves or flowers. . . . We're bound for Yazzieland, Clay! I still can't believe you busted me out of the Escalante jail!"

"You should've seen the look on your face."

"Man oh man . . . God I love this country!"

By day they hid in one of the many slot-canyons that drained toward the Escalante, and they ate from the grub they'd pilfered from the jail kitchen and stashed in their saddlebags. They napped in the shade, but Clay never really slept. He kept listening for the sound of approaching horses, or footsteps. He knew they were out there, the sheriff and Barlow too.

When the moonlight showed on the canyon wall above, they started out of the canyon. Uncle Clay held the horses while Clay sneaked up to the rim and looked all around, keeping low to the ground. Curly knew to keep quiet. All clear. Before long they were up on the slickrock again, riding on the rolling sea of slickrock.

After several hours they heard vehicles, jeeps or trucks, and saw their profiles far off. They were running without headlights this time. "Stay still," Uncle Clay said.

"They'll see us!" Clay whispered. "If we can see them, they can see us."

"Not necessarily," Uncle Clay said. "If we stay real still, from that distance we're going to look like a couple of these junipers."

The motors droned away in the distance, just as Uncle Clay had predicted.

175

A second day they hid, and another night they rode.

With daylight approaching once again, Clay steered for the safety of a nearby canyon. "This way," his uncle said, staying on the beeline across the exposed slickrock toward the east and the lavenders of dawn.

"But Uncle Clay . . . ," he warned, "they can see us up here."

"We're going to be all right," his uncle said, only a little bit tense. "They're going to be tired of looking for us by now. They've gone home for breakfast."

"I sure hope so."

Why were they taking such a chance? Clay thought. It wasn't worth it! They were so close, so close now.

They rode for another half hour. Clay's dread was growing as the daylight was coming on. "It's getting really light, Uncle Clay!"

"Just a little bit farther," his uncle replied. His uncle looked worried now too, but his jaw was set.

Clay was looking all around, all around, and listening. Was he hearing a motor or was he just imagining it?

Still they continued on. The sun was rising. Off to the southeast, he could see a big corral. "Please, Uncle Clay, let's get out of here."

"Just up ahead," was all his uncle said.

As soon as Clay saw this canyon, he didn't have a good feeling about it. It didn't look deep enough or narrow enough to do them much good. It was more like a broad wash. You could see into the bottom of it from a long ways.

"It gets deep soon enough," his uncle said reassuringly.

They started down into the wash. Still, Clay didn't like it. There was no way down on slickrock like there had been into the canyon the day before. They were leaving all kinds of tracks. Why take a risk like this?

They followed the wash downstream until the walls rose

a hundred feet. Still, the wash was wide, and someone up above would see everything. "Let's hurry," he said.

"We'll be okay." His uncle reined his horse in. "Right here. This is a stop I have to make, Clay."

Without saying another word, his uncle tied his horse to a bush right there in the bottom of the wash and started climbing up the hillside.

Clay didn't know what he should do. They had to get down this canyon and fast, and get onto some slickrock where they couldn't be followed. Curly was looking back and forth between him and his uncle moving up the slope, and he was confused too.

Clay scrambled up the slope after him. His uncle was crouching up there at the base of the rimrock where a big slab of rock had fallen down and was leaning back against the rimrock.

He was breathing hard when he reached his uncle. He paused for a second to catch his breath. The soil was dusty and loose, like you find around the cliff ruins. His uncle was crouching at the entrance of the tentlike space under the leaning slab, and he'd taken his hat off. There was a pile of rocks in there, and something else. . . .

Clay leaned closer, and then he saw it. The All-Around Cowboy buckle tucked back in the rocks.

"I had to stop, Clay. I sure hope it isn't going to get us caught, but if I'm never going to come back into this state I knew I had to pay her a visit, one last time."

"I'll run up and keep a lookout," Clay said hurriedly. As much as anything, he thought he should give his uncle privacy for his grief.

It was a a few hundred yards back up the canyon before he found a way up and out. It was broad daylight now and he was terrified. As he was nearing the rim he kept to his belly and crawled up like a lizard. All he meant to do was poke his head over the top.

Up ahead, Curly was growling.

"Quiet, Curly!"

A little ways farther, and he'd be able to peek over the top.

What he found was a big man standing just back from the rim. A man with a deer rifle, a man with a face hard like an anvil and unshaven. A jeep was parked three or four hundred yards away, back by the corral.

"Thought you were pretty smart, didn't you?" The man's voice was hoarse and pitiless.

Clay didn't say anything. All his hopes were dust. Clay stood up and came over the rim, looked around. There was no one but Barlow.

"The sheriff wouldn't stick with it," Barlow sneered. "I knew you were out here somewhere. Your uncle's a rodeo cowboy, that's all he is. I was born out here."

Down the canyon, Uncle Clay had his back turned and wasn't seeing this. He was in the same crouched position. Should he shout to his uncle? Would Barlow shoot? Would Uncle Clay run even if he could?

Uncle Clay wouldn't run with me up here, Clay realized. There's nothing I can do. It's all over.

"Look, Mr. Barlow, why don't you just let him go? He never hurt you, I mean, not you personally."

The man snorted in disgust, and then squinted down the canyon. "What's he doing over there? He's been in that same spot for fifteen minutes."

"Visiting her grave," Clay said quietly.

"Whose grave?" Barlow's voice was harsher than ever.

"Don't you remember? When he came to you to get horses, and his wife was sick? You said she'd just eaten too much frybread, or something like that? Don't you remember?"

Clay saw confusion in Barlow's face at first, and then the memory coming back.

"They think her appendix burst. She died out here."

"I never knew that," Barlow said roughly. "I never heard that from anybody."

"He never talks about it," Clay said. "I learned it from the Navajos."

Barlow stared a long time down the canyon at the man under the rimrock. Then his hard features slackened as the hatred seemed to leave his eyes for a moment. "I'll tell you what, kid . . . ," Barlow said finally, still looking down the canyon. "Just get him out of here . . . just get him out of here for good."

The man turned suddenly on his heel and walked away.

For a moment Clay almost said thanks. No, it was better to say nothing. Even to Uncle Clay, he'd say nothing of what had happened here.

Hurry him down to the river, today. The sheriff might still come looking.

"Now that we've left tracks in this canyon, let's just skedaddle," Uncle Clay said. His eyes were bright and shining but the dust on his cheeks showed the passage of tears. "This is the start of Coyote Canyon. If we keep moving all day, I believe we can cross the river yet this afternoon."

"Fine with me," Clay said. "Let's make tracks, Uncle Clay. Let's make tracks, Curly. I told Russell Yazzie I was going to come back and see him one day—wait till he finds out how soon!"

"A couple days of hard riding and we'll be there. I can smell that wooly mutton roasting from here."

"And I'm going to have a decent present to give my friend."

"What's that?"

"His horse back!"

They dropped into a deeper and deeper canyon. They rode under a natural bridge and they rode under Lobo Arch.

They rode under hanging gardens of ferns and red wildflowers, and dripping springs so convenient they stuck out their mouths and drank from horseback. When they reached the canyon of the Escalante they turned downstream along its sandy shallows.

Past the mouth of Davis Canyon they rode, and Clay remembered a cloudburst and a burro being born. All the while he was scanning the rims a thousand feet above, looking for a girl waving where he guessed she'd be. Soon they'd leave her country and his heart would be left behind as well.

Between the sheer red walls they rode, between the waving willows at the Escalante's edge. No cloudburst coming today. The sky was as blue as the walls were red and the willows were green. "*Bik'é Hozhoni,*" he said aloud.

"Yes, sir," his uncle agreed. "On the beautiful trail we go."

"Just a couple of miles to the river," Clay said, looking up to the rims. "We aren't safe yet."

At last, the coffee-and-cream Colorado. They reined their horses in, and his uncle reached over and shook his hand. "I'll never forget it, Clay. And what do you keep looking up for, anyway?"

"Oh, I'm just checking out the canyon. It sure is deep." In fact, it was so deep he couldn't see up to the Escalante's rims. Even if she was up there he wouldn't see her.

Uncle Clay said it was important to rest the horses before the big swim across the river. They rested too, lying on the riverbank without speaking, thinking about all that had happened. Curly nestled his head against Clay's shoulder and sighed, then closed his eyes.

Just as Clay was thinking the horses must be rested enough and they shouldn't wait any longer, Curly lifted his head and looked around ominously. The tiny dog's brown ears were standing straight up. Clay listened too and thought he heard something, listened again.

At first it sounded far off, like the ocean in a conch shell. Strangely, it was building fast. Clay reached for his hat and got to his feet. Uncle Clay was hearing it too, and he was alarmed.

The sound was swelling, like the Pacific during a storm. In the time it took for Clay to scoop Curly up and turn toward the mustang, the roar was rushing his way, sounding more like a colossal torrent of hailstones, and it seemed to be coming at them off the Escalante's walls.

Clay was fumbling with his shirt buttons, trying to get Curly safely tucked inside for the swim across the river. Uncle Clay, standing by with both horses, was ready to hand him Starbuck's reins.

But before they could mount up, the torrent was upon them. Horses were streaming out of the Escalante and into the canyon mouth, riderless horses with their manes flying. In the lead, that mare blue as a mountain bluebird.

"Holy cow," his uncle said.

Then came the black-and-white dogs, and behind them, the girl on that palomino horse with her long braid flying.

"Got some horses for you!" she called.

Author's Note

While *The Big Wander* is a work of fiction, the idea of a boy, burro, and dog adventuring in the canyon country was inspired by the wanderings of Everett Ruess, a real-life artist and vagabond who has become a legendary figure in the Southwest. The tiny dog who rides the burro's pack in this story is named after Everett's dog, Curly, as a tribute to this remarkable young man who disappeared in the canyons of the Escalante in 1934. His fate remains a mystery.

THIS BOOK
BELONGS TO:

_____

ANNE of GREEN GABLES

BY

Lucy Maud Montgomery

CHILDREN'S CLASSICS

NEW YORK

This 1998 edition is published by Children's Classics™,
an imprint of Random House Value Publishing,
a division of Random House, Inc., New York.

Children's Classics™ and the colophon is a trademark
of Random House, Inc.

Random House
New York • Toronto • London • Sydney • Auckland
www.randomhouse.com

Printed and bound in the United States of America

ISBN 0-517-18968-2

8 7 6 5

*This volume contains the complete and unabridged text of the original edition,
which has been completely reset. The modern reader may be surprised to
discover old-fashioned styles of punctuation and spelling, but these have been
retained in order to convey the flavor and quaintness of the original work.*

The good stars met in your horoscope,
Made you of spirit and fire and dew.
                    —BROWNING

FOREWORD

"There's such a lot of different Annes in me. I sometimes think that is why I'm such a troublesome person. If I was just the one Anne it would be ever so much more comfortable, but then it wouldn't be half so interesting."

Reading *Anne of Green Gables*, we feel there is a vital, living person in the room with us. "All spirit and fire and dew," Lucy Maud Montgomery's Anne is one of the most intriguing heroines in children's literature. She experiences both "the pleasures and pains of life . . . with trebled intensity," living in constant expectation that the next moment will bring adventure. And she is also often reduced to speechlessness by the beauty of sunset, wind, or water. Trying to fit this romantic vision of life into the workaday world of Prince Edward Island, Canada, lands Anne in many comical predicaments. But, as she herself says,

"I never make the same mistake twice. There *must* be a limit to the mistakes one person can make, and when I get to the end of them, then I'll be through with them. That's a very comforting thought."

We first meet Anne when Matthew Cuthbert goes to the train station to pick up the orphan boy he expects is coming to help out on his farm. He finds instead the eleven-year-old girl, sent by mistake from Hopetown Asylum. On the drive home, Anne's pent-up thoughts and feelings spill out. Along with Matthew, we are caught in the spell of Anne's unique voice,

> Isn't it splendid to think of all the things there are to find out about? It just makes me feel glad to be alive . . . . It wouldn't be half so interesting if we knew all about everything, would it? There'd be no scope for the imagination then, would there?"

It is her zest for living that endears Anne to Marilla and Matthew, the elderly sister and brother who do indeed adopt her, and who come to feel the tenderness previously missing from their barren lives. Marilla is "a woman of narrow experience and rigid conscience" with "a saving something about her mouth which, if it had been ever so slightly developed, might have been considered indicative of a sense of humor." Shy Matthew has the "uncomfortable feeling" that all women are "secretly laughing at him." Into their stark world, Anne brings all the varied shadings of fantasy, humor, and poetic insight. She also voices the thoughts Marilla has never permitted herself to think. And, when necessary, she consoles herself by turning life's disappointments into the overblown language of the romance novels she has read,

> "Now you see why I can't be perfectly happy. Nobody could who had red hair . . . . I *cannot* imagine that red hair away. I do my best. I think to myself, 'Now my hair is a glorious black, black as the raven's wing.' But all the time I *know* it is just plain red, and it breaks my heart. It will be my lifelong sorrow."

While we are bewitched by Anne's turn of phrase, we are also led to admire her courage. We wonder how she overcame her earlier life of almost constant hardship to develop her resilience and her determination to taste life to its fullest. The same might be wondered about the author herself, Lucy Maud Montgomery. Raised by strict, elderly grandparents after her mother died when she was only twenty-one months old, Maud, as she like to be called, was forbidden many of the small pleasures allowed her classmates. Yet the earliest diaries of hers that we have (*The Selected Journals of L. M. Montgomery, Volume I: 1889–1910*, Mary Rubio and Elizabeth Waterston, editors, Oxford University Press, Toronto, 1985), record merry doings and her abiding love of nature. We can hear the bubbling voice of Anne, but without the theatrics. However, it was not until early adulthood that Maud trusted her journal to put down her deepest feelings. She recalled of her childhood:

> "For I had already begun to live that strange inner life of fancy which has always existed side by side with my outer life—a life into which I have so often escaped from the dull or painful real.

With the same tenacity with which Anne clings to her appreciation of life's beauties, Maud struggled against great odds to write. She overcame both the bone-chilling cold and exhaustion of one of her years of teaching and the frantic pace of her months spent working on a newspaper to find time to write. But most difficult, she had to deal with the isolation of the almost thirteen years she lived with her grandmother, to whom she returned after her grandfather's death. At the age of twenty-six, she wrote,

> I love bright, cheerful companionship, laughter, sparkling conversation. I get nothing of them. Grandma has always been a reserved, distant woman . . . . My inner life has . . . been lived entirely alone . . . . Sometimes I am conscious of a great *soul loneliness*.

Though Maud wrote constantly, producing many short stories and poems, *Anne of Green Gables* was her first novel. She began the story in the spring of 1904, finding the germ of the idea in a notebook of jottings she had writtten years before: "Elderly couple apply to orphan asylum for a boy. By mistake a girl is sent them." Anne "soon seemed very real to me and took possession of me to an unusual extent," (L. M. Montgomery, *The Alpine Path*, *The Story of My Career*, Fitzhenry & Whiteside Limited, Canada, 1917). Maud decided to write her first full-length book. She finished it in October, 1905, and sent it in turn to five publishers, who all rejected it. Maud put the manuscript away in a hatbox, but, rummaging one winter day, she re-read it and decided to try again. It was accepted by L. C. Page and

Company of Boston, who published it in 1908.

Maud discovered with pleasure that *Anne* was to be a best seller. Mark Twain sent a letter to Maud, calling Anne "the dearest, and most lovable child in fiction since the immortal Alice." The "odder, unexpecteder witch of a child" opened up to young and old a world that is forever morning, with boundless possibilities for delight. Reading *Anne of Green Gables,* we find ourselves rejoicing in the resilience of the human spirit. Though Anne, after one of her narrow escapes, declares,

> " . . . today's mistake is going to cure me of being too romantic . . . . It was probably easy enough in towered Camelot hundreds of years ago, but romance is not appreciated now,"

we may join in Matthew's wishes, not only for Anne, but also for ourselves, "Don't give up all your romance, Anne . . . a little is a good thing—not too much, of course—but keep a little of it, Anne, keep a little of it."

ELLEN S. SHAPIRO

Brooklyn, New York
1987

CHAPTER 1

MRS. RACHEL LYNDE IS SURPRISED

MRS. RACHEL LYNDE lived just where the Avonlea main road dipped down into a little hollow, fringed with alders and ladies' eardrops and traversed by a brook that had its source away back in the woods of the old Cuthbert place; it was reputed to be an intricate, headlong brook in its earlier course through those woods, with dark secrets of pool and cascade; but by the time it reached Lynde's Hollow it was a quiet, well-conducted little stream, for not even a brook could run past Mrs. Rachel Lynde's door without due regard for decency and decorum; it probably was conscious that Mrs. Rachel was sitting at her window, keeping a sharp eye on everything that passed, from brooks and children up, and that if she noticed anything odd or out of place she would never rest until she had ferreted out the whys and wherefores thereof.

There are plenty of people, in Avonlea and out of it, who can attend closely to their neighbors' business by dint of neglecting their own; but Mrs. Rachel Lynde was one of those capable creatures who can manage their own concerns and those of other folks into the bargain. She was a notable housewife; her work was always done and well done; she "ran" the Sewing Circle, helped run the Sunday school, and was the strongest prop of the Church Aid Society and Foreign Missions Auxiliary. Yet with all this Mrs. Rachel found abundant time to sit for hours at her kitchen window, knitting "cotton warp" quilts—she had knitted sixteen of them, as Avonlea housekeepers were wont to tell in awed voices—and keeping a sharp eye on the main road that crossed the hollow and wound up the steep red hill beyond. Since Avonlea occupied a little triangular peninsula jutting out into the Gulf of St. Lawrence, with water on two sides of it, anybody who went out of it or into it had to pass over that hill road and so run the unseen gauntlet of Mrs. Rachel's all-seeing eye.

She was sitting there one afernoon in early June. The sun was coming in at the window warm and bright; the orchard on the slope below the house was in a bridal flush of pinky-white bloom, hummed over by a myriad of bees. Thomas Lynde—a meek little man whom Avonlea people called "Rachel Lynde's husband"—was sowing his late turnip seed on the hill field beyond the barn; and Matthew Cuthbert ought to have been sowing his on the big red brook field away over by Green Gables. Mrs. Rachel knew that he ought because she had heard him tell Peter Morrison the evening before in William J. Blair's store over at Carmody that he meant to sow his turnip seed the next afternoon. Peter had asked him, of course, for Matthew Cuthbert had never been known to volunteer information about anything in his whole life.

And yet here was Matthew Cuthbert, at half-past three on the afternoon of a busy day, placidly driving over the hollow and up the hill; moreover, he wore a white collar and his best suit of clothes, which was plain proof that he was going out of Avonlea; and he had the buggy and the sorrel mare, which betokened that he was going a considerable distance. Now, where was Matthew Cuthbert going and why was he going there?

Had it been any other man in Avonlea, Mrs. Rachel, deftly putting this and that together, might have given a pretty good guess as to both questions. But Matthew so rarely went from home that it must be something pressing and unusual which was taking him; he was the shyest man alive and hated to have to go among strangers or to any place where he might have to talk. Matthew, dressed up with a white collar and driving in a buggy, was something that didn't happen often. Mrs. Rachel, ponder as she might, could make nothing of it and her afternoon's enjoyment was spoiled.

"I'll just step over to Green Gables after tea and find out from Marilla where he's gone and why," the worthy woman finally concluded. "He doesn't generally go to town this time of year and he *never* visits; if he'd run out of turnip seed he wouldn't dress up and take the buggy to go for more; he wasn't driving fast enough to be going for a doctor. Yet something must have happened since last night to start him off. I'm clean puzzled, that's what, and I won't know a minute's peace of mind or conscience until I know what has taken Matthew Cuthbert out of Avonlea today.''

Accordingly after tea Mrs. Rachel set out; she had not far to go; the big, rambling, orchard-embowered house where the Cuthberts lived was a scant quarter of a mile up the road from Lynde's Hollow. To be sure, the long lane made it a good deal further. Matthew Cuthbert's father, as shy and silent as his son after him, had got as far away as he possibly could from his fellow men without actually retreating into the woods when he founded his homestead. Green Gables was built at the furthest edge of his cleared land and there it was to this day, barely visible from the main road along which all the other Avonlea houses were so sociably situated. Mrs. Rachel Lynde did not call living in such a place *living* at all.

''It's just *staying*, that's what,'' she said as she stepped along the deep-rutted, grassy lane bordered with wild rose bushes. ''It's no wonder Matthew and Marilla are both a little odd, living away back here by themselves. Trees aren't much company, though dear knows if they were there'd be enough of them. I'd ruther look at people. To be sure, they seem contented enough; but then, I suppose, they're used to it. A body can get used to anything, even to being hanged, as the Irishman said.''

With this Mrs. Rachel stepped out of the lane into the backyard of Green Gables. Very green and neat and precise was that yard, set about on one side with great patriarchal willows and on the other with prim Lombardies. Not a stray stick nor stone was to be seen, for Mrs. Rachel would have seen it if there had been. Privately she was of the opinion that Marilla Cuthbert swept that yard over as often as she swept her house. One could have eaten a meal off the ground without overbrimming the proverbial peck of dirt.

Mrs. Rachel rapped smartly at the kitchen door and stepped in when bidden to do so. The kitchen at Green Gables was a cheerful apartment—or would have been cheerful if it had not been so painfully clean as to give it something of the appearance of an unused parlour. Its windows looked east and west; through the west one, looking out on the backyard, came a flood of mellow June sunlight; but the east one, whence you got a glimpse of the bloom white cherry-trees in the left orchard and nodding, slender birches down in the hollow by the brook, was greened over by a tangle of vines. Here sat Marilla Cuthbert, when she sat at all, always slightly distrustful of sunshine, which seemed to her too dancing and irresponsible a thing for a world which was meant to be taken seriously; and here she sat now, knitting, and the table behind her was laid for supper.

Mrs. Rachel, before she had fairly closed the door, had taken mental note of everything that was on that table. There were three plates laid, so that Marilla must be expecting some one home with Matthew to tea; but the dishes were everyday dishes and there was only crab-apple preserves and one kind of cake, so that the expected company could not be any particular company. Yet what of Matthew's white collar and the sorrel mare? Mrs. Rachel was getting fairly dizzy with this unusual mystery about quiet, unmysterious Green Gables.

"Good evening, Rachel," Marilla said briskly. "This is a real fine evening, isn't it? Won't you sit down? How are all your folks?"

Something that for lack of any other name might be called friendship existed and always had existed between Marilla Cuthbert and Mrs. Rachel, in spite of—or perhaps because of—their dissimilarity.

Marilla was a tall, thin woman, with angles and without curves; her dark hair showed some gray streaks and was always twisted up in a hard little knot behind with two wire hairpins stuck aggressively through it. She looked like a woman of narrow experience and rigid conscience, which she was; but there was a saving something about her mouth which, if it had been ever so slightly developed, might have been considered indicative of a sense of humour.

"We're all pretty well," said Mrs. Rachel. "I was kind of afraid *you* weren't, though, when I saw Matthew starting off today. I thought maybe he was going to the doctor's."

Marilla's lips twitched understandingly. She had expected Mrs. Rachel up; she had known that the sight of Matthew jaunting off so unaccountably would be too much for her neighbour's curiosity.

"Oh, no, I'm quite well although I had a bad headache yesterday," she said. "Matthew went to Bright River. We're getting a little boy from an orphan asylum in Nova Scotia and he's coming on the train tonight."

If Marilla had said that Matthew had gone to Bright River to meet a kangaroo from Australia Mrs. Rachel could not have been more astonished. She was actually stricken dumb for five seconds. It was unsupposable that Marilla was making fun of her, but Mrs. Rachel was almost forced to suppose it.

"Are you in earnest, Marilla?" she demanded when voice returned to her.

"Yes, of course," said Marilla, as if getting boys from orphan asylums in Nova Scotia were part of the usual spring work on any well-regulated Avonlea farm instead of being an unheard of innovation.

Mrs. Rachel felt that she had received a severe mental jolt. She thought in exclamation points. A boy! Marilla and Matthew Cuthbert of all people adopting a boy! From an orphan asylum! Well, the world was certainly turning upside down! She would be surprised at nothing after this! Nothing!

"What on earth put such a notion into your head?" she demanded disapprovingly.

This had been done without her advice being asked, and must perforce be disapproved.

"Well, we've been thinking about it for some time—all winter in fact," returned Marilla. "Mrs. Alexander Spencer was up here one day before Christmas and she said she was going to get a little girl from the asylum over in Hopetown in the spring. Her cousin lives there and Mrs. Spencer has visited her and knows all about it. So Matthew and I have talked it over off and on ever since. We thought we'd get a boy. Matthew is getting up in years, you know—he's sixty—and he isn't so spry as he once was. His heart troubles him a good deal. And you know how desperate hard it's got to be to get hired help. There's never anybody to be had but those stupid, half-grown little French boys; and as soon as you do get one broke into your ways and taught something he's up and off to the lobster canneries or the States. At first Matthew suggested getting a Barnado boy. But I said 'no' flat to that. 'They may be all right—I'm not saying they're not—but no London street Arabs for me,' I said. 'Give me a native born at least. There'll be a risk, no matter who we get. But I'll feel easier in my mind and sleep sounder at nights if we get a born Canadian.' So in the end we decided to ask Mrs. Spencer to pick us out one when she went over to get her little girl. We heard last week she was going, so we sent her word by Richard Spencer's folks at Carmody to bring us a smart, likely boy of about ten or eleven. We decided that would be the best age—old enough to be of some use in doing chores right off and young enough to be trained up proper. We mean to give him a good home and schooling. We had a telegram from Mrs. Alexander Spencer today—the mailman brought it from the station—saying they were coming on the five-thirty train tonight. So Matthew went to Bright River to meet him. Mrs. Spencer will drop him off there. Of course she goes on to White Sands station herself."

Mrs. Rachel prided herself on always speaking her mind; she proceeded to speak it now, having adjusted her mental attitude to this amazing piece of news.

"Well, Marilla, I'll just tell you plain that I think you're doing a mighty foolish thing—a risky thing, that's what. You don't know what you're getting. You're bringing a strange child into your house and home and you don't know a single thing about him nor what his disposition is like nor what sort of parents he had nor how he's likely to turn out. Why, it was only last week I read in the paper how a man and his wife up west of the Island took a boy out of an orphan asylum and he set fire to the house at night—set it *on purpose*, Marilla—and nearly burnt them to a crisp in their beds. And I know another case where an adopted boy used to suck the eggs—they couldn't break him of it. If you had asked my advice in the matter—which you didn't do, Marilla—I'd have said for mercy's sake not to think of such a thing, that's what."

This Job's comforting seemed neither to offend nor alarm Marilla. She knitted steadily on.

"I don't deny there's something in what you say, Rachel. I've had some qualms myself. But Matthew was terrible set on it. I could see that, so I gave in. It's so seldom Matthew sets his mind on anything that when he does I always feel it's my duty to give in. And as for the risk, there's risks in pretty near everything a body does in this world. There's risks in people's having children of their own if it comes to that—they don't always turn out well. And then Nova Scotia is right close to the Island. It isn't as if we were getting him from England or the States. He can't be much different from ourselves."

"Well, I hope it will turn out all right," said Mrs. Rachel in a tone that plainly indicated her painful doubts. "Only don't say I didn't warn you if he burns Green Gables down or puts strychnine in the well—I heard of a case over in New Brunswick where an orphan asylum child did that and the whole family died in fearful agonies. Only, it was a girl in that instance."

"Well, we're not getting a girl," said Marilla, as if poisoning wells were a purely feminine accomplishment and not to be dreaded in the case of a boy. "I'd never dream of taking a girl to bring up. I wonder at Mrs. Alexander Spencer for doing it. But there, *she* wouldn't shrink from adopting a whole orphan asylum if she took it into her head."

Mrs. Rachel would have liked to stay until Matthew came home with his imported orphan. But reflecting that it would be a good two hours at least before his arrival she concluded to go up the road to Robert Bell's and tell them the news. It would certainly make a sensation second to none, and Mrs. Rachel dearly loved to make a sensation. So she took herself away, somewhat to Marilla's relief, for the latter felt her doubts and fears reviving under the influence of Mrs. Rachel's pessimism.

"Well, of all things that ever were or will be!" ejaculated Mrs. Rachel when she was safely out in the lane. "It does really seem as if I must be dreaming. Well, I'm sorry for that poor young one and no mistake. Matthew and Marilla don't know anything about children and they'll expect him to be wiser and steadier than his own grandfather, if so be's he ever had a grandfather, which is doubtful. It seems uncanny to think of a child at Green Gables somehow; there's never been one there, for Matthew and Marilla were grown up when the new house was built—if they ever *were* children, which is hard to believe when one looks at them. I wouldn't be in that orphan's shoes for anything. My, but I pity him, that's what."

So said Mrs. Rachel to the wild rose bushes out of the fulness of her heart; but if she could have seen the child who was waiting patiently at the Bright River station at that very moment her pity would have been still deeper and more profound.

CHAPTER 2

MATTHEW CUTHBERT IS SURPRISED

MATTHEW CUTHBERT and the sorrel mare jogged comfortably over the eight miles to Bright River. It was a pretty road, running along between snug farmsteads, with now and again a bit of balsamy fir wood to drive through or a hollow where wild plums hung out their filmy bloom. The air was sweet with the breath of many apple orchards and the meadows sloped away in the distance to horizon mists of pearl and purple; while

The little birds sang as if it were
The one day of summer in all the year.

Matthew enjoyed the drive after his own fashion, except during the moments when he met women and had to nod to them—for in Prince Edward Island you are supposed to nod to all and sundry you meet on the road whether you know them or not.

Matthew dreaded all women except Marilla and Mrs. Rachel; he had an uncomfortable feeling that the mysterious creatures were secretly laughing at him. He may have been quite right in thinking so, for he was an odd-looking personage, with an ungainly figure and long iron-gray hair that touched his stooping shoulders, and a full, soft brown beard which he had worn ever since he was twenty. In fact, he had looked at twenty very much as he looked at sixty, lacking a little of the grayness.

When he reached Bright River there was no sign of any train; he thought he was too early, so he tied his horse in the yard of the small Bright River hotel and went over to the station-house. The long platform was almost deserted; the only living creature in sight being a girl who was sitting on a pile of shingles at the extreme end. Matthew, barely noting that it *was* a girl, sidled past her as quickly as possible without looking at her. Had he looked he could hardly have failed to notice the tense rigidity and expectation of her attitude and expression. She was sitting there waiting for something or somebody and, since sitting and waiting was the only thing to do just then, she sat and waited with all her might and main.

Matthew encountered the station-master locking up the ticket-office preparatory to going home for supper, and asked him if the five-thirty train would soon be long.

"The five-thirty train has been in and gone half an hour ago," answered that brisk official. "But there was a passenger dropped off for you—a little girl. She's sitting out there on the shingles. I asked her to go into the ladies' waiting-room, but she informed me gravely that she preferred to stay outside. 'There was more scope for imagination,' she said. She's a case, I should say."

"I'm not expecting a girl," said Matthew blankly. "It's a boy I've come for. He should be here. Mrs. Alexander Spencer was to bring him over from Nova Scotia for me."

The station-master whistled.

"Guess there's some mistake," he said. "Mrs. Spencer came off the train with that girl and gave her into my charge. Said you and your sister were adopting her from an orphan asylum and that you would be along for her presently. That's all *I* know about it—and I haven't got any more orphans concealed hereabouts."

"I don't understand," said Matthew helplessly, wishing that

Marilla was at hand to cope with the situation.

"Well, you'd better question the girl," said the station-master carelessly. "I dare say she'll be able to explain—she's got a tongue of her own, that's certain. Maybe they were out of boys of the brand you wanted."

He walked jauntily away, being hungry, and the unfortunate Matthew was left to do that which was harder for him than bearding a lion in its den—walk up to a girl—a strange girl—an orphan girl—and demand of her why she wasn't a boy. Matthew groaned in spirit as he turned about and shuffled gently down the platform towards her.

She had been watching him ever since he had passed her and she had her eyes on him now. Matthew was not looking at her and would not have seen what she was really like if he had been, but an ordinary observer would have seen this:

A child of about eleven, garbed in a very short, very tight, very ugly dress of yellowish gray wincey. She wore a faded brown sailor hat and beneath the hat, extending down her back, were two braids of very thick, decidedly red hair. Her face was small, white and thin, also much freckled; her mouth was large and so were her eyes, that looked green in some lights and moods and gray in others.

So far, the ordinary observer; an extraordinary observer might have seen that the chin was very pointed and pronounced; that the big eyes were full of spirit and vivacity; that the mouth was sweet-lipped and expressive; that the forehead was broad and full; in short, our discerning extraordinary observer might have concluded that no commonplace soul inhabited the body of this stray woman-child of whom shy Matthew Cuthbert was so ludicrously afraid.

Matthew, however, was spared the ordeal of speaking first, for as soon as she concluded that he was coming to her she stood up, grasping with one thin brown hand the handle of a shabby, old-fashioned carpet-bag; the other she held out to him.

"I suppose you are Mr. Matthew Cuthbert of Green Gables?" she said in a peculiarly clear, sweet voice. "I'm very glad to see you. I was beginning to be afraid you weren't coming for me and I was imagining all the things that might have happened to prevent you. I had made up my mind that if you didn't come for me tonight I'd go down the track to that big wild cherry-tree at the bend, and climb up into it to stay all night. I wouldn't be a bit afraid, and it would be lovely to sleep in a wild cherry-tree all white with bloom in the moonshine, don't you think? You could imagine you were dwelling in marble halls, couldn't you? And I was quite sure you would come for me in the morning, if you didn't tonight.''

Matthew had taken the scrawny little hand awkwardly in his; then and there he decided what to do. He could not tell this child with the glowing eyes that there had been a mistake; he would take her home and let Marilla do that. She couldn't be left at Bright River anyhow, no matter what mistake had been made, so all questions and explanations might as well be deferred until he was safely back at Green Gables.

''I'm sorry I was late,'' he said shyly. ''Come along. The horse is over in the yard. Give me your bag.''

''Oh, I can carry it,'' the child responded cheerfully. ''It isn't heavy. I've got all my worldly goods in it, but it isn't heavy. And if it isn't carried in just a certain way the handle pulls out—so I'd better keep it because I know the exact knack of it. It's an extremely old carpet-bag. Oh, I'm very glad you've come, even if it would have been nice to sleep in a wild cherry-tree. We've got to drive a long piece, haven't we? Mrs. Spencer said it was eight miles. I'm glad because I love driving. Oh, it seems so wonderful that I'm going to live with you and belong to you. I've never belonged to anybody—not really. But the asylum was the worst. I've only been in it four months, but that was enough. I don't suppose you ever were an orphan in an asylum, so you can't possibly understand what it is like. It's worse than anything you could imagine. Mrs. Spencer said it was wicked of me to talk like that, but I didn't mean to be wicked. It's so easy to be wicked without knowing it, isn't it? They were good, you know—the asylum people. But there is so little scope for the imagination in an asylum—only just in the other orphans. It *was* pretty interesting to imagine things about them—to imagine that perhaps the girl who sat next to you was really the daughter of a belted earl, who had been stolen away from her parents in her infancy by a cruel nurse who died before she could confess. I used to lie awake at nights and imagine things like that, because I didn't have time in the day. I guess that's why I'm so thin—I *am* dreadful thin, ain't I? There isn't a pick on my bones. I do love to imagine I'm nice and plump, with dimples in my elbows.''

With this Matthew's companion stopped talking, partly because she was out of breath and partly because they had reached the buggy. Not another word did she say until they had left the village and were driving down a steep little hill, the road part of which had been cut so deeply into the soft soil that the banks, fringed with blooming wild cherry trees and slim white birches, were several feet above their heads.

The child put out her hand and broke off a branch of wild plum that brushed against the side of the buggy.

"Isn't that beautiful? What did that tree, leaning out from the bank, all white and lacy, make you think of?" she asked.

"Well now, I dunno," said Matthew.

"Why, a bride, of course—a bride all in white with a lovely misty veil. I've never seen one, but I can imagine what she would look like. I don't ever expect to be a bride myself. I'm so homely nobody will ever want to marry me—unless it might be a foreign missionary. I suppose a foreign missionary mightn't be very particular. But I do hope that some day I shall have a white dress. That is my highest ideal of earthly bliss. I just love pretty clothes. And I've never had a pretty dress in my life that I can remember—but of course it's all the more to look forward to, isn't it? And then I can imagine that I'm dressed gorgeously. This morning when I left the asylum I felt so ashamed because I had to wear this horrid old wincey dress. All the orphans had to wear them, you know. A merchant in Hopetown last winter donated three hundred yards of wincey to the asylum. Some people said it was because he couldn't sell it, but I'd rather believe that it was out of the kindness of his heart, wouldn't you? When we got on the train I felt as if everybody must be looking at me and pitying me. But I just went to work and imagined that I had on the most beautiful pale blue silk dress—because when you *are* imagining you might as well imagine something worth while—and a big hat all flowers and nodding plumes, and a gold watch, and kid gloves and boots. I felt cheered up right away and I enjoyed my trip to the Island with all my might. I wasn't a bit sick coming over in the boat. Neither was Mrs. Spencer, although she generally is. She said she hadn't time to get sick, watching to see that I didn't fall overboard. She said she never saw the beat of me for prowling about. But if it kept her from being seasick it's a mercy I did prowl, isn't it? And I wanted to see everything that was to be seen on that boat, because I didn't know whether I'd ever have another opportunity. Oh, there are a lot more cherry-trees all in bloom! This Island is the bloomiest place. I just love it already, and I'm so glad I'm going to live here. I've always heard that Prince Edward Island was the prettiest place in the world, and I used to imagine I was living here, but I never really expected I would. It's delightful when your imaginations come true, isn't it? But those red roads are so funny. When we got into the train at Charlottetown and the red roads began to flash past I asked Mrs. Spencer what made them red and she said she didn't know and for pity's sake not to ask her any more questions. She said I must have asked her a thousand already. I suppose I had, too, but how are you going to find out about things if you don't ask questions? And what *does* make the roads red?''

''Well now, I dunno,'' said Matthew.

''Well, that is one of the things to find out sometime. Isn't it splendid to think of all the things there are to find out about? It just makes me feel good to be alive—it's such an interesting world. It wouldn't be half so interesting if we knew all about everything, would it? There'd be no scope for imagination then, would there? But am I talking too much? People are always telling me I do. Would you rather I didn't talk? If you say so I'll stop. I *can* stop when I make up my mind to it, although it's difficult.''

Matthew, much to his own surprise, was enjoying himself. Like most quiet folks he liked talkative people when they were willing to do the talking themselves and did not expect him to keep up his end of it. But he had never expected to enjoy the society of a little girl. Women were bad enough in all conscience, but little girls were worse. He detested the way they had of sidling past him timidly, with sidewise glances, as if they expected him to gobble them up at a mouthful if they ventured to say a word. This was the Avonlea type of well-bred little girl. But this freckled witch was very different, and although he found it rather difficult for his slower intelligence to keep up with her brisk mental processes he thought that he ''kind of liked her chatter.'' So he said as shyly as usual:

''Oh, you can talk as much as you like. I don't mind.''

''Oh, I'm so glad. I know you and I are going to get along together fine. It's such a relief to talk when one wants to and not be told that children should be seen and not heard. I've had that said to me a million times if I have once. And people laugh at me because I use big words. But if you have big ideas you have to use big words to express them, haven't you?''

''Well now, that seems reasonable,'' said Matthew.

''Mrs. Spencer said that my tongue must be hung in the middle. But it isn't—it's firmly fastened at one end. Mrs. Spencer said your place was named Green Gables. I asked her all about it. And she said there were trees all around it. I was gladder than ever. I just love trees. And there weren't any at all about the asylum, only a few poor weeny-teeny things out in front with little whitewashed cagey things about them. They just looked like orphans themselves, those trees did. It used to make me want to cry to look at them. I used to say to them, 'Oh, you *poor* little things! If you were out in a great big woods with other trees all around you and little mosses and Junebells growing over your roots and a brook not far away and birds singing in your branches, you could grow, couldn't you? But you can't where you are. I know just exactly how you feel, little trees.' I felt sorry to leave them behind this morning. You do get so attached to things like that, don't you? Is there a brook anywhere near Green Gables? I forgot to ask Mrs. Spencer that.''

"Well now, yes, there's one right below the house.''

"Fancy! It's always been one of my dreams to live near a brook. I never expected I would, though. Dreams don't often come true, do they? Wouldn't it be nice if they did? But just now I feel pretty nearly perfectly happy. I can't feel exactly perfectly happy because—well, what color would you call this?''

She twitched one of her long glossy braids over her thin shoulder and held it up before Matthew's eyes. Matthew was not used to deciding on the tints of ladies' tresses but in this case there couldn't be much doubt.

"It's red, ain't it?'' he said.

The girl let the braid drop back with a sigh that seemed to come from her very toes and to exhale forth all the sorrows of the ages.

"Yes, it's red,'' she said resignedly. "Now you see why I can't be perfectly happy. Nobody could who had red hair. I don't mind the other things so much—the freckles and the green eyes and my skinniness. I can imagine them away. I can imagine that I have a beautiful rose-leaf complexion and lovely starry violet eyes. But I *cannot* imagine that red hair away. I do my best. I think to myself, 'Now my hair is a glorious black, black as the raven's wing.' But all the time I *know* it is just plain red, and it breaks my heart. It will be my lifelong sorrow. I read of a girl once in a novel who had a lifelong sorrow, but it wasn't red hair. Her hair was pure gold rippling back from her alabaster brow. What is an alabaster brow? I never could find out. Can you tell me?''

"Well now, I'm afraid I can't,'' said Matthew, who was getting a little dizzy. He felt as he had once felt in his rash youth when another boy had enticed him on the merry-go-round at a picnic.

"Well, whatever it was it must have been something nice because she was divinely beautiful. Have you ever imagined what it must feel like to be divinely beautiful?''

"Well now, no, I haven't,'' confessed Matthew ingenuously.

"I have, often. Which would you rather be if you had the choice— divinely beautiful or dazzlingly clever or angelically good?''

"Well now, I—I don't know exactly."

"Neither do I. I can never decide. But it doesn't make much real difference for it isn't likely I'll ever be either. It's certain I'll never be angelically good. Mrs. Spencer says—oh, Mr. Cuthbert! Oh, Mr. Cuthbert!! Oh, Mr. Cuthbert!!!"

That was not what Mrs. Spencer had said; neither had the child tumbled out of the buggy nor had Matthew done anything astonishing. They had simply rounded a curve in the road and found themselves in the "Avenue."

The "Avenue," so called by the Newbridge people, was a stretch of road four or five hundred yards long, completely arched over with huge, wide-spreading apple-trees, planted years ago by an eccentric old farmer. Overhead was one long canopy of snowy fragrant bloom. Below the boughs the air was full of a purple twilight and far ahead a glimpse of painted sunset sky shone like a great rose window at the end of a cathedral aisle.

Its beauty seemed to strike the child dumb. She leaned back in the buggy, her thin hands clasped before her, her face lifted rapturously to the white splendor above. Even when they had passed out and were driving down the long slope to Newbridge she never moved or spoke. Still with rapt face she gazed afar into the sunset west, with eyes that saw visions trooping splendidly across that glowing background. Through Newbridge, a bustling little village where dogs barked at them and small boys hooted and curious faces peered from the windows, they drove, still in silence. When three more miles had dropped away behind them the child had not spoken. She could keep silence, it was evident, as energetically as she could talk.

"I guess you're feeling pretty tired and hungry," Matthew ventured at last, accounting for her long visitation of dumbness with the only reason he could think of. "But we haven't very far to go now—only another mile."

She came out of her reverie with a deep sigh and looked at him with the dreamy gaze of a soul that had been wandering afar, star-led.

"Oh, Mr. Cuthbert," she whispered, "that place we came through—that white place—what was it?"

"Well now, you must mean the Avenue," said Matthew after a few moments' profound reflection. "It is a kind of pretty place."

"Pretty? Oh, pretty doesn't seem the right word to use. Nor beautiful, either. They don't go far enough. Oh, it was wonderful—wonderful. It's the first thing I ever saw that couldn't be improved upon by imagination. It just satisfied me here''—she put one hand on her breast—''it made a queer funny ache and yet it was a pleasant ache. Did you ever have an ache like that, Mr. Cuthbert?''

"Well now, I just can't recollect that I ever had.''

''I have it lots of times—whenever I see anything royally beautiful. But they shouldn't call that lovely place the Avenue. There is no meaning in a name like that. They should call it—let me see—the White Way of Delight. Isn't that a nice imaginative name? When I don't like the name of a place or a person I always imagine a new one and always think of them so. There was a girl at the asylum whose name was Hepzibah Jenkins, but I always imagined her as Rosalia DeVere. Other people may call that place the Avenue, but I shall always call it the White Way of Delight. Have we really only another mile to go before we get home? I'm glad and I'm sorry. I'm sorry because this drive has been so pleasant and I'm always sorry when pleasant things end. Something still pleasanter may come after, but you can never be sure. And it's so often the case that it isn't pleasanter. That has been my experience anyhow. But I'm glad to think of getting home. You see, I've never had a real home since I can remember. It gives me that pleasant ache again just to think of coming to a really truly home. Oh, isn't that pretty!''

They had driven over the crest of a hill. Below them was a pond, looking almost like a river so long and winding was it. A bridge spanned it midway and from there to its lower end, where an amber-hued belt of sand hills shut it in from the dark blue gulf beyond, the water was a glory of many shifting hues—the most spiritual shadings of crocus and rose and ethereal green, with other elusive tintings for which no name has ever been found. Above the bridge the pond ran up into fringing groves of fir and maple and lay all darkly translucent in their wavering shadows. Here and there a wild plum leaned out from the bank like a white-clad girl tiptoeing to her own reflection. From the marsh at the head of the pond came the clear, mournfully-sweet chorus of the frogs. There was a little gray house peering around a white apple orchard on a slope beyond and, although it was not yet quite dark, a light was shining from one of its windows.

"That's Barry's pond," said Matthew.

"Oh, I don't like that name, either. I shall call it—let me see—the Lake of Shining Waters. Yes, that is the right name for it. I know because of the thrill. When I hit on a name that suits exactly it gives me a thrill. Do things ever give you a thrill?''

Matthew ruminated.

"Well now, yes. It always kind of gives me a thrill to see them ugly white grubs that spade up in the cucumber beds. I hate the look of them."

"Oh, I don't think that can be exactly the same kind of a thrill. Do you think it can? There doesn't seem to be much connection between grubs and lakes of shining waters, does there? But why do other people call it Barry's pond?"

"I reckon because Mr. Barry lives up there in that house. Orchard Slope's the name of his place. If it wasn't for that big bush behind it you could see Green Gables from here. But we have to go over the bridge and round by the road, so it's near half a mile further."

"Has Mr. Barry any little girls? Well, not so very little either—about my size."

"He's got one about eleven. Her name is Diana."

"Oh!" with a long indrawing of breath. "What a perfectly lovely name!"

"Well now, I dunno. There's something dreadful heathenish about it, seems to me. I'd ruther Jane or Mary or some sensible name like that. But when Diana was born there was a schoolmaster boarding there and they gave him the naming of her and he called her Diana"

"I wish there had been a schoolmaster like that around when *I* was born, then. Oh, here we are at the bridge. I'm going to shut my eyes tight. I'm always afraid going over bridges. I can't help imagining that perhaps, just as we get to the middle, they'll crumple up like a jack-knife and nip us. So I shut my eyes. But I always have to open them for all when I think we're getting near the middle. Because, you see, if the bridge *did* crumple up I'd want to *see* it crumple. What a jolly rumble it makes! I always like the rumble part of it. Isn't it splendid there are so many things to like in this world? There, we're over. Now I'll look back. Good night, dear Lake of Shining Waters. I always say good night to the things I love, just as I would to people. I think they like it. That water looks as if it was smiling at me."

When they had driven up the further hill and around a corner Matthew said:

"We're pretty near home now. That's Green Gables over—"

"Oh, don't tell me," she interrupted breathlessly, catching at his partially raised arm and shutting her eyes that she might not see his gesture. "Let me guess. I'm sure I'll guess right."

She opened her eyes and looked about her. They were on the crest of a hill. The sun had set some time since, but the landscape was still clear in the mellow afterlight. To the west a dark church spire rose up against a marigold sky. Below was a little valley and beyond a long, gently-rising slope with snug farmsteads scattered along it. From one to another the child's eyes darted, eager and wistful. At last they lingered on one away to the left, far back from the road, dimly white with blossoming trees in the twilight of the surrounding woods. Over it, in the stainless southwest sky, a great crystal-white star was shining like a lamp of guidance and promise.

"That's it, isn't it?" she said, pointing.

Matthew slapped the reins on the sorrel's back delightedly.

"Well now, you've guessed it! But I reckon Mrs. Spencer described it so's you could tell."

"No, she didn't—really she didn't. All she said might just as well have been about most of those other places. I hadn't any real idea what it looked like. But just as soon as I saw it I felt it was home. Oh, it seems as if I must be in a dream. Do you know, my arm must be black and blue from the elbow up, for I've pinched myself so many times today. Every little while a horrible sickening feeling would come over me and I'd be so afraid it was all a dream. Then I'd pinch myself to see if it was real—until suddenly I remembered that even supposing it was only a dream I'd better go on dreaming as long as I could; so I stopped pinching. But it *is* real and we're nearly home."

With a sigh of rapture she relapsed into silence. Matthew stirred uneasily. He felt glad that it would be Marilla and not he who would have to tell this waif of the world that the home she longed for was not to be hers after all. They drove over Lynde's Hollow, where it was already quite dark, but not so dark that Mrs. Rachel could not see them from her window vantage, and up the hill and into the long lane of Green Gables. By the time they arrived at the house Matthew was shrinking from the approaching revelation with an energy he did not understand. It was not of Marilla or himself he was thinking or of the trouble this mistake was probably going to make for them, but of the child's disappointment. When he thought of that rapt light being quenched in her eyes he had an uncomfortable feeling that he was going to assist at murdering something—much the same feeling that came over him when he had to kill a lamb or calf or any other innocent little creature.

The yard was quite dark as they turned into it and the poplar leaves were rustling silkily all round it.

"Listen to the trees talking in their sleep," she whispered, as he lifted her to the ground. ''What nice dreams they must have!''

Then, holding tightly to the carpetbag which contained ''all her worldly goods,'' she followed him into the house.

CHAPTER 3

MARILLA CUTHBERT IS SURPRISED

MARILLA CAME briskly forward as Matthew opened the door. But when her eyes fell on the odd little figure in the stiff, ugly dress, with the long braids of red hair and the eager, luminous eyes, she stopped short in amazement.

''Matthew Cuthbert, who's that?'' she ejaculated. ''Where is the boy?''

''There wasn't any boy,'' said Matthew wretchedly. ''There was only *her*.''

He nodded at the child, remembering that he had never even asked her name.

''No boy! But there *must* have been a boy,'' insisted Marilla. ''We sent word to Mrs. Spencer to bring a boy.''

''Well, she didn't. She brought *her*. I asked the station-master. And I had to bring her home. She couldn't be left there, no matter where the mistake had come in.''

'' Well, this is a pretty piece of business!'' ejaculated Marilla.

During this dialogue the child had remained silent, her eyes roving from one to the other, all the animation fading out of her face. Suddenly she seemed to grasp the full meaning of what had been said. Dropping her precious carpetbag she sprang forward a step and clasped her hands.

"You don't want me!" she cried. "You don't want me because I'm not a boy! I might have expected it. Nobody ever did want me. I might have known it was all too beautiful to last. I might have known nobody really did want me. Oh, what shall I do? I'm going to burst into tears!"

Burst into tears she did. Sitting down on a chair by the table, flinging her arms out upon it, and burying her face in them, she proceeded to cry stormily. Marilla and Matthew looked at each other deprecatingly across the stove. Neither of them knew what to say or do. Finally Marilla stepped lamely into the breach.

"Well, well, there's no need to cry so about it."

"Yes, there *is* need!" The child raised her head quickly, revealing a tear-stained face and trembling lips. "*You* would cry, too, if you were an orphan and had come to a place you thought was going to be home and found that they didn't want you because you weren't a boy. Oh, this is the most *tragical* thing that ever happened to me!"

Something like a reluctant smile, rather rusty from long disuse, mellowed Marilla's grim expression.

"Well, don't cry any more. We're not going to turn you out-of-doors tonight. You'll have to stay here until we investigate this affair. What's your name?"

The child hesitated for a moment.

"Will you please call me Cordelia?" she said eagerly.

"*Call* you Cordelia! Is that your name?"

"No-o-o, it's not exactly my name, but I would love to be called Cordelia. It's such a perfectly elegant name."

"I don't know what on earth you mean. If Cordelia isn't your name, what is?"

"Anne Shirley," reluctantly faltered forth the owner of that name, "but oh, please do call me Cordelia. It can't matter much to you what you call me if I'm only going to be here a little while, can it? And Anne is such an unromantic name."

"Unromantic fiddlesticks!" said the unsympathetic Marilla. "Anne is a real good plain sensible name. You've no need to be ashamed of it."

"Oh, I'm not ashamed of it," explained Anne, "only I like Cordelia better. I've always imagined that my name was Cordelia— at least, I always have of late years. When I was young I used to imagine it was Geraldine, but I like Cordelia better now. But if you call me Anne please call me Anne spelled with an *e*."

"What difference does it make how it's spelled?" asked Marilla with another rusty smile as she picked up the teapot.

"Oh, it makes *such* a difference. It *looks* so much nicer. When you hear a name pronounced can't you always see it in your mind, just as if it was printed out? I can; and A-n-n looks dreadful, but A-n-n-e looks so much more distinguished. If you'll only call me Anne spelled with an *e* I shall try to reconcile myself to not being called Cordelia."

"Very well, then, Anne spelled with an *e*, can you tell us how this mistake came to be made? We sent word to Mrs. Spencer to bring us a boy. Were there no boys at the asylum?''

''Oh, yes, there was an abundance of them. But Mrs. Spencer said *distinctly* that you wanted a girl about eleven years old. And the matron said she thought I would do. You don't know how delighted I was. I couldn't sleep all last night for joy. Oh,'' she added reproachfully, turning to Matthew, ''why didn't you tell me at the station that you didn't want me and leave me there? If I hadn't seen the White Way of Delight and the Lake of Shining Waters it wouldn't be so hard.''

''What on earth does she mean?'' demanded Marilla, staring at Matthew.

''She—she's just referring to some conversation we had on the road,'' said Matthew hastily. ''I'm going out to put the mare in, Marilla. Have tea ready when I come back.''

''Did Mrs. Spencer bring anybody over besides you?'' continued Marilla when Matthew had gone out.

''She brought Lily Jones for herself. Lily is only five years old and she is very beautiful. She has nut-brown hair. If I was very beautiful and had nut-brown hair would you keep me?''

''No. We want a boy to help Matthew on the farm. A girl would be of no use to us. Take off your hat. I'll lay it and your bag on the hall table.''

Anne took off her hat meekly. Matthew came back presently and they sat down to supper. But Anne could not eat. In vain she nibbled at the bread and butter and pecked at the crab-apple preserve out of the little scalloped glass dish by her plate. She did not really make any headway at all.

''You're not eating anything,'' said Marilla sharply, eyeing her as if it were a serious shortcoming.

Anne sighed.

''I can't. I'm in the depths of despair. Can you eat when you are in the depths of despair?''

''I've never been in the depths of despair, so I can't say,'' responded Marilla.

''Weren't you? Well, did you ever try to *imagine* you were in the depths of despair?''

''No, I didn't.''

''Then I don't think you can understand what it's like. It's a very uncomfortable feeling indeed. When you try to eat a lump comes right up in your throat and you can't swallow anything, not even if it was a chocolate caramel. I had one chocolate caramel once two years ago and it was simply delicious. I've often dreamed since then that I had a lot of chocolate caramels, but I always wake up just when I'm going to eat them. I do hope you won't be offended because I can't eat. Everything is extremely nice , but still I cannot eat.''

''I guess she's tired,'' said Matthew, who hadn't spoken since his return from the barn. ''Best put her to bed, Marilla.''

Marilla had been wondering where Anne should be put to bed. She had prepared a couch in the kitchen chamber for the desired and expected boy. But, although it was neat and clean, it did not seem quite the thing to put a girl there somehow. But the spare room was out of the question for such a stray waif, so there remained only the east gable room. Marilla lighted a candle and told Anne to follow her, which Anne spiritlessly did, taking her hat and carpetbag from the hall table as she passed. The hall was fearsomely clean; the little gable chamber in which she presently found herself seemed still cleaner.

Marilla set the candle on a three-legged, three-cornered table and turned down the bedclothes.

''I supose you have a nightgown?'' she questioned.

Anne nodded.

''Yes, I have two. The matron of the asylum made them for me. They're fearfully skimpy. There is never enough to go around in an asylum, so things are always skimpy—at least in a poor asylum like ours. I hate skimpy night-dresses. But one can dream just as well in them as in lovely trailing ones, with frills around the neck, that's one consolation.''

''Well, undress as quick as you can and go to bed. I'll come back in a few minutes for the candle. I daren't trust you to put it out yourself. You'd likely set the place on fire.''

When Marilla had gone Anne looked around her wistfully. The whitewashed walls were so painfully bare and staring that she thought they must ache over their own bareness. The floor was bare, too, except for a round braided mat in the middle such as Anne had never seen before. In one corner was the bed, a high, old-fashioned one, with four dark, low-turned posts. In the other corner was the aforesaid three-cornered table adorned with a fat, red velvet pincushion hard enough to turn the point of the most adventurous pin. Above it hung a little six-by-eight mirror. Midway between table and bed was the window, with an icy white muslin frill over it, and opposite it was the washstand. The whole apartment was of a rigidity not to be described in words, but which sent a shiver to the very marrow of Anne's bones. With a sob she hastily discarded her garments, put on the skimpy nightgown and sprang into bed where she burrowed face downward into the pillow and pulled the clothes over her head. When Marilla came up for the light various skimpy articles of raiment scattered most untidily over the floor and a certain tempestuous appearance of the bed were the only indications of any presence save her own.

She deliberately picked up Anne's clothes, placed them neatly on a prim yellow chair, and then, taking up the candle, went over to the bed.

"Good night," she said, a little awkwardly, but not unkindly.

Anne's white face and big eyes appeared over the bedclothes with a startling suddenness.

"How can you call it a *good* night when you know it must be the very worst night I've ever had?" she said reproachfully.

Then she dived down into invisibility again.

Marilla went slowly down to the kitchen and proceeded to wash the supper dishes. Matthew was smoking—a sure sign of perturbation of mind. He seldom smoked, for Marilla set her face against it as a filthy habit; but at certain times and seasons he felt driven to it and then Marilla winked at the practice, realizing that a mere man must have some vent for his emotions.

"Well, this is a pretty kettle of fish," she said wrathfully. "This is what comes of sending word instead of going ourselves. Robert Spencer's folks have twisted that message somehow. One of us will have to drive over and see Mrs. Spencer tomorrow, that's certain. This girl will have to be sent back to the asylum."

"Yes, I suppose so," said Matthew reluctantly.

"You *suppose* so! Don't you know it?"

"Well now, she's a real nice little thing, Marilla. It's kind of a pity to send her back when she's so set on staying here."

"Matthew Cuthbert, you don't mean to say you think we ought to keep her!"

Marilla's astonishment could not have been greater if Matthew had expressed a predilection for standing on his head.

"Well now, no, I suppose not—not exactly," stammered Matthew, uncomfortably driven into a corner for his precise meaning. "I suppose—we could hardly be expected to keep her."

"I should say not. What good would she be to us?"

"We might be some good to her," said Matthew suddenly and unexpectedly.

"Matthew Cuthbert, I believe that child has bewitched you! I can see as plain as plain that you want to keep her."

"Well now, she's a real interesting little thing," persisted Matthew. "You should have heard her talk coming from the station."

"Oh, she can talk fast enough. I saw that at once. It's nothing in her favor, either. I don't like children who have so much to say. I don't want an orphan girl and if I did she isn't the style I'd pick out. There's something I don't understand about her. No, she's got to be despatched straightway back to where she came from."

"I could hire a French boy to help me," said Matthew, "and she'd be company for you."

"I'm not suffering for company," said Marilla shortly. "And I'm not going to keep her."

"Well now, it's just as you say, of course, Marilla," said Matthew rising and putting his pipe away. "I'm going to bed."

To bed went Matthew. And to bed, when she had put her dishes away, went Marilla, frowning most resolutely. And upstairs, in the east gable, a lonely, heart-hungry, friendless child cried herself to sleep.

——————— CHAPTER 4 ———————

MORNING AT GREEN GABLES

IT WAS broad daylight when Anne awoke and sat up in bed, staring confusedly at the window through which a flood of cheery sunshine was pouring and outside of which something white and feathery waved across glimpses of blue sky.

For a moment she could not remember where she was. First came a delightful thrill, as of something very pleasant; then a horrible remembrance. This was Green Gables and they didn't want her because she wasn't a boy!

But it was morning and, yes, it was a cherry tree in full bloom outside of her window. With a bound she was out of bed and across the floor. She pushed up the sash—it went up stiffly and creakily, as if it hadn't been opened for a long time, which was the case; and it stuck so tight that nothing was needed to hold it up.

Anne dropped on her knees and gazed out into the June morning, her eyes glistening with delight. Oh, wasn't it beautiful? Wasn't it a lovely place? Suppose she wasn't really going to stay here! She would imagine she was. There was scope for imagination here.

A huge cherry tree grew outside, so close that its bough tapped against the house, and it was so thick-set with blossoms that hardly a leaf was to be seen. On both sides of the house was a big orchard, one of apple trees and one of cherry trees, also showered over with blossoms; and their grass was all sprinkled with dandelions. In the garden below were lilac trees purple with flowers, and their dizzily sweet fragrance drifted up to the window on the morning wind.

Below the garden a green field lush with clover sloped down to the hollow where the brook ran and where scores of white birches grew, upspringing airily out of an undergrowth suggestive of delightful possibilities in ferns and mosses and woodsy things generally. Beyond it was a hill, green and feathery with spruce and fir; there was a gap in it where the gray gable end of the little house she had seen from the other side of the Lake of Shining Waters was visible.

Off to the left were the big barns and beyond them, away down over green, low-sloping fields, was a sparkling blue glimpse of sea.

Anne's beauty-loving eyes lingered on it all, taking everything greedily in; she had looked on so many unlovely places in her life, poor child; but this was as lovely as anything she had ever dreamed.

She knelt there, lost to everything but the loveliness around her, until she was startled by a hand on her shoulder. Marilla had come in unheard by the small dreamer.

"It's time you were dressed," she said curtly.

Marilla really did not know how to talk to the child, and her uncomfortable ignorance made her crisp and curt when she did not mean to be.

Anne stood up and drew a long breath.

"Oh, isn't it wonderful?" she said, waving her hand comprehensively at the good world outside.

"It's a big tree," said Marilla, "and it blooms great, but the fruit don't amount to much never—small and wormy."

"Oh, I don't mean just the tree; of course it's lovely—yes, it's *radiantly* lovely—it blooms as if it meant it—but I meant everything, the garden and the orchard and the brook and the woods, the whole big dear world. Don't you feel as if you just loved the world on a morning like this? And I can hear the brook laughing all the way up here. Have you ever noticed what cheerful things brooks are?

They're always laughing. Even in wintertime I've heard them under the ice. I'm so glad there's a brook near Green Gables. Perhaps you think it doesn't make any difference to me when you're not going to keep me, but it does. I shall always like to remember that there is a brook at Green Gables even if I never see it again. If there wasn't a brook I'd be *haunted* by the uncomfortable feeling that there ought to be one. I'm not in the depths of despair this morning. I never can be in the morning. Isn't it a splendid thing that there are mornings? But I feel very sad. I've just been imagining that it was really me you wanted after all and that I was to stay here for ever and ever. It was a great comfort while it lasted. But the worst of imagining things is that the time comes when you have to stop and that hurts.''

"You'd better get dressed and come downstairs and never mind your imaginings,'' said Marilla as soon as she could get a word in edgewise. "Breakfast is waiting. Wash your face and comb your hair. Leave the window up and turn your bedclothes back over the foot of the bed. Be as smart as you can.''

Anne could evidently be smart to some purpose for she was downstairs in ten minutes' time, with her clothes neatly on, her hair brushed and braided, her face washed, and a comfortable consciousness pervading her soul that she had fulfilled all Marilla's requirements. As a matter of fact, however, she had forgotten to turn back the bedclothes.

"I'm pretty hungry this morning,'' she announced, as she slipped into the chair Marilla placed for her. "The world doesn't seem such a howling wilderness as it did last night. I'm so glad it's a sunshiny morning. But I like rainy mornings real well, too. All sorts of mornings are interesting, don't you think? You don't know what's going to happen through the day, and there's so much scope for imagination. But I'm glad it's not rainy today because it's easier to be cheerful and bear up under affliction on a sunshiny day. I feel that I have a good deal to bear up under. It's all very well to read about sorrows and imagine yourself living through them heroically, but it's not so nice when you really come to have them, is it?''

"For pity's sake hold your tongue,'' said Marilla. "You talk entirely too much for a little girl.''

Thereupon Anne held her tongue so obediently and thoroughly that her continued silence made Marilla rather nervous, as if in the presence of something not exactly natural. Matthew also held his tongue,—but this at least was natural,—so that the meal was a very silent one.

As it progressed Anne became more and more abstracted, eating mechanically, with her big eyes fixed unswervingly and unseeingly on the sky outside the window. This made Marilla more nervous than ever; she had an uncomfortable feeling that while this odd child's body might be there at the table her spirit was far away in some remote airy cloudland, borne aloft on the wings of imagination. Who would want such a child about the place?

Yet Matthew wished to keep her, of all unaccountable things! Marilla felt that he wanted it just as much this morning as he had the night before, and that he would go on wanting it. That was Matthew's way—take a whim into his head and cling to it with the most amazing silent persistency—a persistency ten times more potent and effectual in its very silence than if he had talked it out.

When the meal was ended Anne came out of her reverie and offered to wash the dishes.

"Can you wash dishes right?" asked Marilla distrustfully.

"Pretty well. I'm better at looking after children, though. I've had so much experience at that. It's such a pity you haven't any here for me to look after."

"I don't feel as if I wanted any more children to look after than I've got at present. *You're* probably enough in all conscience. What's to be done with you I don't know. Matthew is a most ridiculous man."

"I think he's lovely," said Anne reproachfully. "He is so very sympathetic. He didn't mind how much I talked—he seemed to like it. I felt that he was a kindred spirit as soon as ever I saw him."

"You're both queer enough, if that's what you mean by kindred spirits," said Marilla with a sniff. "Yes, you may wash the dishes. Take plenty of hot water, and be sure you dry them well. I've got enough to attend to this morning for I'll have to drive over to White Sands in the afternoon and see Mrs. Spencer. You'll come with me and we'll settle what's to be done with you. After you've finished the dishes go upstairs and make your bed."

Anne washed the dishes deftly enough, as Marilla, who kept a sharp eye on the process, discerned. Later on she made her bed less successfully, for she had never learned the art of wrestling with a feather tick. But it was done somehow and smoothed down; and then Marilla, to get rid of her, told her she might go out-of-doors and amuse herself until dinnertime.

Anne flew to the door, face alight, eyes glowing. On the very threshold she stopped short, wheeled about, came back and sat down by the table, light and glow as effectually blotted out as if some one had clapped an extinguisher on her.

"What's the matter now?" demanded Marilla.

"I don't dare go out," said Anne, in the tone of a martyr relinquishing all earthly joys. "If I can't stay here there is no use in my loving Green Gables. And if I go out there and get acquainted with all those trees and flowers and the orchard and the brook I'll not be able to help loving it. It's hard enough now, so I won't make it any harder. I want to go out so much—everything seems to be calling to me, 'Anne, Anne, come out to us. Anne, Anne, we want a playmate'— but it's better not. There is no use in loving things if you have to be torn from them, is there? And it's *so* hard to keep from loving things, isn't it? That was why I was so glad when I thought I was going to live here. I thought I'd have so many things to love and nothing to hinder me. But that brief dream is over. I am resigned to my fate now, so I don't think I'll go out for fear I'll get unresigned again. What is the name of that geranium on the window-sill, please?"

"That's the apple-scented geranium."

"Oh, I don't mean that sort of a name. I mean just a name you gave it yourself. Didn't you give it a name? May I give it one then? May I call it—let me see—Bonny would do—may I call it Bonny while I'm here? Oh, do let me!"

"Goodness, I don't care. But where on earth is the sense of naming a geranium?"

"Oh, I like things to have handles even if they are only geraniums. It makes them seem more like people. How do you know but that it hurts a geranium's feelings just to be called a geranium and nothing else? You wouldn't like to be called nothing but a woman all the time. Yes, I shall call it Bonny. I named that cherry tree outside my bedroom window this morning. I called it Snow Queen because it was so white. Of course, it won't always be in blossom, but one can imagine that it is, can't one?"

"I never in all my life saw or heard anything to equal her," muttered Marilla, beating a retreat down cellar after potatoes. "She *is* kind of interesting, as Matthew says. I can feel already that I'm wondering what on earth she'll say next. She'll be casting a spell over me, too. She's cast it over Matthew. That look he gave me when he went out said everything he said or hinted last night over again. I wish he was like other men and would talk things out. A body could answer back then and argue him into reason. But what's to be done with a man who just *looks*?"

Anne had relapsed into reverie, with her chin in her hands and her eyes on the sky, when Marilla returned from her cellar pilgrimage. There Marilla left her until the early dinner was on the table.

"I suppose I can have the mare and buggy this afternoon, Matthew?" said Marilla.

Matthew nodded and looked wistfully at Anne. Marilla intercepted the look and said grimly:

"I'm going to drive over to White Sands and settle this thing. I'll take Anne with me and Mrs. Spencer will probably make arrangments to send her back to Nova Scotia at once. I'll set your tea out for you and I'll be home in time to milk the cows."

Still Matthew said nothing and Marilla had a sense of having wasted words and breath. There is nothing more aggravating than a man who won't talk back—unless it is a woman who won't.

Matthew hitched the sorrel into the buggy in due time and Marilla and Anne set off. Matthew opened the yard gate for them, and as they drove slowly through, he said, to nobody in particular as it seemed:

"Little Jerry Buote from the Creek was here this morning, and I told him I guessed I'd hire him for the summer."

Marilla made no reply, but she hit the unlucky sorrel such a vicious clip with the whip that the fat mare, unused to such treatment, whizzed indignantly down the lane at an alarming pace. Marilla looked back once as the buggy bounced along and saw that aggravating Matthew leaning over the gate, looking wistfully after them.

CHAPTER 5

ANNE'S HISTORY

"DO YOU know," said Anne confidentially, "I've made up my mind to enjoy this drive. It's been my experience that you can nearly always enjoy things if you make up your mind firmly that you will. Of course, you must make it up *firmly*. I am not going to think about going back to the asylum while we're having our drive. I'm just going to think about the drive. Oh, look, there's one little early wild rose out! Isn't it lovely? Don't you think it must be glad to be a rose?

Wouldn't it be nice if roses could talk? I'm sure they could tell us such lovely things. And isn't pink the most bewitching color in the world? I love it, but I can't wear it. Redheaded people can't wear pink, not even in imagination. Did you ever know of anybody whose hair was red when she was young, but got to be another color when she grew up?''

"No, I don't know as I ever did," said Marilla mercilessly, "and I shouldn't think it likely to happen in your case, either."

Anne sighed.

"Well, that is another hope gone. My life is a perfect graveyard of buried hopes. That's a sentence I read in a book once, and I say it over to comfort myself whenever I'm disappointed in anything."

"I don't see where the comforting comes in myself," said Marilla.

"Why, because it sounds so nice and romantic, just as if I were a heroine in a book, you know. I am so fond of romantic things, and a graveyard full of buried hopes is about as romantic a thing as one can imagine, isn't it? I'm rather glad I have one. Are we going across the Lake of Shining Waters today?"

"We're not going over Barry's pond, if that's what you mean by your Lake of Shining Waters. We're going by the shore road."

"Shore road sounds nice," said Anne dreamily. "Is it as nice as it sounds? Just when you said 'shore road' I saw it in a picture in my mind, as quick as that! And White Sands is a pretty name, too; but I don't like it as well as Avonlea. Avonlea is a lovely name. It just sounds like music. How far is it to White Sands?"

"It's five miles; and as you're evidently bent on talking you might as well talk to some purpose by telling me what you know about yourself."

"Oh, what I *know* about myself isn't really worth telling," said Anne eagerly. "If you'll only let me tell you what I *imagine* about myself you'll think it ever so much more interesting."

"No, I don't want any of your imaginings. Just you stick to bald facts. Begin at the beginning. Where were you born and how old are you?"

"I was eleven last March," said Anne, resigning herself to bald facts with a little sigh. "And I was born in Bolingbroke, Nova Scotia. My father's name was Walter Shirley, and he was a teacher in the Bolingbroke High School. My mother's name was Bertha Shirley. Aren't Walter and Bertha lovely names. I'm so glad my parents had nice names. It would be a real disgrace to have a father named— well, say Jedediah, wouldn't it?''

"I guess it doesn't matter what a person's name is as long as he behaves himself," said Marilla, feeling herself called upon to inculcate a good and useful moral.

"Well, I don't know." Anne looked thoughtful. "I read in a book once that a rose by any other name would smell as sweet, but I've never been able to believe it. I don't believe a rose *would* be as nice if it was called a thistle or a skunk cabbage. I suppose my father could have been a good man even if he had been called Jedediah; but I'm sure it would have been a cross. Well, my mother was a teacher in the High School, too, but when she married father she gave up teaching, of course. A husband was enough responsibility. Mrs. Thomas said that they were a pair of babies and as poor as church mice. They went to live in a weeny-teeny little yellow house in Bolingbroke. I've never seen that house, but I've imagined it thousands of times. I think it must have had honeysuckle over the parlor window and lilacs in the front yard and lilies of the valley just inside the gate. Yes, and muslin curtains in all the windows. Muslin curtains give a house such an air. I was born in that house. Mrs. Thomas said I was the homeliest baby she ever saw, I was so scrawny and tiny and nothing but eyes, but that mother thought I was perfectly beautiful. I should think a mother would be a better judge than a poor woman who came in to scrub, wouldn't you? I'm glad she was satisfied with me anyhow; I would feel so sad if I thought I was a disappointment to her—because she didn't live very long after that, you see. She died of fever when I was just three months old. I do wish she'd lived long enough for me to remember calling her mother. I think it would be so sweet to say 'mother,' don't you? And father died four days afterwards from fever, too. That left me an orphan and folks were at their wits' end, so Mrs. Thomas said, what to do with me. You see, nobody wanted me even then. It seems to be my fate. Father and mother had both come from places far away and it was well known they hadn't any relatives living. Finally Mrs. Thomas said she'd take me, though she was poor and had a drunken husband. She brought me up by hand. Do you know if there is anything in being brought up by hand that ought to make people who are brought up that way better than other people? Because whenever I was naughty Mrs. Thomas would ask me how I could be such a bad girl when she had brought me up by hand—reproachful-like.

"Mr. and Mrs. Thomas moved away from Bolingbroke to Marysville, and I lived with them until I was eight years old. I helped look after the Thomas children—there were four of them younger than me—and I can tell you they took a lot of looking after. Then Mr. Thomas was killed falling under a train and his mother offered to take Mrs. Thomas and the children, but she didn't want me. Mrs. Thomas was at *her* wits' end, so she said, what to do with me. Then Mrs. Hammond from up the river came down and said she'd take me, seeing I was handy with children, and I went up the river to live with her in a little clearing among the stumps. It was a very lonesome place. I'm sure I could never have lived there if I hadn't had an imagination. Mr. Hammond worked a little saw-mill up there, and Mrs. Hammond had eight children. She had twins three times. I like babies in moderation, but twins three times in succession is *too much*. I told Mrs. Hammond so firmly, when the last pair came. I used to get so dreadfully tired carrying them about.

"I lived up river with Mrs. Hammond over two years, and then Mr. Hammond died and Mrs. Hammond broke up housekeeping. She divided her children among her relatives and went to the States. I had to go to the asylum at Hopeton, because nobody would take me. They didn't want me at the asylum, either; they said they were overcrowded as it was. But they had to take me and I was there four months until Mrs. Spencer came."

Anne finished up with another sigh, of relief this time. Evidently she did not like talking about her experiences in a world that had not wanted her.

"Did you ever go to school?" demanded Marilla, turning the sorrel mare down the shore road.

"Not a great deal. I went a little the last year I stayed with Mrs. Thomas. When I went up river we were so far from a school that I couldn't walk it in winter and there was vacation in summer, so I could only go in the spring and fall. But of course I went while I was at the asylum. I can read pretty well and I know ever so many pieces of poetry off by heart—'The Battle of Hohenlinden' and 'Edinburgh after Flodden,' and 'Bingen on the Rhine,' and lots of the 'Lady of the Lake' and most of 'The Seasons,' by James Thompson. Don't you just love poetry that gives you a crinkly feeling up and down your back? There is a piece in the Fifth Reader—'The Downfall of Poland'—that is just full of thrills. Of course, I wasn't in the Fifth Reader—I was only in the Fourth—but the big girls used to lend me theirs to read."

"Were those women—Mrs. Thomas and Mrs. Hammond—good to you?" asked Marilla, looking at Anne out of the corner of her eye.

"O-o-o-h," faltered Anne. Her sensitive little face suddenly

flushed scarlet and embarrassment sat on her brow. "Oh, they *meant*
to be—I know they meant to be just as good and kind as possible.
And when people mean to be good to you, you don't mind very much
when they're not quite—always. They had a good deal to worry
them, you know. It's very trying to have a drunken husband, you see;
and it must be very trying to have twins three times in succession,
don't you think? But I feel sure they meant to be good to me."

Marilla asked no more questions. Anne gave herself up to a silent
rapture over the shore road and Marilla guided the sorrel abstractedly
while she pondered deeply. Pity was suddenly stirring in her heart
for the child. What a starved, unloved life she had had—a life of
drudgery and poverty and neglect; for Marilla was shrewd enough to
read between the lines of Anne's history and divine the truth. No
wonder she had been so delighted at the prospect of a real home. It
was a pity she had to be sent back. What if she, Marilla, should
indulge Matthew's unaccountable whim and let her stay? He was set
on it; and the child seemed a nice, teachable little thing.

"She's got too much to say," thought Marilla, "but she might be
trained out of that. And there's nothing rude or slangy in what she
does say. She's ladylike. It's likely her people were nice folks."

The shore road was "woodsy and wild and lonesome." On the
right hand, scrub firs, their spirits quite unbroken by long years of
tussle with the gulf winds, grew thickly. On the left were the steep
red sandstone cliffs, so near the track in places that a mare of less
steadiness than the sorrel might have tried the nerves of the people
behind her. Down at the base of the cliffs were heaps of surf-worn
rocks or little sandy coves inlaid with pebbles as with ocean jewels;
beyond lay the sea, shimmering and blue, and over it soared the
gulls, their pinions flashing silvery in the sunlight.

"Isn't the sea wonderful?" said Anne, rousing from a long,
wide-eyed silence. "Once, when I lived in Marysville, Mr. Thomas
hired an express-wagon and took us all to spend the day at the shore
ten miles away. I enjoyed every moment of that day, even if I had to
look after the children all the time. I lived it over in happy dreams for
years. But this shore is nicer than the Marysville shore. Aren't those
gulls splendid? Would you like to be a gull? I think I would—that is,
if I couldn't be a human girl. Don't you think it would be nice to
wake up at sunrise and swoop down over the water and away out over
that lovely blue all day; and then at night to fly back to one's nest?
Oh, I can just imagine myself doing it. What big house is that just
ahead, please?"

"That's the White Sands Hotel. Mr. Kirke runs it, but the season hasn't begun yet. There are heaps of Americans come there for the summer. They think this shore is just about right."

"I was afraid it might be Mrs. Spencer's place," said Anne mournfully. "I don't want to get there. Somehow, it will seem like the end of everything."

CHAPTER 6

MARILLA MAKES UP HER MIND

GET THERE they did, however, in due season. Mrs. Spencer lived in a big yellow house at White Sands Cove, and she came to the door with surprise and welcome mingled on her benevolent face.

"Dear, dear," she exclaimed, "you're the last folks I was looking for today, but I'm glad to see you. You'll put your horse in? And how are you, Anne?"

"I'm as well as can be expected, thank you," said Anne smilelessly. A blight seemed to have descended on her.

"I suppose we'll stay a little while to rest the mare," said Marilla, "but I promised Matthew I'd be home early. The fact is, Mrs. Spencer, there's been a queer mistake somewhere, and I've come over to see where it is. We sent word, Matthew and I, for you to bring us a boy from the asylum. We told your brother Robert to tell you we wanted a boy ten or eleven years old."

"Marilla Cuthbert, you don't say so!" said Mrs. Spencer in distress. "Why, Robert sent the word down by his daughter Nancy and said you wanted a girl—didn't she, Flora Jane?" appealing to her daughter who had come out to the steps.

"She certainly did, Miss Cuthbert," corroborated Flora Jane earnestly.

"I'm dreadful sorry," said Mrs. Spencer. "It is too bad; but it certainly wasn't my fault, you see, Miss Cuthbert. I did the best I could and I thought I was following your instructions. Nancy is a terrible flighty thing. I've often had to scold her well for her heedlessness."

"It was our own fault," said Marilla resignedly. "We should have come to you ourselves and not left an important message to be passed along by word of mouth in that fashion. Anyhow, the mistake has been made and the only thing to do now it to set it right. Can we send the child back to the asylum? I suppose they'll take her back, won't they?"

"I suppose so," said Mrs. Spencer thoughtfully, "but I don't think it will be necessary to send her back. Mrs. Peter Blewett was up here yesterday, and she was saying to me how much she wished she'd sent by me for a little girl to help her. Mrs. Peter has a large family, you know, and she finds it hard to get help. Anne will be the very girl for her. I call it positively providential."

Marilla did not look as if she thought Providence had much to do with the matter. Here was an unexpectedly good chance to get this unwelcome orphan off her hands, and she did not even feel grateful for it.

She knew Mrs. Peter Blewett only by sight as a small, shrewish-faced woman without an ounce of superfluous flesh on her bones. But she had heard of her. "A terrible worker and driver," Mrs. Peter was said to be; and discharged servant girls told fearsome tales of her temper and stinginess, and her family of pert, quarrelsome children. Marilla felt a qualm of conscience at the thought of handing Anne over to her tender mercies.

"Well, I'll go in and we'll talk the matter over," she said.

"And if there isn't Mrs. Peter coming up the lane this blessed minute!" exclaimed Mrs. Spencer, bustling her guests through the hall into the parlor, where a deadly chill struck them as if the air had been strained so long through dark green, closely drawn blinds that it had lost every particle of warmth it had ever possessed. "That is real lucky, for we can settle the matter right away. Take the armchair, Miss Cuthbert. Anne, you sit here on the ottoman and don't wriggle. Let me take your hats. Flora Jane, go out and put the kettle on. Good afternoon, Mrs. Blewett. We were just saying how fortunate it was you happened along. Let me introduce you two ladies. Mrs. Blewett, Miss Cuthbert. Please excuse me for just a moment. I forgot to tell Flora Jane to take the buns out of the oven."

Mrs. Spencer whisked away, after pulling up the blinds. Anne, sitting mutely on the ottoman, with her hands clasped tightly in her lap, stared at Mrs. Blewett as one fascinated. Was she to be given into the keeping of this sharp-faced, sharp-eyed woman? She felt a lump coming up in her throat and her eyes smarted painfully. She was beginning to be afraid she couldn't keep the tears back when Mrs. Spencer returned, flushed and beaming, quite capable of taking any and every difficulty, physical, mental or spiritual, into consideration and settling it out of hand.

"It seems there's been a mistake about this little girl, Mrs. Blewett," she said. "I was under the impression that Mr. and Miss Cuthbert wanted a little girl to adopt. I was certainly told so. But it seems it was a boy they wanted. So if you're still of the same mind you were yesterday, I think she'll be just the thing for you."

Mrs. Blewett darted her eyes over Anne from head to foot.

"How old are you and what's your name?" she demanded.

"Anne Shirley," faltered the shrinking child, not daring to make any stipulations regarding the spelling thereof, "and I'm eleven years old."

"Humph! You don't look as if there was much to you. But you're wiry. I don't know but the wiry ones are the best after all. Well, if I take you you'll have to be a good girl, you know—good and smart and respectful. I'll expect you to earn your keep, and no mistake about that. Yes, I suppose I might as well take her off your hands, Miss Cuthbert. The baby's awful fractious, and I'm clean worn out attending to him. If you like I can take her right home now."

Marilla looked at Anne and softened at sight of the child's pale face with its look of mute misery—the misery of a helpless little creature who finds itself once more caught in the trap from which it had escaped. Marilla felt an uncomfortable conviction that, if she denied the appeal of that look, it would haunt her to her dying day. Moreover, she did not fancy Mrs. Blewett. To hand a sensitive, "high-strung" child over to such a woman! No, she could not take the responsibility of doing that!

"Well, I don't know," she said slowly. "I didn't say that Matthew and I had absolutely decided that we wouldn't keep her. In fact, I may say that Matthew is disposed to keep her. I just came over to find out how the mistake had occurred. I think I'd better take her home again and talk it over with Matthew. I feel that I oughtn't to decide on anything without consulting him. If we make up our mind not to keep her we'll bring or send her over to you tomorrow night. If we don't you may know that she is going to stay with us. Will that suit you, Mrs. Blewett?"

"I suppose it'll have to," said Mrs. Blewett ungraciously.

During Marilla's speech a sunrise had been dawning on Anne's face. First the look of despair faded out; then came a faint flush of hope; her eyes grew deep and bright as morning stars. The child was quite transfigured; and, a moment later, when Mrs. Spencer and Mrs. Blewett went out in quest of a recipe the latter had come to borrow, she sprang up and flew across the room to Marilla.

"Oh, Miss Cuthbert, did you really say that perhaps you would let me stay at Green Gables?" she said, in a breathless whisper, as if speaking aloud might shatter the glorious possibility. "Did you really say it? Or did I only imagine that you did?"

"I think you'd better learn to control that imagination of yours, Anne, if you can't distinguish between what is real and what isn't," said Marilla crossly. "Yes, you did hear me say just that and no more. It isn't decided yet and perhaps we will conclude to let Mrs. Blewett take you after all. She certainly needs you much more than I do."

"I'd rather go back to the asylum than go to live with her," said Anne passionately. "She looks exactly like a—like a gimlet."

Marilla smothered a smile under the conviction that Anne must be reproved for such a speech.

"A little girl like you should be ashamed of talking so about a lady and a stranger," she said severely. "Go back and sit down quietly and hold your tongue and behave as a good girl should."

"I'll try to do and be anything you want me, if you'll only keep me," said Anne, returning meekly to her ottoman.

When they arrived back at Green Gables that evening Matthew met them in the lane. Marilla from afar had noted him prowling along it and guessed his motive. She was prepared for the relief she read in his face when he saw that she had at least brought Anne back with her. But she said nothing to him, relative to the affair, until they were both out in the yard behind the barn milking the cows. Then she briefly told him Anne's history and the result of the interview with Mrs. Spencer.

"I wouldn't give a dog I liked to that Blewett woman," said Matthew with unusual vim.

"I don't fancy her style myself," admitted Marilla, "but it's that or keeping her ourselves, Matthew. And, since you seem to want her, I suppose I'm willing—or have to be. I've been thinking over the idea until I've got kind of used to it. It seems a sort of duty. I've never brought up a child, especially a girl, and I dare say I'll make a terrible mess of it. But I'll do my best. So far as I'm concerned, Matthew, she may stay."

Matthew's shy face was a glow of delight.

"Well now, I reckoned you'd come to see it in that light, Marilla," he said. "She's such an interesting little thing."

"It'd be more to the point if you could say she was a useful little thing," retorted Marilla, "but I'll make it my business to see she's trained to be that. And mind, Matthew, you're not to go interfering with my methods. Perhaps an old maid doesn't know much about bringing up a child, but I guess she knows more than an old bachelor. So you just leave me to manage her. When I fail it'll be time enough to put your oar in."

"There, there, Marilla, you can have your own way," said Matthew reassuringly. "Only be as good and kind to her as you can without spoiling her. I kind of think she's one of the sort you can do anything with if you only get her to love you."

Marilla sniffed, to express her contempt for Matthew's opinions concerning anything feminine, and walked off to the dairy with the pails.

"I won't tell her tonight that she can stay," she reflected, as she strained the milk into the creamers. "She'd be so excited that she wouldn't sleep a wink. Marilla Cuthbert, you're fairly in for it. Did you ever suppose you'd see the day when you'd be adopting an orphan girl? It's surprising enough; but not so surprising as that Matthew should be at the bottom of it, him that always seemed to have such a mortal dread of little girls. Anyhow, we've decided on the experiment and goodness only knows what will come of it."

—————————— CHAPTER 7 ——————————

ANNE SAYS HER PRAYERS

WHEN MARILLA took Anne up to bed that night she said stiffly:

"Now, Anne, I noticed last night that you threw your clothes all about the floor when you took them off. That is a very untidy habit, and I can't allow it at all. As soon as you take off any article of clothing fold it neatly and place it on the chair. I haven't any use at all for little girls who aren't neat."

"I was so harrowed up in my mind last night that I didn't think about my clothes at all,'' said Anne. ''I'll fold them nicely tonight. They always made us do that at the asylum. Half the time, though, I'd forget, I'd be in such a hurry to get into bed nice and quiet and imagine things.''

''You'll have to remember a little better if you stay here,'' admonished Marilla. ''There, that looks something like. Say your prayers now and get into bed.''

''I never say any prayers,'' announced Anne.

Marilla looked horrified astonishment.

''Why, Anne, what do you mean? Were you never taught to say your prayers? God always wants little girls to say their prayers. Don't you know who God is, Anne?''

'''God is a spirit, infinite, eternal and unchangeable, in His being, wisdom, power, holiness, justice, goodness, and truth,''' responded Anne promptly and glibly.

Marilla looked rather relieved.

''So you do know something then, thank goodness! You're not quite a heathen. Where did you learn that?''

''Oh, at the asylum Sunday-school. They made us learn the whole catechism. I liked it pretty well. There's something splendid about some of the words. 'Infinite, eternal and unchangeable.' Isn't that grand? It has such a roll to it—just like a big organ playing. You couldn't quite call it poetry, I suppose, but it sounds a lot like it, doesn't it?''

''We're not talking about poetry, Anne—we are talking about saying prayers. Don't you know it's a terrible wicked thing not to say your prayers every night? I'm afraid you are a very bad little girl.''

''You'd find it easier to be bad than good if you had red hair,'' said Anne reproachfully. ''People who haven't red hair don't know what trouble is. Mrs. Thomas told me that God made my hair red *on purpose,* and I've never cared about Him since. And anyhow I'd always be too tired at night to bother saying prayers. People who have to look after twins can't be expected to say their prayers. Now, do you honestly think they can?''

Marilla decided that Anne's religious training must be begun at once. Plainly there was no time to be lost.

''You must say your prayers while you are under my roof, Anne.''

''Why, of course, if you want me to,'' assented Anne cheerfully. ''I'd do anything to oblige you. But you'll have to tell me what to say for this once. After I get into bed I'll imagine out a real nice prayer to say always. I believe that it will be interesting, now that I come to think of it.''

"You must kneel down," said Marilla in embarrassment.

Anne knelt at Marilla's knee and looked up gravely.

"Why must people kneel down to pray? If I really wanted to pray I'll tell you what I'd do. I'd go out into the great big field all alone or into the deep, deep woods, and I'd look up into the sky——up—— up——up——into that lovely blue sky that looks as if there was no end to its blueness. And then I'd just *feel* a prayer. Well, I'm ready. What am I to say?"

Marilla felt more embarrassed than ever. She had intended to teach Anne the childish classic, "Now I lay me down to sleep." But she had, as I have told you, the glimmerings of a sense of humor— which is simply another name for the fitness of things; and it suddenly occurred to her that that simple little prayer, sacred to white-robed childhood lisping at motherly knees, was entirely un- suited to this freckled witch of a girl who knew and cared nothing about God's love, since she had never had it translated to her through the medium of human love.

"You're old enough to pray for yourself, Anne," she said finally. "Just thank God for your blessings and ask Him humbly for the things you want."

"Well, I'll do my best,' promised Anne, burying her face in Marilla's lap. "Gracious heavenly Father—that's the way the min- isters say it in church, so I suppose it's all right in a private prayer, isn't it?" she interjected, lifting her head for a moment. "Gracious heavenly Father, I thank Thee for the White Way of Delight and the Lake of Shining Waters and Bonny and the Snow Queen. I'm really extremely grateful for them. And that's all the blessings I can think of just/now to thank Thee for. As for the things I want, they're so numerous that it would take a great deal of time to name them all, so I will only mention the two most important. Please let me stay at Green Gables; and please let me be good-looking when I grow up. I remain,

"Yours respectfully,

"ANNE SHIRLEY.

"There, did I do it all right?" she asked eagerly, getting up. "I could have made it much more flowery if I'd had a little more time to think it over."

Poor Marilla was only preserved from complete collapse by re- membering that it was not irreverence, but simply spiritual ignorance on the part of Anne that was responsible for this extraordinary petition. She tucked the child up in bed, mentally vowing that she should be taught a prayer the very next day, and was leaving the room with the light when Anne called her back.

"I've just thought of it now. I should have said 'Amen' in place of 'yours respectfully,' shouldn't I?—the way the ministers do. I'd forgotten it, but I felt a prayer should be finished off in some way, so I put in the other. Do you suppose it will make any difference?"

"I—I don't suppose it will," said Marilla. "Go to sleep now like a good child. Good night."

"I can say good night tonight with a clear conscience," said Anne, cuddling luxuriously down among her pillows.

Marilla retreated to the kitchen, set the candle firmly on the table, and glared at Matthew.

"Matthew Cuthbert, it's about time somebody adopted that child and taught her something. She's next door to a perfect heathen. Will you believe that she never said a prayer in her life till tonight? I'll send to the manse tomorrow and borrow the Peep of Day series, that's what I'll do. And she shall go to Sunday-school just as soon as I can get some suitable clothes made for her. I foresee that I shall have my hands full. Well, well, we can't get through this world without our share of trouble. I've had a pretty easy life of it so far, but my time has come at last and I suppose I'll just have to make the best of it."

CHAPTER 8

ANNE'S BRINGING-UP IS BEGUN

FOR REASONS best known to herself, Marilla did not tell Anne that she was to stay at Green Gables until the next afternoon. During the forenoon she kept the child busy with various tasks and watched over her with a keen eye while she did them. By noon she had concluded that Anne was smart and obedient, willing to work and quick to learn; her most serious shortcoming seemed to be a tendency to fall into day-dreams in the middle of a task and forget all about it until such times as she was sharply recalled to earth by a reprimand or a catastrophe.

When Anne had finished washing the dinner dishes she suddenly confronted Marilla with the air and expression of one desperately determined to learn the worst. Her thin little body trembled from head to foot; her face flushed and her eyes dilated until they were almost black; she clasped her hands tightly and said in an imploring voice:

"Oh, please, Miss Cuthbert, won't you tell me if you are going to send me away or not? I've tried to be patient all the morning, but I really feel that I cannot bear not knowing any longer. It's a dreadful feeling. Please tell me."

"You haven't scalded the dish-cloth in clean hot water as I told you to do," said Marilla immovably. "Just go and do it before you ask any more questions, Anne."

Anne went and attended to the dish-cloth. Then she returned to Marilla and fastened imploring eyes on the latter's face.

"Well," said Marilla, unable to find any excuse for deferring her explanation longer, "I suppose I might as well tell you. Matthew and I have decided to keep you—that is, if you will try to be a good girl and show yourself grateful. Why, child, whatever is the matter?"

"I'm crying," said Anne in a tone of bewilderment. "I can't think why. I'm glad as glad can be. Oh, *glad* doesn't seem the right word at all. I was glad about the White Way and the cherry blossoms—but this! Oh, it's something more than glad. I'm so happy. I'll try to be so good. It will be up-hill work, I expect, for Mrs. Thomas often told me I was desperately wicked. However, I'll do my very best. But can you tell me why I'm crying?"

"I suppose it's because you're all excited and worked up," said Marilla disapprovingly. "Sit down on that chair and try to calm yourself. I'm afraid you both cry and laugh far too easily. Yes, you can stay here and we will try to do right by you. You must go to school; but it's only a fortnight till vacation so it isn't worthwhile for you to start before it opens again in September."

"What am I to call you?" asked Anne. "Shall I always say Miss Cuthbert? Can I call you Aunt Marilla?"

"No; you'll call me just plain Marilla. I'm not used to being called Miss Cuthbert and it would make me nervous."

"It sounds awfully disrespectful to say just Marilla," protested Anne.

"I guess there'll be nothing disrespectful in it if you're careful to speak respectfully. Everybody, young and old, in Avonlea calls me Marilla except the minister. He says Miss Cuthbert—when he thinks of it."

"I'd love to call you Aunt Marilla," said Anne wistfully. "I've never had an aunt or any relation at all—not even a grandmother. It would make me feel as if I really belonged to you. Can't I call you Aunt Marilla?"

"No. I'm not your aunt and I don't believe in calling people names that don't belong to them."

"But we could imagine you were my aunt."

"I couldn't," said Marilla grimly.

"Do you never imagine things different from what they really are?" asked Anne wide-eyed.

"No."

"Oh!" Anne drew a long breath. "Oh, Miss—Marilla, how much you miss!"

"I don't believe in imagining things different from what they really are," retorted Marilla. "When the Lord puts us in certain circumstances He doesn't mean for us to imagine them away. And that reminds me. Go into the sitting-room, Anne—be sure your feet are clean and don't let any flies in—and bring me out the illustrated card that's on the mantelpiece. The Lord's Prayer is on it and you'll devote your spare time this afternoon to learning it off by heart. There's to be no more of such praying as I heard last night."

"I suppose I was very awkward," said Anne apologetically, "but then, you see, I'd never had any practice. You couldn't really expect a person to pray very well the first time she tried, could you? I thought out a splendid prayer after I went to bed, just as I promised you I would. It was nearly as long as the minister's and so poetical. But would you believe it? I couldn't remember one word when I woke up this morning. And I'm afraid I'll never be able to think out another one as good. Somehow, things are never so good when they're thought out a second time. Have you ever noticed that?"

"Here is something for you to notice, Anne. When I tell you to do a thing I want you to obey me at once and not stand stock-still and discourse about it. Just you go and do as I bid you."

Anne promptly departed for the sitting-room across the hall; she failed to return; after waiting ten minutes Marilla laid down her knitting and marched after her with a grim expression. She found Anne standing motionless before a picture hanging on the wall between the two windows, with her hands clasped behind her, her face uplifted, and her eyes astar with dreams. The white and green light strained through apple-trees and clustering vines outside fell over the rapt little figure with half-unearthly radiance.

"Anne, whatever are you thinking of?" demanded Marilla sharply.

Anne came back to earth with a start.

"That," she said, pointing to the picture—a rather vivid chromo entitled, "Christ Blessing Little Children"—"and I was just imagining I was one of them—that I was the little girl in the blue dress, standing off by herself in the corner as if she didn't belong to anybody, like me. She looks lonely and sad, don't you think? I guess she hadn't any father or mother of her own. But she wanted to be blessed, too, so she just crept shyly up on the outside of the crowd, hoping nobody would notice her—except Him. I'm sure I know just how she felt. Her heart must have beat and her hands must have got cold, like mine did when I asked you if I could stay. She was afraid He mightn't notice her. But it's likely He did, don't you think? I've been trying to imagine it all out—her edging a little nearer all the time until she was quite close to Him; and then He would look at her and put His hand on her hair and oh, such a thrill of joy as would run over her! But I wish the artist hadn't painted Him so sorrowful-looking. All His pictures are like that, if you've noticed. But I don't believe He could really have looked so sad or the children would have been afraid of Him."

"Anne," said Marilla, wondering why she had not broken into this speech long before, "you shouldn't talk that way. It's irreverent—positively irreverent."

Anne's eyes marvelled.

"Why, I felt just as reverent as could be. I'm sure I didn't mean to be irreverent."

"Well, I don't suppose you did—but it doesn't sound right to talk so familiarly about such things. And another thing, Anne, when I send you after something you're to bring it at once and not fall into mooning and imagining before pictures. Remember that. Take that card and come right to the kitchen. Now, sit down in the corner and learn that prayer off by heart."

Anne set the card up against the jugful of apple blossoms she had brought in to decorate the dinner table—Marilla had eyed that decoration askance, but had said nothing—propped her chin on her hands, and fell to studying it intently for several silent minutes.

"I like this," she announced at length. "It's beautiful. I've heard it before—I heard the superintendent of the asylum Sunday-school say it over once. But I didn't like it then. He had such a cracked voice and he prayed it so mournfully. I really felt sure he thought praying was a disagreeable duty. This isn't poetry, but it makes me feel just the same way poetry does. 'Our Father who art in heaven, hallowed be Thy name.' That is just like a line of music. Oh, I'm so glad you thought of making me learn this, Miss—Marilla.''

''Well, learn it and hold your tongue,'' said Marilla shortly.

Anne tipped the vase of apple blossoms near enough to bestow a soft kiss on a pink-cupped bud, and then studied diligently for some moments longer.

''Marilla,'' she demanded presently, ''do you think that I shall ever have a bosom friend in Avonlea?''

''A—a what kind of a friend?''

''A bosom friend—an intimate friend, you know—a really kindred spirit to whom I can confide my inmost soul. I've dreamed of meeting her all my life. I never really supposed I would, but so many of my loveliest dreams have come true all at once that perhaps this one will, too. Do you think it's possible?''

''Diana Barry lives over at Orchard Slope and she's about your age. She's a very nice little girl, and perhaps she will be a playmate for you when she comes home. She's visiting her aunt over at Carmody just now. You'll have to be careful how you behave yourself, though. Mrs. Barry is a very particular woman. She won't let Diana play with any little girl who isn't nice and good.''

Anne looked at Marilla through the apple blossoms, her eyes aglow with interest.

''What is Diana like? Her hair isn't red is it? Oh, I hope not. It's bad enough to have red hair myself, but I positively couldn't endure it in a bosom friend.''

''Diana is a very pretty little girl. She has black eyes and hair and rosy cheeks. And she is good and smart, which is better than being pretty.''

Marilla was as fond of morals as the Duchess in Wonderland, and was firmly convinced that one should be tacked on to every remark made to a child who was being brought up.

But Anne waved the moral inconsequently aside and seized only on the delightful possibilities before it.

''Oh, I'm so glad she's pretty. Next to being beautiful oneself—and that's impossible in my case—it would be best to have a beautiful bosom friend. When I lived with Mrs. Thomas she had a bookcase in her sitting room with glass doors. There weren't any books in it; Mrs. Thomas kept her best china and her preserves there—when she had any preserves to keep. One of the doors was broken. Mr. Thomas smashed it one night when he was slightly intoxicated. But the other was whole and I used to pretend that my reflection in it was another little girl who lived in it. I called her Katie Maurice, and we were very intimate. I used to talk to her by the hour, especially on Sunday, and tell her everything. Katie was the comfort and consolation of my life. We used to pretend that the bookcase was enchanted and that if I only knew the spell I could open the door and step right into the room where Katie Maurice lived, instead of into Mrs. Thomas' shelves of preserves and china. And then Katie Maurice would have taken me by the hand and led me out into a wonderful place, all flowers and sunshine and fairies, and we would have lived there happy for ever after. When I went to live with Mrs. Hammond it just broke my heart to leave Katie Maurice. She felt it dreadfully, too, I know she did, for she was crying when she kissed me good-bye through the bookcase door. There was no bookcase at Mrs. Hammond's. But just up the river a little way from the house there was a long green little valley, and the loveliest echo lived there. It echoed back every word you said, even if you didn't talk a bit loud. So I imagined that it was a little girl called Violetta and we were great friends and I loved her almost as well as I loved Katie Maurice—not quite, but almost, you know. The night before I went to the asylum I said good-bye to Violetta, and oh, her good-bye came back to me in such sad, sad tones. I had become so attached to her that I hadn't the heart to imagine a bosom friend at the asylum, even if there had been any scope for imagination there.''

''I think it's just as well there wasn't,'' said Marilla drily. ''I don't approve of such goings-on. You seem to half believe your own imaginations. It will be well for you to have a real live friend to put such nonsense out of your head. But don't let Mrs. Barry hear you talking about your Katie Maurices and your Violettas or she'll think you tell stories.''

''Oh, I won't. I couldn't talk of them to everybody—their memories are too sacred for that. But I thought I'd like to have you know about them. Oh, look, here's a big bee just tumbled out of an apple blossom. Just think what a lovely place to live—in an apple blossom! Fancy going to sleep in it when the wind was rocking it. If I wasn't a human girl I think I'd like to be a bee and live among the flowers.''

''Yesterday you wanted to be a sea-gull,'' sniffed Marilla. ''I think you are very fickle-minded. I told you to learn that prayer and not talk. But it seems impossible for you to stop talking if you've got anybody that will listen to you. So go up to your room and learn it.''

"Oh, I know it pretty nearly all now—all but just the last line."

"Well, never mind, do as I tell you. Go to your room and finish learning it well, and stay there until I call you down to help me get tea."

"Can I take the apple blossoms with me for company?" pleaded Anne.

"No; you don't want your room cluttered up with flowers. You should have left them on the tree in the first place."

"I did feel a little that way, too," said Anne. "I kind of felt I shouldn't shorten their lovely lives by picking them—I wouldn't want to be picked if I were an apple blossom. But the temptation was *irresistible*. What do you do when you meet with an irresistible temptation?"

"Anne, did you hear me tell you to go to your room?"

Anne sighed, retreated to the east gable, and sat down in a chair by the window.

"There—I know this prayer. I learned that last sentence coming upstairs. Now I'm going to imagine things into this room so that they'll always stay imagined. The floor is covered with a white velvet carpet with pink roses all over it and there are pink silk curtains at the windows. The walls are hung with gold and silver brocade tapestry. The furniture is mahogany. I never saw any mahogany, but it does sound *so* luxurious. This is a couch all heaped with gorgeous silken cushions, pink and blue and crimson and gold, and I am reclining gracefully on it. I can see my reflection in that splendid big mirror hanging on the wall. I am tall and regal, clad in a gown of trailing white lace, with a pearl cross on my breast and pearls in my hair. My hair is of midnight darkness and my skin is a clear ivory pallor. My name is the Lady Cordelia Fitzgerald. No, it isn't—I can't make *that* seem real."

She danced up to the little looking-glass and peered into it. Her pointed freckled face and solemn gray eyes peered back at her.

"You're only Anne of Green Gables," she said earnestly, "and I see you, just as you are looking now, whenever I try to imagine I'm the Lady Cordelia. But it's a million times nicer to be Anne of Green Gables than Anne of nowhere in particular, isn't it?"

She bent forward, kissed her reflection affectionately, and betook herself to the open window.

"Dear Snow Queen, good afternoon. And good afternoon, dear birches down in the hollow. And good afternoon, dear gray house up on the hill. I wonder if Diana is to be my bosom friend. I hope she will, and I shall love her very much. But I must never quite forget Katie Maurice and Violetta. They would feel so hurt if I did and I'd hate to hurt anybody's feelings, even a little bookcase girl's or a little echo girl's. I must be careful to remember them and send them a kiss every day."

Anne blew a couple of airy kisses from her fingertips past the cherry blossoms and then, with her chin in her hands, drifted luxuriously out on a sea of daydreams.

——————————— CHAPTER 9 ———————————

MRS. RACHEL LYNDE IS PROPERLY HORRIFIED

ANNE HAD been a fortnight at Green Gables before Mrs. Lynde arrived to inspect her. Mrs. Rachel, to do her justice, was not to blame for this. A severe and unseasonable attack of grippe had confined that good lady to her house ever since the occasion of her last visit to Green Gables. Mrs. Rachel was not often sick and had a well-defined contempt for people who were; but grippe, she asserted, was like no other illness on earth and could only be interpreted as one of the special visitations of Providence. As soon as her doctor allowed her to put her foot out-of-doors she hurried up to Green Gables, bursting with curiosity to see Matthew's and Marilla's orphan, concerning whom all sorts of stories and suppositions had gone abroad in Avonlea.

Anne had made good use of every waking moment of that fortnight. Already she was acquainted with every tree and shrub about the place. She had discovered that a lane opened out below the apple orchard and ran up through a belt of woodland; and she had explored it to its furthest end in all its delicious vagaries of brook and bridge, fir coppice and wild cherry arch, corners thick with fern, and branching byways of maple and mountain ash.

She had made friends with the spring down in the hollow—that wonderful deep, clear icy-cold spring; it was set about with smooth red sandstones and rimmed in by great palm-like clumps of water fern; and beyond it was a log bridge over the brook.

That bridge led Anne's dancing feet up over a wooded hill beyond, where perpetual twilight reigned under the straight, thick-growing firs and spruces; the only flowers there were myriads of delicate "June bells," those shyest and sweetest of woodland blooms, and a few pale, aerial starflowers, like the spirits of last year's blossoms. Gossamers glimmered like threads of silver among the trees and the fir boughs and tassels seemed to utter friendly speech.

All these raptured voyages of exploration were made in the odd half-hours which she was allowed for play, and Anne talked Matthew and Marilla half-deaf over her discoveries. Not that Matthew complained, to be sure; he listened to it all with a wordless smile of enjoyment on his face; Marilla permitted the "chatter" until she found herself becoming too interested in it, whereupon she always promptly quenched Anne by a curt command to hold her tongue.

Anne was out in the orchard when Mrs. Rachel came, wandering at her own sweet will through the lush, tremulous grasses splashed with ruddy evening sunshine; so that good lady had an excellent chance to talk her illness fully over, describing every ache and pulse-beat with such evident enjoyment that Marilla thought even grippe must bring its compensations. When details were exhausted Mrs. Rachel introduced the real reason of her call.

"I've been hearing some surprising things about you and Matthew."

"I don't suppose you are any more surprised than I am myself," said Marilla. "I'm getting over my surprise now."

"It was too bad there was such a mistake," said Mrs. Rachel sympathetically. "Couldn't you have sent her back?"

"I suppose we could, but we decided not to. Matthew took a fancy to her. And I must say I like her myself—although I admit she has her faults. The house seems a different place already. She's a real bright little thing."

Marilla said more than she had intended to say when she began, for she read disapproval in Mrs. Rachel's expression.

"It's a great responsibility you've taken on yourself," said that lady gloomily, "especially when you've never had any experience with children. You don't know much about her or her real disposition, I suppose, and there's no guessing how a child like that will turn out. But I don't want to discourage you I'm sure, Marilla."

"I'm not feeling discouraged," was Marilla's dry response. "When I make up my mind to do a thing it stays made up. I suppose you'd like to see Anne. I'll call her in."

Anne came running in presently, her face sparkling with the delight of her orchard rovings; but, abashed at finding herself in the unexpected presence of a stranger, she halted confusedly inside the door. She certainly was an odd-looking little creature in the short tight wincey dress she had worn from the asylum, below which her thin legs seemed ungracefully long. Her freckles were more numerous and obtrusive than ever; the wind had ruffled her hatless hair into over-brilliant disorder; it had never looked redder than at that moment.

"Well, they didn't pick you for your looks, that's sure and certain," was Mrs. Rachel Lynde's emphatic comment. Mrs. Rachel was one of those delightful and popular people who pride themselves on speaking their mind without fear or favour. "She's terrible skinny and homely, Marilla. Come here, child, and let me have a look at you. Lawful heart, did anyone ever see such freckles? And hair as red as carrots! Come here, child, I say."

Anne "came there," but not exactly as Mrs. Rachel expected. With one bound she crossed the kitchen floor and stood before Mrs. Rachel, her face scarlet with anger, her lips quivering, and her whole slender form trembling from head to foot.

"I hate you," she cried in a choked voice, stamping her foot on the floor. "I hate you—I hate you—I hate you—" a louder stamp with each assertion of hatred. "How dare you call me skinny and ugly? How dare you say I'm freckled and redheaded? You are a rude, impolite, unfeeling woman!"

"Anne!" exclaimed Marilla in consternation.

But Anne continued to face Mrs. Rachel undauntedly, head up, eyes blazing, hands clenched, passionate indignation exhaling from her like an atmosphere.

"How dare you say such things about me?" she repeated vehemently. "How would you like to have such things said about you? How would you like to be told that you are fat and clumsy and probably hadn't a spark of imagination in you? I don't care if I do hurt your feelings by saying so! I hope I hurt them. You have hurt mine worse than they were ever hurt before even by Mrs. Thomas' intoxicated husband. And I'll *never* forgive you for it, never, never!"

Stamp! Stamp!

"Did anybody ever see such a temper!" exclaimed the horrified Mrs. Rachel.

"Anne, go up to your room and stay there until I come up," said

Marilla, recovering her powers of speech with difficulty.

Anne, bursting into tears, rushed to the hall door, slammed it until the tins on the porch wall outside rattled in sympathy, and fled through the hall and up the stairs like a whirlwind. A subdued slam above told that the door of the east gable had been shut with equal vehemence.

"Well, I don't envy you your job bringing *that* up, Marilla," said Mrs. Rachel with unspeakable solemnity.

Marilla opened her lips to say she knew not what of apology or deprecation. What she did say was a surprise to herself then and ever afterwards.

"You shouldn't have twitted her about her looks, Rachel."

"Marilla Cuthbert, you don't mean to say that you are upholding her in such a terrible display of temper as we've just seen?" demanded Mrs. Rachel indignantly.

"No," said Marilla slowly, "I'm not trying to excuse her. She's been very naughty and I'll have to give her a talking to about it. But we must make allowances for her. She's never been taught what is right. And you *were* too hard on her, Rachel."

Marilla could not help tacking on that last sentence, although she was again surprised at herself for doing it. Mrs. Rachel got up with an air of offended dignity.

"Well, I see that I'll have to be very careful what I say after this, Marilla, since the fine feelings of orphans, brought from goodness knows where, have to be considered before anything else. On, no, I'm not vexed—don't worry yourself. I'm too sorry for you to leave any room for anger in my mind. You'll have your own troubles with that child. But if you'll take my advice—which I suppose you won't do, although I've brought up ten children and buried two—you'll do that 'talking to' you mention with a fair-sized birch switch. I should think *that* would be the most effective language for that kind of a child. Her temper matches her hair I guess. Well, good evening, Marilla. I hope you'll come down to see me often as usual. But you can't expect me to visit here again in a hurry, if I'm liable to be flown at and insulted in such a fashion. It's something new in *my* experience."

Whereat Mrs. Rachel swept out and away—if a fat woman who always waddled *could* be said to sweep away—and Marilla with a very solemn face betook herself to the east gable.

On the way upstairs she pondered uneasily as to what she ought to do. She felt no little dismay over the scene that had just been enacted.

How unfortunate that Anne should have displayed such temper before Mrs. Rachel Lynde, of all people! Then Marilla suddenly became aware of an uncomfortable and rebuking consciousness that she felt more humiliation over this than sorrow over the discovery of such a serious defect in Anne's disposition. And how was she to punish her? The amiable suggestion of the birch switch—to the efficiency of which all of Mrs. Rachel's own children could have borne smarting testimony—did not appeal to Marilla. She did not believe she could whip a child. No, some other method of punishment must be found to bring Anne to a proper realization of the enormity of her offence.

Marilla found Anne face downward on her bed, crying bitterly, quite oblivious of muddy boots on a clean counterpane.

"Anne," she said, not ungently.

No answer.

"Anne," with greater severity, "get off that bed this minute and listen to what I have to say to you."

Anne squirmed off the bed and sat rigidly on a chair beside it, her face swollen and tear-stained and her eyes fixed stubbornly on the floor.

"This is a nice way for you to behave, Anne! Aren't you ashamed of yourself?"

"She hadn't any right to call me ugly and redheaded," retorted Anne, evasive and defiant.

"You hadn't any right to fly into such a fury and talk the way you did to her, Anne. I was ashamed of you—thoroughly ashamed of you. I wanted you to behave nicely to Mrs. Lynde, and instead of that you have disgraced me. I'm sure I don't know why you should lose your temper like that just because Mrs. Lynde said you were red-haired and homely. You say it yourself often enough."

"Oh, but there's such a difference between saying a thing yourself and hearing other people say it," wailed Anne. "You may know a thing is so, but you can't help hoping other people don't quite think it is. I suppose you think I have an awful temper, but I couldn't help it. When she said those things something just rose right up in me and choked me. I *had* to fly out at her."

"Well, you made a fine exhibition of yourself I must say. Mrs. Lynde will have a nice story to tell about you everywhere—and she'll tell it, too. It was a dreadful thing for you to lose your temper like that, Anne."

"Just imagine how you would feel if somebody told you to your face that you were skinny and ugly," pleaded Anne tearfully.

An old remembrance suddenly rose up before Marilla. She had been a very small child when she had heard one aunt say of her to another, "What a pity she is such a dark, homely little thing." Marilla was every day of fifty before the sting had gone out of that memory.

"I don't say that I think Mrs. Lynde was exactly right in saying what she did to you, Anne," she admitted in a softer tone. "Rachel is too outspoken. But that is no excuse for such behavior on your part. She was a stranger and an elderly person and my visitor—all three very good reasons why you should have been respectful to her. You were rude and saucy and"—Marilla had a saving inspiration of punishment—"you must go to her and tell her you are very sorry for your bad temper and ask her to forgive you."

"I can never do that," said Anne determinedly and darkly. "You can punish me in any way you like, Marilla. You can shut me up in a dark, damp dungeon inhabited by snakes and toads and feed me only on bread and water and I shall not complain. But I cannot ask Mrs. Lynde to forgive me."

"We're not in the habit of shutting people up in dark, damp dungeons," said Marilla drily, "especially as they're rather scarce in Avonlea. But apologize to Mrs. Lynde you must and shall and you'll stay here in your room until you can tell me you're willing to do it."

"I shall have to stay here for ever then," said Anne mournfully, "because I can't tell Mrs. Lynde I'm sorry I said those things to her. How can I? I'm *not* sorry. I'm sorry I've vexed you; but I'm *glad* I told her just what I did. It was a great satisfaction. I can't say I'm sorry when I'm not, can I? I can't even *imagine* I'm sorry."

"Perhaps your imagination will be in better working order by the morning," said Marilla, rising to depart. "You'll have the night to think over your conduct in and come to a better frame of mind. You said you would try to be a very good girl if we kept you at Green Gables, but I must say it hasn't seemed very much like it this evening."

Leaving this Parthian shaft to rankle in Anne's stormy bosom, Marilla descended to the kitchen, grievously troubled in mind and vexed in soul. She was as angry with herself as with Anne, because, whenever she recalled Mrs. Rachel's dumfounded countenance her lips twitched with amusement and she felt a most reprehensible desire to laugh.

CHAPTER 10

ANNE'S APOLOGY

MARILLA SAID nothing to Matthew about the affair that evening; but when Anne proved still refractory the next morning an explanation had to be made to account for her absence from the breakfast table. Marilla told Matthew the whole story, taking pains to impress him with a due sense of the enormity of Anne's behaviour.

"It's a good thing Rachel Lynde got a calling down; she's a meddlesome old gossip," was Matthew's consolatory rejoinder.

"Matthew Cuthbert, I'm astonished at you. You know that Anne's behaviour was dreadful, and yet you take her part! I suppose you'll be saying next thing that she oughtn't to be punished at all."

"Well now—no—not exactly," said Matthew uneasily. "I reckon she ought to be punished a little. But don't be too hard on her, Marilla. Recollect she hasn't ever had any one to teach her right. You're—you're going to give her something to eat, aren't you?"

"When did you ever hear of me starving people into good behaviour?" demanded Marilla indignantly. "She'll have her meals regular, and I'll carry them up to her myself. But she'll stay up there until she's willing to apologize to Mrs. Lynde, and that's final, Matthew."

Breakfast, dinner, and supper were very silent meals—for Anne still remained obdurate. After each meal Marilla carried a well-filled tray to the east gable and brought it down later on not noticeably depleted. Matthew eyed its last descent with a troubled eye. Had Anne eaten anything at all?

When Marilla went out that evening to bring the cows from the back pasture, Matthew, who had been hanging about the barns and watching, slipped into the house with the air of a burglar and crept upstairs. As a general thing Matthew gravitated between the kitchen and the little bedroom off the hall where he slept; once in a while he ventured uncomfortably into the parlour or sitting-room when the minister came to tea. But he had never been upstairs in his own house since the spring he helped Marilla paper the spare bedroom, and that was four years ago.

He tiptoed along the hall and stood for several minutes outside the door of the east gable before he summoned courage to tap on it with his fingers and then open the door to peep in.

Anne was sitting on the yellow chair by the window, gazing mournfully out into the garden. Very small and unhappy she looked, and Matthew's heart smote him. He softly closed the door and tiptoed over to her.

"Anne," he whispered, as if afraid of being overheard,"how are you making it, Anne?"

Anne smiled wanly.

"Pretty well. I imagine a good deal, and that helps to pass the time. Of course, it's rather lonesome. But then, I may as well get used to that."

Anne smiled again, bravely facing the long years of solitary imprisonment before her.

Matthew recollected that he must say what he had come to say without loss of time, lest Marilla return prematurely.

"Well now, Anne, don't you think you'd better do it and have it over with?" he whispered. "It'll have to be done sooner or later, you know, for Marilla's a dreadful determined woman—dreadful determined, Anne. Do it right off, I say, and have it over."

"Do you mean apologize to Mrs. Lynde?"

"Yes—apologize—that's the very word," said Matthew eagerly. "Just smooth it over so to speak. That's what I was trying to get at."

"I suppose I could do it to oblige you," said Anne thoughtfully. "It would be true enough to say I am sorry, because I *am* sorry now. I wasn't a bit sorry last night. I was mad clear through, and I stayed mad all night. I know I did because I woke up three times and I was just furious every time. But this morning it was all over. I wasn't in a temper any more—and it left a dreadful sort of goneness, too. I felt so ashamed of myself. But I just couldn't think of going and telling Mrs. Lynde so. It would be so humiliating. I made up my mind I'd stay shut up here for ever rather than do that. But still—I'd do anything for you—if you really want me to—"

"Well now, of course I do. It's terrible lonesome downstairs without you. Just go and smooth it over—that's a good girl."

"Very well," said Anne resignedly. "I'll tell Marilla as soon as she comes in that I've repented."

"That's right—that's right, Anne. But don't tell Marilla I said anything about it. She might think I was putting my oar in and I promised not to do that."

"Wild horses won't drag the secret from me," promised Anne solemnly. "How would wild horses drag a secret from a person anyhow?"

But Matthew was gone, scared at his own success. He fled hastily to the remotest corner of the horse pasture lest Marilla should suspect what he had been up to. Marilla herself, upon her return to the house, was agreeably surprised to hear a plaintive voice calling, "Marilla," over the banisters.

"Well?" she said, going into the hall.

"I'm sorry I lost my temper and said rude things, and I'm willing to go and tell Mrs. Lynde so."

"Very well." Marilla's crispness gave no sign of her relief. She had been wondering what under the canopy she should do if Anne did not give in. "I'll take you down after milking."

Accordingly, after milking, behold Marilla and Anne walking down the lane, the former erect and triumphant, the latter drooping and dejected. But half-way down Anne's dejection vanished as if by enchantment. She lifted her head and stepped lightly along, her eyes fixed on the sunset sky and an air of subdued exhilaration about her. Marilla beheld the change disapprovingly. This was no meek penitent such as it behooved her to take into the presence of the offended Mrs. Lynde.

"What are you thinking of, Anne?" she asked sharply.

"I'm imagining out what I must say to Mrs. Lynde," answered Anne dreamily.

This was satisfactory—or should have been so. But Marilla could not rid herself of the notion that something in her scheme of punishment was going askew. Anne had no business to look so rapt and radiant.

Rapt and radiant Anne continued until they were in the very presence of Mrs. Lynde, who was sitting knitting by her kitchen window. Then the radiance vanished. Mournful penitence appeared on every feature. Before a word was spoken Anne suddenly went down on her knees before the astonished Mrs. Rachel and held out her hands beseechingly.

"Oh, Mrs. Lynde, I am so extremely sorry," she said with a quiver in her voice. "I could never express all my sorrow, no, not if I used up a whole dictionary. You must just imagine it. I behaved terribly to you—and I've disgraced the dear friends, Matthew and Marilla, who have let me stay at Green Gables although I'm not a boy. I'm a dreadfully wicked and ungrateful girl, and I deserve to be punished and cast out by respectable people for ever. It was very wicked of me to fly into a temper because you told me the truth. It *was* the truth; every word you said was true. My hair is red and I'm freckled and skinny and ugly. What I said to you was true, too, but I shouldn't have said it. Oh, Mrs. Lynde, please, please, forgive me. If you refuse it will be a lifelong sorrow to me. You wouldn't like to inflict a lifelong sorrow on a poor little orphan girl, would you, even if she had a dreadful temper? Oh, I am sure you wouldn't. Please say you forgive me, Mrs. Lynde.''

Anne clasped her hands together, bowed her head, and waited for the word of judgment.

There was no mistaking her sincerity—it breathed in every tone of her voice. Both Marilla and Mrs. Lynde recognized its unmistakable ring. But the former understood in dismay that Anne was actually enjoying her valley of humiliation—was revelling in the thoroughness of her abasement. Where was the wholesome punishment upon which she, Marilla, had plumed herself? Anne had turned it into a species of positive pleasure.

Good Mrs. Lynde, not being overburdened with perception, did not see this. She only perceived that Anne had made a very thorough apology and all resentment vanished from her kindly, if somewhat officious, heart.

"There, there, get up child," she said heartily. "Of course I forgive you. I guess I was a little too hard on you, anyway. But I'm such an outspoken person. You just mustn't mind me, that's what. It can't be denied your hair is terrible red; but I knew a girl once—went to school with her, in fact—whose hair was every mite as red as yours when she was young, but when she grew up it darkened to a real handsome auburn. I wouldn't be a mite surprised if yours did, too—not a mite.''

"Oh, Mrs. Lynde!'' Anne drew a long breath as she rose to her feet. "You have given me a hope. I shall always feel that you are a benefactor. Oh, I could endure anything if I only thought my hair would be a handsome auburn when I grew up. It would be so much easier to be good if one's hair was a handsome auburn, don't you think? And now may I go out into your garden and sit on that bench under the apple trees while you and Marilla are talking? There is so much more scope for imagination out there.''

"Laws, yes, run along, child. And you can pick a bouquet of them white June lilies over in the corner if you like.''

As the door closed behind Anne Mrs. Lynde got briskly up to light a lamp.

"She's a real odd little thing. Take this chair, Marilla; it's easier than the one you've got; I just keep that for the hired boy to sit on. Yes, she certainly is an odd child, but there is something kind of taking about her after all. I don't feel so surprised at you and Matthew keeping her as I did—nor so sorry for you, either. She may turn out all right. Of course, she has a queer way of expressing herself—a little too—well, too kind of forcible, you know; but she'll likely get over that now that she's come to live among civilized folks. And then, her temper's pretty quick, I guess; but there's one comfort, a child that has a quick temper, just blaze up and cool down, ain't never likely to be sly or deceitful. Preserve me from a sly child, that's what. On the whole, Marilla, I kind of like her.''

When Marilla went home Anne came out of the fragrant twilight of the orchard with a sheaf of white narcissi in her hands.

''I apologized pretty well, didn't I?'' she said proudly as they went down the lane. ''I thought since I had to do it I might as well do it thoroughly.''

''You did it thoroughly, all right enough,'' was Marilla's comment. Marilla was dismayed at finding herself inclined to laugh over the recollection. She had also an uneasy feeling that she ought to scold Anne for apologizing so well; but then that was ridiculous! She compromised with her conscience by saying severely:

''I hope you won't have occasion to make many more such apologies. I hope you'll try to control you temper now, Anne.''

''That wouldn't be so hard if people wouldn't twit me about my looks,'' said Anne with a sigh. ''I don't get cross about other things; but I'm *so* tired of being twitted about my hair and it just makes me boil right over. Do you suppose my hair will really be a handsome auburn when I grow up?''

''You shouldn't think so much about your looks, Anne. I'm afraid you are a very vain little girl.''

''How can I be vain when I know I'm homely?'' protested Anne. ''I love pretty things; and I hate to look in the glass and see something that isn't pretty. It makes me feel so sorrowful—just as I feel when I look at any ugly thing. I pity it because it isn't beautiful.''

''Handsome is as handsome does,'' quoted Marilla.

''I've had that said to me before, but I have my doubts about it,'' remarked skeptical Anne, sniffing at her narcissi. ''Oh, aren't these flowers sweet! It was lovely of Mrs. Lynde to give them to me. I have no hard feelings against Mrs. Lynde now. It gives you a lovely, comfortable feeling to apologize and be forgiven, doesn't it? Aren't the stars bright tonight? If you could live in a star, which one would you pick? I'd like that lovely clear big one away over there above that dark hill.''

''Anne, do hold your tongue,'' said Marilla, thoroughly worn out trying to follow the gyrations of Anne's thoughts.

Anne said no more until they turned into their own lane. A little gypsy wind came down it to meet them, laden with the spicy perfume of young dew-wet ferns. Far up in the shadows a cheerful light gleamed out through the trees from the kitchen at Green Gables. Anne suddenly came close to Marilla and slipped her hand into the older woman's hard palm.

"It's lovely to be going home and know it's home," she said. "I love Green Gables already, and I never loved any place before. No place ever seemed like home. Oh, Marilla, I'm so happy. I could pray right now and not find it a bit hard."

Something warm and pleasant welled up in Marilla's heart at touch of that thin little hand in her own—a throb of the maternity she had missed, perhaps. Its very unaccustomedness and sweetness disturbed her. She hastened to restore her sensations to their normal calm by inculcating a moral.

"If you'll be a good girl you'll always be happy, Anne. And you should never find it hard to say your prayers."

"Saying one's prayers isn't exactly the same thing as praying," said Anne meditatively. "But I'm going to imagine that I'm the wind that is blowing up there in those tree-tops. When I get tired of the trees I'll imagine I'm gently waving down here in the ferns—and then I'll fly over to Mrs. Lynde's garden and set the flowers dancing—and then I'll go with one great swoop over the clover field—and then I'll blow over the Lake of Shining Waters and ripple it all up into little sparkling waves. Oh, there's so much scope for imagination in a wind! So I'll not talk any more just now, Marilla."

"Thank be to goodness for that," breathed Marilla in devout relief.

CHAPTER 11

ANNE'S IMPRESSIONS OF SUNDAY-SCHOOL

"WELL, HOW do you like them?" said Marilla.

Anne was standing in the gable-room, looking solemnly at three new dresses spread out on the bed. One was of snuffy colored gingham which Marilla had been tempted to buy from a peddler the preceding summer because it looked so serviceable; one was of black-and-white checked sateen which she had picked up at a bargain counter in the winter; and one was a stiff print of an ugly blue shade which she had purchased that week at a Carmody store.

She had made them herself, and they were all made alike—plain skirts fulled tightly to plain waists, with sleeves as plain as waist and skirt and tight as sleeves could be.

"I'll imagine that I like them," said Anne soberly.

"I don't want you to imagine it," said Marilla, offended. "Oh, I can see you don't like the dresses! What is the matter with them? Aren't they neat and clean and new?"

"Yes."

"Then why don't you like them?"

"They're—they're not—pretty," Anne said reluctantly.

"Pretty!" Marilla sniffed. "I didn't trouble my head about getting pretty dresses for you. I don't believe in pampering vanity, Anne, I'll tell you that right off. Those dresses are good, sensible, serviceable dresses, without any frills or furbelows about them, and they're all you'll get this summer. The brown gingham and the blue print will do you for school when you begin to go. The sateen is for church and Sunday school. I'll expect you to keep them neat and clean and not to tear them. I should think you'd be grateful to get most anything after those skimpy wincey things you've been wearing."

"Oh, I *am* grateful," protested Anne. "But I'd be ever so much gratefuller if—if you'd made just one of them with puffed sleeves. Puffed sleeves are so fashionable now. It would give me such a thrill, Marilla, just to wear a dress with puffed sleeves."

"Well, you'll have to do without your thrill. I hadn't any material to waste on puffed sleeves. I think they are ridiculous-looking things anyhow. I prefer the plain, sensible ones."

"But I'd rather look ridiculous when everybody else does than plain and sensible all by myself," persisted Anne mournfully.

"Trust you for that! Well, hang those dresses carefully up in your closet, and then sit down and learn the Sunday school lesson. I got a quarterly from Mr. Bell for you and you'll go to Sunday school tomorrow," said Marilla, disappearing downstairs in high dudgeon.

Anne clasped her hands and looked at the dresses.

"I did hope there would be a white one with puffed sleeves," she whispered disconsolately. "I prayed for one, but I didn't much expect it on that account. I didn't suppose God would have time to bother about a ittle orphan girl's dress. I knew I'd just have to depend on Marilla for it. Well, fortunately I can imagine that one of them is of snow-white muslin with lovely lace frills and three-puffed sleeves.''

The next morning warnings of a sick headache prevented Marilla from going to Sunday school with Anne.

''You'll have to go down and call for Mrs. Lynde. Anne,'' she said. ''She'll see that you get into the right class. Now, mind you behave yourself properly. Stay to preaching afterwards and ask Mrs. Lynde to show you our pew. Here's a cent for collection. Don't stare at people and don't fidget. I shall expect you to tell me the text when you come home.''

Anne started off irreproachably, arrayed in the stiff black-and-white sateen, which, while decent as regards length and certainly not open to the charge of skimpiness, contrived to emphasize every corner and angle of her thin figure. Her hat was a little, flat, glossy, new sailor, the extreme plainness of which had likewise much disappointed Anne, who had permitted herself secret visions of ribbon and flowers. The latter, however, were supplied before Anne reached the main road, for, being confronted halfway down the lane with a golden frenzy of wind-stirred buttercups and a glory of wild roses, Anne promptly and liberally garlanded her hat with a heavy wreath of them. Whatever other people might have thought of the result it satisfied Anne, and she tripped gaily down the road, holding her ruddy head with its decoration of pink and yellow very proudly.

When she reached Mrs. Lynde's house she found that lady gone. Nothing daunted Anne proceeded onward to the church alone. In the porch she found a crowd of little girls, all more or less gaily attired in whites and blues and pinks, and all staring with curious eyes at this stranger in their midst, with her extraordinary head adornment. Avonlea little girls had already heard queer stories about Anne; Mrs. Lynde said she had an awful temper; Jerry Buote, the hired boy at Green Gables, said she talked all the time to herself or to the trees and flowers like a crazy girl. They looked at her and whispered to each other behind their quarterlies. Nobody made any friendly advances, then or later on when the opening exercises were over and Anne found herself in Miss Rogerson's class.

Miss Rogerson was a middle-aged lady who had taught a Sunday school class for twenty years. Her method of teaching was to ask the printed questions from the quarterly and look sternly over its edge at

THEY LOOKED AT HER AND WHISPERED TO EACH OTHER.

the particular little girl she thought ought to answer the question. She looked often at Anne, and Anne, thanks to Marilla's drilling, answered promptly; but it may be questioned if she understood very much about either question or answer.

She did not think she liked Miss Rogerson, and she felt very miserable; every other little girl in the class had puffed sleeves. Anne felt that life was really not worth living without puffed sleeves.

"Well, how did you like Sunday school?" Marilla wanted to know when Anne came home. Her wreath having faded, Anne had discarded it in the lane, so Marilla was spared the knowledge of that for a time.

"I didn't like it a bit. It was horrid."

"Anne Shirley!" said Marilla rebukingly.

Anne sat down on the rocker with a long sigh, kissed one of Bonny's leaves, and waved her hand to a blossoming fuchsia.

"They might have been lonesome while I was away," she explained. "And now about the Sunday school. I behaved well, just as you told me. Mrs. Lynde was gone, but I went right on myself. I went into the church, with a lot of other little girls, and I sat in the corner of a pew by the window while the opening exercises went on. Mr. Bell made an awfully long prayer. I would have been dreadfully tired before he got through if I hadn't been sitting by that window. But it looked right out on the Lake of Shining Waters, so I just gazed at that and imagined all sorts of splendid things."

"You shouldn't have done anything of the sort. You should have listened to Mr. Bell."

"But he wasn't talking to me," protested Anne. "He was talking to God and he didn't seem to be very much interested in it, either. I think he thought God was too far off to make it worth while. I said a little prayer myself, though. There was a long row of white birches hanging over the lake and the sunshine fell down through them, 'way, 'way down, deep into the water. Oh, Marilla, it was like a beautiful dream! It gave me a thrill and I just said, 'Thank you for it, God,' two or three times."

"Not out loud, I hope," said Marilla anxiously.

"Oh, no, just under my breath. Well, Mr. Bell did get through at last and they told me to go into the classroom with Miss Rogerson's class. There were nine other girls in it. They all had puffed sleeves. I tried to imagine mine were puffed, too, but I couldn't. Why couldn't I? It was as easy as could be to imagine they were puffed when I was alone in the east gable, but it was awfully hard there among the others who had really truly puffs.''

''You shouldn't have been thinking about your sleeves in Sunday school. You should have been attending to the lesson. I hope you knew it.''

''Oh, yes; and I answered a lot of questions. Miss Rogerson asked ever so many. I don't think it was fair for her to do all the asking. There were lots I wanted to ask her, but I didn't like to because I didn't think she was a kindred spirit. Then all the other little girls recited a paraphrase. She asked me if I knew any. I told her I didn't, but I could recite, 'The Dog at His Master's Grave' if she liked. That's in the Third Royal Reader. It isn't a really truly religious piece of poetry, but it's so sad and melancholy that it might as well be. She said it wouldn't do and she told me to learn the nineteenth paraphrase for next Sunday. I read it over in church afterwards and it's splendid. There are two lines in particular that just thrill me.

> *Quick as the slaughtered squadrons fell*
> *In Midian's evil day.*

I don't know what 'squadrons' means nor 'Midian,' either, but it sounds *so* tragical. I can hardly wait until next Sunday to recite it. I'll practise it all the week. After Sunday school I asked Miss Rogerson—because Mrs. Lynde was too far away—to show me your pew. I sat just as still as I could and the text was Revelations, third chapter, second and third verses. It was a very long text. If I was a minister I'd pick the short, snappy ones. The sermon was awfully long, too. I suppose the minister had to match it to the text. I didn't think he was a bit interesting. The trouble with him seems to be that he hasn't enough imagination. I didn't listen to him very much. I just let my thoughts run and I thought of the most surprising things.''

Marilla felt helplessly that all this should be sternly reproved, but she was hampered by the undeniable fact that some of the things Anne had said, especially about the minister's sermons and Mr. Bell's prayers, were what she herself had really thought deep down in her heart for years, but had never given expression to. It almost seemed to her that those secret, unuttered, critical thoughts had suddenly taken visible and accusing shape and form in the person of this outspoken morsel of neglected humanity.

CHAPTER 12

A SOLEMN VOW AND PROMISE

IT WAS not until the next Friday that Marilla heard the story of the flower-wreathed hat. She came home from Mrs. Lynde's and called Anne to account.

"Anne, Mrs. Rachel says you went to church last Sunday with your hat rigged out ridiculous with roses and buttercups. What on earth put you up to such a caper? A pretty-looking object you must have been!"

"Oh. I know pink and yellow aren't becoming to me," began Anne.

"Becoming fiddlesticks! It was putting flowers on your hat at all, no matter what color they were, that was ridiculous. You are the most aggravating child!"

"I don't see why it's any more ridiculous to wear flowers on your hat than on your dress," protested Anne. "Lots of little girls there had bouquets pinned on their dresses. What was the difference?"

Marilla was not to be drawn from the safe concrete into dubious paths of the abstract.

"Don't answer me back like that, Anne. It was very silly of you to do such a thing. Never let me catch you at such a trick again. Mrs. Rachel says she thought she would sink through the floor when she saw you come in all rigged out like that. She couldn't get near enough to tell you to take them off till it was too late. She says people talked about it something dreadful. Of course they would think I had no better sense than to let you go decked out like that."

"Oh, I'm so sorry," said Anne, tears welling into her eyes. "I never thought you'd mind. The roses and buttercups were so sweet and pretty I thought they'd look lovely on my hat. Lots of the little girls had artificial flowers on their hats. I'm afraid I'm going to be a dreadful trial to you. Maybe you'd better send me back to the asylum. That would be terrible; I don't think I could endure it; most likely I would go into consumption; I'm so thin as it is, you see. But that would be better than being a trial to you."

"Nonsense," said Marilla, vexed at herself for having made the child cry. "I don't want to send you back to the asylum, I'm sure. All I want is that you should behave like other little girls and not make yourself ridiculous. Don't cry any more. I've got some news for you. Diana Barry came home this afternoon. I'm going up to see if I can borrow a skirt pattern from Mrs. Barry, and if you like you can come with me and get acquainted with Diana.''

Anne rose to her feet, with clasped hands, the tears still glistening on her cheeks; the dish-towel she had been hemming slipped unheeded to the floor.

''Oh, Marilla, I'm frightened—now that it has come I'm actually frightened. What if she shouldn't like me! It would be the most tragical disappointment of my life.''

''Now, don't get into a fluster. And I do wish you wouldn't use such long words. It sounds so funny in a little girl. I guess Diana'll like you well enough. It's her mother you've got to reckon with. If she doesn't like you it won't matter how much Diana does. If she had heard about your outburst to Mrs. Lynde and going to church with buttercups round your hat I don't know what she'll think of you. You must be polite and well-behaved, and don't make any of your startling speeches. For pity's sake, if the child isn't actually trembling!''

Anne *was* trembling. Her face was pale and tense.

''Oh, Marilla, you'd be excited, too, if you were going to meet a little girl you hoped would be your bosom friend and whose mother mightn't like you,'' she said as she hastened to get her hat.

They went over to Orchard Slope by the short cut across the brook and up the firry hill grove. Mrs. Barry came to the kitchen door in answer to Marilla's knock. She was a tall, black-eyed, black-haired woman, with a very resolute mouth. She had the reputation of being very strict with her children.

''How do you do, Marilla?'' she said cordially. ''Come in. And this is the little girl you have adopted, I suppose?''

''Yes, this is Anne Shirley,'' said Marilla.

''Spelled with an *e*,'' gasped Anne, who, tremulous and excited as she was, was determined there should be no misunderstanding on that important point.

Mrs. Barry, not hearing or not comprehending, merely shook hands and said kindly:

''How are you?''

''I am well in body although considerably rumpled in spirit, thank you, ma'am,'' said Anne gravely. Then aside to Marilla in an audible whisper, ''There wasn't anything startling in that, was there, Marilla?''

Diana was sitting on the sofa, reading a book which was dropped when the callers entered. She was a very pretty little girl, with her mother's black eyes and hair, and rosy cheeks, and the merry expression which was her inheritance from her father.

"This is my little girl, Diana," said Mrs. Barry. "Diana, you might take Anne out into the garden and show her your flowers. It will be better for you than straining your eyes over that book. She reads entirely too much——" this to Marilla as the little girls went out—"and I can't prevent her, for her father aids and abets her. She's always poring over a book. I'm glad she has the prospect of a playmate—perhaps it will take her more out-of-doors."

Outside in the garden, which was full of mellow sunset light streaming through the dark old firs to the west of it, stood Anne and Diana, gazing bashfully at one another over a clump of gorgeous tiger lilies.

The Barry garden was a bowery wilderness of flowers which would have delighted Anne's heart at any time less fraught with destiny. It was encircled by huge old willows and tall firs, beneath which flourished flowers that loved the shade. Prim, right-angled paths, neatly bordered with clam-shells, intersected it like moist red ribbons and in the beds between old-fashioned flowers ran riot. There were rosy bleeding-hearts and great splendid crimson peonies; white, fragrant narcissi and thorny, sweet Scotch roses; pink and blue and white columbines and lilac-tinted Bouncing Bets; clumps of southern-wood and ribbon grass and mint; purple Adam-and-Eve, daffodils, and masses of sweet clover white with its delicate, fragrant, feathery sprays; scarlet lightning that shot its fiery lances over prim white musk-flowers; a garden it was where sunshine lingered and bees hummed, and winds, beguiled into loitering, purred and rustled.

"Oh, Diana," said Anne at last, clasping her hands and speaking almost in a whisper, "do you think—oh, do you think you can like me a little—enough to be my bosom friend?"

Diana laughed. Diana always laughed before she spoke.

"Why, I guess so," she said frankly. "I'm awfully glad you've come to live at Green Gables. It will be jolly to have somebody to play with. There isn't any other girl who lives near enough to play with, and I've no sisters big enough."

"Will you swear to be my friend for ever and ever?" demanded Anne eagerly.

Diana looked shocked.

"Why, it's dreadfully wicked to swear," she said rebukingly.

"Oh no, not my kind of swearing. There are two kinds, you know."

"I never heard of but one kind," said Diana doubtfully.

"There really is another. Oh, it isn't wicked at all. It just means vowing and promising solemnly."

"Well, I don't mind doing that," agreed Diana, relieved. "How do you do it?"

"We must join hands—so," said Anne gravely. "It ought to be over running water. We'll just imagine this path is running water. I'll repeat the oath first. I solemnly swear to be faithful to my bosom friend, Diana Barry, as long as the sun and moon shall endure. Now you say it and put my name in."

Diana repeated the "oath" with a laugh fore and aft. Then she said:

"You're a queer girl, Anne. I heard before that you were queer. But I believe I'm going to like you real well."

When Marilla and Anne went home Diana went with them as far as the log bridge. The two little girls walked with their arms about each other. At the brook they parted with many promises to spend the next afternoon together.

"Well, did you find Diana a kindred spirit?" asked Marilla as they went up through the Garden of Green Gables.

"Oh, yes," sighed Anne, blissfully unconscious of any sarcasm on Marilla's part. "Oh, Marilla, I'm the happiest girl on Prince Edward Island this very moment. I assure you I'll say my prayers with a right goodwill tonight. Diana and I are going to build a playhouse in Mr. William Bell's birch grove tomorrow. Can I have those broken pieces of china that are out in the wood-shed? Diana's birthday is in February and mine is in March. Don't you think that is a very strange coincidence? Diana is going to lend me a book to read. She says it's perfectly splendid and tremenjusly exciting. She's going to show me a place back in the woods where rice lilies grow. Don't you think Diana has got very soulful eyes? I wish I had soulful eyes. Diana is going to teach me to sing a song called 'Nelly in the Hazel Dell.' She's going to give me a picture to put up in my room; it's a perfectly beautiful picture, she says—a lovely lady in a pale blue silk dress. A sewing-maching agent gave it to her. I wish I had something to give Diana. I'm an inch taller than Diana, but she is ever so much fatter; she says she'd like to be thin because it's so much more graceful, but I'm afraid she only said it to soothe my feelings. We're going to the shore some day to gather shells. We have agreed to call the spring down by the log bridge the Dryad's Bubble. Isn't that a perfectly elegant name? I read a story once about a spring called that. A dryad is a sort of grown-up fairy, I think."

"Well, all I hope is you won't talk Diana to death," said Marilla.

"But remember this in all your planning, Anne. You're not going to play all the time nor most of it. You'll have your work to do and it'll have to be done first."

Anne's cup of happiness was full, and Matthew caused it to overflow. He had just got home from a trip to the store at Carmody, and he sheepishly produced a small parcel from his pocket and handed it to Anne, with a deprecatory look at Marilla.

"I heard you say you liked chocolate sweeties, so I got you some," he said.

"Humph," sniffed Marilla. "It'll ruin her teeth and stomach. There, there, child, don't look so dismal. You can eat those, since Matthew has gone and got them. He'd better have brought you some peppermints. They're wholesomer. Don't sicken yourself eating them all at once now."

"Oh, no, indeed, I won't," said Anne eagerly. "I'll just eat one tonight, Marilla. And I can give Diana half of them, can't I? The other half will taste twice as sweet to me if I give some to her. It's delightful to think I have something to give her."

"I will say it for the child," said Marilla when Anne had gone to her gable, "she isn't stingy. I'm glad, for of all faults I detest stinginess in a child. Dear me, it's only three weeks since she came, and it seems as if she'd been here always. I can't imagine the place without her. Now, don't be looking I-told-you-so, Matthew. That's bad enough in a woman, but isn't to be endured in a man. I'm perfectly willing to own up that I'm glad I consented to keep the child and that I'm getting fond of her, but don't you rub it in, Matthew Cuthbert."

----------- CHAPTER 13 -----------

THE DELIGHTS OF ANTICIPATION

"I T'S TIME Anne was in to do her sewing," said Marilla, glancing at the clock and then out into the yellow August afternoon where everything drowsed in the heat. "She stayed playing with Diana more than half and hour more'n I gave her leave to; and now she's perched out there on the woodpile talking to Matthew, nineteen to the dozen, when she knows perfectly well that she ought to be at her work. And of course he's listening to her like a perfect ninny. I never saw such an infatuated man. The more she talks and the odder the things she says, the more he's delighted evidently. Anne Shirley, you come right in here this minute, do you hear me!''

A series of staccato taps on the west window brought Anne flying in from the yard, eyes shining, cheeks faintly flushed with pink, unbraided hair streaming behind her in a torrent of brightness.

''Oh, Marilla,'' she exclaimed breathlessly, ''there's going to be a Sunday-school picnic next week—in Mr. Harmon Andrews' field, right near the Lake of Shining Waters. And Mrs. Superintendent Bell and Mrs. Rachel Lynde are going to make ice-cream—think of it, Marilla—*ice-cream!* And oh, Marilla, can I go to it?''

''Just look at the clock, if you please, Anne. What time did I tell you to come in?''

''Two o'clock—but isn't it splendid about the picnic, Marilla? Please can I go? Oh, I've never been to a picnic—I've dreamed of picnics, but I've never—''

''Yes, I told you to come at two o'clock. And it's a quarter to three. I'd like to know why you didn't obey me, Anne.''

''Why, I meant to, Marilla, as much as could be. But you have no idea how fascinating Idlewild is. And then, of course, I had to tell Matthew about the picnic. Matthew is such a sympathetic listener. Please can I go?''

''You'll have to learn to resist the fascination of Idle-whatever-you-call-it. When I tell you to come in at a certain time I mean that time and not half an hour later. And you needn't stop to discourse with sympathetic listeners on your way, either. As for the picnic, of course you can go. You're a Sunday-school scholar, and it's not likely I'd refuse to let you go when all the other little girls are going.''

''But—but,'' faltered Anne, ''Diana says that everybody must take a basket of things to eat. I can't cook, as you know, Marilla, and—and—I don't mind going to a picnic without puffed sleeves so much, but I'd feel terribly humiliated if I had to go without a basket. It's been preying on my mind ever since Diana told me.''

''Well, it needn't prey any longer. I'll bake you a basket.''

''Oh, you dear good Marilla. Oh, you are so kind to me. Oh, I'm so much obliged to you.''

Getting through with her ''ohs'' Anne cast herself into Marilla's arms and rapturously kissed her sallow cheek. It was the first time in her whole life that childish lips had voluntarily touched Marilla's face. Again that sudden sensation of startling sweetness thrilled her. She was secretly vastly pleased at Anne's impulsive caress, which was probably the reason why she said brusquely:

"There, there, never mind your kissing nonsense. I'd sooner see you doing strictly as you're told. As for cooking, I mean to begin giving you lessons in that some of these days. But you're so feather-brained, Anne, I've been waiting to see if you'd sober down a little and learn to be steady before I begin. You've got to keep your wits about you in cooking and not stop in the middle of things to let your thoughts rove over all creation. Now, get out your patchwork and have your square done before tea-time."

"I do *not* like patchwork," said Anne dolefully, hunting out her workbasket and sitting down before a little heap of red and white diamonds with a sigh. "I think some kinds of sewing would be nice; but there's no scope for imagination in patchwork. It's just one little seam after another and you never seem to be getting anywhere. But of course I'd rather be Anne of Green Gables sewing patchwork than Anne of any other place with nothing to do but play. I wish time went as quick sewing patches as it does when I'm playing with Diana, though. Oh, we do have such elegant times, Marilla. I have to furnish most of the imagination, but I'm well able to do that. Diana is simply perfect in every other way. You know that little piece of land across the brook that runs up between our farm and Mr. Barry's. It belongs to Mr. William Bell, and right in the corner there is a little ring of white birch trees—the most romantic spot, Marilla. Diana and I have our playhouse there. We call it Idlewild. Isn't that a poetical name? I assure you it took me some time to think it out. I stayed awake nearly a whole night before I invented it. Then, just as I was dropping off to sleep, it came like an inspiration. Diana was *enraptured* when she heard it. We have got our house fixed up elegantly. You must come and see it Marilla—won't you? We have great big stones, all covered with moss, for seats, and boards from tree to tree for shelves. And we have all our dishes on them. Of course, they're broken but it's the easiest thing in the world to imagine that they are whole. There's a piece of a plate with a spray of red and yellow ivy on it that is especially beautiful. We keep it in the parlor and we have the fairy glass there, too. The fairy glass is as lovely as a dream. Diana found it out in the woods behind their chicken house. It's all full of rainbows—just little young rainbows that haven't grown big yet—and Diana's mother told her it was broken off a hanging lamp they once had. But it's nicer to imagine the fairies lost it one night when they had a ball, so we call it the fairy glass. Matthew is going to make us a table. Oh, we have named that little round pool over in Mr. Barry's field Willowmere. I got that name out of the book Diana lent me. That was a thrilling book, Marilla. The heroine had five lovers. I'd be satisfied with one, wouldn't you? She was very handsome and she went through great tribulations. She could faint as easy as anything. I'd love to be able to faint, wouldn't you, Marilla? It's so romantic. But I'm really very healthy for all I'm so thin. I believe I'm getting fatter, though. Don't you think I am? I look at my elbows every morning when I get up to see if any dimples are coming. Diana is having a new dress made with elbow sleeves. She is going to wear it to the picnic. Oh, I do hope it will be fine next Wednesday. I don't feel that I could endure the disappointment if anything happened to prevent me from getting to the picnic. I suppose I'd live through it, but I'm certain it would be a lifelong sorrow. It wouldn't matter if I got to a hundred picnics in after years; they wouldn't make up for missing this one. They're going to have boats on the Lake of Shining Waters—and ice-cream as I told you. I have never tasted ice-cream. Diana tried to explain what it was like, but I guess ice-cream is one of those things that are beyond imagination.''

''Anne, you have talked even on for ten minutes by the clock,'' said Marilla. ''Now, just for curiosity's sake, see if you can hold your tongue for the same length of time.''

Anne held her tongue as desired. But for the rest of the week she talked picnic and thought picnic and dreamed picnic. On Saturday it rained and she worked herself up into such a frantic state lest it should keep on raining until and over Wednesday, that Marilla made her sew an extra patchwork square by way of steadying her nerves.

On Sunday Anne confided to Marilla on the way home from church that she grew actually cold all over with excitement when the minister announced the picnic from the pulpit.

''Such a thrill as went up and down my back, Marilla! I don't think I'd ever really believed until then that there was honestly going to be a picnic. I couldn't help fearing I'd only imagined it. But when a minster says a thing in the pulpit you just have to believe it.''

''You set your heart too much on things, Anne,'' said Marilla with a sigh. ''I'm afraid there'll be a great many disappointments in store for you through life.''

''Oh, Marilla, looking forward to things is half the pleasure of them,'' exclaimed Anne. ''You mayn't get the things themselves; but nothing can prevent you from having the fun of looking forward to them. Mrs. Lynde says, 'Blessed are they who expect nothing for they shall not be disappointed.' But I think it would be worse to expect nothing than to be disappointed.''

Marilla wore her amethyst brooch to church that day as usual. Marilla always wore her amethyst brooch to church. She would have thought it rather sacrilegious to leave it off—as bad as forgetting her Bible or her collection dime. That amethyst brooch was Marilla's most treasured possession. A sea-faring uncle had given it to her mother who in turn had bequeathed it to Marilla. It was an old-fashioned oval, containing a braid of her mother's hair, surrounded by a border of very fine amethysts. Marilla knew too little about precious stones to realize how fine the amethysts actually were; but she thought them very beautiful and was always pleasantly conscious of their violet shimmer at her throat, above her good brown satin dress, even although she could not see it.

Anne had been smitten with delighted admiration when she first saw that brooch.

''Oh, Marilla, it's a perfectly elegant brooch. I don't know how you can pay attention to the sermon or the prayers when you have it on. *I* couldn't, I know. I think amethysts are just sweet. They are what I used to think diamonds were like. Long ago, before I had seen a diamond, I read about them and I tried to imagine what they would be like. I thought they would be lovely glimmering purple stones. When I saw a real diamond in a lady's ring one day I was so disappointed I cried. Of course, it was very lovely but it wasn't my idea of a diamond. Will you let me hold the brooch for one minute, Marilla? Do you think amethysts can be the souls of good violets?''

CHAPTER 14

ANNE'S CONFESSION

ON THE Monday evening before the picnic Marilla came down from her room with a troubled face.

''Anne,'' she said to that small personage, who was shelling peas by the spotless table and singing ''Nelly of the Hazel Dell'' with a vigour and expression that did credit to Diana's teaching, ''did you see anything of my amethyst brooch? I though I stuck it in my pincushion when I came home from church yesterday evening, but I can't find it anywhere."

"I—I saw it this afternoon when you were away at the Aid Society," said Anne, a little slowly. "I was passing your door when I saw it on the cushion, so I went in to look at it."

"Did you touch it?" said Marilla sternly.

"Y-e-e-s," admitted Anne, "I took it up and I pinned it on my breast just to see how it would look."

"You had not business to do anything of the sort. It's very wrong in a little girl to meddle. You shouldn't have gone into my room in the first place and you shouldn't have touched a brooch that didn't belong to you in the second. Where did you put it?"

"Oh, I put it back on the bureau. I hadn't it on a minute. Truly, I didn't mean to meddle, Marilla. I didn't think about its being wrong to go in and try on the brooch; but I see now that it was and I'll never do it again. That's one good thing about me. I never do the same naughty thing twice."

"You didn't put it back," said Marilla. "That brooch isn't anywhere on the bureau. You've taken it out or something, Anne."

"I *did* put it back," said Anne quickly—pertly, Marilla thought. "I don't just remember whether I stuck it on the pincushion or laid it in the china tray. But I'm perfectly certain I put it back."

"I'll go and have another look," said Marilla, determining to be just. "If you put that brooch back it's there still. If it isn't I'll know you didn't, that's all!"

Marilla went to her room and made a thorough search, not only over the bureau but in every other place she thought the brooch might possibly be. It was not to be found and she returned to the kitchen.

"Anne, the brooch is gone. By your own admission you were the last person to handle it. Now, what have you done with it? Tell me the truth at once. Did you take it out and lose it?"

"No, I didn't," said Anne solemnly, meeting Marilla's angry gaze squarely. "I never took the brooch out of your room and that is the truth, if I was to be led to the block for it—although I'm not very certain what a block is. So there, Marilla."

Anne's "so there" was only intended to emphasize her assertion, but Marilla took it as a display of defiance.

"I believe you are telling me a falsehood, Anne," she said sharply. "I know you are. There now, don't say anything more unless you are prepared to tell the whole truth. Go to your room and stay there until you are ready to confess.''

''Will I take the peas with me?'' said Anne meekly.

''No, I'll finish shelling them myself. Do as I bid you.''

When Anne had gone Marilla went about her evening tasks in a very disturbed state of mind. She was worried about her valuable brooch. What if Anne had lost it? And how wicked of the child to deny having taken it, when anybody could see she must have! With such an innocent face, too!

''I don't know what I wouldn't sooner have had happen,'' thought Marilla, as she nervously shelled the peas. ''Of course, I don't suppose she meant to steal it or anything like that. She's just taken it to play with or help along that imagination of hers. She must have taken it, that's clear, for there hasn't been a soul in that room since she was in it, by her own story, until I went up tonight. And the brooch is gone, there's nothing surer. I suppose she has lost it and is afraid to own up for fear she'll be punished. It's a dreadful thing to think she tells falsehoods. It's a far worse thing than her fit of temper. It's a fearful responsibility to have a child in your house you can't trust. Slyness and untruthfulness—that's what she has displayed. I declare I feel worse about that than about the brooch. If she'd only have told the truth about it I wouldn't mind so much.''

Marilla went to her room at intervals all through the evening and searched for the brooch, without finding it. A bed-time visit to the east gable produced no result. Anne persisted in denying that she knew anything about the brooch but Marilla was only the more firmly convinced that she did.

She told Matthew the story the next morning. Matthew was confounded and puzzled; he could not so quickly lose faith in Anne but he had to admit that circumstances were against her.

''You're sure it hasn't fell down behind the bureau?'' was the only suggestion he could offer.

''I've moved the bureau and I've taken out the drawers and I've looked in every crack and cranny,'' was Marilla's positive answer. ''The brooch is gone and that child has taken it and lied about it. That's the plain, ugly truth, Matthew Cuthbert, and we might as well look it in the face.''

''Well now, what are you going to do about it?'' Matthew asked forlornly, feeling secretly thankful that Marilla and not he had to deal with the situation. He felt no desire to put his oar in this time.

''She'll stay in her room until she confesses,'' said Marilla grimly, remembering the success of this method in the former case.

"Then we'll see. Perhaps we'll be able to find the brooch if she'll only tell where she took it; but in any case she'll have to be severely punished, Matthew."

"Well now, you'll have to punish her," said Matthew, reaching for his hat. "I've nothing to do with it, remember. You warned me off yourself."

Marilla felt deserted by everyone. She could not even go to Mrs. Lynde for advice. She went up to the east gable with a very serious face and left it with a face more serious still. Anne steadfastly refused to confess. She persisted in asserting that she had not taken the brooch. The child had evidently been crying and Marilla felt a pang of pity which she sternly repressed. By night she was, as she expressed it, "beat out."

"You'll stay in this room until you confess, Anne. You can make up your mind to that," she said firmly.

"But the picnic is tomorrow, Marilla," cried Anne. "You won't keep me from going to that, will you? Then I'll stay here as long as you like afterwards *cheerfully*. But I *must* go to the picnic."

"You'll not go to picnics nor anywhere else until you've confessed, Anne."

"Oh, Marilla," gasped Anne.

But Marilla had gone out and shut the door.

Wednesday morning dawned as bright and fair as if expressly made to order for the picnic. Birds sang around Green Gables; the Madonna lilies in the garden sent out whiffs of perfume that entered in on viewless winds at every door and window, and wandered through halls and rooms like spirits of benediction. The birches in the hollow waved joyful hands as if watching for Anne's usual morning greeting from the east gable. But Anne was not at her window. When Marilla took her breakfast up to her she found the child sitting primly on her bed, pale and resolute, with tight-shut lips and gleaming eyes.

"Marilla, I'm ready to confess."

"Ah!" Marilla laid down her tray. Once again her method had succeeded; but her success was very bitter to her. "Let me hear what you have to say then, Anne."

"I took the amethyst brooch," said Anne, as if repeating a lesson she had learned. "I took it just as you said. I didn't mean to take it when I went in. But it did look so beautiful, Marilla, when I pinned it on my breast that I was overcome by an irresistible temptation. I imagined how perfectly thrilling it would be to take it to Idlewild and play I was the Lady Cordelia Fitzgerald. It would be so much easier to imagine I was Lady Cordelia if I had a real amethyst brooch on. Diana and I made necklaces of roseberries but what are roseberries compared to amethysts? So I took the brooch. I thought I could put it back before you came home. I went all the way around by the road to lengthen out the time. When I was going over the bridge across the Lake of Shining Waters I took the brooch off to have another look at it. Oh, how it did shine in the sunlight! And then, when I was leaning over the bridge, it just slipped through my fingers—so—and went down—down—down, all purply-sparkling, and sank forevermore beneath the Lake of Shining Waters. And that's the best I can do at confessing, Marilla.''

Marilla felt hot anger surge up into her heart again. This child had taken and lost her treasured amethyst brooch and now sat there calmly reciting the details thereof without the least apparent compunction or repentance.

''Anne, this is terrible,'' she said, trying to speak calmly. ''You are the very wickedest girl I ever heard of.''

''Yes, I suppose I am,'' agreed Anne tranquilly. ''And I know I'll have to be punished. It'll be your duty to punish me, Marilla. Won't you please get it over right off because I'd like to go the picnic with nothing on my mind.''

''Picnic, indeed! You'll go to no picnic today, Anne Shirley. That shall be your punishment. And it isn't half severe enough either for what you've done!''

''Not go to the picnic!'' Anne sprang to her feet and clutched Marilla's hand. ''But you *promised* me I might! Oh, Marilla, I must go to the picnic. That was why I confessed. Punish me any way you like but that. Oh, Marilla, please, please, let me go to the picnic. Think of the ice-cream! For anything you know I may never have a chance to taste ice-cream again.''

Marilla disengaged Anne's clinging hands stonily.

''You needn't plead, Anne. You are not going to the picnic and that's final. No, not a word.''

Anne realized that Marilla was not to be moved. She clasped her hands together, gave a piercing shriek, and then flung herself face downwards on the bed, crying and writhing in an utter abandonment of disappointment and despair.

''For land's sake!'' gasped Marilla, hastening from the room. ''I believe the child is crazy. No child in her senses would behave as she does. If she isn't she's utterly bad. Oh dear, I'm afraid Rachel was right from the first. But I've put my hand to the plough and I won't look back.''

That was a dismal morning. Marilla worked fiercely and scrubbed the porch and the dairy shelves when she could find nothing else to do. Neither the shelves nor the porch needed it—but Marilla did. Then she went out and raked the yard.

When dinner was ready she went to the stairs and called Anne. A tear-stained face appeared, looking tragically over the banisters.

"Come down to your dinner, Anne."

"I don't want any dinner, Marilla," said Anne sobbingly. "I couldn't eat anything. My heart is broken. You'll feel remorse of conscience some day, I expect, for breaking it, Marilla, but I forgive you. Remember when the time comes that I forgive you. But please don't ask me to eat anything, especially boiled pork and greens. Boiled pork and greens are so unromantic when one is in affliction."

Exasperated Marilla returned to the kitchen and poured out her tale of woe to Matthew, who, between his sense of justice and his unlawful sympathy with Anne, was a miserable man.

"Well now, she shouldn't have taken the brooch, Marilla, or told stories about it," he admitted, mournfully surveying his plateful of unromantic pork and greens as if he, like Anne, thought it a food unsuited to crises of feeling, "but she's such a little thing—such an interesting little thing. Don't you think it's pretty rough not to let her go to the picnic when she's so set on it?"

"Matthew Cuthbert, I'm amazed at you. I think I've let her off entirely too easy. And she doesn't appear to realize how wicked she's been at all—that's what worries me most. If she'd really felt sorry it wouldn't be so bad. And you don't seem to realize it, neither; you're making excuses for her all the time to yourself—I can see that."

"Well now, she's such a little thing," feebly reiterated Matthew. "And there should be allowances made, Marilla. You know she's never had any bringing up."

"Well, she's having it now," retorted Marilla.

The retort silenced Matthew if it did not convince him. That dinner was a very dismal meal. The only cheerful thing about it was Jerry Buote, the hired boy, and Marilla resented his cheerfulness as a personal insult.

When her dishes were washed and her bread sponge set and her hens fed Marilla remembered that she had noticed a small rent in her best black lace shawl when she had taken it off on Monday afternoon on returning from the Ladies' Aid. She would go and mend it.

The shawl was in a box in her trunk. As Marilla lifted it out, the sunlight, falling through the vines that clustered thickly about the window, struck upon something caught in the shawl—something that glittered and sparkled in facets of violet light. Marilla snatched at it with a gasp. It was the amethyst brooch, hanging to a thread of the lace by its catch!

"Dear life and heart," said Marilla blankly, "what does this mean? Here's my brooch safe and sound that I thought was at the bottom of Barry's pond. Whatever did that girl mean by saying she took it and lost it? I declare I believe Green Gables is bewitched. I remember now that when I took off my shawl Monday afternoon I laid it on the bureau for a minute. I suppose the brooch got caught in it somehow. Well!"

Marilla betook herself to the east gable, brooch in hand. Anne had cried herself out and was sitting dejectedly by the window.

"Anne Shirley," said Marilla solemnly, "I've just found my brooch hanging to my black lace shawl. Now I want to know what that rigmarole you told me this morning meant."

"Why, you said you'd keep me here until I confessed," returned Anne wearily, "and so I decided to confess because I was bound to get to the picnic. I thought out a confession last night after I went to bed and made it as interesting as I could. And I said it over and over so that I wouldn't forget it. But you wouldn't let me go to the picnic after all, so all my trouble was wasted."

Marilla had to laugh in spite of herself. But her conscience pricked her.

"Anne, you do beat all! But I was wrong—I see that now. I shouldn't have doubted your word when I'd never known you to tell a story. Of course, it wasn't right for you to confess to a thing you hadn't done—it was very wrong to do so. But I drove you to it. So if you'll forgive me, Anne, I'll forgive you and we'll start square again. And now get yourself ready for the picnic."

Anne flew up like a rocket.

"Oh, Marilla, isn't it too late?"

"No, it's only two o'clock. They won't be more than well gathered yet and it'll be an hour before they have tea. Wash your face and comb your hair and put on your gingham. I'll fill a basket for you. There's plenty of stuff baked in the house. And I'll get Jerry to hitch up the sorrel and drive you down to the picnic ground."

"Oh, Marilla," exclaimed Anne, flying to the washstand. "Five minutes ago I was so miserable I was wishing I'd never been born and now I wouldn't change places with an angel!"

That night a thoroughly happy, completely tired out Anne returned to Green Gables in a state of beatification impossible to describe.

"Oh, Marilla, I've had a perfectly scrumptious time. Scrumptious is a new word I learned today. I heard Mary Alice Bell use it. Isn't it very expressive? Everything was lovely. We had a splendid tea and then Mr. Harmon Andrews took us all for a row on the Lake of Shining Waters—six of us at a time. And Jane Andrews fell overboard. She was leaning out to pick water lilies and if Mr. Andrews hadn't caught her by her sash just in the nick of time she'd have fallen in and prob'ly been drowned. I wish it had been me. It would have been such a romantic experience to have been nearly drowned. It would be such a thrilling tale to tell. And we had the ice-cream. Words fail me to describe that ice-cream. Marilla, I assure you it was sublime."

That evening Marilla told the whole story to Matthew over her stocking basket.

"I'm willing to own up that I made a mistake," she concluded candidly, "but I've learned a lesson. I have to laugh when I think of Anne's 'confession,' although I suppose I shouldn't for it really was a falsehood. But it doesn't seem as bad as the other would have been, somehow, and anyhow I'm responsible for it. That child is hard to understand in some respects. But I believe she'll turn out all right yet. And there's one thing certain, no house will ever be dull that she's in."

CHAPTER 15

A TEMPEST IN THE SCHOOL TEAPOT

"WHAT A splendid day!" said Anne, drawing a long breath. "Isn't it good just to be alive on a day like this? I pity the people who aren't born yet for missing it. They may have good days, of course, but they can never have this one. And it's splendider still to have such a lovely way to go to school by, isn't it?"

"It's a lot nicer than going round by the road; that is so dusty and hot," said Diana practically, peeping into her dinner basket and mentally calculating if the three juicy, toothsome, raspberry tarts reposing there were divided among ten girls how many bites each girl would have.

The little girls of Avonlea school always pooled their lunches, and to eat three raspberry tarts all alone or even to share them only with one's chum would have forever and ever branded as "awful mean" the girl who did it. And yet, when tarts were divided among ten girls you just got enough to tantalize you.

The way Anne and Diana went to school *was* a pretty one. Anne thought those walks to and from school with Diana couldn't be improved upon even by imagination. Going around by the main road would have been so unromantic; but to go by Lover's Lane and Willowmere and Violet Vale and the Birch Path was romantic, if ever anything was.

Lover's Lane opened out below the orchard at Green Gables and stretched far up into the woods to the end of the Cuthbert farm. It was the way by which the cows were taken to the back pasture and the wood hauled home in winter. Anne had named it Lover's Lane before she had been a month at Green Gables.

"Not that lovers ever really walk there," she explained to Marilla, "but Diana and I are reading a perfectly magnificent book and there's a Lover's Lane in it. So we want to have one, too. And it's a very pretty name, don't you think? So romantic! We can imagine the lovers into it, you know. I like that lane because you can think out loud there without people calling you crazy."

Anne, starting out alone in the morning, went down Lover's Lane as far as the brook. Here Diana met her, and the two little girls went on up the lane under the leafy arch of maples—"maples are such sociable trees," said Anne; "they're always rustling and whispering to you,"—until they came to a rustic bridge. Then they left the lane and walked through Mr. Barry's back field and past Willowmere. Beyond Willowmere came Violet Vale—a little green dimple in the shadow of Mr. Andrew Bell's big woods. "Of course there are no violets there now," Anne told Marilla, "but Diana says there are millions of them in spring. Oh, Marilla, can't you just imagine you see them? It actually takes away my breath. I named it Violet Vale. Diana says she never saw the beat of me for hitting on fancy names for places. It's nice to be clever at something, isn't it? But Diana named the Birch Path. She wanted to, so I let her; but I'm sure I could have found something more poetical than plain Birch Path. Anybody can think of a name like that. But the Birch Path is one of the prettiest places in the world, Marilla.''

It was. Other people besides Anne thought so when they stumbled on it. It was a little narrow, twisting path, winding down over a long hill straight through Mr. Bell's woods, where the light came down sifted through so many emerald screens that it was as flawless as the heart of a diamond. It was fringed in all its length with slim young birches, white-stemmed and lissom boughed; ferns and starflowers and wild lilies-of-the-valley and scarlet tufts of pigeon berries grew thickly along it; and always there was a delightful spiciness in the air and music of bird calls and the murmur and laugh of wood winds in the trees overhead. Now and then you might see a rabbit skipping across the road if you were quiet—which, with Anne and Diana, happened about once in a blue moon. Down in the valley the path came out to the main road and then it was just up the spruce hill to the school.

The Avonlea school was a whitewashed building low in the eaves and wide in the windows, furnished inside with comfortable substantial old-fashioned desks that opened and shut, and were carved all over their lids with the initials and hieroglyphics of three generations of school-children. The schoolhouse was set back from the road and behind it was a dusky fir wood and a brook where all the children put their bottles of milk in the morning to keep cool and sweet until dinner hour.

Marilla had seen Anne start off to school on the first day of September with many secret misgivings. Anne was such an odd girl. How would she get on with the other children? And how on earth would she ever manage to hold her tongue during school hours?

Things went better than Marilla feared, however. Anne came home that evening in high spirits.

"I think I'm going to like school here," she announced. "I don't think much of the master, though. He's all the time curling his moustache and making eyes at Prissy Andrews. Prissy is grown-up, you know. She's sixteen and she's studying for the entrance examination into Queen's Academy at Charlottetown next year. Tillie Boulter says that the master is *dead gone* on her. She's got a beautiful complexion and curly brown hair and she does it up so elegantly. She sits in the long seat at the back and he sits there, too, most of the time—to explain her lessons, he says. But Ruby Gillis says she saw him writing something on her slate and when Prissy read it she blushed as red as a beet and giggled; and Ruby Gillis says she doesn't believe it had anything to do with the lesson.''

"Anne Shirley, don't let me hear you talking about your teacher in that way again," said Marilla sharply. "You don't go to school to criticize the master. I guess he can teach *you* something and it's your business to learn. And I want you to understand right off that you are not to come home telling tales about him. That is something I won't encourage. I hope you were a good girl."

"Indeed I was," said Anne comfortably. "It wasn't so hard as you might imagine, either. I sit with Diana. Our seat is right by the window and we can look down to the Lake of Shining Waters. There are a lot of nice girls in school and we had scrumptious fun playing at dinner time. It's so nice to have a lot of little girls to play with. But of course I like Diana best and always will. I *adore* Diana. I'm dreadfully far behind the others. They're all in the fifth book and I'm only in the fourth. I feel that it's kind of a disgrace. But there's not one of them has such an imagination as I have and I soon found that out. We had reading and geography and Canadian History and dictation today. Mr. Phillips said my spelling was disgraceful and he held up my slate so that everybody could see it, all marked over. I felt so mortified, Marilla; he might have been politer to a stranger, I think. Ruby Gillis gave me an apple and Sophia Sloane lent me a lovely pink card with 'May I see you home?' on it. I'm to give it back to her tomorrow. And Tillie Boulter let me wear her bead ring all the afternoon. Can I have some of those pearl beads off the old pincushion in the garret to make myself a ring? And oh Marilla, Jane Andrews told me that Minnie MacPherson told her that she heard Prissy Andrews tell Sara Gillis that I had a very pretty nose. Marilla, that is the first compliment I have ever had in my life and you can't imagine what a strange feeling it gave me. Marilla, have I really a pretty nose? I know you'll tell me the truth."

"Your nose is well enough," said Marilla shortly. Secretly she thought Anne's nose was a remarkably pretty one; but she had no intention of telling her so.

That was three weeks ago and all had gone smoothly so far. And now, this crisp September morning, Anne and Diana were tripping blithely down the Birch Path, two of the happiest little girls in Avonlea.

"I guess Gilbert Blythe will be in school today," said Diana. "He's been visiting his cousins over in New Brunswick all summer and he only came home Saturday night. He's *aw'fly* handsome, Anne. And he teases the girls something terrible. He just torments our lives out."

Diana's voice indicated that she rather liked having her life tormented out than not.

"Gilbert Blythe?" said Anne. "Isn't it his name that's written up on the porch wall with Julia Bell's and a big 'Take Notice' over them?"

"Yes," said Diana, tossing her head, "but I'm sure he doesn't like Julia Bell so very much. I've heard him say he studied the multiplication table by her freckles."

"Oh, don't speak about freckles to me," implored Anne. "It isn't delicate when I've got so many. But I do think that writing take-notices up on the wall about the boys and girls is the silliest ever. I should just like to see anybody dare to write my name up with a boy's. Not, of course," she hastened to add, "that anybody would."

Anne sighed. She didn't want her name written up. But it was a little humiliating to know that there was no danger of it.

"Nonsense," said Diana, whose black eyes and glossy tresses had played such havoc with the hearts af Avonlea schoolboys that her name figured on the porch walls in half a dozen take-notices. "It's only meant as a joke. And don't you be too sure your name won't ever be written up. Charlie Sloane is *dead gone* on you. He told his mother—his *mother* mind you—that you were the smartest girl in school. That's better than being good-looking."

"No, it isn't," said Anne, feminine to the core. "I'd rather be pretty than clever. And I hate Charlie Sloane. I can't bear a boy with goggle eyes. If anyone wrote my name up with his I'd *never* get over it, Diana Barry. But it *is* nice to keep head of your class."

"You'll have Gilbert in your class after this," said Diana, "and he's used to being head of his class, I can tell you. He's only in the fourth book although he's nearly fourteen. Four years ago his father was sick and had to go out to Alberta for his health and Gilbert went with him. They were there three years and Gil didn't go to school hardly any until they came back. You won't find it so easy to keep head after this, Anne."

"I'm glad," said Anne quickly. "I couldn't really feel proud of keeping head of little boys and girls of just nine or ten. I got up yesterday spelling 'ebullition.' Josie Pye was head and, mind you, she peeped in her book. Mr. Phillips didn't see her—he was looking at Prissy Andrews—but I did. I just swept her a look of freezing scorn and she got as red as a beet and spelled it wrong after all."

"Those Pye girls are cheats all round," said Diana indignantly, as they climbed the fence of the main road. "Gertie Pye actually went and put her milk bottle in my place in the brook yesterday. Did you ever? I don't speak to her now.''

When Mr. Phillips was in the back of the room hearing Prissy Andrews' Latin Diana whispered to Anne,

''That's Gilbert Blythe sitting right across the aisle from you, Anne. Just look at him and see if you don't think he's handsome.''

Anne looked accordingly. She had a good chance to do so, for the said Gilbert Blythe was absorbed in stealthily pinning the long yellow braid of Ruby Gillis, who sat in front of him, to the back of her seat. He was a tall boy, with curly brown hair, roguish hazel eyes and a mouth twisted into a teasing smile. Presently Ruby Gillis started up to take a sum to the master; she fell back into her seat with a little shriek, believing that her hair was pulled out by the roots. Everybody looked at her and Mr. Phillips glared so sternly that Ruby began to cry. Gilbert had whisked the pin out of sight and was studying his history with the soberest face in the world; but when the commotion subsided he looked at Anne and winked with inexpressible drollery.

''I think your Gilbert Blythe *is* handsome,'' confided Anne to Diana, ''but I think he's very bold. It isn't good manners to wink at a strange girl.''

But it was not until the afternoon that things really began to happen.

Mr. Phillips was back in the corner explaining a problem in algebra to Prissy Andrews and the rest of the scholars were doing pretty much as they pleased, eating green apples, whispering, drawing pictures on their slates, and driving crickets, harnessed to strings, up and down the aisle. Gilbert Blythe was trying to make Anne Shirley look at him and failing utterly, because Anne was at that moment totally oblivious, not only of the very existence of Gilbert Blythe, but of every other scholar in Avonlea school and of Avonlea school itself. With her chin propped on her hands and her eyes fixed on the blue glimpse of the Lake of Shining Waters that the west window afforded, she was far away in a gorgeous dreamland, hearing and seeing nothing save her own wonderful visions.

Gilbert Blythe wasn't used to putting himself out to make a girl look at him and meeting with failure. She *should* look at him, that red-haired Shirley girl with the little pointed chin and the big eyes that weren't like the eyes of any other girl in Avonlea school.

Gilbert reached across the aisle, picked up the end of Anne's long red braid, held it out at arm's length and said in a piercing whisper,

"Carrots! Carrots!"

Then Anne looked at him with a vengeance!

She did more than look. She sprang to her feet, her bright fancies fallen into cureless ruin. She flashed one indignant glance at Gilbert from eyes whose angry sparkle was swiftly quenched in equally angry tears.

"You mean, hateful boy!" she exclaimed passionately. "How dare you!"

And then——Thwack! Anne had brought her slate down on Gilbert's head and cracked it—slate, not head—clear across.

Avonlea school always enjoyed a scene. This was an especially enjoyable one. Everybody said, "Oh" in horrified delight. Diana gasped. Ruby Gillis, who was inclined to be hysterical, began to cry. Tommy Sloane let his team of crickets escape him altogether while he stared open-mouthed at the tableau.

Mr. Phillips stalked down the aisle and laid his hand heavily on Anne's shoulder.

"Anne Shirley, what does this mean?" he said angrily.

Anne returned no answer. It was asking too much of flesh and blood to expect her to tell before the whole school that she had been called "carrots." Gilbert it was who spoke up stoutly.

"It was my fault, Mr. Phillips. I teased her."

Mr. Phillips paid no heed to Gilbert.

"I am sorry to see a pupil of mine displaying such a temper and such a vindictive spirit," he said in a solemn tone, as if the mere fact of being a pupil of his ought to root out all evil passions from the hearts of small imperfect mortals. "Anne, go and stand on the platform in front of the blackboard for the rest of the afternoon."

Anne would have infinitely preferred a whipping to this punishment, under which her sensitive spirit quivered as from a whiplash. With a white, set face she obeyed. Mr. Phillips took a chalk crayon and wrote on the blackboard above her head.

"Ann Shirley has a very bad temper. Ann Shirley must learn to control her temper," and then read it aloud so that even the primer class, who couldn't read writing, should understand it.

Anne stood there the rest of the afternoon with that legend above her. She did not cry or hang her head. Anger was still too hot in her heart for that and it sustained her amid all her agony of humiliation. With resentful eyes and passion-red cheeks she confronted alike Diana's sympathetic gaze and Charlie Sloane's indignant nods and Josie Pye's malicious smiles. As for Gilbert Blythe, she would not even look at him. She would *never* look at him again! She would never speak to him!!

When school was dismissed Anne marched out with her red head held high. Gilbert Blythe tried to intercept her at the porch door.

"I'm awful sorry I made fun of your hair, Anne," he whispered contritely, "Honest I am. Don't be mad for keeps, now."

Anne swept by disdainfully, without look or sign of hearing. "Oh, how could you, Anne? breathed Diana as they went down the road, half reproachfully, half admiringly. Diana felt that *she* could never have resisted Gilbert's plea.

"I shall never forgive Gilbert Blythe," said Anne firmly. "And Mr. Phillips spelled my name without an *e*, too. The iron has entered into my soul, Diana."

Diana hadn't the least idea what Anne meant but she understood it was something terrible.

"You mustn't mind Gilbert making fun of your hair," she said soothingly. "Why, he makes fun of all the girls. He laughs at mine because it's so black. He's called me a crow a dozen times; and I never heard him apologize for anything before, either."

"There's a great deal of difference between being called a crow and being called carrots," said Anne with dignity. "Gilbert Blythe has hurt my feelings *excruciatingly,* Diana."

It is possible the matter might have blown over without more excruciation if nothing else had happened. But when things begin to happen they are apt to keep on.

Avonlea scholars often spent noon hour picking gum in Mr. Bell's spruce grove over the hill and across his big pasture field. From there they could keep an eye on Eben Wright's house where the master boarded. When they saw Mr. Phillips emerging therefrom they ran for the schoolhouse; but the distance being about three times longer than Mr. Wright's lane they were very apt to arrive there, breathless and gasping, some three minutes too late.

On the following day Mr. Phillips was seized with one of his spasmodic fits of reform and announced, before going home to dinner, that he should expect to find all the scholars in their seats when he returned. Anyone who came in late would be punished.

All the boys and some of the girls went to Mr. Bell's spruce grove as usual, fully intending to stay only long enough to "pick a chew." But spruce groves are seductive and yellow nuts of gum beguiling; they picked and loitered and strayed; and as usual the first thing that recalled them to a sense of the flight of time was Jimmy Glover

THWACK! ANNE BROUGHT HER SLATE DOWN ON GILBERT'S HEAD.

shouting from the top of a patriarchal old spruce, "Master's coming."

The girls, who were on the ground, started first and managed to reach the schoolhouse in time but without a second to spare. The boys, who had to wriggle hastily down from the tress, were later; and Anne, who had not been picking gum at all but was wandering happily in the far end of the grove, waist deep among the bracken, singing softly to herself, with a wreath of rice lilies on her hair as if she were some wild divinity of the shadowy places, was latest of all. Anne could run like a deer, however; run she did with the impish result that she overtook the boys at the door and was swept into the schoolhouse among them just as Mr. Phillips was in the act of hanging up his hat.

Mr. Phillips' brief reforming energy was over; he didn't want the bother of punishing a dozen pupils; but it was necessary to do someting to save his word, so he looked about for a scapegoat and found it in Anne, who had dropped into her seat, gasping for breath, with her forgotten lily wreath hanging askew over one ear and giving her a particularly rakish and dishevelled appearance.

"Anne Shirley, since you seem to be so fond of the boys' company we shall indulge your taste for it this afternoon," he said sarcastically. "Take those flowers out of your hair and sit with Gilbert Blythe." The other boys snickered. Diana, turning pale with pity, plucked the wreath from Anne's hair and squeezed her hand. Anne stared at the master as if turned to stone.

"Did you hear what I said, Anne?" queried Mr. Phillips sternly.

"Yes, sir," said Anne slowly, "but I didn't suppose you really meant it."

"I assure you I did,"—still with the sarcastic inflection which all the children, and Anne especially, hated. It flicked on the raw. "Obey me at once."

For a moment Anne looked as if she meant to disobey. Then, realizing that there was no help for it, she rose haughtily, stepped across the aisle, sat down beside Gilbert Blythe, and buried her face in her arms on the desk. Ruby Gillis, who got a glimpse of it as it went down, told the others going home from school that she'd "acksually never seen anything like it—it was so white, with awful little red spots in it."

To Anne, this was as the end of all things. It was bad enough to be singled out for punishment from among a dozen equally guilty ones; it was worse still to be sent to sit with a boy; but that that boy should be Gilbert Blythe was heaping insult on injury to a degree utterly unbearable. Anne felt that she could *not* bear it and it would be of no use to try. Her whole being seethed with shame and anger and humiliation.

At first the other scholars looked and whispered and giggled and nudged. But as Anne never lifted her head and as Gilbert worked fractions as if his whole soul was absorbed in them and them only, they soon returned to their own tasks and Anne was forgotten. When Mr. Phillips called the history class out Anne should have gone; but Anne did not move, and Mr. Phillips, who had been writing some verse "To Priscilla" before he called the class, was thinking about an obstinate rhyme still and never missed her. Once, when nobody was looking, Gilbert took from his desk a little pink candy heart with a gold motto on it, "You are sweet," and slipped it under the curve of Anne's arm. Whereupon Anne arose, took the pink heart gingerly between the tips of her fingers, dropped it on the floor, ground it to powder beneath her heel, and resumed her position without deigning to bestow a glance on Gilbert.

When school went out Anne marched to her desk, ostentatiously took out everything therein, books and writing tablet, pen and ink, testament and arithmetic, and piled them neatly on her cracked slate.

"What are you taking all those things home for, Anne?" Diana wanted to know, as soon as they were out on the road. She had not dared to ask the question before.

"I am not coming back to school any more," said Anne.

Diana gasped and stared at Anne to see if she meant it.

"Will Marilla let you stay home?" she asked.

"She'll have to," said Anne. "I'll *never* go to school to that man again."

"Oh, Anne!" Diana looked as if she were ready to cry. "I do think you're mean. What shall I do? Mr. Phillips will make me sit with that horrid Gertie Pye—I know he will because she is sitting alone. Do come back, Anne."

"I'd do almost anything in the world for you, Diana," said Anne sadly. "I'd let myself be torn limb from limb if it would do you any good. But I can't do this, so please don't ask it. You harrow up my very soul."

"Just think of all the fun you will miss," mourned Diana. "We are going to build the loveliest new house down by the brook; and we'll be playing ball next week and you've never played ball, Anne. It's tremenjusly exciting. And we're going to learn a new song——

Jane Andrews is practising it up now; and Alice Andrews is going to bring a new Pansy book next week and we're all going to read it out loud, chapter about, down by the brook. And you know you are so fond of reading out loud, Anne.''

Nothing moved Anne in the least. Her mind was made up. She would not go to school to Mr. Phillips again; she told Marilla so when she got home.

''Nonsense,'' said Marilla.

"It isn't nonsense at all," said Anne gazing at Marilla with solemn, reproachful eyes. ''Don't you understand, Marilla? I've been insulted.''

''Insulted fiddlesticks! You'll go to school tomorrow as usual.''

''Oh, no.'' Anne shook her head gently. ''I'm not going back, Marilla. I'll learn my lessons at home and I'll be as good as I can be and hold my tongue all the time if it's possible at all. But I will not go back to school I assure you.''

Marilla saw something remarkably like unyielding stubbornness looking out of Anne's small face. She understood that she would have trouble in overcoming it; but she resolved wisely to say nothing more just then.

''I'll run down and see Rachel about it this evening,'' she thought. ''There's no use reasoning with Anne now. She's too worked up and I've an idea she can be awful stubborn if she takes the notion. Far as I can make out from her story, Mr. Phillips has been carrying matters with a rather high hand. But it would never do to say so to her. I'll just talk it over with Rachel. She's sent ten children to school and she ought to know something about it. She'll have heard the whole story, too, by this time.''

Marilla found Mrs. Lynde knitting quilts as industriously and cheerfully as usual.

''I suppose you know what I've come about,'' she said, a little shamefacedly.

Mrs. Rachel nodded.

''About Anne's fuss in school, I reckon,'' she said. ''Tillie Boulter was in on her way home from school and told me about it.''

''I don't know what to do with her,'' said Marilla. ''She declares she won't go back to school. I never saw a child so worked up. I've been expecting trouble ever since she started to school. I knew things were going too smooth to last. She's so high-strung. What would you advise, Rachel?''

''Well, since you've asked my advice, Marilla,'' said Mrs. Lynde amiably—Mrs. Lynde dearly loved to be asked for advice—''I'd just

humor her a little at first, that's what I'd do. It's my belief that Mr.
Phillips was in the wrong. Of course, it doesn't do to say so to the
children, you know. And of course he did right to punish her
yesterday for giving way to temper. But today it was different. The
others who were late should have been punished as well as Anne,
that's what. And I don't believe in making the girls sit with the boys
for punishment. It isn't modest. Tille Boulter was real indignant. She
took Anne's part right through and said all the scholars did, too.
Anne seems real popular among them, somehow. I never thought
she'd take with them so well.''

''Then you really think I'd better let her stay home,'' said Marilla
in amazement.

''Yes. That is, I wouldn't say school to her again until she said it
herself. Depend upon it, Marilla, she'll cool off in a week or so and
be ready enough to go back of her own accord, that's what, while, if
you were to make her go back right off, dear knows what freak or
tantrum she'd take next and make more trouble than ever. The less
fuss made the better, in my opinion. She won't miss much by not
going to school, as far as *that* goes. Mr. Phillips isn't any good at all as
a teacher. The order he keeps is scandalous, that's what, and he
neglects the young fry and puts all his time on those big scholars he's
getting ready for Queen's. He'd never have got the school for
another year if his uncle hadn't been a trustee—*the* trustee, for he just
leads the other two around by the nose, that's what. I declare, I don't
know what education in this Island is coming to.''

Mrs. Rachel shook her head, as much as to say if she were only at
the head of the educational system of the Province things would be
much better managed.

Marilla took Mrs. Rachel's advice and not another word was said
to Anne about going back to school. She learned her lessons at home,
did her chores, and played with Diana in the chilly purple autumn
twilights; but when she met Gilbert Blythe on the road or encountered him in Sunday-school she passed him by with an icy contempt
that was no whit thawed by his evident desire to appease her. Even
Diana's efforts as a peacemaker were of no avail. Anne had evidently
made up her mind to hate Gilbert Blythe to the end of life.

As much as she hated Gilbert, however, did she love Diana, with
all the love of her passionate little heart, equally intense in its likes
and dislikes. One evening Marilla, coming in from the orchard with a
basket of apples, found Anne sitting alone by the east window in the
twilight, crying bitterly.

''Whatever's the matter now, Anne?'' she asked.

"It's about Diana," sobbed Anne luxuriously. "I love Diana so, Marilla. I cannot ever live without her. But I know very well when we grow up that Diana will get married and go away and leave me. And oh, what shall I do? I hate her husband—I just hate him furiously. I've been imagining it all out—the wedding and everything—Diana dressed in snowy garments, with a veil, and looking beautiful and regal as a queen; and me the bridesmaid, with a lovely dress, too, and puffed sleeves, but with a breaking heart hid beneath my smiling face. And then bidding Diana good-by-e-e—" Here Anne broke down entirely and wept with increasing bitterness.

Marilla turned quickly away to hide her twitching face; but it was no use; she collapsed on the nearest chair and burst into such a hearty and unusual peal of laughter that Matthew, crossing the yard outside, halted in amazement. When had he heard Marilla laugh like that before?

"Well, Anne Shirley," said Marilla as soon as she could speak, "if you must borrow trouble, for pity's sake borrow it handier home. I should think you had an imagination, sure enough."

CHAPTER 16

DIANA IS INVITED TO TEA WITH TRAGIC RESULTS

OCTOBER WAS a beautiful month at Green Gables, when the birches in the hollow turned as golden as sunshine and the maples behind the orchard were royal crimson and the wild cherry-trees along the lane put on the loveliest shades of dark red and bronzy green, while the fields sunned themselves in aftermaths.

Anne revelled in the world of color about her.

"Oh, Marilla," she exclaimed one Saturday morning, coming dancing in with her arms full of gorgeous boughs. "I'm so glad I live in a world where there are Octobers. It would be terrible if we just skipped from September to November, wouldn't it? Look at these maple branches. Don't they give you a thrill—several thrills? I'm going to decorate my room with them."

"Messy things," said Marilla, whose aesthetic sense was not

noticeably developed. "You clutter up your room entirely too much with out-of-doors stuff, Anne. Bedrooms were made to sleep in."

"Oh, and dream in too, Marilla. And you know one can dream so much better in a room where there are pretty things. I'm going to put these boughs in the old blue jug and set them on my table."

"Mind you don't drop leaves all over the stairs then. I'm going to a meeting of the Aid Society at Carmody this afternoon, Anne, and I won't likely be home before dark. You'll have to get Matthew and Jerry their supper, so mind you don't forget to put the tea to draw until you sit down at the table as you did last time."

"It was dreadful of me to forget," said Anne apologetically, "but that was the afternoon I was trying to think of a name for Violet Vale and it crowded other things out. Matthew was so good. He never scolded a bit. He put the tea down himself and said we could wait awhile as well as not. And I told him a lovely fairy story while we were waiting, so he didn't find the time long at all. It was a beautiful fairy story, Marilla. I forgot the end of it, so I made up an end for it myself and Matthew said he couldn't tell where the join came in."

"Matthew would think it all right, Anne, if you took a notion to get up and have dinner in the middle of the night. But you keep your wits about you this time. And—I don't really know if I'm doing right—it may make you more addle-pated than ever—but you can ask Diana to come over and spend the afternoon with you and have tea here."

"Oh, Marilla!" Anne clasped her hands. "How perfectly lovely! You *are* able to imagine things after all or else you'd never have understood how I've longed for that very thing. It will seem so nice and grown-uppish. No fear of my forgetting to put the tea to draw when I have company. Oh, Marilla, can I use the rosebud spray tea-set?"

"No, indeed! The rosebud tea-set! Well, what next? You know I never use that except for the minister or the Aids. You'll put down the old brown tea-set. But you can open the little yellow crock of cherry preserves. It's time it was being used anyhow—I believe it's beginning to work. And you can cut some fruit-cake and have some of the cookies and snaps."

"I can just imagine myself sitting down at the head of the table and pouring out the tea," said Anne, shutting her eyes ecstatically. "And asking Diana if she takes sugar! I know she doesn't but of course I'll ask her just as if I didn't know. And then pressing her to take another piece of fruit-cake and another helping of preserves.

Oh, Marilla, it's a wonderful sensation just to think of it. Can I take her into the spare room to lay off her hat when she comes? And then into the parlor to sit?''

''No. The sitting-room will do for you and your company. But there's a bottle half full of raspberry cordial that was left over from the church social the other night. It's on the second shelf of the sitting-room closet and you and Diana can have it if you like, and a cooky to eat with it along in the afternoon, for I daresay Matthew'll be late coming in to tea since he's hauling potatoes to the vessel.''

Anne flew down to the hollow, past the Dryad's Bubble and up the spruce path to Orchard Slope, to ask Diana to tea. As a result, just after Marilla had driven off to Carmody, Diana came over, dressed in her second best dress and looking exactly as it is proper to look when asked out to tea. At other times she was wont to run into the kitchen without knocking; but now she knocked primly at the front door. And when Anne, dressed in *her* second best, as primly opened it, both little girls shook hands as gravely as if they had never met before. This unnatural solemnity lasted until after Diana had been taken to the east gable to lay off her hat and then had sat for ten minutes in the sitting-room, toes in position.

''How is your mother?'' inquired Anne politely, just as if she had not seen Mrs. Barry picking apples that morning in excellent health and spirits.

''She is very well, thank you. I suppose Mr. Cuthbert is hauling potatoes to the *Lily Sands* this afternoon, is he?'' said Diana, who had ridden down to Mr. Harmon Andrews' that morning in Matthew's cart.

''Yes. Our potato crop is very good this year. I hope your father's potato crop is good, too.''

''It is fairly good, thank you. Have you picked many of your apples yet?''

''Oh, ever so many,'' said Anne, forgetting to be dignified and jumping up quickly. ''Let's go out to the orchard and get some of the Red Sweetings, Diana. Marilla says we can have all that are left on the tree. Marilla is a very generous woman. She said we could have fruit-cake and cherry preserves for tea. But it isn't good manners to tell your company what you are going to give them to eat, so I won't tell you what she said we could have to drink. Only it begins with an *r* and a *c* and it's a bright red color. I love bright red drinks, don't you? They taste twice as good as any other color.''

The orchard, with its great sweeping boughs that bent to the ground with fruit, proved so delightful that the little girls spent most of the afternoon in it, sitting in a grassy corner where the frost had spared the green and the mellow autumn sunshine lingered warmly, eating apples and talking as hard as they could. Diana had much to tell Anne of what went on in school. She had to sit with Gertie Pye and she hated it; Gertie squeaked her pencil all the time and it just made her—Diana's—blood run cold; Ruby Gillis had charmed all her warts away, true's you live, with a magic pebble that old Mary Joe from the Creek gave her. You had to rub the warts with the pebble and then throw it away over your left shoulder at the time of the new moon and the warts would all go. Charlie Sloane's name was written up with Em White's on the porch wall and Em White was *awful mad* about it; Sam Boulter had "sassed" Mr. Phillips in class and Mr. Phillips whipped him and Sam's father came to the school and dared Mr. Phillips to lay a hand on one of his children again; and Mattie Andrews had a new red hood and a blue crossover with tassels on it and the airs she put on about it were perfectly sickening; and Lizzie Wright didn't speak to Mamie Wilson because Mamie Wilson's grown-up sister had cut out Lizzie Wright's grown-up sister with her beau; and everybody missed Anne so and wished she'd come to school again; and Gilbert Blythe—

But Anne didn't want to hear about Gilbert Blythe. She jumped up hurriedly and said suppose they go in and have some raspberry cordial.

Anne looked on the second shelf of the room pantry but there was no bottle of raspberry cordial there. Search revealed it away back on the top shelf. Anne put it on a tray and set it on the table with a tumbler.

"Now, please help yourself, Diana," she said politely. "I don't believe I'll have any just now. I don't feel as if I wanted any after all those apples."

Diana poured herself out a tumblerful, looked at its bright red hue admiringly, and then sipped it daintily.

"That's awfully nice raspberry cordial, Anne," she said. "I didn't know raspberry cordial was so nice."

"I'm real glad you like it. Take as much as you want. I'm going to run out and stir the fire up. There are so many responsibilities on a person's mind when they're keeping house, isn't there?"

When Anne came back from the kitchen Diana was drinking her second glassful of cordial; and, being entreated thereto by Anne, she offered no particular objection to the drinking of a third. The tumblerfuls were generous ones and the raspberry cordial was certainly very nice.

"The nicest I ever drank," said Diana. "It's ever so much nicer than Mrs. Lynde's although she brags of hers so much. It doesn't taste a bit like hers."

"I should think Marilla's raspberry cordial would prob'ly be much nicer than Mrs. Lynde's," said Anne loyally. "Marilla is a famous cook. She is trying to teach me to cook but I assure you, Diana, it is uphill work. There's so little scope for imagination in cookery. You have to go by rules. The last time I made a cake I forgot to put the flour in. I was thinking the loveliest story about you and me, Diana. I thought you were desperately ill with smallpox and everybody deserted you, but I went boldly to your bedside and nursed you back to life; and then I took the smallpox and died and I was buried under those poplar trees in the graveyard and you planted a rosebush by my grave and watered it with your tears; and you never, never forgot the friend of your youth who sacrificed her life for you. Oh, it was a pathetic tale, Diana. The tears just rained down over my cheeks while I mixed the cake. But I forgot the flour and the cake was a dismal failure. Flour is so essential to cakes, you know. Marilla was very cross and I don't wonder. I'm a great trial to her. She was terribly mortified about the pudding sauce last week. We had a plum pudding for dinner on Tuesday and there was half the pudding and a pitcherful of sauce left over. Marilla said there was enough for another dinner and told me to set it on the pantry shelf and cover it. I meant to cover it just as much as could be, Diana, but when I carried it in I was imagining I was a nun—of course I'm a Protestant but I imagined I was a Catholic—taking the veil to bury a broken heart in cloistered seclusion; and I forgot all about covering the pudding sauce. I thought of it next morning and ran to the pantry. Diana, fancy if you can my extreme horror at finding a mouse drowned in that pudding sauce! I lifted the mouse out with a spoon and threw it in the yard and then I washed the spoon in three waters. Marilla was out milking and I fully intended to ask her when she came in if I'd give the sauce to the pigs; but when she did come in I was imagining that I was a frost fairy going through the woods turning the trees red and yellow, whichever they wanted to be, so I never thought about the pudding sauce again and Marilla sent me out to pick apples. Well, Mr. and Mrs. Chester Ross from Spencervale came here that morning. You know they are very stylish people, especially Mrs. Chester Ross. When Marilla called me in dinner was ready and everybody was at the table. I tried to be as polite and dignified as I could be, for I wanted Mrs. Chester Ross to think I was a ladylike little girl even if I wasn't pretty. Everything went right until I saw Marilla coming with the plum pudding in one hand and the pitcher of pudding sauce, *warmed up,* in the other. Diana, that was a terrible moment. I remembered everything and I just stood up in my place and shrieked out, 'Marilla, you mustn't use that pudding sauce. There was a mouse drowned in it. I forgot to tell you before.' Oh, Diana, I shall never forget that awful moment if I live to be a hundred. Mrs. Chester Ross just *looked* at me and I thought I would sink through the floor with mortification. She is such a perfect housekeeper and fancy what she must have thought of us. Marilla turned red as fire but she never said a word—then. She just carried that sauce and pudding out and brought in some strawberry preserves. She even offered me some, but I couldn't swallow a mouthful. It was like heaping coals of fire on my head. After Mrs. Chester Ross went away Marilla gave me a dreadful scolding. Why, Diana, what it the matter?''

Diana had stood up very unsteadily; then she sat down again, putting her hands to her head.

"I'm—I'm awful sick," she said, a little thickly. "I—I—must go right home."

"Oh, you mustn't dream of going home without your tea," cried Anne in distress. "I'll get it right off—I'll go and put the tea down this very minute."

"I must go home," repeated Diana, stupidly but determinedly.

"Let me get you a lunch anyhow," implored Anne. "Let me give you a bit of fruit-cake and some of the cherry preserves. Lie down on the sofa for a little while and you'll be better. Where do you feel bad?"

"I must go home," said Diana, and that was all she would say. In vain Anne pleaded.

"I never heard of company going home without tea," she mourned. "Oh, Diana, do you suppose that it's possible you're really taking the smallpox? If you are I'll go and nurse you, you can depend on that. I'll never forsake you. But I do wish you'd stay till after tea. Where do you feel bad?"

"I'm awful dizzy," said Diana.

And indeed, she walked very dizzily. Anne, with tears of disappointment in her eyes, got Diana's hat and went with her as far as the Barry yard fence. Then she wept all the way back to Green Gables, where she sorrowfully put the remainder of the raspberry cordial back into the pantry and got tea for Matthew and Jerry, with all the zest gone out of the performance.

The next day was Sunday and as the rain poured down in torrents from dawn till dusk Anne did not stir abroad from Green Gables. Monday afternoon Marilla sent her down to Mrs. Lynde's on an errand. In a very short space of time Anne came flying back up the lane, with tears rolling down her cheeks. Into the kitchen she dashed and flung herself downward on the sofa in an agony.

"Whatever has gone wrong now, Anne?" queried Marilla in doubt and dismay. "I do hope you haven't gone and been saucy to Mrs. Lynde again."

No answer from Anne save more tears and stormier sobs!

"Anne Shirley, when I ask you a question I want to be answered. Sit right up this very minute and tell me what you are crying about."

Anne sat up, tragedy personified.

"Mrs. Lynde was up to see Mrs. Barry today and Mrs. Barry was in an awful state," she wailed. "She says that I set Diana *drunk* Saturday and sent her home in a disgraceful condition. And she says I must be a thoroughly bad, wicked little girl and she's never, never going to let Diana play with me again. Oh, Marilla, I'm just overcome with woe."

Marilla stared in blank amazement.

"Set Diana drunk!" she said when she found her voice. "Anne, are you or Mrs. Barry crazy? What on earth did you give her?"

"Not a thing but raspberry cordial," sobbed Anne. "I never thought raspberry cordial would set people drunk, Marilla,—not even if they drank three big tumblerfuls as Diana did. Oh, it sounds so—so—like Mrs. Thomas' husband! But I didn't mean to set her drunk."

"Drunk fiddlesticks!" said Marilla, marching to the sitting-room pantry. There on the shelf was a bottle which she at once recognized as one containing some of her three year old homemade currant wine for which she was celebrated in Avonlea, although certain of the stricter sort, Mrs. Barry among them, disapproved strongly of it. And at the same time Marilla recollected that she had put the bottle of raspberry cordial down in the cellar instead of in the pantry as she had told Anne.

She went back to the kitchen with the wine bottle in her hand. Her face was twitching in spite of herself.

"Anne, you certainly have a genius for getting into trouble. You went and gave Diana currant wine instead of raspberry cordial.

Didn't you know the difference yourself?''

"I never tasted it," said Anne. "I thought it was the cordial. I meant to be so—so—hospitable. Diana got awfully sick and had to go home. Mrs. Barry told Mrs. Lynde she was simply dead drunk. She just laughed silly like when her mother aksed what was the matter and went to sleep and slept for hours. Her mother smelled her breath and knew she was drunk. She had a fearful headache all day yesterday. Mrs. Barry is so indignant. She will never believe but what I did it on purpose.''

"I should think she would better punish Diana for being so greedy as to drink three glassfuls of anything," said Marilla shortly. "Why, three of those big glasses would have made her sick even if it had only been cordial. Well, this story will be a nice handle for those folks who are so down on me for making currant wine, although I haven't made any for three years ever since I found out that the minister didn't approve. I just kept that bottle for sickness. There, there, child, don't cry. I can't see as you were to blame although I'm sorry it happened so.''

"I must cry," said Anne. "My heart is broken. The stars in their courses fight against me, Marilla. Diana and I are parted forever. Oh, Marilla, I little dreamed of this when first we swore our vows of friendship.''

"Don't be foolish, Anne. Mrs. Barry will think better of it when she finds you're not really to blame. I suppose she thinks you've done it for a silly joke or something of that sort. You'd best go up this evening and tell her how it was.''

"My courage fails me at the thought of facing Diana's injured mother," sighed Anne. "I wish you'd go, Marilla. You're so much more dignified than I am. Likely she'd listen to you quicker than to me.''

"Well, I will," said Marilla, reflecting that it would probably be the wiser course. "Don't cry any more, Anne. It will be all right.''

Marilla had changed her mind about its being all right by the time she got back from Orchard Slope. Anne was watching for her coming and flew to the porch door to meet her.

"Oh, Marilla, I know by your face that it's been no use," she said sorrowfully. "Mrs. Barry won't forgive me?''

"Mrs. Barry, indeed!" snapped Marilla. "Of all the unreasonable women I ever saw she's the worst. I told her it was all a mistake and you weren't to blame, but she just simply didn't believe me. And she rubbed it well in about my currant wine and how I'd always said it couldn't have the least effect on anybody. I just told her plainly that currant wine wasn't meant to be drunk three tumblerfuls at a time and that if a child I had to do with was so greedy I'd sober her up with a right good spanking.''

Marilla whisked into the kitchen, grievously disturbed, leaving a very much distracted little soul in the porch behind her. Presently Anne stepped out bare-headed into the chill autumn dusk; very determinedly and steadily she took her way down through the sere clover field over the log bridge and up through the spruce grove, lighted by a pale little moon hanging low over the western woods. Mrs. Barry, coming to the door in answer to a timid knock, found a white-lipped, eager-eyed suppliant on the doorstep.

Her face hardened. Mrs. Barry was a woman of strong prejudices and dislikes, and her anger was of the cold, sullen sort which is always hardest to overcome. To do her justice, she really believed Anne had made Diana drunk out of sheer malice prepense, and she was honestly anxious to preserve her little daughter from the contamination of further intimacy with such a child.

"What do you want?" she said stiffly.

Anne clasped her hands.

"Oh, Mrs. Barry, please forgive me. I did not mean to—to—intoxicate Diana. How could I? Just imagine if you were a poor little orphan girl that kind people had adopted and you had just one bosom friend in all the world. Do you think you would intoxicate her on purpose? I thought it was only raspberry cordial. I was firmly convinced it was raspberry cordial. Oh, please don't say that you won't let Diana play with me any more. If you do you will cover my life with a dark cloud of woe.''

This speech, which would have softened good Mrs. Lynde's heart in a twinkling, had no effect on Mrs. Barry except to irritate her still more. She was suspicious of Anne's big words and dramatic gestures and imagined that the child was making fun of her. So she said, coldly and cruelly:

"I don't think you are a fit little girl for Diana to associate with. You'd better go home and behave yourself.''

Anne's lip quivered.

"Won't you let me see Diana just once to say farewell?'' she implored.

"Diana has gone over to Carmody with her father," said Mrs. Barry, going in and shutting the door.

Anne went back to Green Gables calm with despair.

"My last hope is gone," she told Marilla. "I went up and saw Mrs. Barry myself and she treated me very insultingly. Marilla, I do *not* think she is a well-bred woman. There is nothing more to do except pray and I haven't much hope that that'll do much good because, Marilla, I do not believe that God Himself can do very much with such an obstinate person as Mrs. Barry.''

"Anne, you shouldn't say such things," rebuked Marilla, striving to overcome that unholy tendency to laughter which she was dismayed to find growing upon her. And indeed, when she told the whole story to Matthew that night, she did laugh heartily over Anne's tribulations.

But when she slipped into the east gable before going to bed and found that Anne had cried herself to sleep an unaccustomed softness crept into her face.

"Poor little soul," she murmured, lifting a loose curl of hair from the child's tear-stained face. Then she bent down and kissed the flushed cheek on the pillow.

CHAPTER 17

A NEW INTEREST IN LIFE

THE NEXT afternoon Anne, bending over her patchwork at the kitchen window, happened to glance out and beheld Diana down by the Dryad's Bubble beckoning mysteriously. In a trice Anne was out of the house and flying down to the hollow, astonishment and hope struggling in her expressive eyes. But the hope faded when she saw Diana's dejected countenance.

"Your mother hasn't relented?" she gasped.

Diana shook her head mournfully.

"No; and oh, Anne, she says I'm never to play with you again. I've cried and cried and I told her it wasn't your fault, but it wasn't any use. I had ever such a time coaxing her to let me come down and say good-bye to you. She said I was only to stay ten minutes and she's timing me by the clock.''

"Ten minutes isn't very long to say an eternal farewell in," said Anne tearfully. "Oh, Diana, will you promise faithfully never to forget me, the friend of your youth, no matter what dearer friends may caress thee?''

"Indeed I will," sobbed Diana, "and I'll never have another

bosom friend—I don't want to have. I couldn't love anybody as I love you.''

''Oh, Diana,'' cried Anne, clasping her hands, ''do you *love* me?''

''Why, of course I do. Didn't you know that?''

''No.'' Anne drew a long breath. ''I thought you *liked* me of course, but I never hoped you *loved* me. Why, Diana, I didn't think anybody could love me. Nobody ever has loved me since I can remember. Oh, this is wonderful! It's a ray of light which will forever shine on the darkness of a path severed from thee, Diana. Oh, just say it once again.''

''I love you devotedly, Anne,'' said Diana stanchly, ''and I always will, you may be sure of that.''

''And I will always love thee, Diana,'' said Anne, solemnly extending her hand. ''In the years to come thy memory will shine like a star over my lonely life, as that last story we read together says. Diana, wilt thou give me a lock of thy jet-black tresses in parting to treasure forevermore?''

''Have you got anything to cut it with?'' queried Diana, wiping away the tears which Anne's affecting accents had caused to flow afresh, and returning to practicalities.

''Yes. I've got my patchwork scissors in my apron pocket fortunately,'' said Anne. She solemnly clipped one of Diana's curls. ''Fare thee well, my beloved friend. Henceforth we must be as strangers living side by side. But my heart will ever be faithful to thee.''

Anne stood and watched Diana out of sight, mournfully waving her hand to the latter whenever she turned to look back. Then she returned to the house, not a little consoled for the time being by this romantic parting.

''It is all over,'' she informed Marilla. ''I shall never have another friend. I'm really worse off than ever before, for I haven't Katie Maurice and Violetta now. And even if I had it wouldn't be the same. Somehow, little dream girls are not satisfying after a real friend. Diana and I had such an affecting farewell down by the spring. It will be sacred in my memory forever. I used the most pathetic language I could think of and said 'thou' and 'thee.' 'Thou' and 'thee' seem so much more romantic than 'you.' Diana gave me a lock of her hair and I'm going to sew it up in a little bag and wear it around my neck all .my life. Please see that it is buried with me, for I don't believe I'll live very long. Perhaps when she sees me lying cold and dead before her Mrs. Barry may feel remorse for what she has done and will let Diana come to my funeral.''

''I don't think there is much fear of your dying of grief as long as you can talk, Anne,'' said Marilla unsympathetically.

The following Monday Anne surprised Marilla by coming down from her room with her basket of books on her arm and her lips primmed up into a line of determination.

''I'm going back to school,'' she announced. ''That is all there is left in life for me, now that my friend has been ruthlessly torn from me. In school I can look at her and muse over days departed.''

''You'd better muse over your lessons and sums,'' said Marilla, concealing her delight at this development of the situation. ''If you're going back to school I hope we'll hear no more of breaking slates over people's heads and such carryings-on. Behave yourself and do just what your teacher tells you.''

''I'll try to be a model pupil,'' agreed Anne dolefully. ''There won't be much fun in it, I expect. Mr. Phillips said Minnie Andrews was a model pupil and there isn't a spark of imagination or life in her. She is just dull and poky and never seems to have a good time. But I feel so depressed that perhaps it will come easy to me now. I'm going round by the road. I couldn't bear to go by the Birch Path all alone. I should weep bitter tears if I did.''

Anne was welcomed back to school with open arms. Her imagination had been sorely missed in games, her voice in the singing, and her dramatic ability in the perusal aloud of books at dinner hour. Ruby Gillis smuggled three plums over to her during testament reading; Ella May Macpherson gave her an enormous yellow pansy cut from the covers of a floral catalogue—a species of desk decoration much prized in Avonlea school. Sophia Sloane offered to teach her a perfectly elegant new pattern of knit lace, *so* nice for trimming aprons. Katie Boulter gave her a perfume bottle to keep slate-water in and Julia Bell copied carefully on a piece of pale pink paper, scalloped on the edges, the following effusion:

TO ANNE
When twilight drops her curtain down
And pins it with a star
Remember that you have a friend
Though she may wander far.

"It's so nice to be appreciated," sighed Anne rapturously to Marilla that night.

The girls were not the only scholars who "appreciated" her. When Anne went to her seat after dinner hour—she had been told by Mr. Phillips to sit with the model Minnie Andrews—she found on her desk a big luscious "strawberry apple." Anne caught it up all ready to take a bite, when she remembered that the only place in Avonlea where strawberry apples grew was in the old Blythe orchard on the other side of the Lake of Shining Waters. Anne dropped the apple as if it were a red-hot coal and ostentatiously wiped her fingers on her handkerchief. The apple lay untouched on her desk until the next morning, when little Timothy Andrews, who swept the school and kindled the fire, annexed it as one of his perquisites. Charlie Sloane's slate pencil, gorgeously bedizened with striped red and yellow paper, costing two cents where ordinary pencils cost only one, which he sent up to her after dinner hour, met with a more favorable reception. Anne was graciously pleased to accept it and rewarded the donor with a smile which exalted that infatuated youth straightway into the seventh heaven of delight and caused him to make such fearful errors in his dictation that Mr. Phillips kept him after to rewrite it.

But as,

> *The Caesar's pageant shorn of Brutus' bust*
> *Did but of Rome's best son remind her more*

so the marked absence of any tribute or recognition from Diana Barry, who was sitting with Gertie Pye, embittered Anne's little triumph.

"Diana might just have smiled at me once, I think," she mourned to Marilla that night. But the next morning a note, most fearfully and wonderfully twisted and folded, and a small parcel, were passed across to Anne.

"Dear Anne," ran the former, "Mother says I'm not to play with you or talk to you even in school!. It isn't my fault and don't be cross at me, because I love you as much as ever. I miss you awfully to tell all my secrets to and I don't like Gertie Pye one bit. I made you one of the new bookmarkers out of red tissue paper. They are awfully fashionable now and only three girls in school know how to make them. When you look at it remember

> "Your true friend,
> "DIANA BARRY"

Anne read the note, kissed the bookmark, and despatched a prompt reply back to the other side of the school.

"MY OWN DARLING DIANA:—

"Of course I am not cross at you because you have to obey your mother. Our spirits can commune. I shall keep your lovely present forever. Minnie Andrews is a very nice little girl—although she has no imagination—but after having been Diana's busum friend I cannot be Minnie's. Please excuse mistakes because my spelling isn't very good yet, although much improoved.

> "Yours until death us do part,
> "ANNE or CORDELIA SHIRLEY.

"P.S. I shall sleep with your letter under my pillow tonight.

> "A. or C.S."

Marilla pessimistically expected more trouble since Anne had again begun to go to school. But none developed. Perhaps Anne caught something of the "model" spirit from Minnie Andrews; at least she got on very well with Mr. Phillips thenceforth. She flung herself into her studies heart and soul, determined not to to be outdone in any class by Gilbert Blythe. The rivalry between them was soon apparent; it was entirely good-natured on Gilbert's side; but it is much to be feared that the same thing cannot be said of Anne, who had certainly an unpraiseworthy tenacity for holding grudges. She was as intense in her hatreds as in her loves. She would not stoop to admit that she meant to rival Gilbert in his school work, because that would have been to acknowledge his existence which Anne persistently ignored; but the rivalry was there and honors fluctuated between them. Now Gilbert was head of the spelling class; now Anne, with a toss of her long red braids, spelled him down. One morning Gilbert had all his sums done correctly and had his name written on the blackboard on the roll of honor; the next morning Anne, having wrestled wildly with decimals the entire evening before, would be first. One awful day they were ties and their names were written up together. It was almost as bad as a "take-notice" and Anne's mortification was as evident as Gilbert's satisfaction. When the written examinations at the end of each month were held the suspense was terrible. The first month Gilbert came out three marks ahead. The second Anne beat him by five. But her triumph was marred by the fact that Gilbert congratulated her heartily before the whole school. It would have been ever so much sweeter to her if he had felt the sting of his defeat.

Mr. Phillips might not be a very good teacher; but a pupil so inflexibly determined on learning as Anne was could hardly escape making progress under any kind of a teacher. By the end of the term Anne and Gilbert were both promoted into the fifth class and allowed to begin studying the elements of "the branches"—by which Latin, geometry, French and algebra were meant. In geometry Anne met her Waterloo.

"It's perfectly awful stuff, Marilla," she groaned. "I'm sure I'll never be able to make head or tail of it. There is no scope for imagination in it at all. Mr. Phillips says I'm the worst dunce he ever saw at it. And Gil—I mean some of the others are so smart at it. It is extremely mortifying, Marilla. Even Diana gets along better than I do. But I don't mind being beaten by Diana. Even although we meet as strangers now I still love her with an *inextinguishable* love. It makes me very sad at times to think about her. But really, Marilla, one can't stay sad very long in such an interesting world, can one?"

CHAPTER 18

ANNE TO THE RESCUE

ALL THINGS great are wound up with all things little. At first glance it might not seem that the decision of a certain Canadian Premier to include Prince Edward Island in a political tour could have much or anything to do with the fortunes of little Anne Shirley at Green Gables. But it had.

It was in January the Premier came, to address his loyal supporters and such of his non-supporters as chose to be present at the monster mass meeting held in Charlottetown. Most of the Avonlea people were on the Premier's side of politics; hence, on the night of the meeting nearly all the men and a goodly proportion of the women had gone to town, thirty miles away. Mrs. Rachel Lynde had gone too. Mrs. Rachel Lynde was a red-hot politician and couldn't have believed that the political rally could be carried through without her, although she was on the opposite side of politics. So she went to town and took her husband—Thomas would be useful in looking after the horse—and Marilla Cuthbert with her. Marilla had a sneaking interest in politics herself, and as she thought it might be her only chance to see a real live Premier, she promptly took it, leaving Anne and Matthew to keep house until her return the following day.

Hence, while Marilla and Mrs. Rachel were enjoying themselves hugely at the mass meeting, Anne and Matthew had the cheerful kitchen at Green Gables all to themselves. A bright fire was glowing in the old-fashioned Waterloo stove and blue-white frost crystals were shining on the window-panes. Matthew nodded over a *Farmers' Advocate* on the sofa and Anne at the table studied her lessons with grim determination, despite sundry wistful glances at the clock shelf, where lay a new book that Jane Andrews had lent her that day. Jane had assured her that it was warranted to produce any number of thrills, or words to that effect, and Anne's fingers tingled to reach out for it. But that would mean Gilbert Bythe's triumph on the morrow. Anne turned her back on the clock shelf and tried to imagine it wasn't there.

"Matthew, did you ever study geometry when you went to school?"

"Well now, no, I didn't," said Matthew, coming out of his doze with a start.

"I wish you had," sighed Anne, "because then you'd be able to sympathize with me. You can't sympathize properly if you've never studied it. It is casting a cloud over my whole life. I'm such a dunce at it, Matthew."

"Well now, I dunno," said Matthew soothingly. "I guess you're all right at anything. Mr. Phillips told me last week in Blair's store at Carmody that you was the smartest scholar in school and was making rapid progress. 'Rapid progress' was his very words. There's them as runs down Teddy Phillips and says he ain't much of a teacher; but I guess he's all right."

Matthew would have thought any one who praised Anne was "all right."

"I'm sure I'd get on better with geometry if only he wouldn't change the letters," complained Anne. "I learn the proposition off by heart, and then he draws it on the blackboard and puts different letters from what are in the book and I get all mixed up. I don't think a teacher should take such a mean advantage, do you? We're studying agriculture now and I've found out at last what makes the roads red. It's a great comfort. I wonder how Marilla and Mrs. Lynde are enjoying themselves. Mrs. Lynde says Canada is going to the dogs the way things are being run at Ottawa, and that it's an awful warning to the electors. She says if women were allowed to vote we would soon see a blessed change. What way do you vote, Matthew?"

"Conservative," said Matthew promptly. To vote Conservative was part of Matthew's religion.

"Then I'm Conservative too," said Anne decidely. "I'm glad, because Gil—because some of the boys in school are Grits. I guess Mr. Phillips is a Grit too, because Prissy Andrews' father is one, and Ruby Gillis says that when a man is courting he always has to agree with the girl's mother in religion and her father in politics. Is that true, Matthew?"

"Well now, I dunno," said Matthew.

"Did you ever go courting, Matthew?"

"Well, now, no, I dunno's I ever did," said Matthew, who had certainly never thought of such a thing in his whole existence.

Anne reflected with her chin in her hands.

"It must be rather interesting, don't you think, Matthew? Ruby Gillis says when she grows up she's going to have ever so many beaus on the string and have them all crazy about her; but I think that would be too exciting. I'd rather have just one in his right mind. But Ruby Gillis knows a great deal about such matters because she has so many big sisters, and Mrs. Lynde says the Gillis girls have gone off like hot cakes. Mr. Phillips goes up to see Prissy Andrews nearly every evening. He says it is to help her with her lessons, but Miranda Sloane is studying for Queen's, too, and I should think she needed help a lot more than Prissy because she's ever so much stupider, but he never goes to help her in the evenings at all. There are a great many things in this world that I can't understand very well, Matthew."

"Well now, I dunno as I comprehend them all myself," acknowledged Matthew.

"Well, I suppose I must finish up my lessons. I won't allow myself to open that new book Jane lent me until I'm through. But it's a terrible temptation, Matthew. Even when I turn my back on it I can see it there just as plain. Jane said she cried herself sick over it. I love a book that makes me cry. But I think I'll carry that book into the sitting-room and lock it in the jam closet and give you the key. And you must *not* give it to me, Matthew, until my lessons are done, not even if I implore you on my bended knees. It's all very well to say resist temptation, but it's ever so much easier to resist it if you can't get the key. And then shall I run down the cellar and get some russets, Matthew? Wouldn't you like some russets?''

''Well now, I dunno but what I would,'' said Matthew, who never ate russets but knew Anne's weakness for them.

Just as Anne emerged triumphantly from the cellar with her plateful of russets came the sound of flying footsteps on the icy board walk outside and the next moment the kitchen door was flung open and in rushed Diana Barry, white-faced and breathless, with a shawl wrapped hastily around her head. Anne promptly let go of her candle and plate in her surprise, and plate, candle, and apples crashed together down the cellar ladder and were found at the bottom embedded in melted grease, the next day, by Marilla, who gathered them up and thanked mercy the house hadn't been set on fire.

''Whatever is the matter, Diana?'' cried Anne. ''Has your mother relented at last?''

''Oh, Anne, do come quick,'' implored Diana nervously. ''Minnie May is awful sick—she's got croup, Young Mary Joe says—and father and mother are away to town and there's nobody to go for the doctor. Minnie May is awful bad and Young Mary Joe doesn't know what to do—and oh, Anne, I'm so scared!''

Matthew, without a word, reached out for cap and coat, slipped past Diana and away into the darkness of the yard.

''He's gone to harness the sorrel mare to go to Carmody for the doctor,'' said Anne, who was hurrying on hood and jacket. ''I know it as well as if he'd said so. Matthew and I are such kindred spirits I can read his thoughts without words at all.''

''I don't believe he'll find the doctor at Carmody,'' sobbed Diana. ''I know that Doctor Blair went to town and I guess Doctor Spencer would go too. Young Mary Joe never saw anybody with croup and Mrs. Lynde is away. Oh, Anne!''

''Don't cry, Di,'' said Anne cheerily. ''I know exactly what to do for croup. You forget that Mrs. Hammond had twins three times. When you look after three pairs of twins you naturally get a lot of experience. They all had croup regularly. Just wait till I get the ipecac bottle—you mayn't have any at your house. Come on now.''

The two litle girls hastened out hand in hand and hurried through Lovers' Lane and across the crusted field beyond, for the snow was too deep to go by the shorter wood way. Anne, although sincerely sorry for Minnie May, was far from being insensible to the romance of the situation and to the sweetness of once more sharing that romance with a kindred spirit.

The night was clear and frosty, all ebony of shadow and silver of snowy slope; big stars were shining over the silent fields; here and there the dark pointed firs stood up with snow powdering their branches and the wind whistling through them. Anne thought it was truly delightful to go skimming through all this mystery and loveliness with your bosom friend who had been so long estranged.

Minnie May, aged three, was really very sick. She lay on the kitchen sofa, feverish and restless, while her hoarse breathing could be heard all over the house. Young Mary Joe, a buxom, broad-faced French girl from the Creek, whom Mrs. Barry had engaged to stay with the children during her absence, was helpless and bewildered, quite incapable of thinking what to do, or doing it if she thought of it.

Anne went to work with skill and promptness.

''Minnie may has croup all right; she's pretty bad, but I've seen them worse. First we must have lots of hot water. I declare, Diana, there isn't more than a cupful in the kettle! There, I've filled it up, and, Mary Joe, you may put some wood in the stove. I don't want to hurt your feelings, but it seems to me you might have thought of this before if you'd any imagination. Now, I'll undress Minnie May and put her to bed, and you try to find some soft flannel cloths, Diana. I'm going to give her a dose of ipecac first of all.''

Minnie May did not take kindly to the ipecac, but Anne had not brought up three pairs of twins for nothing. Down that ipecac went, not only once, but many times during the long, anxious night when the two little girls worked patiently over the suffering Minnie May, and Young Mary Joe, honestly anxious to do all she could, kept on a roaring fire and heated more water than would have been needed for a hospital of croupy babies.

It was three o'clock when Matthew came with the doctor, for he had been obliged to go all the way to Spencervale for one. But the pressing need for assistance was past. Minnie May was much better and was sleeping soundly.

''I was awfully near giving up in despair,'' explained Anne. ''She got worse and worse until she was sicker than ever the Hammond twins were, even the last pair. I actually thought she was going to choke to death. I gave her every drop of ipecac in that bottle, and when the last dose went down I said to myself—not to Diana or Young Mary Joe, because I didn't want to worry them any more than they were worried, but I had to say it to myself just to relieve my feelings—'This is the last lingering hope and I fear 'tis a vain one.' But in about three minutes she coughed up the phlegm and began to get better right away. You must just imagine my relief, doctor, because I can't express it in words. You know there are some things that cannot be expressed in words.''

"Yes, I know,'' nodded the doctor. He looked at Anne as if he were thinking some things about her that couldn't be expressed in words. Later on, however, he expressed them to Mr. and Mrs. Barry.

"That little red-headed girl they have over at Cuthbert's is as smart as they make 'em. I tell you she saved that baby's life, for it would have been too late by the time I got here. She seems to have a skill and presence of mind perfectly wonderful in a child of her age. I never saw anything like the eyes of her when she was explaining the case out to me.''

Anne had gone home in the wonderful, white-frosted winter morning, heavy-eyed from loss of sleep, but still talking unweariedly to Matthew as they crossed the long white field and walked under the glittering fairy arch of the Lovers' Lane maples.

"Oh, Matthew, isn't it a wonderful morning? The world looks like something God had just imagined for His own pleasure, doesn't it? Those trees look as if I could blow them away with a breath—pouf! I'm so glad I live in a world where there are white frosts, aren't you? And I'm so glad Mrs. Hammond had three pairs of twins after all. If she hadn't I mightn't have known what to do for Minnie May. I'm real sorry I was ever cross with Mrs. Hammond for having twins. But, oh, Matthew, I'm so sleepy. I can't go to school. I just know I couldn't keep my eyes open and I'd be so stupid. But I hate to stay home for Gil—some of the others will get head of the class, and it's so hard to get up again—although of course the harder it is the more satisfaction you have when you do get up, haven't you?''

"Well now, I guess you'll manage all right,'' said Matthew, looking at Anne's white little face and the dark shadows under her eyes. "You just go right to bed and have a good sleep. I'll do all the chores.''

Anne accordingly went to bed and slept so long and soundly that it was well on in the white and rosy winter afternoon when she awoke and descended to the kitchen where Marilla, who had arrived home in the meantime, was sitting knitting.

"Oh, did you see the Premier?" exclaimed Anne at once. "What did he look like, Marilla?"

"Well, he never got to be Premier on account of his looks," said Marilla. "Such a nose as that man had! But he can speak. I was proud of being a Conservative. Rachel Lynde, of course, being a Liberal, had no use for him. Your dinner is in the oven, Anne; and you can get yourself some blue plum preserve out of the pantry. I guess you're hungry. Matthew has been telling me about last night. I must say it was fortunate you knew what to do. I wouldn't have had any idea myself, for I never saw a case of croup. There now, never mind talking till you've had your dinner. I can tell by the look of you that you're just full up with speeches, but they'll keep."

Marilla had something to tell Anne, but she did not tell it just then, for she knew if she did Anne's consequent excitement would lift her clear out of the region of such material matters as appetite or dinner. Not until Anne had finished her saucer of blue plums did Marilla say:

"Mrs. Barry was here this afternoon, Anne. She wanted to see you, but I wouldn't wake you up. She says you saved Minnie May's life, and she is very sorry she acted as she did in that affair of the currant wine. She says she knows now you didn't mean to set Diana drunk, and she hopes you'll forgive her and be good friends with Diana again. You're to go over this evening if you like, for Diana can't stir outside the door on account of a bad cold she caught last night. Now, Anne Shirley, for pity's sake don't fly clean up into the air."

The warning seemed not unnecessary, so uplifted and aerial was Anne's expression and attitude as she sprang to her feet, her face irradiated with the flame of her spirit.

"Oh, Marilla, can I go right now—without washing my dishes? I'll wash them when I come back, but I cannot tie myself down to anything so unromantic as dish-washing at this thrilling moment."

"Yes, yes, run along," said Marilla indulgently. "Anne Shirley—are you crazy? Come back this instant and put something on you. I might as well call to the wind. She's gone without a cap or wrap. Look at her tearing through the orchard with her hair streaming. It'll be a mercy if she doesn't catch her death of cold."

Anne came dancing home in the purple winter twilight across the snowy places. Afar in the southwest was the great shimmering, pearl-like sparkle of an evening star in a sky that was pale golden and ethereal rose over gleaming white spaces and dark glens of spruce. The tinkles of sleigh-bells among the snowy hills came like elfin chimes through the frosty air, but their music was not sweeter than the song in Anne's heart and on her lips.

"You see before you a perfectly happy person, Marilla," she announced. "I'm perfectly happy—yes, in spite of my red hair. Just at present I have a soul above red hair. Mrs. Barry kissed me and cried and said she was so sorry and she could never repay me. I felt fearfuly embarrassed, Marilla, but I just said as politely as I could, 'I have no hard feelings for you, Mrs. Barry. I assure you once for all that I did not mean to intoxicate Diana and henceforth I shall cover the past with the mantle of oblivion.' That was a pretty dignified way of speaking, wasn't it, Marilla? I felt that I was heaping coals of fire on Mrs. Barry's head. And Diana and I had a lovely afternoon. Diana showed me a new fancy crochet stitch her aunt over at Carmody taught her. Not a soul in Avonlea knows it but us, and we pledged a solemn vow never to reveal it to any one else. Diana gave me a beautiful card with a wreath of roses on it and a verse of poetry:

> *If you love me as I love you*
> *Nothing but death can part us two.*

And that is true, Marilla. We're going to ask Mr. Phillips to let us sit together in school again, and Gertie Pye can go with Minnie Andrews. We had an elegant tea. Mrs. Barry had the very best china set out, Marilla, just as if I was real company. I can't tell you what a thrill it gave me. Nobody ever used their very best china on my account before. And we had fruit-cake and pound-cake and doughnuts and two kinds of preserves, Marilla. And Mrs. Barry asked me if I took tea and said, 'Pa, why don't you pass the biscuits to Anne?' It must be lovely to be grown up, Marilla, when just being treated as if you were is so nice."

"I don't know about that," said Marilla with a brief sigh.

"Well, anyway, when I am grown up," said Anne decidely, "I'm always going to talk to little girls as if they were, too, and I'll never laugh when they use big words. I know from sorrowful experience how that hurts one's feelings. After tea Diana and I made taffy. The taffy wasn't very good, I suppose because neither Diana nor I had ever made any before. Diana left me to stir it while she buttered the plates and I forgot and let it burn; and then when we set it out on the platform to cool the cat walked over one plate and that had to be thrown away. But the making of it was splendid fun. Then when I came home Mrs. Barry asked me to come over as often as I could and Diana stood at the window and threw kisses to me all the way down to Lovers' Lane. I assure you, Marilla, that I feel like praying tonight and I'm going to think out a special brand new prayer in honor of the occasion.''

------------ **CHAPTER 19** ------------

A CONCERT, A CATASTROPHE, AND A CONFESSION

"MARILLA, CAN I go over to see Diana just for a minute?'' asked Anne, running breathlessly down from the east gable one February evening.

"I don't see what you want to be traipsing about after dark for,'' said Marilla shortly. "You and Diana walked home from school together and then stood down there in the snow for half an hour more, your tongues going the whole blessed time, clickety-clack. So I don't think you're very badly off to see her again.''

"But she wants to see me,'' pleaded Anne. "She has something very important to tell me.''

"How do you know she has?''

"Because she just signalled to me from her window. We have arranged a way to signal with our candles and cardboard. We set the candle on the windowsill and make flashes by passing the cardboard back and forth. So many flashes mean a certain thing. It was my idea, Marilla.''

"I'll warrant you it was,'' said Marilla emphatically. "And the next thing you'll be setting fire to the curtains with your signalling nonsense.''

"Oh, we're very careful, Marilla. And it's so interesting. Two flashes mean, 'Are you there?' Three means 'yes' and four 'no.' Five mean, 'Come over as soon as possible because I have something important to reveal.' Diana has just signalled five flashes, and I'm really suffering to know what it is.''

"Well, you needn't suffer any longer," said Marilla sarcastically. "You can go, but you're to be back here in just ten minutes, remember that."

Anne did remember it and was back in the stipulated time, although probably no mortal will ever know just what it cost her to confine the discussion of Diana's important communication within the limits of ten minutes. But at least she had made good use of them.

"Oh, Marilla, what do you think? You know tomorrow is Diana's birthday. Well, her mother told her she could ask me to go home with her from school and stay all night with her. And her cousins are coming over from Newbridge in a big pung sleigh to go to the Debating Club concert at the hall tomorrow night. And they are going to take Diana and me to the concert—if you'll let me go, that is. You will, won't you, Marilla? Oh, I feel so excited."

"You can calm down then, because you're not going. You're better at home in your own bed, and as for that Club concert, it's all nonsense, and little girls should not be allowed to go out to such places at all."

"I'm sure the Debating Club is a most respectable affair," pleaded Anne.

"I'm not saying it isn't. But you're not going to begin gadding about to concerts and staying out all hours of the night. Pretty doings for children. I'm surprised at Mrs. Barry's letting Diana go."

"But it's such a very special occasion," mourned Anne, on the verge of tears. "Diana has only one birthday in a year. It isn't as if birthdays were common things, Marilla. Prissy Andrews is going to recite 'Curfew Must Not Ring Tonight.' That is such a good moral piece, Marilla, I'm sure it would do me lots of good to hear it. And the choir are going to sing four lovely pathetic songs that are pretty near as good as hymns. And oh, Marilla, the minister is going to take part; yes, indeed, he is; he's going to give an address. That will be just about the same thing as a sermon. Please, mayn't I go, Marilla?"

"You heard what I said, Anne, didn't you? Take off your boots now and go to bed. It's past eight."

"There's just one more thing, Marilla," said Anne, with the air of producing the last shot in her locker. "Mrs. Barry told Diana that we might sleep in the spare-room bed. Think of the honor of your little Anne being put in the spare-room bed."

"It's an honor you'll have to get along without. Go to bed, Anne, and don't let me hear another word out of you."

When Anne, with tears rolling over her cheeks, had gone sorrowfully upstairs, Matthew, who had been apparently sound asleep on the lounge during the whole dialogue, opened his eyes and said decidedly:

"Well now, Marilla, I think you ought to let Anne go."

"I don't then," retorted Marilla. "Who's bringing this child up, Matthew, you or me?"

"Well now, you," admitted Matthew.

"Don't interfere then."

"Well now, I ain't interfering. It ain't interfering to have your own opinion. And my opinion is that you ought to let Anne go."

"You'd think I ought to let Anne go to the moon if she took the notion, I've no doubt," was Marilla's amiable rejoinder. "I might have let her spend the night with Diana, if that was all. But I don't approve of this concert plan. She'd go there and catch cold like as not, and have her head filled up with nonsense and excitement. It would unsettle her for a week. I understand that child's disposition and what's good for it better than you, Matthew."

"I think you ought to let Anne go," repeated Matthew firmly. Argument was not his strong point, but holding fast to his opinion certainly was. Marilla gave a gasp of helplessness and took refuge in silence. The next morning, when Anne was washing the breakfast dishes in the pantry, Matthew paused on his way out to the barn to say to Marilla again:

"I think you ought to let Anne go, Marilla.

For a moment Marilla looked things not lawful to be uttered. Then she yielded to the inevitable and said tartly:

"Very well, she can go, since nothing else'll please you."

Anne flew out of the pantry, dripping dish-cloth in hand.

"Oh, Marilla, Marilla, say those blessed words again."

"I guess once is enough to say them. This is Matthew's doings and I wash my hands of it. If you catch pneumonia sleeping in a strange bed or coming out of that hot hall in the middle of the night, don't blame me, blame Matthew. Anne Shirley, you're dripping greasy water all over the floor. I never saw such a careless child."

"Oh, I know I'm a great trial to you, Marilla," said Anne repentantly. "I make so many mistakes. But then just think of all the mistakes I don't make, although I might. I'll get some sand and scrub up the spots before I go to school. Oh, Marilla, my heart was just set on going to that concert. I never was to a concert in my life, and when the other girls talk about them in school I feel so out of it. You didn't know just how I felt about it, but you see Matthew did. Matthew understands me, and it's so nice to be understood, Marilla.''

Anne was too excited to do herself justice as to lessons that morning in school. Gilbert Blythe spelled her down in class and left her clear out of sight in mental arithmetic. Anne's consequent humiliation was less than it might have been, however, in view of the concert and the spare-room bed. She and Diana talked so constantly about it all day that with a stricter teacher than Mr. Phillips dire disgrace must inevitably have been their portion.

Anne felt that she could not have borne it if she had not been going to the concert, for nothing else was discussed that day in school. The Avonlea Debating Club, which met fortnightly all winter, had had several smaller free entertainments; but this was to be a big affair, admission ten cents, in aid of the library. The Avonlea young people had been practising for weeks, and all the scholars were especially interested in it by reason of older brothers and sisters who were going to take part. Everybody in school over nine years of age expected to go, except Carrie Sloane, whose father shared Marilla's opinions about small girls going out to night concerts. Carrie Sloane cried into her grammar all the afternoon and felt that life was not worth living.

For Anne the real excitement began with the dismissal of school and increased therefrom in crescendo until it reached to a crash of positive ecstasy in the concert itself. They had a ''perfectly elegant tea;'' and then came the delicious occupation of dressing in Diana's little room upstairs. Diana did Anne's front hair in the new pompadour style and Anne tied Diana's bows with the especial knack she possessed; and they experimented with at least half a dozen different ways of arranging their back hair. At last they were ready, cheeks scarlet and eyes glowing with excitement.

True, Anne could not help a little pang when she contrasted her plain black tam and shapeless, tight-sleeved home-made gray cloth coat with Diana's jaunty fur cap and smart little jacket. But she remembered in time that she had an imagination and could use it.

Then Diana's cousins, the Murrays from Newbridge, came; they all crowded into the big pung sleigh, among straw and furry robes. Anne revelled in the drive to the hall, slipping along over the satin-smooth roads with the snow crisping under the runners. There was a magnificent sunset, and the snowy hills and deep blue water of the St. Lawrence Gulf seemed to rim in the splendor like a huge bowl of pearl and sapphire brimmed with wine and fire. Tinkles of sleigh-bells and distant laughter, that seemed like the mirth of wood elves, came from every quarter.

"Oh, Diana," breathed Anne, squeezing Diana's mittened hand under the fur robe, "isn't it all like a beautiful dream? Do I really look the same as usual? I feel so different that it seems to me it must show in my looks."

"You look awfully nice," said Diana, who having just received a compliment from one of her cousins, felt that she ought to pass it on. "You've got the loveliest color."

The program that night was a series of "thrills" for at least one listener in the audience, and, as Anne assured Diana, every succeeding thrill was thrillier than the last. When Prissy Andrews, attired in a new pink silk waist with a string of pearls about her smooth white throat and real carnations in her hair—rumor whispered that the master had sent all the way to town for them for her—"climbed the slimy ladder, dark without one ray of light," Anne shivered in luxurious sympathy; when the choir sang "Far Above the Gentle Daisies" Anne gazed at the ceiling as if it were frescoed with angels; when Sam Sloane proceeded to explain and illustate "How Sockery Set a Hen" Anne laughed until people sitting near her laughed too, more out of sympathy with her than with amusement at a selection that was rather threadbare even in Avonlea; and when Mr. Phillips gave Mark Antony's oration over the dead body of Caesar in the most heart-stirring tones—looking at Prissy Andrews at the end of every sentence—Anne felt that she could rise and mutiny on the spot if but one roman citizen led the way.

Only one number on the program failed to interest her. When Gilbert Blythe recited "Bingen on the Rhine" Anne picked up Rhoda Murray's library book and read it until he had finished, when she sat rigidly stiff and motionless while Diana clapped her hands until they tingled.

It was eleven when they got home, sated with dissipation, but with the exceeding sweet pleasure of talking it all over still to come. Everybody seemed asleep and the house was dark and silent. Anne and Diana tiptoed into the parlor, a long narrow room out of which the spare room opened. It was pleasantly warm and dimly lighted by the embers of a fire in the grate.

"Let's undress here," said Diana. "It's so nice and warm."

"Hasn't it been a delightful time?" sighed Anne rapturously "It must be splendid to get up and recite there. Do you suppose we will ever be asked to do it, Diana?"

"Yes, of course, some day. They're always wanting the big scholars to recite. Gilbert Bythe does often and he's only two years older than us. Oh, Anne, how could you pretend not to listen to him? When he came to the line,

There's another, not *a sister*

he looked right down at you.''

''Diana,'' said Anne with dignity, ''you are my bosom friend, but I cannot allow even you to speak to me of that person. Are you ready for bed? Let's run a race and see who'll get to the bed first.''

The suggestion appealed to Diana. The two little white-clad figures flew down the long room, through the spare-room door, and bounded on the bed at the same moment. And then—something—moved beneath them, there was a gasp and a cry—and somebody said in muffled accents:

''Merciful goodness!''

Anne and Diana were never able to tell just how they got off that bed and out of the room. They only knew that after one frantic rush they found themselves tiptoeing shiveringly upstairs.

''Oh, who was it—*what* was it?'' whispered Anne, her teeth chattering with cold and fright.

''It was Aunt Josephine,'' said Diana, gasping with laughter. ''Oh, Anne, it was Aunt Josephine, however she came to be there. Oh, and I know she will be furious. It's dreadful—it's really dreadful—but did you ever know anything so funny, Anne?''

''Who is your Aunt Josephine?''

''She's father's aunt and she lives in Charlottetown. She's awfully old—seventy anyhow—and I don't believe she was *ever* a little girl. We were expecting her out for a visit, but not so soon. She's awfully prim and proper and she'll scold dreadfully about this, I know. Well, we'll have to sleep with Minnie May—and you can't think how she kicks.''

Miss Josephine Barry did not appear at the early breakfast the next morning. Mrs. Barry smiled kindly at the two little girls.

''Did you have a good time last night? I tried to stay awake until you came home, for I wanted to tell you Aunt Josephine had come and that you would have to go upstairs after all, but I was so tired I fell alseep. I hope you didn't disturb your aunt, Diana.''

Diana preserved a discreet silence, but she and Anne exchanged furtive smiles of guilty amusement across the table. Anne hurried home after breakfast and so remained in blissful ignorance of the disturbance which presently resulted in the Barry household until the late afternoon, when she went down to Mrs. Lynde's on an errand for Marilla.

"So you and Diana nearly frightened poor old Miss Barry to death last night?" said Mrs. Lynde severely, but with a twinkle in her eye. "Mrs. Barry was here a few minutes ago on her way to Carmody. She's feeling real worried over it. Old Miss Barry was in a terrible temper when she got up this morning—and Josephine Barry's temper is no joke, I can tell you that. She wouldn't speak to Diana at all."

"It wasn't Diana's fault," said Anne contritely. "It was mine. I suggested racing to see who would get into bed first."

"I knew it!" said Mrs. Lynde with the exultation of a correct guesser. "I knew the idea came out of your head. Well, it's made a nice lot of trouble, that's what. Old Miss Barry came out to stay for a month, but she declared she won't stay another day and is going right back to town tomorrow, Sunday and all as it is. She'd have gone today if they could have taken her. She had promised to pay for a quarter's music lessons for Diana, but now she is determined to do nothing at all for such a tomboy. Oh, I guess they had a lively time of it there this morning. The Barrys must feel cut up. Old Miss Barry is rich and they'd like to keep on the good side of her. Of course, Mrs. Barry didn't say just that to me, but I'm a pretty good judge of human nature, that's what."

"I'm such an unlucky girl," mourned Anne. "I'm always getting into scrapes myself and getting my best friends—people I'd shed my heart's blood for—into them, too. Can you tell me why it is so, Mrs. Lynde?"

"It's because you're too heedless and impulsive, child, that's what. You never stop to think—whatever comes into your head to say or do you say or do it without a moment's reflection."

"Oh, but that's the best of it," protested Anne. "Something just flashes into your mind, so exciting, and you must out with it. If you stop to think it over you spoil it all. Haven't you never felt that yourself, Mrs. Lynde?"

No, Mrs. Lynde had not. She shook her head sagely.

"You must learn to think a little, Anne, that's what. The proverb you need to go by is 'look before you leap'—especially into spare-room beds."

Mrs. Lynde laughed comfortably over her mild joke, but Anne remained pensive. She saw nothing to laugh at in the situation, which to her eyes appeared very serious. When she left Mrs. Lynde's she took her way across the crusted fields to Orchard Slope. Diana met her at the kitchen door.

"Your Aunt Josephine was very cross about it, wasn't she?" whispered Anne.

"Yes," answered Diana, stifling a giggle with an apprehensive glance over her shoulder at the closed sitting-room door. "She was fairly dancing with rage, Anne. Oh, how she scolded. She said I was the worst-behaved girl she ever saw and that my parents ought to be ashamed of the way they had brought me up. She says she won't stay and I'm sure I don't care. But father and mother do."

"Why didn't you tell them it was my fault?" demanded Anne.

"It's likely I'd do such a thing, isn't it?" said Diana with just scorn. "I'm no telltale, Anne Shirley, and anyhow I was just as much to blame as you."

"Well, I'm going in to tell her myself," said Anne resolutely.

Diana stared.

"Anne Shirley, you'd never! why——she'll eat you alive!"

"Don't frighten me any more than I am frightened," implored Anne. "I'd rather walk up to a cannon's mouth. But I've got to do it, Diana. It was my fault and I've got to confess. I've had practice in confessing fortunately."

"Well, she's in the room," said Diana. "You can go in if you want to. I wouldn't dare. And I don't believe you'll do a bit of good."

With this encouragement Anne bearded the lion in its den—that is to say, walked resolutely up to the sitting-room door and knocked faintly. A sharp "Come in" followed.

Miss Josephine Barry, thin, prim and rigid, was knitting fiercely by the fire, her wrath quite unappeased and her eyes snapping through her gold-rimmed glasses. She wheeled around in her chair expecting to see Diana, and beheld a white-faced girl whose great eyes were brimmed up with a mixture of desperate courage and shrinking terror.

"Who are you?" demanded Miss Josephine Barry without ceremony.

"I'm Anne of Green Gables," said the small visitor tremulously, clasping her hands with her characteristic gesture, "and I've come to confess, if you please."

"Confess what?"

"That it was all my fault about jumping into bed on you last night. I suggested it. Diana would never have thought of such a thing, I am sure. Diana is a very ladylike girl, Miss Barry. So you must see how unjust it is to blame her."

"Oh, I must, hey? I rather think Diana did her share of the

jumping at least. Such carryings-on in a respectable house!''

"But we were only in fun," persisted Anne. "I think you ought to forgive us, Miss Barry, now that we've apologized. And anyhow, please forgive Diana and let her have her music lessons. Diana's heart is set on her music lessons, Miss Barry, and I know too well what it is to set your heart on a thing and not get it. If you must be cross with anyone, be cross with me. I've been so used in my early days to having people cross at me that I can endure it much better than Diana can."

Much of the snap had gone out of the old lady's eyes by this time and was replaced by a twinkle of amused interest. But she still said severely:

"I don't think it is any excuse for you that you were only in fun. Little girls never indulged in that kind of fun when I was young. You don't know what it is to be awakened out of a sound sleep, after a long and arduous journey, by two great girls coming bounce down on you."

"I don't *know*, but I can *imagine*," said Anne eagerly. "I'm sure it must have been very disturbing. But then, there is our side of it too. Have you any imagination, Miss Barry? If you have, just put yourself in our place. We didn't know there was anybody in that bed and you nearly scared us to death. It was simply awful the way we felt. And then we couldn't sleep in the spare room after being promised. I suppose you are used to sleeping in spare rooms. But just imagine what you would feel like if you were a little orphan girl who had never had such an honor."

All the snap had gone by this time. Miss Barry actually laughed— a sound which caused Diana, waiting in speechless anxiety in the kitchen outside, to give a great gasp of relief.

"I'm afraid my imagination is a little rusty—it's so long since I used it," she said. "I dare say your claim to sympathy is just as strong as mine. It all depends on the way we look at it. Sit down here and tell me about yourself."

"I am very sorry I can't," said Anne firmly. "I would like to, because you seem like an interesting lady, and you might even be a kindred spirit although you don't look very much like it. But it is my duty to go home to Miss Marilla Cuthbert. Miss Marilla Cuthbert is a very kind lady who has taken me to bring up properly. She is doing her best, but it is very discouraging work. You must not blame her because I jumped on the bed. But before I go I do wish you would tell me if you will forgive Diana and stay just a long as you meant to in Avonlea."

"I think perhaps I will if you will come over and talk to me occasionally," said Miss Barry.

That evening Miss Barry gave Diana a silver bangle bracelet and told the senior members of the household that she had unpacked her valise.

"I've made up my mind to stay simply for the sake of getting better acquainted with that Anne-girl," she said frankly. "She amuses me, and at my time of life an amusing person is a rarity."

Marilla's only comment when she heard the story was, "I told you so." This was for Matthew's benefit.

Miss Barry stayed her month out and over. She was a more agreeable guest than usual, for Anne kept her in good humor. They became firm friends.

When Miss Barry went away she said:

"Remember, you Anne-girl, when you come to town you're to visit me and I'll put you in my very sparest spare-room bed to sleep."

"Miss Barry was a kindred spirit, after all," Anne confided to Marilla. "You wouldn't think so to look at her, but she is. You don't find it right out at first, as in Matthew's case, but after a while you come to see it. Kindred spirits are not so scarce as I used to think. It's splendid to find out there are so many of them in the world."

CHAPTER 20

A GOOD IMAGINATION GONE WRONG

SPRING HAD come once more to Green Gables—the beautiful, capricious, reluctant Canadian spring, lingering along through April and May in a succession of sweet, fresh, chilly days, with pink sunsets and miracles of resurrection and growth. The maples in Lovers' Lane were red-budded and little curly ferns pushed up around the Dryad's Bubble. Away up in the barrens, behind Mr. Silas Sloane's place, the Mayflowers blossomed out, pink and white stars of sweetness under their brown leaves. All the school girls and boys had one golden afternoon gathering them, coming home in the clear, echoing twilight with arms and baskets full of flowery spoil.

"I'm so sorry for people who live in lands where there are no

Mayflowers," said Anne. "Diana says perhaps they have something better, but there couldn't be anything better than Mayflowers, could there, Marilla? And Diana says if they don't know what they are like they don't miss them. But I think that is the saddest thing of all. I think it would be *tragic*, Marilla, not to know what Mayflowers are like and *not* to miss them. Do you know what I think Mayflowers are, Marilla? I think they must be the soul of the flowers that died last summer and this is their heaven. But we had a splendid time today, Marilla. We had our lunch down in a big mossy hollow by an old well—such a *romantic* spot. Charlie Sloane dared Arty Gillis to jump over it, and Arty did because he wouldn't take a dare. Nobody would in school. It is very *fashionable* to dare. Mr. Phillips gave all the Mayflowers he found to Prissy Andrews and I heard him say 'sweets to the sweet.' He got that out of a book, I know; but it shows he has some imagination. I was offered some Mayflowers too, but I rejected them with scorn. I can't tell you the person's name because I have vowed never to let it cross my lips. We made wreaths of the Mayflowers and put them on our hats; and when the time came to go home we marched in procession down the road, two by two, with our bouquets and wreaths, singing 'My Home on the Hill.' Oh, it was so thrilling, Marilla. All Mr. Silas Sloane's folks rushed out to see us and everybody we met on the road stopped and stared after us. We made a real sensation."

"Not much wonder! Such silly doings!" was Marilla's response.

After the Mayflowers came the violets, and Violet Vale was empurpled with them. Anne walked through it on her way to school with reverent steps and worshipping eyes, as if she trod on holy ground.

"Somehow," she told Diana, "when I'm going through here I don't really care whether Gil—whether anybody gets ahead of me in class or not. But when I'm up in school it's all different and I care as much as ever. There's such a lot of different Annes in me. I sometimes think that is why I'm such a troublesome person. If I was just the one Anne it would be ever so much more comfortable, but then it wouldn't be half so interesting."

One June evening, when the orchards were pink-blossomed again, when the frogs were singing silverly sweet in the marshes about the head of the Lake of Shining Waters, and the air as full of the savor of clover fields and balsamic fir woods, Anne was sitting by her gable window. She had been studying her lessons, but it had grown too dark to see the book, so she had fallen into wide-eyed reverie, looking out past the boughs of the Snow Queen, once more bestarred with its tufts of blossom.

In all essential respects the little gable chamber was unchanged. The walls were as white, the pincushion as hard, the chairs as stiffly and yellowly upright as ever. Yet the whole character of the room was altered. It was full of a new vital, pulsing personality that seemed to pervade it and to be quite independent of schoolgirl books and dresses and ribbons, and even of the cracked blue jug full of apple blossoms on the table. It was as if all the dreams, sleeping and waking, of its vivid occupant had taken a visible although immaterial form and had tapestried the bare room with splendid filmy tissues of rainbow and moonshine. Presently Marilla came briskly in with some of Anne's freshly ironed school aprons. She hung them over a chair and sat down with a short sigh. She had had one of her headaches that afternoon, and although the pain had gone she felt weak and "tuckered out," as she expressed it. Anne looked at her with eyes limpid with sympathy.

"I do truly wish I could have had the headache in your place, Marilla. I would have endured it joyfully for your sake."

"I guess you did your part in attending to the work and letting me rest," said Marilla. "You seem to have got on fairly well and made fewer mistakes than usual. Of course it wasn't exactly necessary to starch Matthew's handkerchiefs! And most people when they put a pie in the oven to warm up for dinner take it out and eat it when it gets hot instead of leaving it to be burned to a crisp. But that doesn't seem to be your way evidently."

Headaches always left Marilla somewhat sarcastic.

"Oh, I'm so sorry," said Anne penitently. "I never thought about that pie from the moment I put it in the oven till now, although I felt *instinctively* that there was something missing on the dinner table. I was firmly resolved, when you left me in charge this morning, not to imagine anything, but keep my thoughts on facts. I did pretty well until I put the pie in, and then an irresistible temptation came to me to imagine I was an enchanted princess shut up in a lonely tower with a handsome knight riding to my rescue on a coal-black steed. So that is how I came to forget the pie. I didn't know I starched the handkerchiefs. All the time I was ironing I was trying to think of a name for a new island Diana and I have discovered up the brook. It's the most ravishing spot, Marilla. There are two maple trees on it and the brook flows right around it. At last it struck me that it would be splendid to call it Victoria Island because we found it on the Queen's birthday. Both Diana and I are very loyal. But I'm very sorry about that pie and the handkerchiefs. I wanted to be extra good today because it's an anniversary. Do you remember what happened this day last year, Marilla?"

"No, I can't think of anything special."

"Oh, Marilla, it was the day I came to Green Gables. I shall never forget it. It was the turning point in my life. Of course it wouldn't seem so important to you. I've been here for a year and I've been so happy. Of course, I've had my troubles, but one can live down troubles. Are you sorry you kept me, Marilla?"

"No, I can't say I'm sorry," said Marilla, who sometimes wondered how she could have lived before Anne came to Green Gables, "no, not exactly sorry. If you've finished your lessons, Anne, I want you to run over and ask Mrs. Barry if she'll lend me Diana's apron pattern."

"Oh—it's—too dark," cried Anne.

"Too dark? Why, it's only twilight. And goodness knows you've gone over enough after dark."

"I'll go over early in the morning," said Anne eagerly. "I'll get up at sunrise and go over, Marilla."

"What has got into your head now, Anne Shirley? I want that pattern to cut out your new apron this evening. Go at once and be smart, too."

"I'll have to go around by the road, then," said Anne, taking up her hat reluctantly.

"Go by the road and waste half an hour! I'd like to catch you!"

"I can't go through the Haunted Wood, Marilla," cried Anne desperately.

Marilla stared.

"The Haunted Wood! Are you crazy? What under the canopy is the Haunted Wood?"

"The spruce wood over the brook," said Anne in a whisper.

"Fiddlesticks! There is no such thing as a haunted wood anywhere. Who has been telling you such stuff?"

"Nobody," confessed Anne. "Diana and I just imagined the wood was haunted. All the places around here are so—so—*commonplace*. We just got this up for our own amusement. We began it in April. A haunted wood is so very romantic, Marilla. We chose the spruce grove because it's so gloomy. Oh, we have imagined the most harrowing things. There's a white lady walks along the brook just about this time of the night and wrings her hands and utters wailing cries. She appears when there is to be a death in the family. And the ghost of a little murdered child haunts the corner up by Idlewild; it creeps up behind you and lays its cold fingers on your hand—so. Oh, Marilla, it gives me a shudder to think of it. And there's a headless man stalks up and down the path and skeletons glower at you between the boughs. Oh, Marilla, I wouldn't go through the Haunted Wood after dark now for anything. I'd be sure that white things would reach out from behind the trees and grab me.''

"Did ever any one hear the like!" ejaculated Marilla, who had listened in dumb amazement. "Anne Shirley, do you mean to tell me you believe all that wicked nonsense of your own imagination?"

"Not believe *exactly*" faltered Anne. "At least, I don't believe it in daylight. But after dark, Marilla, it's different. That is when ghosts walk."

"There are no such things as ghosts, Anne."

"Oh, but there are, Marilla," cried Anne eagerly. "I know people who have seen them. And they are respectable people. Charlie Sloane says that his grandmother saw his grandfather driving home the cows one night after he'd been buried for a year. You know Charlie Sloane's grandmother wouldn't tell a story for anything. She's a very religious woman. And Mrs. Thomas' father was pursued home one night by a lamb of fire with its head cut off hanging by a strip of skin. He said he knew it was the spirit of his brother and that it was warning he would die within nine days. He didn't, but he died two years after, so you see it was really true. And Ruby Gillis says—"

"Anne Shirley," interrupted Marilla firmly, "I never want to hear you talking in this fashion again. I've had my doubts about that imagination of yours right along, and if this is going to be the outcome of it, I won't countenance any such doings. You'll go right over to Barry's, and you'll go through that spruce grove, just for a lesson and a warning to you. And never let me hear a word out of your head about haunted woods again."

Anne might plead and cry as she liked—and did, for her terror was very real. Her imagination had run away with her and she held the spruce grove in mortal dread after nightfall. But Marilla was inexorable. She marched the shrinking ghostseer down to the spring and ordered her to proceed straightway over the bridge and into the dusky retreats of wailing ladies and headless spectres beyond.

"Oh, Marilla, how can you be so cruel?" sobbed Anne. "What would you feel like if a white thing did snatch me up and carry me off?"

"I'll risk it," said Marilla unfeelingly. "You know I always mean what I say. I'll cure you of imagining ghosts into places. March, now.''

Anne marched. That is, she stumbled over the bridge and went shuddering up the horrible dim path beyond. Anne never forgot that walk. Bitterly did she repent the license she had given to her imagination. The goblins of her fancy lurked in every shadow about her, reaching out their cold, fleshless hands to grasp the terrified small girl who had called them into being. A white strip of birch bark blowing up from the hollow over the brown floor of the grove made her heart stand still. The long-drawn wail of two old boughs rubbing against each other brought out the perspiration in beads on her forehead. The swoop of bats in the darkness over her was as the wings of unearthly creatures. When she reached Mr. William Bell's field she fled across it as if pursued by an army of white things, and arrived at the Barry kitchen door so out of breath that she could hardly gasp out her request for the apron pattern. Diana was away so that she had no excuse to linger. The dreadful return journey had to be faced. Anne went back over it with shut eyes, preferring to take the risk of dashing her brains out among the boughs to that of seeing a white thing. When she finally tumbled over the log bridge she drew one long shivering breath of relief.

"Well, so nothing caught you?" said Marilla unsympathetically.

"Oh, Mar—Marilla," chattered Anne, "I'll b-b-be cont-t-tented with c-c-commonplace places after this.''

CHAPTER 21

A NEW DEPARTURE IN FLAVORINGS

"DEAR ME, there is nothing but meetings and partings in this world, as Mrs. Lynde says," remarked Anne plaintively, putting her slate and books down on the kitchen table on the last day of June and wiping her red eyes with a very damp handkerchief. "Wasn't it fortunate, Marilla, that I took an extra handkerchief to school today? I had a presentiment that it would be needed.''

"I never thought you were so fond of Mr. Phillips that you'd require two handkerchiefs to dry your tears just because he was going away," said Marilla.

"I don't think I was crying because I was really so very fond of him," reflected Anne. "I just cried because all the others did. It was Ruby Gillis started it. Ruby Gillis has always declared she hated Mr. Phillips, but just as soon as he got up to make his farewell speech she burst into tears. Then all the girls began to cry, one after the other. I tried to hold out, Marilla. I tried to remember the time Mr. Phillips made me sit with Gil—with a boy; and the time he spelled my name without an *e* on the blackboard; and how he said I was the worst dunce he ever saw at geometry and laughed at my spelling; and all the times he had been so horrid and sarcastic; but somehow I couldn't, Marilla, and I just had to cry too. Jane Andrews has been talking for a month about how glad she'd be when Mr. Phillips went away and she declared she'd never shed a tear. Well, she was worse than any of us and had to borrow a handkerchief from her brother—of course the boys didn't cry—because she hadn't brought one of her own, not expecting to need it. Oh, Marilla, it was heartrending. Mr. Phillips made such a beautiful farewell speech beginning, 'The time has come for us to part.' It was very affecting. And he had tears in hs eyes too, Marilla. Oh, I felt dreadfully sorry and remorseful for all the times I'd talked in school and drawn pictures of him on my slate and made fun of him and Prissy. I can tell you I wished I'd been a model pupil like Minnie Andrews. *She* hadn't anything on her conscience. The girls cried all the way home from school. Carrie Sloane kept saying every few minutes, 'The time has come for us to part,' and that would start us off again whenever we were in any danger of cheering up. I do feel dreadfully sad, Marilla. But one can't feel quite in the depths of despair with two months vacation before them, can they, Marilla? And besides, we met the new minister and his wife coming from the station. For all I was feeling so bad about Mr. Phillips going away I couldn't help taking a little interest in a new minister, could I? His wife is very pretty. Not exactly regally lovely, of course—it wouldn't do, I suppose, for a minister to have a regally lovely wife, because it might set a bad example. Mrs. Lynde says the minister's wife over at Newbridge sets a very bad example because she dresses so fashionably. Our new minister's wife was dressed in blue muslin with lovely puffed sleeves and a hat trimmed with roses. Jane Andrews said she thought puffed sleeves were too worldly for a minister's wife, but I didn't make any such uncharitable remark, Marilla, because I know what it is to long for puffed sleeves. Besides, she's only been a minister's wife for a little while, so one should make allowances, shouldn't they? They are going to board with Mrs. Lynde until the manse is ready."

If Marilla, in going down to Mrs. Lynde's that evening, was actuated by any motive save her avowed one of returning the quilting-frames she had borrowed the preceding winter, it was an amiable weakness shared by most of the Avonlea people. Many a thing Mrs. Lynde had lent, sometimes never expecting to see it again, came home that night in charge of the borrowers thereof. A new minister, and moreover a minister with a wife, was a lawful object of curiosity in a quiet little country settlement where sensations were few and far between.

Old Mr. Bentley, the minister whom Anne had found lacking in imagination, had been pastor of Avonlea for eighteen years. He was a widower when he came, and a widower he remained, despite the fact that gossip regularly married him to this, that or the other one, every year of his sojourn. In the preceding February he had resigned his charge and departed amid the regrets of his people, most of whom had the affection born of long intercourse for their good old minister in spite of his shortcomings as an orator. Since then the Avonlea church had enjoyed a variety of religious dissipation in listening to the many and various candidates and "supplies" who came Sunday after Sunday to preach on trial. These stood or fell by the judgment of the fathers and mothers in Israel; but a certain small, red-haired girl who sat meekly in the corner of the old Cuthbert pew also had her opinions about them and discussed the same in full with Matthew, Marilla always declining from principle to criticize ministers in any shape or form.

"I don't think Mr. Smith would have done, Matthew," was Anne's final summing up. "Mrs. Lynde says his delivery was so poor, but I think his worst fault was just like Mr. Bentley's—he had no imagination. And Mr. Terry had too much; he let it run away with him just as I did mine in the matter of the Haunted Wood. Besides, Mrs. Lynde says his theology wasn't sound. Mr. Gresham was a very good man and a very religious man, but he told too many funny stories and made the people laugh in church; he was undignified, and you must have some dignity about a minister, mustn't you, Matthew? I thought Mr. Marshall was decidedly attractive; but Mrs. Lynde says he isn't married, or even engaged, because she made special inquiries about him, and she says it would never do to have a young unmarried minister in Avonlea, because he might marry in the congregation and that would make trouble. Mrs. Lynde is a very far-seeing woman, isn't she, Matthew? I'm very glad they've called Mr. Allan. I liked him because his sermon was interesting and he prayed as if he meant it and not just as if he did it because he was in the habit of it. Mrs. Lynde says he isn't perfect, but she says she supposes we couldn't expect a perfect minister for seven hundred and fifty dollars a year, and anyhow his theology is sound because she questioned him thoroughly on all the points of doctrine. And she knows his wife's people and they are most respectable and the women are all good housekeepers. Mrs. Lynde says that sound doctrine in the man and good housekeeping in the woman make an ideal combination for a minister's family.''

The new minister and his wife were a young, pleasant-faced couple, still in their honeymoon, and full of all good and beautiful enthusiasms for their chosen life-work. Avonlea opened its heart to them from the start. Old and young liked the frank, cheerful young man with his high ideals, and the bright, gentle little lady who assumed the mistress-ship of the manse. With Mrs. Allan Anne fell promptly and whole-heartedly in love. She had discovered another kindred spirit.

"Mrs. Allan is perfectly lovely," she announced one Sunday afternoon. "She's taken our class and she's a splendid teacher. She said right away she didn't think it was fair for the teacher to ask all the questions, and you know, Marilla, that is exactly what I've always thought. She said we could ask her any question we liked, and I asked ever so many. I'm good at asking questions, Marilla."

"I believe you," was Marilla's emphatic comment.

"Nobody else asked any except Ruby Gillis, and she asked if there was to be a Sunday school picnic this summer. I didn't think that was a very proper question to ask because it hadn't any connection with the lesson—the lesson was about Daniel in the lion's den—but Mrs. Allan just smiled and said she thought there would be. Mrs. Allan has a lovely smile; she has such *exquisite* dimples in her cheeks. I wish I had dimples in my cheeks, Marilla. I'm not half so skinny as I was when I came here, but I have no dimples yet. If I had perhaps I could influence people for good. Mrs. Allan said we ought always to try to influence other people for good. She talked so nice about everything. I never knew before that religion was such a cheerful thing. I always thought it was kind of melancholy, but Mrs. Allan's isn't, and I'd like to be a Christian if I could be one like her. I wouldn't want to be one like Mr. Superintendent Bell."

"It's very naughty of you to speak so about Mr. Bell," said Marilla severely. "Mr. Bell is a real good man."

"Oh, of course he's good," agreed Anne, "but he doesn't seem to get any comfort out of it. If I could be good I'd dance and sing all day because I was glad of it. I suppose Mrs. Allan is too old to dance and sing and of course it wouldn't be dignified in a minister's wife. But I can just feel she's glad she's a Christian and that she'd be one even if she could get to heaven without it.''

"I suppose we must have Mr. and Mrs. Allan up to tea some day soon," said Marilla reflectively. ''They've been most everywhere but here. Let me see. Next Wednesday would be a good time to have them. But don't say a word to Matthew about it, for if he knew they were coming he'd find some excuse to be away that day. He'd got so used to Mr. Bentley he didn't mind him, but he's going to find it hard to get acquainted with a new minister, and a new minister's wife will frighten him to death.''

"I'll be as secret as the dead," assured Anne. ''But oh, Marilla, will you let me make a cake for the occasion? I'd love to do something for Mrs. Allan, and you know I can make a pretty good cake by this time.''

"You can make a layer cake," promised Marilla.

Monday and Tuesday great preparations went on at Green Gables. Having the minister and his wife to tea was a serious and important undertaking, and Marilla was determined not to be eclipsed by any of the Avonlea housekeepers. Anne was wild with excitement and delight. She talked it all over with Diana Tuesday night in the twilight, as they sat on the big red stones by the Dryad's Bubble and made rainbows in the water with little twigs dipped in fir balsam.

"Everything is ready, Diana, except my cake which I'm to make in the morning, and the baking-powder biscuits which Marilla will make just before tea-time. I assure you, Diana, that Marilla and I have had a busy two days of it. It's such a responsibility having a minister's family to tea. I never went through such an experience before. You should just see our pantry. It's a sight to behold. We're going to to have jellied chicken and cold tongue. We're to have two kinds of jelly, red and yellow, and whipped cream and lemon pie, and cherry pie, and three kinds of cookies, and fruitcake, and Marilla's famous yellow plum reserves that she keeps especially for ministers, and pound cake and layer cake, and biscuits as aforesaid; and new bread and old both, in case the minister is dyspeptic and can't eat new. Mrs. Lynde says ministers are mostly dyspeptic, but I don't think Mr. Allan has been a minister long enough for it to have had a bad effect on him. I just grow cold when I think of my layer cake. Oh, Diana, what if it shouldn't be good! I dreamed last night that I was chased all around by a fearful goblin with a big layer cake for a head.''

''It'll be good, all right,'' assured Diana, who was a very comfortable sort of friend. ''I'm sure that piece of the one you made that we had for lunch in Idlewild two weeks ago was perfectly elegant.''

''Yes; but cakes have such a terrible habit of turning out bad just when you especially want them to be good,'' sighed Anne, setting a particularly well-balsamed twig afloat. ''However, I suppose I shall just have to trust to Providence and be careful to put in the flour. Oh, look, Diana, what a lovely rainbow! Do you suppose the dryad will come out after we go away and take it for a scarf?''

''You know there is no such thing as a dryad,'' said Diana. Diana's mother had found out about the Haunted Wood and had been decidedly angry over it. As a result Diana had abstained from any further imitative flights of imagination and did not think it prudent to cultivate a spirit of belief even in harmless dryads.

''But it's so easy to imagine there is,'' said Anne. ''Every night, before I go to bed, I look out of my window and wonder if the dryad is really sitting here, combing her locks with the spring for a mirror. Sometimes I look for her footprints in the dew in the morning. Oh, Diana, don't give up your faith in the dryad!''

Wednesday morning came. Anne got up at sunrise because she was too excited to sleep. She had caught a severe cold in the head by reason of her dabbling in the spring on the preceding evening; but nothing short of absolute pneumonia could have quenched her interest in culinary matters that morning. After breakfast she proceeded to make her cake. When she finally shut the oven door upon it she drew a long breath.

''I'm sure I haven't forgotten anything this time, Marilla. But do you think it will rise? Just suppose perhaps the baking-powder isn't good? I used it out of the new can. And Mrs. Lynde says you can never be sure of getting good baking-powder nowadays when everything is so adulterated. Mrs. Lynde says the Government ought to take the matter up, but she says we'll never see the day when a Tory Government will do it. Marilla, what if that cake doesn't rise?''

''We'll have plenty without it,'' was Marilla's unimpassioned way of looking at the subject.

The cake did rise, however, and came out of the oven as light and feathery as golden foam. Anne, flushed with delight, clapped it together with layers of ruby jelly and, in imagination, saw Mrs. Allan eating it and possibly asking for another piece!

"You'll be using the best tea set, of course, Marilla," she said. "Can I fix up the table with ferns and wild roses?"

"I think that's all nonsense," sniffed Marilla. "In my opinion it's the eatables that matter and not flummery decorations."

"Mrs. Barry had *her* table decorated," said Anne, who was not entirely guiltless of the wisdom of the serpent, "and the minister paid her an elegant compliment. He said it was a feast for the eye as well as the palate."

"Well, do as you like," said Marilla, who was quite determined not to be surpassed by Mrs. Barry or anybody else. "Only mind you leave enough room for the dishes and the food."

Anne laid herself out to decorate in a manner and after a fashion that should leave Mrs. Barry's nowhere. Having abundance of roses and ferns and a very artistic taste of her own, she made that tea table such a thing of beauty that when the minister and his wife sat down to it they exclaimed in chorus over its loveliness.

"It's Anne's doings," said Marilla, grimly just; and Anne felt that Mrs. Allan's approving smile was almost too much happiness for this world.

Matthew was there, having been inveigled into the party only goodness and Anne knew how. He had been in such a state of shyness and nervousness that Marilla had given him up in despair, but Anne took him in hand so successfully that he now sat at the table in his best clothes and white collar and talked to the minister not uninterestingly. He never said a word to Mrs. Allan, but that perhaps was not to be expected.

All went merry as a marriage bell until Anne's layer cake was passed. Mrs. Allan, having already been helped to a bewildering variety, declined it. But Marilla, seeing the disappointment on Anne's face, said smilingly:

"Oh, you must take a piece of this, Mrs. Allan. Anne made it on purpose for you."

"In that case I must sample it," laughed Mrs. Allan, helping herself to a plump triangle, as did also the minister and Marilla.

Mrs. Allan took a mouthful of hers and a most peculiar expression crossed her face; not a word did she say, however, but steadily ate away at it. Marilla saw the expression and hastened to taste the cake.

"Anne Shirley!" she exclaimed, "what on earth did you put into that cake?"

"Nothing but what the recipe said, Marilla," cried Anne with a look of anguish. "Oh, isn't it all right?"

"All right! It's simply horrible. Mrs. Allan, don't try to eat it. Anne, taste it yourself. What flavoring did you use?"

"Vanilla," said Anne, her face scarlet with mortification after tasting the cake. "Only vanilla. Oh, Marilla, it must have been the baking powder. I had my suspicions of that bak—"

"Baking-powder fiddlesticks! Go and bring me the bottle of vanilla you used."

Anne fled to the pantry and returned with a small bottle partially filled with a brown liquid and labelled yellowly, "Best Vanilla."

Marilla took it, uncorked, it smelled it.

"Mercy on us, Anne, you've flavored that cake with *anodyne liniment*. I broke the liniment bottle last week and poured what was left into an old empty vanilla bottle. I suppose it's partly my fault—I should have warned you—but for pity's sake why couldn't you have smelled it?"

Anne dissolved into tears under this double disgrace.

"I couldn't—I had such a cold!" and with this she fairly fled to the gable chamber, where she cast herself on the bed and wept as one who refuses to be comforted.

Presently a light step sounded on the stairs and somebody entered the room.

"Oh, Marilla," sobbed Anne without looking up, "I'm disgaced for ever. I shall never be able to live this down. It will get out—things always do get out in Avonlea. Diana will ask me how my cake turned out and I shall have to tell her the truth. I shall always be pointed at as the girl who flavored a cake with anodyne liniment. Gil—the boys in school will never get over laughing at it. Oh, Marilla, if you have a spark of Christian pity don't tell me that I must go down and wash the dishes after this. I'll wash them when the minister and his wife are gone, but I cannot ever look Mrs. Allan in the face again. Perhaps she'll think I tried to poison her. Mrs. Lynde says she knows an orphan girl who tried to poison her benefactor. But the liniment isn't poisonous. It's meant to be taken internally—although not in cakes. Won't you tell Mrs. Allan so, Marilla?"

"Suppose you jump up and tell her so yourself," said a merry voice.

Anne flew up, to find Mrs. Allan standing by her bed, surveying her with laughing eyes.

"My dear little girl, you mustn't cry like this," she said, genuinely disturbed by Anne's tragic face. "Why, it's all just a funny mistake that anybody might make."

"Oh, no, it takes me to make such a mistake," said Anne forlornly. "And I wanted to have that cake so nice for you, Mrs. Allan."

"Yes, I know, dear. And I assure you I appreciate your kindness and thoughtfulness just as much as if it had turned out all right. Now, you mustn't cry any more, but come down with me and show me your flower garden. Miss Cuthbert tells me you have a little plot all your own. I want to see it, for I'm very much interested in flowers."

Anne permitted herself to be led down and comforted, reflecting that it was really providential that Mrs. Allan was a kindred spirit. Nothing more was said about the liniment cake, and when the guests went away Anne found that she had enjoyed the evening more than could have been expected, considering that terrible incident. Nevertheless she sighed deeply.

"Marilla, isn't it nice to think that tomorrow is a new day with no mistakes in it yet?"

"I'll warrant you'll make plenty in it," said Marilla. "I never saw your beat for making mistakes, Anne."

"Yes, and well I know it," admitted Anne mournfully. "But have you ever noticed one encouraging thing about me, Marilla? I never make the same mistake twice."

"I don't know as that's much benefit when you're always making new ones."

"Oh, don't you see, Marilla? There *must* be a limit to the mistakes one person can make, and when I get to the end of them, then I'll be through with them. That's a very comforting thought."

"Well, you'd better go and give that cake to the pigs," said Marilla. "It isn't fit for any human to eat, not even Jerry Buote."

CHAPTER 22

ANNE IS INVITED OUT TO TEA

AND WHAT are your eyes popping out of your head about now?" asked Marilla, when Anne had just come in from a run to the post office. "Have you discovered another kindred spirit?"

Excitement hung around Anne like a garment, shone in her eyes, kindled in every feature. She had come dancing up the lane, like a wind-blown sprite, through the mellow sunshine and lazy shadows of the August evening.

"No, Marilla, but oh, what do you think? I am invited to tea at the manse tomorrow afternoon! Mrs. Allan left the letter for me at the post-office. Just look at it, Marilla. 'Miss Anne Shirley, Green Gables.' That is the first time I was ever called 'Miss.' Such a thrill as it gave me! I shall cherish it for ever among my choicest treasures."

"Mrs. Allan told me she meant to have all the members of her Sunday school class to tea in turn," said Marilla, regarding the wonderful event very coolly. "You needn't get in such a fever over it. Do learn to take things calmly, child."

For Anne to take things calmly would have been to change her nature. All "spirit and fire and dew," as she was, the pleasures and pains of life came to her with trebled intensity. Marilla felt this and was vaguely troubled over it, realizing that the ups and downs of existence would probably bear hardly on this impulsive soul and not sufficiently understanding that the equally great capacity for delight might more than compensate. Therefore Marilla conceived it to be her duty to drill Anne into a tranquil uniformity of disposition as impossible and alien to her as to a dancing sunbeam in one of the brook shallows. She did not make much headway, as she sorrowfully admitted to herself. The downfall of some dear hope or plan punged Anne into "deeps of affliction." The fulfilment thereof exalted her to dizzy realms of delight. Marilla had almost begun to despair of ever fashioning this waif of the world into her model little girl of demure manners and prim deportment. Neither would she have believed that she really liked Anne much better as she was.

Anne went to bed that night speechless with misery because Matthew had said the wind was round northeast and he feared it would be a rainy day tomorrow. The rustle of the poplar leaves about the house worried her, it sounded so like pattering raindrops, and the dull, faraway roar of the gulf, to which she listened delightedly at other times, loving its strange, sonorous, haunting rhythm, now seemed like a prophecy of storm and disaster to a small maiden who particularly wanted a fine day. Anne thought that the morning would never come.

But all things have an end, even nights before the day on which you are invited to take tea at the manse. The morning, in spite of

Matthew's predictions, was fine and Anne's spirits soared to their highest.

"Oh, Marilla, there is something in me today that makes me just love everybody I see," she exclaimed as she washed the breakfast dishes. "You don't know how good I feel! Wouldn't it be nice if it could last? I believe I could be a model child if I were just invited out to tea every day. But oh, Marilla, it's a solemn occasion, too. I feel so anxious. What if I shouldn't behave properly? You know I never had tea at a manse before, and I'm not sure that I know all the rules of etiquette, although I've been studying the rules given in the Etiquette Department of the *Family Herald* ever since I came here. I'm so afraid I'll do something silly or forget to do something I should do. Would it be good manners to take a second helping of anything if you wanted to *very* much?"

"The trouble with you, Anne, is that you're thinking too much about yourself. You should just think of Mrs. Allan and what would be nicest and most agreeable for her," said Marilla, hitting for once in her life on a very sound and pithy piece of advice. Anne instantly realized this.

"You are right, Marilla. I'll try not to think about myself at all."

Anne evidently got through her visit without any serious breach of "etiquette" for she came home through the twilight, under a great, high-sprung sky gloried over with trails of saffron and rosy cloud, in a beatified state of mind and told Marilla all about it happily, sitting on the big red sandstone slab at the kitchen door with her tired curly head in Marilla's gingham lap.

A cool wind was blowing down over the long harvest fields from the rims of firry western hills and whistling through the poplars. One clear star hung above the orchard and the fireflies were flitting over in Lovers' Lane, in and out among the ferns and rustling boughs. Anne watched them as she talked and somehow felt that wind and stars and fireflies were all tangled up together into something unutterably sweet and enchanting.

"Oh, Marilla, I've had a most *fascinating* time. I feel that I have not lived in vain and I shall always feel like that even if I should never be invited to tea at a manse again. When I got there Mrs. Allan met me at the door. She was dressed in the sweetest dress of pale pink organdy, with dozens of frills and elbow sleeves, and she looked just like a seraph. I really think I'd like to be a minister's wife when I grow up, Marilla. A minister mightn't mind my red hair because he wouldn't be thinking of such worldly things. But then of course one would have to be naturally good and I'll never be that, so I suppose there's no use in thinking about it. Some people are naturally good, you know, and others are not. I'm one of the others. Mrs. Lynde says I'm full of original sin. No matter how hard I try to be good I can never make such a success of it as those who are naturally good. It's a good deal like geometry, I expect. But don't you think the trying so hard ought to count for something? Mrs. Allan is one of the naturally good people. I love her passionately. You know there are some people, like Matthew and Mrs. Allan, that you can love right off without any trouble. And there are others, like Mrs. Lynde, that you have to try very hard to love. You know you *ought* to love them because they know so much and are such active workers in the church, but you have to keep reminding yourself of it all the time or else you forget. There was another little girl at the manse to tea, from the White Sands Sunday school. Her name was Lauretta Bradley, and she was a very nice little girl. Not exactly a kindred spirit, you know, but still very nice. We had an elegant tea, and I think I kept all the rules of etiquette pretty well. After tea Mrs. Allan played and sang and she got Lauretta and me to sing, too. Mrs. Allan says I have a good voice and she says I must sing in the Sunday school choir after this. You can't think how I was thrilled at the mere thought. I've longed so to sing in the Sunday school choir, as Diana does, but I feared it was an honor I could never aspire to. Lauretta had to go home early because there is a big concert in the White Sands hotel tonight and her sister is to recite at it. Lauretta says that the Americans at the hotel give a concert every fortnight in aid of the Charlottetown hospital, and they ask lots of the White Sands people to recite. Lauretta said she expected to be asked herself some day. I just gazed at her in awe. After she had gone Mrs. Allan and I had a heart-to-heart talk. I told her everything——about Mrs. Thomas and the twins and Katie Maurice and Violetta and coming to Green Gables and my troubles over geometry. And would you believe it, Marilla? Mrs. Allan told me she was a dunce at geometry, too. You don't know how that encouraged me. Mrs. Lynde came to the manse just before I left, and what do you think, Marilla? The trustees have hired a new teacher and it's a lady. Her name is Miss Muriel Stacy. Isn't that a romantic name? Mrs. Lynde says they've never had a female teacher in Avonlea before and she thinks it is a dangerous innovation. But I think it will be splendid to have a lady teacher, and I really don't see how I'm going to live through the two weeks before school begins, I'm so impatient to see her.

CHAPTER 23

ANNE COMES TO GRIEF IN AN AFFAIR OF HONOR

ANNE HAD to live through more than two weeks, as it happened. Almost a month having elapsed since the liniment cake episode, it was high time for her to get into fresh trouble of some sort, little mistakes, such as absent-mindedly emptying a pan of skim milk into a basket of yarn balls in the pantry instead of into the pigs' bucket, and walking clean over the edge of the log bridge into the brook while wrapped in imaginative reverie, not really being worth counting.

A week after the tea at the manse Diana Barry gave a party.

"Small and select," Anne assured Marilla. "Just the girls in our class."

They had a very good time and nothing untoward happened until after tea, when they found themselves in the Barry garden, a little tired of all their games and ripe for any enticing form of mischief which might present itself. This presently took the form of "daring."

Daring was the fashionable amusement among the Avonlea small fry just then. It had begun among the boys, but soon spread to the girls, and all the silly things that were done in Avonlea that summer because the doers thereof were "dared" to do them would fill a book by themselves.

First of all Carrie Sloane dared Ruby Gillis to climb to a certain point in the huge old willow tree before the front door; which Ruby Gillis, albeit in mortal dread of the fat green caterpillars with which said tree was infested and with the fear of her mother before her eyes if she should tear her new muslin dress, nimbly did, to the discomfiture of the aforesaid Carrie Sloane.

Then Josie Pye dared Jane Andrews to hop on her left leg around the garden without stopping once or putting her right foot to the ground; which Jane Andrews gamely tried to do, but gave out at the third corner and had to confess herself defeated.

Josie's triumph being rather more pronounced than good taste permitted, Anne Shirley dared her to walk along the top of the board fence which bounded the garden to the east. Now, to "walk" board fences requires more skill and steadiness of head and heel than one might suppose who has never tried it. But Josie Pye, if deficient in some qualities that make for popularity, had at least a natural and inborn gift, duly cultivated, for walking board fences. Josie walked the Barry fence with an airy unconcern which seemed to imply that a little thing like that wasn't worth a "dare." Reluctant admiration greeted her exploit, for most of the other girls could appreciate it, having suffered many things themselves in their efforts to walk fences. Josie descended from her perch, flushed with victory, and darted a defiant glance at Anne.

Anne tossed her red braids.

"I don't think it's such a very wonderful thing to walk a little, low, board fence," she said. "I knew a girl in Marysville who could walk the ridge-pole of a roof."

"I don't believe it," said Josie flatly. "I don't believe anybody could walk a ridge-pole. *You* couldn't anyhow."

"Couldn't I?" cried Anne rashly.

"Then I dare you to do it," said Josie defiantly. "I dare you to climb up there and walk the ridge-pole of Mr. Barry's kitchen roof."

Anne turned pale, but there was clearly only one thing to be done. She walked towards the house, where a ladder was leaning against the kitchen roof. All the fifth-class girls said, "Oh!" partly in excitement, partly in dismay.

Don't you do it, Anne," entreated Diana. "You'll fall off and be killed. Never mind Josie Pye. It isn't fair to dare anybody to do anything so dangerous."

"I must do it. My honor is at stake," said Anne solemnly. "I shall walk that ridge-pole, Diana, or perish in the attempt. If I am killed you are to have my pearl bead ring."

Anne climbed the ladder amid breathless silence, gained the ridge-pole, balanced herself uprightly on that precarious footing, and started to walk along it, dizzily conscious that she was uncomfortably high up in the world and that walking ridge-poles was not a thing in which your imagination helped you out much. Nevertheless, she managed to take several steps before the catastrophe came. Then she swayed, lost her balance, stumbled, staggered and fell, sliding down over the sun-baked roof and crashing off it through the tangle of Virginia creeper beneath—all before the dismayed circle below could give a simultaneous, terrified shriek.

If Anne had tumbled off the roof on the side up which she ascended, Diana would probably have fallen heir to the pearl bead ring then and there. Fortunately she fell on the other side, where the roof extended down over the porch so nearly to the ground that a fall therefrom was a much less serious thing. Nevertheless, when Diana and the other girls had rushed frantically around the house—except

Ruby Gillis, who remained as if rooted to the ground and went into hysterics—they found Anne lying all white and limp among the wreck and ruin of the Virginia creeper.

"Anne, are you killed?" shrieked Diana, throwing herself on her knees beside her friend. "Oh, Anne, dear Anne, speak just one word to me and tell me if you're killed."

To the immense relief of all the girls, and especially of Josie Pye, who, in spite of lack of imagination, had been seized with horrible visions of a future branded as the girl who was the cause of Anne Shirley's early and tragic death, Anne sat dizzily up and answered uncertainly:

"No, Diana, I am not killed, but I think I am rendered unconscious."

"Where?" sobbed Carrie Sloane. "Oh, where, Anne?"

Before Anne could answer, Mrs. Barry appeared on the scene. At sight of her Anne tried to scramble to her feet, but sank back again with a sharp little cry of pain.

"What's the matter? Where have you hurt yourself?" demanded Mrs. Barry.

"My ankle," gasped Anne. "Oh, Diana, please find your father and ask him to take me home. I know I can never walk there. And I'm sure I couldn't hop so far on one foot when Jane couldn't even hop around the garden."

Marilla was out in the orchard picking a panful of summer apples when she saw Mr. Barry coming over the log bridge and up the slope, with Mrs. Barry beside him and a whole procession of little girls trailing after him. In his arms he carried Anne, whose head lay limply against his shoulder.

At that moment Marilla had a revelation. In the sudden stab of fear that pierced to her very heart she realized what Anne had come to mean to her. She would have admitted that she liked Anne—nay, that she was very fond of Anne. But now she knew as she hurried wildly down the slope that Anne was dearer to her than anything on earth.

"Mr. Barry, what has happened to her?" she gasped, more white and shaken than the self-contained, sensible Marilla had been for many years.

Anne herself answered, lifting her head.

"Don't be frightened, Marilla. I was walking the ridge-pole and I fell off. I expect I have sprained my ankle. But, Marilla, I might have broken my neck. Let us look on the bright side of things."

"I might have known you'd go and do something of the sort when

"I SHALL WALK THAT RIDGE-POLE, OR PERISH IN THE ATTEMPT."

I let you go to that party," said Marilla, sharp and shrewish in her very relief. "Bring her in here, Mr. Barry, and lay her on the sofa. Mercy me, the child has gone and fainted!"

It was quite true. Overcome by the pain of her injury, Anne had one more of her wishes granted to her. She had fainted dead away.

Matthew, hastily summoned from the harvest field, was straightway despatched for the doctor, who in due time came, to discover that the injury was more serious than they had supposed. Anne's ankle was broken.

That night, when Marilla went up the the east gable, where a white-faced girl was lying, a plaintive voice greeted her from the bed.

"Aren't you very sorry for me, Marilla?"

"It was your own fault," said Marilla, twitching down the blind and lighting a lamp.

"And that is just why you should be sorry for me," said Anne, "because the thought that it *is* all my own fault is what makes it so hard. If I could blame it on anybody I would feel so much better. But what would you have done, Marilla, if you had been dared to walk a ridge-pole?"

" I'd have stayed on good firm ground and let them dare away. Such absurdity!" said Marilla.

Anne sighed.

"But you have such strength of mind, Marilla. I haven't. I just felt that I couldn't bear Josie Pye's scorn. She would have crowed over me all my life. And I think I have been punished so much that you needn't be very cross with me, Marilla. It's not a bit nice to faint, after all. And the doctor hurt me dreadfully when he was setting my ankle. I won't be able to go around for six or seven weeks and I'll miss the new lady teacher. She won't be new anymore by the time I'm able to go to school. And Gil—everbody will get ahead of me in class. Oh, I am an afflicted mortal. But I'll try to bear it all bravely if only you won't be cross with me, Marilla."

"There, there, I'm not cross," said Marilla. "You're an unlucky child, there's no doubt about that; but, as you say, you'll have the suffering of it. Here now, try and eat some supper."

"Isn't it fortunate I've got such an imagination?" said Anne. "It will help me through splendidly, I expect. What do people who haven't any imagination do when they break their bones, do you suppose, Marilla?"

Anne had good reason to bless her imagination many a time and oft during the tedious seven weeks that followed. But she was not

solely dependent on it. She had many visitors and not a day passed
without one or more of the schoolgirls dropping in to bring her
flowers and books and tell her all the happenings in the juvenile
world of Avonlea.

"Everybody has been so good and kind, Marilla," sighed Anne
happily, on the day when she could first limp across the floor. "It
isn't very pleasant to be laid up, but there *is* a bright side to it,
Marilla. You find out how many friends you have. Why, even
Superintendent Bell came to see me, and he's really a very fine man.
Not a kindred spirit, of course; but still I like him and I'm awfully
sorry I ever criticized his prayers. I believe now he really does mean
them, only he has got into the habit of saying them as if he didn't. He
could get over that if he'd take a little trouble. I gave him a good
broad hint. I told him how hard I tried to make my own little private
prayers interesting. He told me all about the time he broke his ankle
when he was a boy. It does seem so strange to think of Superintendent Bell ever being a boy. Even my imagination has its limits for I
can't imagine *that*. When I try to imagine him as a boy I see him with
gray whiskers and spectacles, just as he looks in Sunday school, only
small. Now, it's so easy to imagine Mrs. Allan as a little girl. Mrs.
Allan has been to see me fourteen times. Isn't that something to be
proud of, Marilla? When a minister's wife has so many claims on her
time! She is such a cheerful person to have visit you, too. She never
tells you it's your own fault and she hopes you'll be a better girl on
account of it. Mrs. Lynde always told me that when she came to see
me; and she said it in a kind of way that made me feel she might hope
I'd be a better girl, but didn't really believe I would. Even Josie Pye
came to see me. I received her as politely as I could, because I think
she was sorry she dared me to walk a ridge-pole. If I had been killed
she would have had to carry a dark burden of remorse all her life.
Diana has been a faithful friend. She's been over every day to cheer
my lonely pillow. But oh, I shall be so glad when I can go to school
for I've heard such exciting things about the new teacher. The girls
all think she is perfectly sweet. Diana says she has the loveliest fair
curly hair and such fascinating eyes. She dresses beautifully, and her
sleeve puffs are bigger than anybody else's in Avonlea. Every
other Friday afternoon she has recitations and everybody has to say a
piece or take part in a dialogue. Oh, it's just glorious to think of it.
Josie Pye says she hates it, but that is just because Josie has so little
imagination. Diana and Ruby Gillis and Jane Andrews are preparing
a dialogue, called 'A Morning Visit,' for next Friday. And the Friday
afternoons they don't have recitations Miss Stacy takes them all to

the woods for a 'field' day and they study ferns and flowers and birds. And they have physical culture exercises every morning and evening. Mrs. Lynde says she never heard of such goings-on and it all comes of having a lady teacher. But I think it must be splendid and I believe I shall find that Miss Stacy is a kindred spirit.''

''There's one thing plain to be seen, Anne,'' said Marilla, ''and that is that your fall off the Barry roof hasn't injured your tongue at all.''

CHAPTER 24

MISS STACY AND HER PUPILS GET UP A CONCERT

IT WAS October again when Anne was ready to go back to school—a glorious October, all red and gold, with mellow mornings when the valleys were filled with delicate mists as if the spirit of autumn had poured them in for the sun to drain—amethyst, pearl, silver rose, and smoke-blue. The dews were so heavy that the fields glistened like cloth of silver and there were such heaps of rustling leaves in the hollows of many-stemmed woods to run crisply through. The Birch Path was a canopy of yellow and the ferns were sear and brown all along it. There was a tang in the very air that inspired the hearts of small maidens tripping, unlike snails, swiftly and willingly to school; and it *was* jolly to be back again at the little brown desk beside Diana, with Ruby Gillis nodding across the aisle and Carrie Sloane sending up notes and Julie Bell passing a ''chew'' of gum down from the back seat. Anne drew a long breath of happiness as she sharpened her pencil and arranged her picture cards in her desk. Life was certainly very interesting.

In the new teacher she found another true and helpful friend. Miss Stacy was a bright, sympathetic young woman with the happy gift of winning and holding the affections of her pupils and bringing out the best that was in them mentally and morally. Anne expanded like a flower under this wholesome influence and carried home to the admiring Matthew and the critical Marilla glowing accounts of school work and aims.

''I love Miss Stacy with my whole heart, Marilla. She is so ladylike and she has such a sweet voice. When she pronounces my name I feel *instinctively* that she's spelling it with an *e*. We had recitations this afternoon. I just wish you could have been there to hear me recite 'Mary, Queen of Scots.' I just put my whole soul into it. Ruby Gillis told me coming home that the way I said the line, 'Now for my father's arm, she said, my woman's heart farewell,' just made her blood run cold.''

''Well now, you might recite for me some of these days, out in the barn,'' suggested Matthew.

''Of course I will,'' said Anne meditatively, ''but I won't be able to do it so well, I know. It won't be so exciting as it is when you have a whole schoolful before you hanging breathlessly on your words. I know I won't be able to make your blood run cold.''

''Mrs. Lynde says it made *her* blood run cold to see the boys climbing to the very tops of those big trees on Bell's hill after crows' nests last Friday,'' said Marilla. ''I wonder at Miss Stacy for encouraging it.''

''But we wanted a crow's nest for nature study,'' explained Anne. ''That was on our field afternoon. Field afternoons are splendid, Marilla. And Miss Stacy explains everything so beautifully. We have to write compositions on our field afternoons and I write the best ones.''

''It's very vain of you to say so then. You'd better let your teacher say it.''

''But she *did* say it, Marilla. And indeed I'm not vain about it. How can I be, when I'm such a dunce at geometry? Although I'm really beginning to see through it a little, too. Miss Stacy makes it so clear. Still, I'll never be good at it and I assure you it is a humbling reflection. But I love writing compositions. Mostly Miss Stacy lets us choose our own subjects; but next week we are to write a composition on some remarkable person. It's hard to choose among so many remarkable people who have lived. Mustn't it be splendid to be remarkable and have compositions written about you after you're dead? Oh, I would dearly love to be remarkable. I think when I grow up I'll be a trained nurse and go with the Red Crosses to the field of battle as a messenger of mercy. That is, if I don't go out as a foreign missionary. That would be very romantic, but one would have to be very good to be a missionary, and that would be a stumbling-block. We have physical culture exercises every day, too. They make you graceful and promote digestion.''

''Promote fiddlesticks!'' said Marilla, who honestly thought it was all nonsense.

But all the field afternoons and recitation Fridays and physical culture contortions paled before a project which Miss Stacy brought forward in November. This was that the scholars of Avonlea school should get up a concert and hold it in the hall on Christmas night, for the laudable purpose of helping to pay for a schoolhouse flag. The pupils one and all taking graciously to this plan, the preparations for a program were begun at once. And of all the excited performers-elect none was so excited as Anne Shirley, who threw herself into the undertaking heart and soul, hampered as she was by Marilla's disapproval. Marilla thought it all rank foolishness.

"It's just filling your heads up with nonsense and taking time that ought to be put on your lessons," she grumbled. "I don't approve of children's getting up concerts and racing about to practices. It makes them vain and forward and fond of gadding."

"But think of the worthy object," pleaded Anne. "A flag will cultivate a spirit of patriotism, Marilla."

"Fudge! There's precious little patriotism in the thoughts of any of you. All you want is a good time."

"Well, when you can combine patriotism and fun, isn't it all right? Of course it's real nice to be getting up a concert. We're going to have six choruses and Diana is to sing a solo. I'm in two dialogues—'The Society fo the Suppression of Gossip' and 'The Fairy Queen.' The boys are going to have a dialogue, too. And I'm to have two recitations, Marilla. I just tremble when I think of it, but it's a nice thrilly kind of tremble. And we're to have a tableau at the last—'Faith, Hope and Charity.' Diana and Ruby and I are to be in it, all draped in white with flowing hair. I'm to be Hope, with my hands clasped—so—and my eyes uplifted. I'm going to practise my recitations in the garret. Don't be alarmed if you hear me groaning. I have to groan heartrendingly in one of them, and it's really hard to get up a good artistic groan, Marilla. Josie Pye is sulky because she didn't get the part she wanted in the dialogue. She wanted to be the fairy queen. That would have been ridiculous, for who ever heard of a fairy queen as fat as Josie? Fairy queens must be slender. Jane Andrews is to be the queen and I am to be one of her maids of honor. Josie says she thinks a red-haired fairy is just as ridiculous as a fat one, but I do not let myself mind what Josie says. I'm to have a wreath of white roses on my hair and Ruby Gillis is going to lend me her slippers because I haven't any of my own. It's necessary for fairies to have slippers, you know. You couldn't imagine a fairy wearing boots, could you? Especially with copper toes? We are going to decorate the hall with creeping spruce and fir mottoes with pink tissue-paper roses in them. And we are all to march in two by two after the audience is seated, while Emma White plays a march on the organ. Oh, Marilla, I know you aren't so enthusiastic about it as I am, but don't you hope your little Anne will distinguish herself?''

''All I hope is that you'll behave yourself. I'll be heartily glad when all this fuss is over and you'll be able to settle down. You are simply good for nothing just now with your head stuffed full of dialogues and groans and tableaus. As for your tongue, it's a marvel it's not clean worn out.''

Anne sighed and betook herself to the back yard, over which a young new moon was shining through the leafless poplar boughs from an apple-green western sky, and where Matthew was splitting wood. Anne perched herself on a block and talked the concert over with him, sure of an appreciative and sympathetic listener in this instance at least.

''Well now, I reckon it's going to be a pretty good concert. And I expect you'll do your part fine,'' he said, smiling down into her eager, vivacious little face. Anne smiled back at him. Those two were the best of friends and Matthew thanked his stars many a time and oft that he had nothing to do with bringing her up. That was Marilla's exclusive duty; if it had been his he would have been worried over frequent conflicts between inclination and said duty. As it was, he was free to ''spoil Anne''—Marilla's phrasing—as much as he liked. But it was not such a bad arrangement after all; a little ''appreciation'' sometimes does quite as much good as all the conscientious ''bringing up'' in the world.

CHAPTER 25

MATTHEW INSISTS ON PUFFED SLEEVES

MATTHEW WAS having a bad ten minutes of it. He had come into the kitchen, in the twilight of a cold, gray December evening, and had sat down in the wood-box corner to take off his heavy boots, unconscious of the fact that Anne and a bevy of her schoolmates were having a practice of ''The Fairy Queen'' in the sitting-room. Presently they came trooping through the hall and out into the kitchen, laughing and chattering gaily. They did not see Matthew, who shrank bashfully back into the shadows beyond the wood-box with a boot in one hand and a bootjack in the other, and he watched them shyly for the aforesaid ten minutes as they put on caps and jackets and talked about the dialogue and the concert. Anne stood among them, bright-eyed and animated as they; but Matthew suddenly became conscious that there was something about her different from her mates. And what worried Matthew was that the difference impressed him as being something that should not exist. Anne had a brighter face, and bigger, starrier eyes, and more delicate features than the others; even shy, unobservant Matthew had learned to take note of these things; but the difference that disturbed him did not consist in any of these respects. Then in what did it consist?

Matthew was haunted by this question long after the girls had gone, arm in arm, down the long, hard-frozen lane and Anne had betaken herself to her books. He could not refer it to Marilla, who, he felt, would be quite sure to sniff scornfully and remark that the only difference she saw between Anne and the other girls was that they sometimes kept their tongues quiet while Anne never did. This, Matthew felt, would be no great help.

He had recourse to his pipe that evening to help him study it out, much to Marilla's disgust. After two hours of smoking and hard reflection Matthew arrived at a solution of his problem. Anne was not dressed like the other girls!

The more Matthew thought about the matter the more he was convinced that Anne never had been dressed like the other girls—never since she had come to Green Gables. Marilla kept her clothed in plain, dark dresses, all made after the same unvarying pattern. If Matthew knew there was such a thing as fashion in dress it is as much as he did; but he was quite sure that Anne's sleeves did not look at all like the sleeves the other girls wore. He recalled the cluster of little girls he had seen around her that evening—all gay in waists of red and blue and pink and white—and he wondered why Marilla always kept her so plainly and soberly gowned.

Of course, it must be all right. Marilla knew best and Marilla was bringing her up. Probably some wise, inscrutable motive was to be served thereby. But surely it would do not harm to let the child have one pretty dress—something like Diana Barry always wore. Matthew decided that he would give her one; that surely could not be objected to as an unwarranted putting in of his oar. Christmas was only a fortnight off. A nice new dress would be the very thing for a present. Matthew, with a sigh of satisfaction, put away his pipe and went to bed, while Marilla opened all the doors and aired the house.

The very next evening Matthew betook himself to Carmody to buy the dress, determined to get the worst over and have done with it. It would be, he felt assured, no trifling ordeal. There were some things Matthew could buy and prove himself no mean bargainer; but he knew he would be at the mercy of shopkeepers when it came to buying a girl's dress.

After much cogitation Matthew resolved to go to Samuel Lawson's store instead of William Blair's. To be sure, the Cuthberts always had gone to William Blair's; it was almost as much a matter of conscience with them as to attend the Presbyterian church and vote Conservative. But William Blair's two daughters frequently waited on customers there and Matthew held them in absolute dread. He could contrive to deal with them when he knew exactly what he wanted and could point it out; but in such a matter as this, requiring explanation and consultation, Matthew felt that he must be sure of a man behind the counter. So he would go to Lawson's where Samuel or his son would wait on him.

Alas! Matthew did not know that Samuel, in the recent expansion of his business, had set up a lady clerk also; she was a niece of his wife's and a very dashing young person indeed, with a huge, drooping pompadour, big, rolling brown eyes, and a most extensive and bewildering smile. She was dressed with exceeding smartness and wore several bangle bracelets that glittered and rattled and tinkled with every movement of her hands. Matthew was covered with confusion at finding her there at all; and those bangles completely wrecked his wits at one fell swoop.

"What can I do for you this evening, Mr. Cuthbert?" Miss Lucilla Harris inquired, briskly and ingratiatingly, tapping the counter with both hands.

"Have you any—any—well now, say any garden rakes?" stammered Matthew.

Miss Harris looked somewhat surprised, as well she might, to hear a man inquiring for garden rakes in the middle of December.

"I believe we have one or two left over," she said, "but they're upstairs in the lumber room. I'll go and see."

During her absence Matthew collected his scattered senses for another effort.

When Miss Harris returned with the rake and cheerfully inquired: "Anything else tonight, Mr. Cuthbert?" Matthew took his courage in both hands and replied: "Well now, since you suggest it, I might as well—take—that is—look at—buy some—some hayseed."

Miss Harris had heard Matthew Cuthbert called odd. She now concluded that he was entirely crazy.

"We only keep hayseed in the spring," she explained loftily. "We've none on hand just now."

"Oh, certainly—certainly—just as you say," stammered unhappy Matthew, seizing the rake and making for the door. At the threshold he recollected that he had not paid for it and he turned miserably back. While Miss Harris was counting out his change he rallied his powers for a final desperate attempt.

"Well now—if it isn't too much trouble—I might as well—that is—I'd like to look at—at—some sugar."

"White or brown?" queried Miss Harris patiently.

"Oh—well now—brown," said Matthew feebly.

"There's a barrel of it over there," said Miss Harris, shaking her bangles at it. "It's the only kind we have."

"I'll—I'll take twenty pounds of it," said Matthew, with beads of perspiration standing on his forehead.

Matthew had driven halfway home before he was his own man again. It had been a gruesome experience, but it served him right, he thought, for committing the heresy of going to a strange store. When he reached home he hid the rake in the toolhouse, but the sugar he carried in to Marilla.

"Brown sugar!" exclaimed Marilla. "Whatever possessed you to get so much? You know I never use it except for the hired man's porridge or black fruit-cake. Jerry's gone and I've made my cake long ago. It's not good sugar, either—it's coarse and dark—William Blair doesn't ususally keep sugar like that."

"I—I thought it might come in handy sometime," said Matthew, making good his escape.

When Matthew came to think the matter over he decided that a woman was required to cope with the situation. Marilla was out of the question. Matthew felt sure she would throw cold water on his project at once. Remained only Mrs. Lynde; for of no other woman in Avonlea would Matthew have dared to ask advice. To Mrs. Lynde he went accordingly, and that good lady promptly took the matter out of the harassed man's hands.

"Pick out a dress for you to give Anne? To be sure I will. I'm going to Carmody tomorrow and I'll attend to it. Have you something particular in mind? No? Well, I'll just go by my own judgment then.

I believe a nice rich brown would just suit Anne, and William Blair has some new gloria in that's real pretty. Perhaps you'd like me to make it up for her, too, seeing that if Marilla was to make it Anne would probably get wind of it before the time and spoil the surprise? Well, I'll do it. No, it isn't a mite of trouble. I like sewing. I'll make it to fit my niece, Jenny Gillis, for she and Anne are as like as two peas as far as figure goes.''

''Well now, I'm much obliged,'' said Matthew, ''and—and—I dunno—but I'd like—I think they make the sleeves different nowadays to what they used to be. If it wouldn't be asking too much I—I'd like them made in the new way.''

''Puffs? Of course. You needn't worry a speck more about it, Matthew. I'll make it up in the very latest fashion,'' said Mrs. Lynde. To herself she added when Matthew had gone:

''It'll be a real satisfaction to see that poor child wearing something decent for once. The way Marilla dresses her is positively ridiculous, that's what, and I've ached to tell her so plainly a dozen times. I've held my tongue though, for I can see Marilla doesn't want advice and she thinks she knows more about bringing children up than I do for all she's an old maid. But that's always the way. Folks that has brought up children know that there's no hard and fast method in the world that'll suit every child. But them as never have think it's all as plain and easy as Rule of Three—just set your three terms down so fashion, and the sum'll work out correct. But flesh and blood don't come under the head of arithmetic and that's where Marilla Cuthbert makes her mistake. I suppose she's trying to cultivate a spirit of humility in Anne by dressing her as she does; but it's more likely to cultivate envy and discontent. I'm sure the child must feel the difference between her clothes and the other girls'. But to think of Matthew taking notice of it! That man is waking up after being asleep for over sixty years.''

Marilla knew all the following fortnight that Matthew had something on his mind, but what it was she could not guess, until Christmas Eve, when Mrs. Lynde brought up the new dress. Marilla behaved pretty well on the whole, although it is very likely she distrusted Mrs. Lynde's diplomatic explanation that she had made the dress because Matthew was afraid Anne would find out about it too soon if Marilla made it.

''So this is what Matthew has been looking so mysterious over and grinning about to himself for two weeks, is it?'' she said a little stiffly but tolerantly. ''I knew he was up to some foolishness. Well, I must say I don't think Anne needed any more dresses. I made her three good, warm, serviceable ones this fall, and anything more is sheer extravagance. There's enough material in those sleeves alone to make a waist, I declare there is. You'll just pamper Anne's vanity, Matthew, and she's as vain as a peacock now. Well, I hope she'll be satisfied at last, for I know she's been hankering after those silly sleeves ever since they came in, although she never said a word after the first. The puffs have been getting bigger and more ridiculous right along; they're as big as balloons now. Next year anybody who wears them will have to go through a door sideways.''

Christmas morning broke on a beautiful white world. It had been a very mild December and people had looked forward to a green Christmas; but just enough snow fell softly in the night to transfigure Avonlea. Anne peeped out from her frosted gable window with delighted eyes. The firs in the Haunted Wood were all feathery and wonderful; the birches and wild cherry-trees were outlined in pearl; the ploughed fields were stretches of snowy dimples; and there was a crisp tang in the air that was glorious. Anne ran downstairs singing until her voice reechoed through Green Gables.

''Merry Christmas, Marilla! Merry Christmas, Matthew! Isn't it a lovely Christmas? I'm so glad it's white. Any other kind of Christmas doesn't seem real, does it? I don't like green Christmases. They're *not* green—they're just nasty faded browns and grays. What makes people call them green? Why—why—Matthew, is that for me? Oh, Matthew!''

Matthew had sheepishly unfolded the dress from its paper swathings and held it out with a deprecatory glance at Marilla, who feigned to be contemptuously filling the teapot, but nevertheless watched the scene out of the corner of her eye with a rather interested air.

Anne took the dress and looked at it in reverent silence. Oh, how pretty it was—a lovely soft brown gloria with all the gloss of silk; a skirt with dainty frills and shirrings; a waist elaborately pintucked in the most fashionable way, and a little ruffle of filmy lace at the neck. But the sleeves—they were the crowning glory! Long elbow cuffs, and above them two beautiful puffs divided by rows of shirring and bows of brown silk ribbon.

''That's a Christmas present for you, Anne,'' said Matthew shyly. ''Why—why Anne, don't you like it? Well now—well now.''

For Anne's eyes had suddenly filled with tears.

''*Like* it! Oh, Matthew!'' Anne laid the dress over a chair and clasped her hands. ''Matthew, it's perfectly exquisite. Oh, I can never thank you enough. Look at those sleeves! Oh, it seems to me this must be a happy dream.''

''Well, well, let us have breakfast,'' interrupted Marilla. ''I must say, Anne, I don't think you needed the dress; but since Matthew has got it for you, see that you take good care of it. There's a hair ribbon Mrs. Lynde left for you. It's brown to match the dress. Come now, sit in.''

''I don't see how I'm going to eat breakfast,'' said Anne rapturously. ''Breakfast seems so commonplace at such an exciting moment. I'd rather feast my eyes on that dress. I'm so glad that puffed sleeves are still fashionable. It did seem to me that I'd never get over it if they went out before I had a dress with them. I'd never have felt quite satisfied, you see. It was lovely of Mrs. Lynde to give me the ribbon, too. I feel that I ought to be a very good girl indeed. It's at times like this I'm sorry I'm not a model little girl; and I always resolve that I will be in future. But somehow it's hard to carry out your resolutions when irresistible temptations come. Still, I really will make an extra effort after this.''

When the commonplace breakfast was over Diana appeared, crossing the white log bridge in the hollow, a gay little figure in her crimson ulster. Anne flew down the slope to meet her.

''Merry Christmas, Diana! And oh, it's a wonderful Christmas. I've something splendid to show you. Matthew has given me the loveliest dress, with *such* sleeves. I couldn't even imagine any nicer.''

''I've got something more for you,'' said Diana breathlessly. ''Here—this box. Aunt Josephine sent us out a big box with ever so many things in it—and this is for you. I'd have brought it over last night, but it didn't come until after dark, and I never feel very comfortable coming through the Haunted Wood in the dark now.''

Anne opened the box and peeped in. First a card with ''For the Anne-girl and Merry Christmas,'' written on it; and then, a pair of the daintiest little kid slippers, with beaded toes and satin bows and glistening buckles.

''Oh,'' said Anne, ''Diana, this is too much. I must be dreaming.''

''*I* call it providential,'' said Diana. ''You won't have to borrow Ruby's slippers now, and that's a blessing, for they're two sizes too big for you, and it would be awful to hear a fairy shuffling. Josie Pye would be delighted. Mind you, Rob Wright went home with Gertie Pye from the practice night before last. Did you ever hear anything equal to that?''

All the Avonlea scholars were in a fever of excitement that day, for the hall had to be decorated and a last grand rehearsal held.

The concert came off in the evening and was a pronounced success. The little hall was crowded; all the performers did excellently well, but Anne was the bright particular star of the occasion, as even envy, in the shape of Josie Pye, dared not deny.

"Oh, hasn't it been a brilliant evening?" sighed Anne, when it was all over and she and Diana were walking home together under a dark, starry sky.

"Everything went off very well," said Diana practically. "I guess we must have made as much as ten dollars. Mind you, Mr. Allan is going to send an account of it to the Charlottetown papers."

"Oh, Diana, will we really see our names in print? It makes me thrill to think of it. Your solo was perfectly elegant, Diana. I felt prouder than you did when it was encored. I just said to myself, 'It is my dear bosom friend who is so honored.' "

"Well, your recitations just brought down the house, Anne. That sad one was simply splendid."

"Oh, I was so nervous, Diana. When Mr. Allan called out my name I really cannot tell how I ever got up on that platform. I felt as if a million eyes were looking at me and through me, and for one dreadful moment I was sure I couldn't begin at all. Then I thought of my lovely puffed sleeves and took courage. I knew that I must live up to those sleeves, Diana. So I started in, and my voice seemed to be coming from ever so far away. I just felt like a parrot. It's providential that I practiced those recitations so often up in the garret, or I'd never have been able to get through. Did I groan all right?"

"Yes, indeed, you groaned lovely," assured Diana.

"I saw old Mrs. Sloane wiping away tears when I sat down. It was splendid to think I had touched somebody's heart. It's so romantic to take part in a concert, isn't it? Oh, it's been a very memorable occasion indeed."

"Wasn't the boys' dialogue fine?" said Diana. "Gilbert Blythe was just splendid. Anne, I do think it's awful mean the way you treat Gil. Wait till I tell you. When you ran off the platform after the fairy dialogue one of your roses fell out of your hair. I saw Gil pick it up and put it in his breast-pocket. There now. You're so romantic that I'm sure you ought to be pleased at that."

"It's nothing to me what that person does," said Anne loftily. "I simply never waste a thought on him, Diana."

That night Marilla and Matthew, who had been out to a concert for the first time in twenty years, sat for awhile by the kitchen fire after Anne had gone to bed.

"Well now, I guess our Anne did as well as any of them," said Matthew proudly.

"Yes, she did," admitted Marilla. "She's a bright child, Matthew. And she looked real nice, too. I've been kind of opposed to this concert scheme, but I suppose there's no real harm in it after all. Anyhow, I was proud of Anne tonight, although I'm not going to tell her so."

"Well now, I was proud of her and I did tell her so 'fore she went upstairs," said Matthew. "We must see what we can do for her some of these days, Marilla. I guess she'll need something more than Avonlea school by and by."

"There's time enough to think of that," said Marilla. "She's only thirteen in March. Though tonight it struck me she was growing quite a big girl. Mrs. Lynde made that dress a mite too long, and it makes Anne look so tall. She's quick to learn and I guess the best thing we can do for her will be to send her to Queen's after a spell. But nothing need be said about that for a year or two yet."

"Well now, it'll do no harm to be thinking it over off and on," said Matthew. "Things like that are all the better for lots of thinking over."

CHAPTER 26

THE STORY CLUB IS FORMED

JUNIOR AVONLEA found it hard to settle down to humdrum existence again. To Anne in particular things seemed fearfully flat, stale, and unprofitable after the goblet of excitement she had been sipping for weeks. Could she go back to the former quiet pleasures of those far-away days before the concert? At first, as she told Diana, she did not really think she could.

"I'm positively certain, Diana, that life can never be quite the same again as it was in those olden days," she said mournfully, as if referring to a period of at least fifty years back. "Perhaps after a while I'll get used to it, but I'm afraid concerts spoil people for everyday life. I suppose that is why Marilla disapproves of them. Marilla is such a sensible woman. It must be a great deal better to be sensible;

but still, I don't believe I'd really like to be a sensible person, because they are so unromantic. Mrs. Lynde says there is no danger of my ever being one, but you can never tell. I feel just now that I may grow up to be sensible yet. But perhaps that is only because I'm tired. I simply couldn't sleep last night for ever so long. I just lay awake and imagined the concert over and over again. That's one splendid thing about such affairs—it's so lovely to look back to them.''

Eventually, however, Avonlea school skipped back into its old groove and took up its old interests. To be sure, the concert left traces. Ruby Gillis and Emma White, who had quarrelled over a point of precedence in their platform seats, no longer sat at the same desk, and a promising friendship of three years was broken up. Josie Pye and Julia Bell did not ''speak'' for three months, because Josie Pye had told Bessie Wright that Julia Bell's bow when she got up to recite made her think of a chicken jerking up its head, and Bessie told Julia. None of the Sloanes would have any dealings with the Bells, because the Bells had declared that the Sloanes had too much to do in the program, and the Sloanes had retorted that the Bells were not capable of doing the little they had to do properly. Finally, Charlie Sloane fought Moody Spurgeon MacPherson, because Moody Spurgeon had said that Anne Shirley put on airs about her recitations, and Moody Spurgeon was ''licked;'' consequently Moody Spurgeon's sister, Ella May, would not ''speak'' to Anne Shirley all the rest of the winter. With the exception of these trifling frictions, work in Miss Stacy's little kingdom went on with regularity and smoothness.

The winter weeks slipped by. It was an unusually mild winter, with so little snow that Anne and Diana could go to school nearly every day by way of the Birch Path. On Anne's birthday they were tripping lightly down it, keeping eyes and ears alert amid all their chatter, for Miss Stacy had told them that they must soon write a composition on ''A Winter's Walk in the Woods,'' and it behooved them to be observant.

''Just think, Diana, I'm thirteen years old today,'' remarked Anne in an awed voice. ''I can scarcely realize that I'm in my teens. When I woke this morning it seemed to me that everything must be different. You've been thirteen for a month, so I suppose it doesn't seem such a novelty to you as it does to me. It makes life seem so much more interesting. In two more years I'll be really grown up. It's a great comfort to think that I'll be able to use big words then without being laughed at.''

"Ruby Gillis says she means to have a beau as soon as she's fifteen," said Diana.

"Ruby Gillis thinks of nothing but beaus," said Anne disdainfully. "She's actually delighted when any one writes her name up in a take-notice for all she pretends to be so mad. But I'm afraid that is an uncharitable speech. Mrs. Allan says we should never make uncharitable speeches; but they do slip out so often before you think, don't they? I simply can't talk about Josie Pye without making an uncharitable speech, so I never mention her at all. You may have noticed that. I'm trying to be as much like Mrs. Allan as I possibly can, for I think she's perfect. Mr. Allan thinks so too. Mrs. Lynde says he just worships the ground she treads on and she doesn't really think it right for a minister to set his affections so much on a mortal being. But then, Diana, even ministers are human and have their besetting sins just like everybody else. I had such an interesting talk with Mrs. Allan about besetting sins last Sunday afternoon. There are just a few things it's proper to talk about on Sundays and that is one of them. My besetting sin is imagining too much and forgetting my duties. I'm striving very hard to overcome it and now that I'm really thirteen perhaps I'll get on better."

"In four more years we'll be able to put our hair up," said Diana. "Alice Bell is only sixteen and she is wearing hers up, but I think that's ridiculous. I shall wait until I'm seventeen."

"If I had Alice Bell's crooked nose," said Anne decidely, "I wouldn't—but there! I won't say what I was going to because it was extremely uncharitable. Besides, I was comparing it with my own nose and that's vanity. I'm afraid I think too much about my nose ever since I heard that compliment about it long ago. It really is a great comfort to me. Oh, Diana, look, there's a rabbit. That's something to remember for our woods composition. I really think the woods are just as lovely in winter as in summer. They're so white and still, as if they were asleep and dreaming pretty dreams."

"I won't mind writing that composition when its time comes," sighed Diana. "I can manage to write about the woods, but the one we're to hand in Monday is terrible. The idea of Miss Stacy telling us to write a story out of our own heads!"

"Why it's as easy as a wink," said Anne.

"It's easy for you because you have an imagination," retorted Diana, "but what would you do if you had been born without one? I suppose you have your composition all done?"

Anne nodded, trying hard not to look virtuously complacent and failing miserably.

"I wrote it last Monday evening. It's called 'The Jealous Rival; or, in Death Not Divided.' I read it to Marilla and she said it was stuff and nonsense. Then I read it to Matthew and he said it was fine. That is the kind of critic I like. It's a sad, sweet story. I just cried like a child while I was writing it. It's about two beautiful maidens called Cordelia Montmorency and Geraldine Seymour who live in the same village and were devotedly attached to each other. Cordelia was a regal brunette with a coronet of midnight hair and duskly flashing eyes. Geraldine was a queenly blonde with hair like spun gold and velvety purple eyes."

"I never saw anybody with purple eyes," said Diana dubiously.

"Neither did I. I just imagined them. I wanted something out of the common. Geraldine had an alabaster brow, too. I've found out what an alabaster brow is. That is one of the advantages of being thirteen. You know so much more than you did when you were only twelve."

"Well, what became of Cordelia and Geraldine?" asked Diana, who was beginning to feel rather interested in their fate.

"They grow in beauty side by side until they were sixteen. Then Bertram DeVere came to their native village and fell in love with the fair Geraldine. He saved her life when her horse ran away with her in a carriage, and she fainted in his arms and he carried her home three miles; because, you understand, the carriage was all smashed up. I found it rather hard to imagine the proposal because I had no experience to go by. I asked Ruby Gillis if she knew anything about how men proposed because I thought she'd likely be an authority on the subject, having so many sisters married. Ruby told me she was hid in the hall pantry when Malcolm Andrews proposed to her sister Susan. She said Malcolm told Susan that his dad had given him the farm in his own name and then said, 'What do you say, darling pet, if we get hitched this fall?' And Susan said, 'Yes—no—I don't know—let me see,'—and there they were, engaged as quick as that. But I didn't think that sort of a proposal was a very romantic one, so in the end I had to imagine it out as well as I could. I made it very flowery and poetical and Bertram went on his knees, although Ruby Gillis says it isn't done nowadays. Geraldine accepted him in a speech a page long. I can tell you I took a lot of trouble with that speech. I rewrote it five times and I look upon it as my masterpiece. Bertram gave her a diamond ring and a ruby necklace and told her they would go to Europe for a wedding tour, for he was immensely wealthy. But then, alas, shadows began to darken over their path.

Cordelia was secretly in love with Bertram herself and when Geraldine told her about the engagement she was simply furious, especially when she saw the necklace and the diamond ring. All her affection for Geraldine turned to bitter hate and she vowed that she should never marry Bertram. But she pretended to be Geraldine's friend the same as ever. One evening they were standing on the bridge over a rushing turbulent stream and Cordelia, thinking they were alone, pushed Geraldine over the brink with a wild, mocking 'Ha, ha, ha.' But Bertram saw it all and he at once plunged into the current, exclaiming, 'I will save thee, my peerless Geraldine.' But alas, he had forgotten he couldn't swim and they were both drowned, clasped in each other's arms. Their bodies were washed ashore soon afterwards. They were buried in the one grave and their funeral was most imposing, Diana. It's so much more romantic to end a story up with a funeral than a wedding. As for Cordelia, she went insane with remorse and was shut up in a lunatic asylum. I thought that was a poetical retribution for her crime.''

''How perfectly lovely!'' sighed Diana, who belonged to Matthew's school of critics. ''I don't see how you can make up such thrilling things out of your own head, Anne. I wish my imagination was as good as yours.''

''It would be if you'd only cultivate it,'' said Anne cheeringly. ''I've just thought of a plan, Diana. Let you and I have a story club all our own and write stories for practice. I'll help you along until you can do them by yourself. You ought to cultivate your imagination, you know. Miss Stacy says so. Only we must take the right way. I told her about the Haunted Wood, but she said we went the wrong way about it in that.''

This was how the story club came into existence. It was limited to Diana and Anne at first, but soon it was extended to include Jane Andrews and Ruby Gillis and one or two others who felt that their imaginations needed cultivating. No boys were allowed in it—although Ruby Gillis opined that their admission would make it more exciting—and each member had to produce one story a week.

''It's extremely interesting,'' Anne told Marilla. ''Each girl has to read her story out loud and then we talk it over. We are going to keep them all sacredly and have them to read to our descendants. We each write under a nom-de-plume. Mine is Rosamond Montmorency. All the girls do pretty well. Ruby Gillis is rather sentimental. She puts too much love-making into her stories and you know too much is worse than too little. Jane never puts any because she says it makes her feel so silly when she has to read it out loud. Jane's stories are extremely sensible. Then Diana puts too many murders into hers. She says most of the time she doesn't know what to do with the people so she kills them off to get rid of them. I mostly always have to tell them what to write about, but that isn't hard for I've millions of ideas.''

''I think this story-writing business is the foolishest yet,'' scoffed Marilla. ''You'll get a pack of nonsense into your heads and waste time that should be put on your lessons. Reading stories is bad enough but writing them is worse.''

''But we're so careful to put a moral into them all, Marilla,'' explained Anne. ''I insist upon that. All the good people are rewarded and all the bad ones are suitably punished. I'm sure that must have a wholesome effect. The moral is the great thing. Mr. Allan says so. I read one of my stories to him and Mrs. Allan and they both agreed that the moral was excellent. Only they laughed in the wrong places. I like it better when people cry. Jane and Ruby almost always cry when I come to the pathetic parts. Diana wrote her Aunt Josephine about our club and her Aunt Josephine wrote back that we were to send her some of our stories. So we copied out four of our very best and sent them. Miss Josephine Barry wrote back that she had never read anything so amusing in her life. That kind of puzzled us because the stories were all very pathetic and almost everybody died. But I'm glad Miss Barry liked them. It shows our club is doing some good in the world. Mrs. Allan says that ought to be our object in everything. I do really try to make it my object but I forget so often when I'm having fun. I hope I shall be a little like Mrs. Allan when I grow up. Do you think there is any prospect of it, Marilla?''

''I shouldn't say there was a great deal,'' was Marilla's encouraging answer. ''I'm sure Mrs. Allan was never such a silly, forgetful little girl as you are.''

''No; but she wasn't always so good as she is now either,'' said Anne seriously. ''She told me so herself—that is, she said she was a dreadful mischief when she was a girl and was always getting into scrapes. I felt so encouraged when I heard that. Is it very wicked of me, Marilla, to feel encouraged when I hear that other people have been bad and mischievous? Mrs. Lynde says it is. Mrs. Lynde says she always feels shocked when she hears of any one ever having been naughty, no matter how small they were. Mrs. Lynde says she once heard a minister confess that when he was a boy he stole a strawberry tart out of his aunt's pantry and she never had any respect for that minister again. Now, I wouldn't have felt that way. I'd have thought that it was real noble of him to confess it, and I'd have thought what an encouraging thing it would be for small boys nowadays who do naughty things and are sorry for them to know that perhaps they may grow up to be ministers in spite of it. That's how I'd feel, Marilla.''

''The way I feel at present, Anne,'' said Marilla, ''is that it's high time you had those dishes washed. You've taken half an hour longer than you should with all your chattering. Learn to work first and talk afterwards.''

CHAPTER 27

VANITY AND VEXATION OF SPIRIT

MARILLA, WALKING home one late April evening from an Aid meeting, realized that the winter was over and gone with the thrill of delight that spring never fails to bring to the oldest and saddest as well as to the youngest and merriest. Marilla was not given to the subjective analysis of her thoughts and feelings. She probably imagined that she was thinking about the Aids and their missionary box and the new carpet for the vestry-room, but under these reflections was a harmonious consciousness of red fields smoking into pale-purply mists in the declining sun, of long, sharp-pointed fir shadows falling over the meadow beyond the brook, of still crimson-budded maples around a mirror-like wood-pool, of a wakening in the world and a stir of hidden pulses under the gray sod. The spring was abroad in the land and Marilla's sober, middle-aged step was lighter and swifter because of its deep, primal gladness.

Her eyes dwelt affectionately on Green Gables, peering through its network of trees and reflecting the sunlight back from its windows in several little coruscations of glory. Marilla, as she picked her steps along the damp lane, thought that it was really a satisfaction to know that she was going home to a briskly snapping wood fire and a table nicely spread for tea, instead of to the cold comfort of old Aid meeting evenings before Anne had come to Green Gables.

Consequently, when Marilla entered her kitchen and found the fire black out, with no sign of Anne anywhere, she felt justly disappointed and irritated. She had told Anne to be sure and have tea ready at five o'clock, but now she must hurry to take off her second-best dress and prepare the meal herself against Matthew's return from ploughing.

"I'll settle Miss Anne when she comes home," said Marilla grimly, as she shaved up kindlings with a carving knife and more vim than was strictly necessary. Matthew had come in and was waiting patiently for his tea in his corner. "She's gadding off somewhere with Diana, writing stories or practising dialogues or some such tomfoolery, and never thinking once about the time or her duties. She's just got to be pulled up short and sudden on this sort of thing. I don't care if Mrs. Allan does say she's the brightest and sweetest child she ever knew. She may be bright and sweet enough, but her head is full of nonsense and there's never any knowing what shape it'll break out in next. Just as soon as she grows out of one freak she takes up with another. But there! Here I am saying the very thing I was so riled with Rachel Lynde for saying at the Aid today. I was real glad when Mrs. Allan spoke up for Anne, for if she hadn't I know I'd have said something too sharp to Rachel before everybody. Anne's got plenty of faults, goodness knows, and far be it from me to deny it. But I'm bringing her up and not Rachel Lynde, who'd pick faults in the Angel Gabriel himself if he lived in Avonlea. Just the same, Anne has no business to leave the house like this when I told her she was to stay home this afternoon and look after things. I must say, with all her faults, I never found her disobedient or untrustworthy before and I'm real sorry to find her so now."

"Well now, I dunno," said Matthew, who, being patient and wise, and above all, hungry, had deemed it best to let Marilla talk her wrath out unhindered, having learned by experience that she got through with whatever work was on hand much quicker if not delayed by untimely argument. "Perhaps you're judging her too hasty, Marilla. Don't call her untrustworthy until you're sure she has disobeyed you. Mebbe it can all be explained—Anne's a great hand at explaining."

"She's not here when I told her to stay," retorted Marilla. "I reckon she'll find it hard to explain *that* to my satisfaction. Of course I knew you'd take her part, Matthew. But I'm bringing her up, not you."

It was dark when supper was ready, and still no sign of Anne, coming hurriedly over the log bridge or up Lovers' Lane, breathless and repentant with a sense of neglected duties. Marilla washed and put away the dishes grimly. Then, wanting a candle to light her down cellar, she went up to the east gable for the one that generally stood on Anne's table. Lighting it, she turned around to see Anne herself lying on the bed, face downward among the pillows.

"Mercy on us," said astonished Marilla, "have you been asleep, Anne?"

"No," was the muffled reply.

"Are you sick then?" demanded Marilla anxiously, going over to the bed.

Anne cowered deeper into her pillows as if desirous of hiding herself for ever from mortal eyes.

"No. But please, Marilla, go away and don't look at me. I'm in the depths of despair and I don't care who gets head in class or writes the best composition or sings in the Sunday school choir any more. Little things like that are of no importance now because I don't suppose I'll ever be able to go anywhere again. My career is closed. Please, Marilla, go away and don't look at me."

"Did any one ever hear the like?" the mystified Marilla wanted to know. "Anne Shirley, whatever is the matter with you? What have you done? Get right up this minute and tell me. This minute, I say. There now, what is it?"

Anne had slid to the floor in despairing obedience.

"Look at my hair, Marilla," she whispered.

Accordingly, Marilla lifted her candle and looked scrutinizingly at Anne's hair, flowing in heavy masses down her back. It certainly had a very strange appearance.

"Anne Shirley, what have you done to your hair? Why, its *green!*"

Green it might be called, if it were any earthly color—a queer, dull, bronzy green, with streaks here and there of the original red to heighten the ghastly effect. Never in all her life had Marilla seen anything so grotesque as Anne's hair at that moment.

"Yes, it's green," moaned Anne. "I thought nothing could be as bad as red hair. But now I know it's ten times worse to have green hair. Oh, Marilla, you little know how utterly wretched I am."

"I little know how you got into this fix, but I mean to find out," said Marilla. "Come right down to the kitchen—it's too cold up here—and tell me just what you've done. I've been expecting something queer for some time. You haven't got into any scrape for over two months, and I was sure another one was due. Now, then, what did you do to your hair?''

''I dyed it.''

''Dyed it! Dyed your hair! Anne Shirley, didn't you know it was a wicked thing to do?''

''Yes, I knew it was a little wicked,'' admitted Anne. ''But I thought it was worth while to be a little wicked to get rid of red hair. I counted the cost, Marilla. Besides, I meant to be extra good in other ways to make up for it.''

''Well,'' said Marilla sarcastically, ''if I'd decided it was worth while to dye my hair I'd have dyed it a decent color at least. I wouldn't have dyed it green.''

''But I didn't mean to dye it green, Marilla,'' protested Anne dejectedly. ''If I was wicked I meant to be wicked to some purpose. He said it would turn my hair a beautiful raven black—he positively assured me that it would. How could I doubt his word, Marilla? I know what it feels like to have your word doubted. And Mrs. Allan says we should never suspect any one of not telling us the truth unless we have proof that they're not. I have proof now—green hair is proof enough for anybody. But I hadn't then and I believed every word he said *implicitly*.''

''Who said? Who are you talking about?''

''The pedlar that was here this afternoon. I bought the dye from him.''

''Anne Shirley, how often have I told you never to let one of those Italians in the house! I don't believe in encouraging them to come around at all.''

''Oh, I didn't let him in the house. I remembered what you told me, and I went out, carefully shut the door, and looked at his things on the step. Besides, he wasn't an Italian——he was a German. He had a big box full of very interesting things and he told me he was working hard to make enough money to bring his wife and children out from Germany. He spoke so feelingly about them that it touched my heart. I wanted to buy something from him to help him in such a worthy object. Then all at once I saw the bottle of hair dye. The pedlar said it was warranted to dye any hair a beautiful raven black and wouldn't wash off. In a trice I saw myself with beautiful raven black hair and the temptation was irresistible. But the price of the bottle was seventy-five cents and I had only fifty cents left out of my chicken money. I think the pedlar had a very kind heart, for he said that, seeing it was me, he'd sell it for fifty cents and that was just giving it away. So I bought it, and as soon as he had gone I came up here and applied it with an old hair-brush as the directions said. I used up the whole bottle, and oh, Marilla, when I saw the dreadful color it turned my hair I repented of being wicked, I can tell you. And I've been repenting ever since.''

''Well, I hope you'll repent to good purpose,'' said Marilla severely, ''and that you've got your eyes opened to where your vanity has led you, Anne. Goodness knows what's to be done. I suppose the first thing is to give your hair a good washing and see if that will do any good.''

Accordingly, Anne washed her hair, scrubbing it vigorously with soap and water, but for all the difference it made she might as well have been scouring its original red. The pedlar had certainly spoken the truth when he declared that the dye wouldn't wash off, however his veracity might be impeached in other respects.

''Oh, Marilla, what shall I do?'' questioned Anne in tears. ''I can never live this down. People have pretty well forgotten my other mistakes—the liniment cake and setting up Diana drunk and flying into a temper with Mrs. Lynde. But they'll never forget this. They will think I am not respectable. Oh, Marilla, 'what a tangled web we weave when first we practise to deceive.' That is poetry, but it is true. And oh, how Josie Pye will laugh! Marilla, I *cannot* face Josie Pye. I am the unhappiest girl in Prince Edward Island.''

Anne's unhappiness continued for a week. During that time she went nowhere and shampooed her hair every day. Diana alone of outsiders knew the fatal secret, but she promised solemnly never to tell, and it may be stated here and now that she kept her word. At the end of the week Marilla said decidedly:

''It's no use, Anne. That is fast dye if ever there was any. Your hair must be cut off; there is no other way. You can't go out with it looking like that.''

Anne's lips quivered, but she realized the bitter truth of Marilla's remarks. With a dismal sigh she went for the scissors.

''Please cut it off at once, Marilla, and have it over. Oh, I feel that my heart is broken. This is such an unromantic affliction. The girls in books lose their hair in fevers or sell it to get money for some good deed, and I'm sure I wouldn't mind losing my hair in some such fashion half so much. But there is nothing comforting in having your hair cut off because you've dyed it a dreadful color, is there? I'm going to weep all the time you're cutting it off, if it won't interfere. It seems such a tragic thing.''

Anne wept then, but later on, when she went upstairs and looked in the glass, she was calm with despair. Marilla had done her work thoroughly and it had been necessary to shingle the hair as closely as possible. The result was not becoming, to state the case as mildly as may be. Anne promptly turned her glass to the wall.

"I'll never, never look at myself again until my hair grows," she exclaimed passionately.

Then she suddenly righted the glass.

"Yes, I will, too. I'd do penance for being wicked that way. I'll look at myself every time I come to my room and see how ugly I am. And I won't try to imagine it away, either. I never thought I was vain about my hair, of all things, but now I know I was, in spite of its being red, because it was so long and thick and curly. I expect something will happen to my nose next.''

Anne's clipped head made a sensation in school on the following Monday, but to her relief nobody guessed the real reason for it, not even Josie Pye, who, however, did not fail to inform Anne that she looked like a perfect scarecrow.

"I didn't say anything when Josie said that to me," Anne confided that evening to Marilla, who was lying on the sofa after one of her headaches, "because I thought it was part of my punishment and I ought to bear it patiently. It's hard to be told you look like a scarecrow and I wanted to say something back. But I didn't. I just swept her one scornful look and then I forgave her. It makes you feel very virtuous when you forgive people, doesn't it? I mean to devote all my energies to being good after this and I shall never try to be beautiful again. Of course it's better to be good. I know it is, but it's sometimes so hard to believe a thing even when you know it. I do really want to be good, Marilla, like you and Mrs. Allan and Miss Stacy, and grow up to be a credit to you. Diana says when my hair begins to grow to tie a black velvet ribbon around my head with a bow at one side. She says she thinks it will be very becoming. I will call it a snood—that sounds so romantic. But am I talking too much, Marilla? Does it hurt your head?''

"My head is better now. It was terrible bad this afternoon, though. These headaches of mine are getting worse and worse. I'll have to see a doctor about them. As for your chatter, I don't know that I mind it—I've got so used to it.''

Which was Marilla's way of saying that she liked to hear it.

CHAPTER 28

AN UNFORTUNATE LILY MAID

"OF COURSE you must be Elaine, Anne," said Diana. "I could never have the courage to float down there."

"Nor I," said Ruby Gillis with a shiver. "I don't mind floating down when there's two or three of us in the flat and we can sit up. It's fun then. But to lie down and pretend I was dead—I just couldn't. I'd die really of fright."

"Of course it would be romantic," conceded Jane Andrews. "But I know I couldn't keep still. I'd be popping up ever minute or so to see where I was and if I wasn't drifting too far out. And you know, Anne, that would spoil the effect."

"But it's so ridiculous to have a red-headed Elaine," mourned Anne. "I'm not afraid to float down and I'd *love* to be Elaine. But it's ridiculous just the same. Ruby ought to be Elaine because she is so fair and has such lovely long golden hair—Elaine had 'all her bright hair streaming down,' you know. And Elaine was the lily maid. Now, a red-haired person cannot be a lily maid."

"Your complexion is just as fair as Ruby's," said Diana earnestly, "and your hair is ever so much darker than it used to be before you cut it."

"Oh, do you really think so?" exclaimed Anne, flushing sensitively with delight. "I've sometimes thought it was myself—but I never dared to ask anyone for fear she would tell me it wasn't. Do you think it could be called auburn now, Diana?"

"Yes, and I think it is real pretty," said Diana, looking admiringly at the short, silky curls that clustered over Anne's head and were held in place by a very jaunty black velvet ribbon and bow.

They were standing on the bank of the pond, below Orchard Slope, where a little headland fringed with birches ran out from the bank; at its tip was a small wooden platform built out into the water for the convenience of fishermen and duck hunters. Ruby and Jane were spending the midsummer afternoon with Diana, and Anne had come over to play with them.

Anne and Diana had spent most of their playtime that summer on and about the pond. Idlewild was a thing of the past, Mr. Bell having ruthlessly cut down the little circle of trees in his back pasture in the spring. Anne had sat among the stumps and wept, not without an eye to the romance of it; but she was speedily consoled, for, after all, as she and Diana said, big girls of thirteen, going on fourteen, were too old for such childish amusements as playhouses, and there were more fascinating sports to be found about the pond. It was splendid to fish for trout over the bridge and the two girls learned to row themselves about in the little flat-bottomed dory Mr. Barry kept for duck shooting.

It was Anne's idea that they dramatize Elaine. They had studied Tennyson's poem in school the preceding winter, the Superintendent of Education having prescribed it in the English course for the Prince Edward Island schools. They had analyzed and parsed it and torn it to pieces in general until it was a wonder there was any meaning at all left in it for them, but at least the fair lily maid and Lancelot and Guinevere and King Arthur had become very real people to them, and Anne was devoured by secret regret that she had not been born in Camelot. Those days, she said, were so much more romantic than the present.

Anne's plan was hailed with enthusiasm. The girls had discovered that if the flat were pushed off from the landing-place it would drift down with the current under the bridge and finally strand itself on another headland lower down which ran out at a curve in the pond. They had often gone down like this and nothing could be more convenient for playing Elaine.

"Well, I'll be Elaine," said Anne, yielding reluctantly, for, although she would have been delighted to play the principal character, yet her artistic sense demanded fitness for it and this, she felt, her limitations made impossible. "Ruby, you must be King Arthur and Jane will be Guinevere and Diana must be Lancelot. But first you must be the brothers and the father. We can't have the old dumb servitor because there isn't room for two in the flat when one is lying down. We must pall the barge all its length in blackest samite. That old black shawl of your mother's will be just the thing, Diana."

The black shawl having been procured, Anne spread it over the flat and then lay down on the bottom, with closed eyes and hands folded over her breast.

"Oh, she does look really dead," whispered Ruby Gillis nervously, watching the still, white little face under the flickering shadows of the birches. "It makes me feel frightened, girls. Do you suppose it's really right to act like this? Mrs. Lynde says that all play-acting is abominably wicked."

"Ruby, you shouldn't talk about Mrs. Lynde," said Anne severely. "It spoils the effect because this is hundreds of years before Mrs. Lynde was born. Jane, you arrange this. It's silly for Elaine to be talking when she's dead."

Jane rose to the occasion. Cloth of gold for coverlet there was none, but an old piano scarf of yellow Japanese crêpe was an excellent substitute. A white lily was not obtainable just then, but the effect of a tall blue iris placed in one of Anne's folded hands was all that could be desired.

"Now, she's all ready," said Jane. "We must kiss her quiet brows and, Diana, you say, 'Sister, farewell for ever,' and Ruby, you say, 'Farewell, sweet sister,' both of you as sorrowfully as you possibly can. Anne, for goodness sake smile a little. You know Elaine 'lay as though she smiled.' That's better. Now push the flat off."

The flat was accordingly pushed off, scraping roughly over an old embedded stake in the process. Diana and Jane and Ruby only waited long enough to see it caught in the current and headed for the bridge before scampering up through the woods, across the road, and down to the lower headland where, as Lancelot and Guinevere and the King, they were to be in readiness to receive the lily maid.

For a few minutes Anne, drifting slowly down, enjoyed the romance of her situation to the full. Then something happened not at all romantic. The flat began to leak. In a very few moments it was necessary for Elaine to scramble to her feet, pick up her cloth of gold coverlet and pall of blackest samite and gaze blankly at a big crack in the bottom of her barge through which the water was literally pouring. That sharp stake at the landing had torn off the strip of batting nailed on the flat. Anne did not know this, but it did not take her long to realize that she was in a dangerous plight. At this rate the flat would fill and sink long before it could drift to the lower headland. Where were the oars? Left behind at the landing!

Anne gave one gasping little scream which nobody ever heard; she was white to the lips, but she did not lose her self-possession. There was one chance—just one.

"I was horribly frightened," she told Mrs. Allan the next day, "and it seemed like years while the flat was drifting down to the bridge and the water rising in it every moment. I prayed, Mrs. Allan, most earnestly, but I didn't shut my eyes to pray, for I knew the only way God could save me was to let the flat float close enought to one of the bridge piles for me to climb up on it. You know the piles are just old tree trunks and there are lots of knots and old branch stubs on them. It was proper to pray, but I had to do my part by watching out and right well I knew it. I just said, 'Dear God, please take the flat close to a pile and I'll do the rest,' over and over again. Under such circumstances you don't think much about making a flowery prayer. But mine was answered, for the flat bumped right into a pile for a minute and I flung the scarf and the shawl over my shoulder and scrambled up on a big providential stub. And there I was, Mrs. Allan, clinging to that slippery old pile with no way of getting up or down. It was a very unromantic position, but I didn't think about that at the time. You don't think much about romance when you have just escaped from a watery grave. I said a grateful prayer at once and then I gave all my attention to holding on tight, for I knew I should probably have to depend on human aid to get back to dry land.''

The flat drifted under the bridge and then promptly sank in midstream. Ruby, Jane, and Diana, already awaiting it on the lower headland, saw it disappear before their very eyes and had not a doubt but that Anne had gone down with it. For a moment they stood still, white as sheets, frozen with horror at the tragedy; then, shrieking at the tops of their voices, they started on a frantic run up through the woods, never pausing as they crossed the main road to glance the way of the bridge. Anne, clinging desperately to her precarious foothold, saw their flying forms and heard their shrieks. Help would soon come, but meanwhile her position was a very uncomfortable one.

The minutes passed by, each seeming an hour to the unfortunate lily maid. Why didn't somebody come? Where had the girls gone? Suppose they had fainted, one and all! Suppose nobody ever came! Suppose she grew so tired and cramped that she could hold on no longer! Anne looked at the wicked green depths below her, wavering with long, oily shadows, and shivered. Her imagination began to suggest all manner of gruesome possibilities to her.

Then, just as she thought she really could not endure the ache in her arms and wrists another moment, Gilbert Blythe came rowing under the bridge in Harmon Andrews' dory!

Gilbert glanced up and, much to his amazement, beheld a little white scornful face looking down upon him with big, frightened but also scornful gray eyes.

''Anne Shirley! How on earth did you get there?'' he exclaimed.

Without waiting for an answer he pulled close to the pile and extended his hand. There was no help for it; Anne, clinging to Gilbert Blythe's hand, scrambled down into the dory, where she sat, drabbled and furious, in the stern with her arms full of dripping shawl

HE PULLED CLOSE TO THE PILE AND EXTENDED HIS HAND.

and wet crêpe. It was certainly extremely difficult to be dignified under the circumstances!

"What has happened, Anne?" asked Gilbert, taking up his oars.

"We were playing Elaine," explained Anne frigidly, without even looking at her rescuer, "and I had to drift down to Camelot in the barge—I mean the flat. The flat began to leak and I climbed out on the pile. The girls went for help. Will you be kind enough to row me to the landing?"

Gilbert obligingly rowed to the landing and Anne, disdaining assistance, sprang nimbly on shore.

"I'm very much obliged to you," she said haughtily as she turned away. But Gilbert had also sprung from the boat and now laid a detaining hand on her arm.

"Anne," he said hurriedly, "look here. Can't we be good friends? I'm awfully sorry I made fun of your hair that time. I didn't mean to vex you and I only meant it for a joke. Besides, it's so long ago. I think your hair is awfully pretty now—honest I do. Let's be friends."

For a moment Anne hesitated. She had an odd, newly awakened consciousness under all her outraged dignity that the half-shy, half-eager expression in Gilbert's hazel eyes was something that was very good to see. Her heart gave a quick, queer little beat. But the bitterness of her old grievance promptly stiffened up her wavering determination. That scene of two years before flashed back into her recollection as vividly as if it had taken place yesterday. Gilbert had called her "carrots" and had brought about her disgrace before the whole school. Her resentment, which to other and older people might be as laughable as its cause, was in no whit allayed and softened by time seemingly. She hated Gilbert Blythe! She would never forgive him!

"No," she said coldly, "I shall never be friends with you, Gilbert Blythe; and I don't want to be!"

"All right!" Gilbert sprang into his skiff with an angry color in his cheeks. "I'll never ask you to be friends again, Anne Shirley. And I don't care either!"

He pulled away with swift defiant strokes, and Anne went up the steep, ferny little path under the maples. She held her head very high, but she was conscious of an odd feeling of regret. She almost wished she had answered Gilbert differently. Of course, he had insulted her terribly, but still—! Altogether, Anne rather thought it would be a relief to sit down and have a good cry. She was really quite unstrung, for the reaction from her fright and cramped clinging was making itself felt.

Half-way up the path she met Jane and Diana rushing back to the pond in a state narrowly removed from positive frenzy. They had found nobody at Orchard Slope, both Mr. and Mrs. Barry being away. Here Ruby Gillis had succumbed to hysterics, and was left to recover from them as best she might, while Jane and Diana flew through the Haunted Wood and across the brook to Green Gables. There they had found nobody either, for Marilla had gone to Carmody and Matthew was making hay in the back field.

"Oh, Anne," gasped Diana, fairly falling on the former's neck and weeping with relief and delight, "Oh, Anne—we thought—you were—drowned—and we felt like murderers—because we had made—you be—Elaine. And Ruby is in hysterics—oh, Anne, how did you escape?"

"I climbed up on one of the piles," explained Anne wearily, "and Gilbert Blythe came along in Mr. Andrews' dory and brought me to land."

"Oh, Anne, how splendid of him! Why, it's so romantic!" said Jane, finding breath enough for utterance at last. "Of course you'll speak to him after this."

"Of course I won't," flashed Anne with a momentary return of her old spirit. "And I don't want ever to hear the word romantic again, Jane Andrews. I'm awfully sorry you were so frightened, girls. It is all my fault. I feel sure I was born under an unlucky star. Everything I do gets me or my dearest friends into a scrape. We've gone and lost your father's flat, Diana, and I have a presentiment that we'll not be allowed to row on the pond any more."

Anne's presentiment proved more trustworthy than presentiments are apt to do. Great was the consternation in the Barry and Cuthbert households when the events of the afternoon became known.

"Will you *ever* have any sense, Anne?" groaned Marilla.

"Oh, yes, I think I will, Marilla," returned Anne optimistically. A good cry, indulged in the grateful solitude of the east gable, had soothed her nerves and restored her to her wonted cheerfulness. "I think my prospects of becoming sensible are brighter now than ever."

"I don't see how," said Marilla.

"Well," explained Anne, "I've learned a new and valuable lesson today. Ever since I came to Green Gables I've been making mistakes, and each mistake has helped to cure me of some great shortcoming. The affair of the amethyst brooch cured me of meddling with things that didn't belong to me. The Haunted Wood mistake cured me of letting my imagination run away with me. The liniment cake mistake cured me of carelessness in cooking. Dyeing my hair cured me of vanity. I never think about my hair and nose now—at least, very seldom. And today's mistake is going to cure me of being too romantic. I have come to the conclusion that it is no use trying to be romantic in Avonlea. It was probably easy enough in towered Camelot hundreds of years ago, but romance is not appreciated now. I feel quite sure that you will soon see a great improvement in me in this respect, Marilla.''

"I'm sure I hope so,'' said Marilla skeptically.

But Matthew, who had been sitting mutely in his corner, laid a hand on Anne's shoulder when Marilla had gone out.

"Don't give up all your romance, Anne,'' he whispered shyly, "a little of it is a good thing—not too much, of course—but keep a little of it, Anne, keep a little of it.''

CHAPTER 29

AN EPOCH IN ANNE'S LIFE

ANNE WAS bringing the cows home from the back pasture by way of Lovers' Lane. It was a September evening and all the gaps and clearings in the woods were brimmed up with ruby sunset light. Here and there the lane was splashed with it, but for the most part it was already quite shadowy beneath the maples, and the spaces under the firs were filled with a clear violet dusk like airy wine. The winds were out in their tops, and there is no sweeter music on earth than that which the wind makes in the fir-trees at evening.

The cows swung placidly down the lane, and Anne followed them dreamily, repeating aloud the battle canto from "Marmion"— which had also been part of their English course the preceding winter and which Miss Stacy had made them learn off by heart—and exulting in its rushing lines and the clash of spears in its imagery. When she came to the lines:

> *The stubborn spearsmen still made good*
> *Their dark impenetrable wood,*

she stopped in ecstasy to shut her eyes that she might the better fancy herself one of that heroic ring. When she opened them again it was to behold Diana coming through the gate that led into the Barry field and looking so important that Anne instantly divined there was news to be told. But betray too eager curiosity she would not.

"Isn't this evening just like a purple dream, Diana? It makes me so glad to be alive. In the mornings I always think the mornings are best; but when evening comes I think it's lovelier still."

"It's a very fine evening," said Diana, "but oh, I have such news, Anne. Guess. You can have three guesses."

"Charlotte Gillis is going to be married in the church after all and Mrs. Allan wants us to decorate it," cried Anne.

"No. Charlotte's beau won't agree to that, because nobody ever has been married in the church yet, and he thinks it would seem too much like a funeral. It's too mean, because it would be such fun. Guess again."

"Jane's mother is going to let her have a birthday party?"

Diana shook her head, her black eyes dancing with merriment.

"I can't think what it can be," said Anne in despair, "unless it's that Moody Spurgeon MacPherson saw you home from prayer-meeting last night. Did he?"

"I should think not," exclaimed Diana indignantly. "I wouldn't be likely to boast of it if he did, the horrid creature! I knew you couldn't guess it. Mother had a letter from Aunt Josephine today, and Aunt Josephine wants you and me to go to town next Tuesday and stop with her for the Exhibition. There!"

"Oh, Diana," whispered Anne, finding it necessary to lean up against a maple-tree for support, "do you really mean it? But I'm afraid Marilla won't let me go. She will say that she can't encourage gadding about. That was what she said last week when Jane invited me to go with them in their double-seated buggy to the American concert at the White Sands Hotel. I wanted to go, but Marilla said I'd better be home learning my lessons and so would Jane. I was bitterly disappoined, Diana. I felt so heart-broken that I wouldn't say my prayers when I went to bed. But I repented of that and got up in the middle of the night and said them."

"I'll tell you," said Diana, "we'll get mother to ask Marilla. She'll be more likely to let you go then; and if she does we'll have the time of our lives, Anne. I've never been to an Exhibition, and it's so aggravating to hear the other girls talking about their trips. Jane and Ruby have been twice, and they're going this year again.''

''I'm not going to think about it at all until I know whether I can go or not,'' said Anne resolutely. ''If I did and then was disappointed, it would be more than I could bear. But in case I do go I'm very glad my new coat will be ready by that time. Marilla didn't think I needed a new coat. She said my old one would do very well for another winter and that I ought to be satisfied with having a new dress. The dress is very pretty, Diana—navy blue and made so fashionably. Marilla always makes my dresses fashionably now, because she says she doesn't intend to have Matthew going to Mrs. Lynde to make them. I'm so glad. It is ever so much easier to be good if your clothes are fashionable. At least, it is easier for me. I suppose it doesn't make such a difference to naturally good people. But Matthew said I must have a new coat, so Marilla bought a lovely piece of blue broadcloth, and it's being made by a real dressmaker over at Carmody. It's to be done Saturday night, and I'm trying not to imagine myself walking up the church aisle on Sunday in my new suit and cap, because I'm afraid it isn't right to imagine such things. But it just slips into my mind in spite of me. My cap is so pretty. Matthew bought it for me the day we were over at Carmody. It is one of those little blue velvet ones that are all the rage, with gold cord and tassels. Your new hat is elegant, Diana, and so becoming. When I saw you come into church last Sunday my heart swelled with pride to think you were my dearest friend. Do you suppose it's wrong for us to think so much about clothes? Marilla says it is very sinful. But it *is* such an interesting subject, isn't it?''

Marilla agreed to let Anne go to town, and it was arranged that Mr. Barry should take the girls in on the following Tuesday. As Charlottetown was thirty miles away and Mr. Barry wished to go and return the same day, it was necessary to make a very early start. But Anne counted it all joy, and was up before sunrise on Tuesday morning. A glance from her window assured her that the day would be fine, for the eastern sky behind the firs of the Haunted Wood was all silvery and cloudless. Through the gap in the trees a light was shining in the western gable of Orchard Slope, a token that Diana was also up.

Anne was dressed by the time Matthew had the fire on and had the breakfast ready when Marilla came down, but for her own part was much too excited to eat. After breakfast the jaunty new cap and jacket were donned, and Anne hastened over the brook and up through the firs to Orchard Slope. Mr. Barry and Diana were waiting for her, and they were soon on the road.

It was a long drive, but Anne and Diana enjoyed every minute of it. It was delightful to rattle along over the moist roads in the early red sunlight that was creeping across the shorn harvest fields. The air was fresh and crisp, and little smoke-blue mists curled throught the valleys and floated off from the hills. Sometimes the road went through the woods where maples were beginning to hang out scarlet banners; sometimes it crossed rivers on bridges that made Anne's flesh cringe with the old, half-delightful fear; sometimes it wound along a harbor shore and passed by a little cluster of weather-gray fishing huts; again it mounted to hills whence a far sweep of curving upland or misty blue sky could be seen; but wherever it went there was much of interest to discuss. It was almost noon when they reached town and found their way to "Beechwood." It was quite a fine old mansion, set back from the street in a seclusion of green elms and branching beeches. Miss Barry met them at the door with a twinkle in her sharp black eyes.

"So you've come to see me at last, you Anne-girl." she said. "Mercy, child, how you have grown! You're taller than I am, I declare. And you're ever so much better-looking than you used to be, too. But I dare say you know that without being told."

"Indeed I didn't," said Anne radiantly. "I know I'm not so freckled as I used to be, so I've much to be thankful for, but I really hadn't dared to hope there was any other improvement. I'm so glad you think there is, Miss Barry."

Miss Barry's house was furnished with "great magnificence," as Anne told Marilla afterwards. The two little country girls were rather abashed by the splendor of the parlor where Miss Barry left them when she went to see about dinner.

"Isn't it just like a palace?" whispered Diana. "I never was in Aunt Josephine's house before, and I'd no idea it was so grand. I just wish Julia Bell could see this—she puts on such airs about her mother's parlor."

"Velvet carpet," sighed Anne luxuriously, *"and* silk curtains! I've dreamed of such things, Diana. But do you know I don't believe I feel very comfortable with them after all. There are so many things in this room and all so splendid that there is no scope for imagination. That is one consolation when you are poor—there are so many more things you can imagine about."

Their sojourn in town was something that Anne and Diana dated from for years. From first to last it was crowded with delights.

On Wednesday Miss Barry took them to the Exhibition grounds and kept them there all day.

"It was splendid," Anne related to Marilla later on. "I never imagined anything so interesting. I don't really know which department was the most interesting. I think I liked the horses and the flowers and the fancy work best. Josie Pye took first prize for knitted lace. I was real glad she did. And I was glad that I felt glad, for it shows I'm improving, don't you think, Marilla, when I can rejoice in Josie's success? Mr. Harmon Andrews took second prize for Gravenstein apples and Mr. Bell took first prize for a pig. Diana said she thought it was ridiculous for a Sunday-school superintendent to take a prize in pigs, but I don't see why. Do you? She said she would always think of it after this when he was praying so solemnly. Clara Louise MacPherson took a prize for painting, and Mrs. Lynde got first prize for home-made butter and cheese. So Avonlea was pretty well represented, wasn't it? Mrs. Lynde was there that day, and I never knew how much I really liked her until I saw her familiar face among all those strangers. There were thousands of people there, Marilla. It made me feel dreadfully insignificant. And Miss Barry took us up to the grand stand to see the horse-races. Mrs. Lynde wouldn't go; she said horse-racing was an abomination, and she being a church-member, thought it her bounden duty to set a good example by staying away. But there were so many there I don't believe Mrs. Lynde's absence would ever be noticed. I don't think, though, that I ought to go very often to horse-races, because they *are* awfully fascinating. Diana got so excited that she offered to bet me ten cents that the red horse would win. I didn't believe he would, but I refused to bet, because I wanted to tell Mrs. Allan all about everything, and I felt sure it wouldn't do to tell her that. It's always wrong to do anything you can't tell the minister's wife. It's as good as an extra conscience to have a minister's wife for your friend. And I was very glad I didn't bet, because the red horse *did* win, and I would have lost ten cents. So you see that virture was its own reward. We saw a man go up in a balloon. I'd love to go up in a balloon, Marilla; it would be simply thrilling; and we saw a man selling fortunes. You paid him ten cents and a little bird picked out your fortune for you. Miss Barry gave Diana and me ten cents each to have our fortunes told. Mine was that I would marry a dark-complected man who was very wealthy, and I would go across water to live. I looked carefully at all the dark men I saw after that, but I didn't care much for any of them, and anyhow I suppose it's too early to be looking out for him yet. Oh, it was a never-to-be-forgotten day, Marilla. I was so tired I couldn't sleep at night. Miss Barry put us in the spare room, according to promise. It was an elegant room, Marilla, but somehow sleeping in a spare room isn't what I used to think it was. That's the worst part of growing up, and I'm beginning to realize it. The things you wanted so much when you were a child don't seem half so wonderful to you when you get them.''

Thursday the girls had a drive in the park, and in the evening Miss Barry took them to a concert in the Academy of Music, where a noted prima donna was to sing. To Anne the evening was a glittering vision of delight.

"Oh, Marilla, it was beyond description. I was so excited I couldn't even talk, so you may know what it was like. I just sat in enraptured silence. Madame Selitsky was perfectly beautiful, and wore white satin and diamonds. But when she began to sing I never thought about anything else. Oh, I can't tell you how I felt. But it seemed to me that it could never be hard to be good any more. I felt like I do when I look up to the stars. Tears came into my eyes, but, oh, they were such happy tears. I was so sorry when it was all over, and I told Miss Barry I didn't see how I was ever to return to common life again. She said she thought if we went over to the restaurant across the street and had an ice-cream it might help me. That sounded so prosaic; but to my surprise I found it true. The ice-cream was so delicious, Marilla, and it was so lovely and dissipated to be sitting there eating it at eleven o'clock at night. Diana said she believed she was born for city life. Miss Barry asked me what my opinion was, but I said I would have to think it over very seriously before I could tell her what I really thought. So I thought it over after I went to bed. That is the best time to think things out. And I came to the conclusion, Marilla, that I wasn't born for city life and that I was glad of it. It's nice to be eating ice-cream at brilliant restaurants at eleven o'clock at night once in awhile; but as a regular thing I'd rather be in the east gable at eleven, sound asleep, but kind of knowing even in my sleep that the stars were shining outside and that the wind was blowing in the firs across the brook. I told Miss Barry so at breakfast the next morning and she laughed. Miss Barry generally laughed at anything I said, even when I said the most solemn things. I don't think I liked it, Marilla, because I wasn't trying to be funny. But she is a most hospitable lady and treated us royally.''

Friday brought going-home time, and Mr. Barry drove in for the girls.

"Well, I hope you've enjoyed yourselves," said Miss Barry, as she bade them good-bye.

"Indeed we have," said Diana.

"And you, Anne-girl?"

"I've enjoyed every minute of the time," said Anne, throwing her arms impulsively about the old woman's neck and kissing her wrinkled cheek. Diana would never have dared to do such a thing, and felt rather aghast at Anne's freedom. But Miss Barry was pleased, and she stood on her veranda and watched the buggy out of sight. Then she went back into her big house with a sigh. It seemed very lonely, lacking those fresh young lives. Miss Barry was a rather selfish old lady, if the truth must be told, and had never cared much for anybody but herself. She valued people as they were of service to her or amused her. Anne had amused her, and consequently stood high in the old lady's good graces. But Miss Barry found herself thinking less about Anne's quaint speeches than of her fresh enthusiasms, her transparent emotions, her little winning ways, and the sweetness of her eyes and lips.

"I thought Marilla Cuthbert was an old fool when I heard she'd adopted a girl out of an orphan asylum," she said to herself, "but I guess she didn't make much of a mistake after all. If I'd a child like Anne in the house all the time I'd be a better and happier woman."

Anne and Diana found the drive home as pleasant as the drive in—pleasanter, indeed, since there was the delightful consciousness of home waiting at the end of it. It was sunset when they passed through White Sands and turned into the shore road. Beyond, the Avonlea hills came out darkly against the saffron sky. Behind them the moon was rising out of the sea that grew all radiant and transfigured in her light. Every little cove along the curving road was a marvel of dancing ripples. The waves broke with a soft swish on the rocks below them, and the tang of the sea was in the strong, fresh air.

"Oh, but it's good to be alive and to be going home," breathed Anne.

When she crossed the log bridge over the brook the kitchen light of Green Gables winked her a friendly welcome back, and through the open door shone the hearth fire, sending out its warm red glow athwart the chilly autumn night. Anne ran blithely up the hill and into the kitchen, where a hot supper was waiting on the table.

"So, you've got back?" said Marilla, folding up her knitting.

"Yes, and, oh, it's so good to be back," said Anne joyously. "I could kiss everything, even to the clock. Marilla, a broiled chicken! You don't mean to say you cooked that for me!"

"Yes, I did," said Marilla. "I thought you'd be hungry after such a drive and need something real appetizing. Hurry and take off your things, and we'll have supper as soon as Matthew comes in. I'm glad you've got back, I must say. It's been fearful lonesome here without you, and I never put in four longer days."

After supper Anne sat before the fire between Matthew and Marilla, and gave them a full account of her visit.

"I've had a splendid time," she concluded happily, "and I feel that it marks an epoch in my life. But the best of it all was the coming home."

CHAPTER 30

THE QUEEN'S CLASS IS ORGANIZED

MARILLA LAID her knitting on her lap and leaned back in her chair. Her eyes were tired, and she thought vaguely that she must see about having her glasses changed the next time she went to town, for her eyes had grown tired very often of late.

It was nearly dark, for the full November twilight had fallen around Green Gables, and the only light in the kitchen came from the dancing red flames in the stove.

Anne was curled up Turk-fashion on the hearth-rug, gazing into that joyous glow where the sunshine of a hundred summers was being distilled from the maple cord-wood. She had been reading, but her book had slipped to the floor, and now she was dreaming, with a smile on her parted lips. Glittering castles in Spain were shaping themselves out of the mists and rainbows of her lively fancy; adventures wonderful and enthralling were happening to her in cloud-land—adventures that always turned out triumphantly and never involved her in scrapes like those of actual life.

Marilla looked at her with a tenderness that would never have been suffered to reveal itself in any clearer light than that soft mingling of fireshine and shadow. The lesson of a love that should display itself easily in spoken word and open look was one Marilla could never learn. But she had learned to love this slim, gray-eyed girl with an affection all the deeper and stronger from its very undemonstrativeness. Her love made her afraid of being unduly indulgent, indeed. She had an uneasy feeling that it was rather sinful to set one's heart so intensely on any human creature as she had set hers on Anne, and perhaps she performed a sort of unconscious penance for this by being stricter and more critical than if the girl had been less dear to her. Certainly Anne herself had no idea how Marilla loved her. She sometimes thought wistfully that Marilla was very hard to please and distinctly lacking in sympathy and understanding. But she always checked the thought reproachfully, remembering what she owed to Marilla.

"Anne," said Marilla abruptly, "Miss Stacy was here this afternoon when you were out with Diana."

Anne came back from her other world with a start and a sigh.

"Was she? Oh, I'm so sorry I wasn't in. Why didn't you call me, Marilla? Diana and I were only over in the Haunted Wood. It's lovely in the woods now. All the little wood things—the ferns and the satin leaves and the crackerberries—have gone to sleep, just as if somebody had tucked them away until spring under a blanket of leaves. I think it was a little gray fairy with a rainbow scarf that came tiptoeing along the last moonlight night and did it. Diana wouldn't say much about that, though. Diana has never forgotten the scolding her mother gave her about imagining ghosts into the Haunted Wood. It had a very bad effect on Diana's imagination. It blighted it. Mrs. Lynde says Myrtle Bell is a blighted being. I asked Ruby Gillis why Myrtle was blighted, and Ruby said she guessed it was because her young man had gone back on her. Ruby Gillis thinks of nothing but young men, and the older she gets the worse she is. Young men are all very well in their place, but it doesn't do to drag them into everything, does it? Diana and I are thinking seriously of promising each other that we will never marry but be nice old maids and live together forever. Diana hasn't quite made up her mind though, because she thinks perhaps it would be nobler to marry some wild, dashing, wicked young man and reform him. Diana and I talk a great deal about serious subjects now, you now. We feel that we are so much older than we used to be that it isn't becoming to talk of childish matters. It's such a solemn thing to be almost fourteen, Marilla. Miss Stacy took all us girls who are in our teens down to the brook last Wednesday, and talked to us about it. She said we couldn't be too careful what habits we formed and what ideals we acquired in our teens, because by the time we were twenty our characters would be developed and the foundation laid for our whole future life. And she said if the foundation was shaky we could never build anything really worth while on it. Diana and I talked the matter over coming home from school. We felt extremely solemn, Marilla. And we decided that we would try to be very careful indeed and form respectable habits and learn all we could and be as sensible as possible, so that by the time we were twenty our characters would be properly developed. It's perfectly appalling to think of being twenty, Marilla. It sounds so fearfully old and grown up. But why was Miss Stacy here this afternoon?''

''That is what I want to tell you, Anne, if you'll ever give me a chance to get a a word in edgewise. She was talking about you.''

''About me?'' Anne looked rather scared. Then she flushed and exclaimed:

''Oh, I know what she was saying. I meant to tell you, Marilla, honestly I did, but I forgot. Miss Stacy caught me reading 'Ben Hur' in school yesterday afternoon when I should have been studying my Canadian history. Jane Andrews lent it to me. I was reading it at dinner hour, and I had just got to the chariot-race when school went in. I was simply wild to know how it turned out—although I felt sure 'Ben Hur' must win, because it wouldn't be poetical justice if he didn't—so I spread the history open on my desk lid and then tucked 'Ben-Hur' between the desk and my knee. It just looked as if I were studying Canadian history, you know, while all the while I was revelling in 'Ben Hur.' I was so interested in it that I never noticed Miss Stacy coming down the aisle until all at once I just looked up and there she was looking down at me, so reproachful like. I can't tell you how ashamed I felt, Marilla, especially when I heard Josie Pye giggling. Miss Stacy took 'Ben Hur' away, but she never said a word then. She kept me in at recess and talked to me. She said I had done very wrong in two respects. First, I was wasting the time I ought to have put on my studies; and secondly I was deceiving my teacher in trying to make it appear I was reading a history when it was a story-book instead. I had never realized until that moment, Marilla, that what I was doing was deceitful. I was shocked. I cried bitterly, and asked Miss Stacy to forgive me and I'd never do such a thing again; and I offered to do penance by never so much as looking at 'Ben Hur' for a whole week, not even to see how the chariot-race turned out. But Miss Stacy said she wouldn't require that, and she forgave me freely. So I think it wasn't very kind of her to come up here to you about it after all.''

"Miss Stacy never mentioned such a thing to me, Anne, and it's only your guilty conscience that's the matter with you. You have no business to be taking storybooks to school. You read too many novels, anyhow. When I was a girl I wasn't so much as allowed to look at a novel.''

"Oh, how can you call 'Ben Hur' a novel when it's really such a religious book?'' protested Anne. "Of course it's a little too exciting to be proper reading for Sunday, and I only read it on weekdays. And I never read *any* book now unless either Miss Stacy or Mrs. Allan thinks it is a proper book for a girl of thirteen and three-quarters to read. Miss Stacy made me promise that. She found me reading a book one day called, 'The Lurid Mystery of the Haunted Hall.' It was one Ruby Gillis had lent me, and oh, Marilla, it was so fascinating and creepy. It just curdled the blood in my veins. But Miss Stacy said it was a very silly, unwholesome book, and she asked me not to read any more of it or any like it. It's really wonderful, Marilla, what you can do when you're truly anxious to please a certain person.''

"Well, I guess I'll light the lamp and get to work,'' said Marilla. "I see plainly that you don't want to hear what Miss Stacy had to say. You're more interested in the sound of your own tongue than in anything else.''

"Oh, indeed, Marilla, I do want to hear it,'' cried Anne contritely. "I won't say another word—not one. I know I talk too much, but I am really trying to overcome it, and although I say far too much, yet if you only knew how many things I want to say and don't, you'd give me some credit for it. Please tell me, Marilla.''

"Well, Miss Stacy wants to organize a class among her advanced students who mean to study for the entrance examination into Queen's. She intends to give them extra lessons for an hour after school. And she came to ask Matthew and me if we would like to have you join it. What do you think about it yourself, Anne? Would you like to go to Queen's and pass for a teacher?''

"Oh, Marilla!'' Anne straightened to her knees and clasped her hands. "It's been the dream of my life—that is, for the last six months, ever since Ruby and Jane began to talk of studying for the entrance. But I didn't say anything about it, because I supposed it would be perfectly useless. I'd love to be a teacher. But won't it be dreadfully expensive? Mr. Andrews says it cost him one hundred and fifty dollars to put Prissy through, and Prissy wasn't a dunce in geometry.''

"I guess you needn't worry about that part of it. When Matthew and I took you to bring up we resolved we would do the best we could for you and give you a good education. I believe in a girl being fitted to earn her own living whether she ever has to or not. You'll always have a home at Green Gables as long as Matthew and I are here, but nobody knows what is going to happen in this uncertain world, and it's just as well to be prepared. So you can join the Queen's class if you like, Anne.''

"Oh, Marilla, thank you." Anne flung her arms about Marilla's waist and looked up earnestly into her face. "I'm extremely grateful to you and Matthew. And I'll study as hard as I can and do my very best to be a credit to you. I warn you not to expect much in geometry, but I think I can hold my own in anything else if I work hard.''

"I dare say you'll get along well enough. Miss Stacy says you are bright and diligent.'' Not for worlds would Marilla have told Anne just what Miss Stacy had said about her; that would have been to pamper vanity. "You needn't rush to any extreme of killing yourself over your books. There is no hurry. You won't be ready to try the entrance for a year and a half yet. But it's well to begin in time and be thoroughly grounded, Miss Stacy says.''

"I shall take more interest than ever in my studies now," said Anne blissfully, "because I have a purpose in life. Mr. Allan says everybody should have a purpose in life and pursue it faithfully. Only he says we must first make sure that it is a worthy purpose. I would call it a worthy purpose to want to be a teacher like Miss Stacy, wouldn't you, Marilla? I think it's a very noble profession.''

The Queen's class was organized in due time. Gilbert Blythe, Anne Shirley, Ruby Gillis, Jane Andrews, Josie Pye, Charlie Sloane, and Moody Spurgeon MacPherson joined it. Diana Barry did not, as her parents did not intend to send her to Queen's. This seemed nothing short of a calamity to Anne. Never, since the night on which Minnie May had had the croup, had she and Diana been separated in anything. On the evening when the Queen's class first remained in school for the extra lessons and Anne saw Diana go slowly out with the others, to walk home alone through the Birch Path and Violet Vale, it was all the former could do to keep her seat and refrain from rushing impulsively after her chum. A lump came into her throat, and she hastily retired behind the pages of her uplifted Latin grammar to hide the tears in her eyes. Not for worlds would Anne have had Gilbert Blythe or Josie Pye see those tears.

"But, oh, Marilla, I really felt that I had tasted the bitterness of death, as Mr. Allan said in his sermon last Sunday, when I saw Diana go out alone," she said mournfully that night. "I thought how splendid it would have been if Diana had only been going to study for the Entrance, too. But we can't have things perfect in this imperfect world, as Mrs. Lynde says. Mrs. Lynde isn't exactly a comforting person sometimes, but there's no doubt she says a great many very true things. And I think the Queen's class is going to be extremely interesting. Jane and Ruby are just going to study to be teachers. That is the height of their ambition. Ruby says she will only teach for two years after she gets through, and then she intends to be married. Jane says she will devote her life to teaching, and never, never marry, because you are paid a salary for teaching, but a husband won't pay you anything, and growls if you ask for a share in the egg and butter money. I expect Jane speaks from mournful experience, for Mrs. Lynde says that her father is a perfect old crank, and meaner than second skimmings. Josie Pye says she is just going to college for education's sake, because she won't have to earn her own living; she says of course it is different with orphans who are living on charity—— *they* have to hustle. Moody Spurgeon is going to be a minister. Mrs. Lynde says he couldn't be anything else with a name like that to live up to. I hope it isn't wicked of me, Marilla, but really the thought of Moody Spurgeon being a minister makes me laugh. He's such a funny-looking boy with that big fat face, and his little blue eyes, and his ears sticking out like flaps. But perhaps he will be more intellectual-looking when he grows up. Charlie Sloane says he's going to go into politics and be a member of Parliament, but Mrs. Lynde says he'll never succeed at that, because the Sloanes are all honest people, and it's only rascals that get on in politics nowadays.''

''What is Gilbert Blythe going to be?'' queried Marilla, seeing that Anne was opening her Caesar.

''I don't happen to know what Gilbert Blythe's ambition in life is—if he has any,'' said Anne scornfully.

There was open rivalry between Gilbert and Anne now. Previously the rivalry had been rather one-sided, but there was no longer any doubt that Gilbert was as determined to be first in class as Anne was. He was a foeman worthy of her steel. The other members of the class tacitly acknowledged their superiority, and never dreamed of trying to compete with them.

Since the day by the pond when she had refused to listen to his plea for forgiveness, Gilbert, save for the aforesaid determined rivalry, had evinced no recognition whatever of the existence of Anne Shirley. He talked and jested with the other girls, exchanged books and puzzles with them, discussed lessons and plans, sometimes walked home with one or the other of them from prayer meeting or Debating Club. But Anne Shirley he simply ignored, and Anne found out that it is not pleasant to be ignored. It was in vain that she told herself with a toss of her head that she did not care. Deep down in her wayward, feminine little heart she knew that she did care, and that if she had that chance of the Lake of Shining Waters again she would answer very differently. All at once, as it seemed, and to her secret dismay, she found that the old resentment she had cherished against him was gone—gone just when she most needed its sustaining power. It was in vain that she recalled every incident and emotion of that memorable occasion and tried to feel the old satisfying anger. That day by the pond had witnessed its last spasmodic flicker. Anne realized that she had forgiven and forgotten without knowing it. But it was too late.

And at least neither Gilbert nor anybody else, not even Diana, should ever suspect how sorry she was and how much she wished she hadn't been so proud and horrid! She determined to "shroud her feelings in deepest oblivion," and it may be stated here and now that she did it, so successfully that Gilbert, who possibly was not quite so indifferent as he seemed, could not console himself with any belief that Anne felt his retaliatory scorn. The only poor comfort he had was that she snubbed Charlie Sloane, unmercifully, continually and undeservedly.

Otherwise the winter passed away in a round of pleasant duties and studies. For Anne the days slipped by like golden beads on the necklace of the year. She was happy, eager, interested; there were lessons to be learned and honors to be won; delightful books to read; new pieces to be practised for the Sunday school choir; pleasant Saturday afternoons at the manse with Mrs. Allan; and then, almost before Anne realized it, spring had come again to Green Gables. And all the world was abloom once more.

Studies palled just a wee bit then; the Queen's class, left behind in school while the others scattered to green lanes and leafy wood-cuts and meadow byways, looked wistfully out of the windows and discovered that Latin verbs and French exercises had somehow lost the tang and zest they had possessed in the crisp winter months. Even Anne and Gilbert lagged and grew indifferent. Teacher and taught were alike glad when the term was ended and the glad vacation days stretched rosily before them.

"But you've done good work this past year," Miss Stacy told them on the last evening, "and you deserve a good, jolly vacation.

Have the best time you can in the out-of-door world and lay in a good stock of health and vitality and ambition to carry you through next year. It will be the tug of war, you know—the last year before the Entrance.''

"Are you going to be back next year, Miss Stacy?" asked Josie Pye.

Josie Pye never scrupled to ask questions; in this instance the rest of the class felt grateful to her; none of them would have dared to ask it of Miss Stacy, but all wanted to, for there had been alarming rumors running at large through the school for some time that Miss Stacy was not coming back the next year—that she had been offered a position in the graded school of her own home district and meant to accept. The Queen's class listened in breathless suspense for her answer.

"Yes, I think I will," said Miss Stacy. "I thought of taking another school, but I have decided to come back to Avonlea. To tell the truth, I've grown so interested in my pupils here that I found I couldn't leave them. So I'll stay and see you through.''

"Hurrah!" said Moody Spurgeon. Moody Spurgeon had never been so carried away by his feelings before, and he blushed uncomfortably every time he thought about it for a week.

"Oh, I'm so glad," said Anne with shining eyes. "Dear Miss Stacy, it would be perfectly dreadful if you didn't come back. I don't believe I could have the heart to go on with my studies at all if another teacher came here.''

When Anne got home that night she stacked all her text-books away in an old trunk in the attic, locked it, and threw the key into the blanket box.

"I'm not even going to look at a school book in vacation," she told Marilla. "I've studied as hard all the term as I possibly could and I've pored over that geometry until I know every proposition in the first book off by heart, even when the letters *are* changed. I just feel tired of everything sensible and I'm going to let my imagination run riot for the summer. Oh, you needn't be alarmed, Marilla. I'll only let it run riot within reasonable limits. But I want to have a real good jolly time this summer, for maybe it's the last summer I'll be a little girl. Mrs. Lynde says that if I keep stretching out next year as I've done this I'll have to put on longer skirts. She says I'm all running to legs and eyes. And when I put on longer skirts I shall feel that I have to live up to them and be very dignified. It won't even do to believe in fairies then, I'm afraid; so I'm going to believe in them with all my whole heart this summer. I think we're going to have a very gay vacation. Ruby Gillis is going to have a birthday party soon and there's the Sunday school picnic and the missionary concert next month. And Mr. Barry says that some evening he'll take Diana and me over to the White Sands Hotel and have dinner there. They have dinner there in the evening, you know. Jane Andrews was over once last summer and she says it was a dazzling sight to see the electric lights and the flowers and all the lady guests in such beautiful dresses. Jane says it was her first glimpse into high life and she'll never forget it to her dying day."

Mrs. Lynde came up the next afternoon to find out why Marilla had not been at the Aid meeting on Thursday. When Marilla was not at Aid meeting people knew there was something wrong at Green Gables.

"Matthew had a bad spell with his heart Thursday," Marilla explained, "and I didn't feel like leaving him. Oh, yes, he's all right again, now, but he takes them spells oftener than he used to and I'm anxious about him. The doctor says he must be careful to avoid excitement. That's easy enough, for Matthew doesn't go about looking for excitement by any means and never did, but he's not to do any very heavy work either and you might as well tell Matthew not to breathe as not to work. Come and lay off your things, Rachel. You'll stay to tea?"

"Well, seeing you're so pressing, perhaps I might as well stay," said Mrs. Rachel, who had not the slightest intention of doing anything else.

Mrs. Rachel and Marilla sat comfortably in the parlor while Anne got the tea and made hot biscuits that were light and white enough to defy even Mrs. Rachel's criticism.

"I must say Anne has turned out a real smart girl," admitted Mrs. Rachel, as Marilla accompanied her to the end of the lane at sunset. "She must be a great help to you."

"She is," said Marilla, "and she's real steady and reliable now. I used to be afraid she'd never get over her feather-brained ways, but she has and I wouldn't be afraid to trust her in anything now."

"I never would have thought she'd have turned out so well that first day I was here three years ago," said Mrs. Rachel. "Lawful heart, shall I ever forget that tantrum of hers! When I went home that night I says to Thomas, says I, 'Mark my words, Thomas, Marilla Cuthbert'll live to rue the step she's took.' But I was mistaken and I'm real glad of it. I ain't one of those kind of people, Marilla, as can never be brought to own up that they've made a mistake. No, that never was my way, thank goodness. I did make a mistake in judging Anne, but it weren't no wonder, for an odder, unexpecteder witch of a child there never was in this world, that's what. There was no ciphering her out by the rules that worked with other children. It's nothing short of wonderful how she's improved these three years, but especially in looks. She's a real pretty girl got to be, though I can't say I'm overly partial to that pale, big-eyed style myself. I like more snap and color, like Diana Barry has or Ruby Gillis. Ruby Gillis' looks are real showy. But somehow—I don't know how it is but when Anne and them are together, though she ain't half as handsome, she makes them look kind of common and overdone—something like them white June lilies she calls narcissus alongside of the big, red peonies, that's what.''

CHAPTER 31

WHERE THE BROOK AND RIVER MEET

ANNE HAD her ''good'' summer and enjoyed it whole-heartedly. She and Diana fairly lived outdoors, revelling in all the delights that Lovers' Lane and the Dryad's Bubble and Willowmere and Victoria Island afforded. Marilla offered no objections to Anne's gipsyings. The Spencervale doctor who had come the night Minnie May had the croup met Anne at the house of a patient one afternoon early in vacation, looked her over sharply, screwed up his mouth, shook his head, and sent a message to Marilla Cuthbert by another person. It was:

''Keep that red-headed girls of yours in the open air all summer and don't let her read books until she gets more spring into her step.''

This message frightened Marilla wholesomely. She read Anne's death warrant by consumption in it unless it was scrupulously obeyed. As a result, Anne had the golden summer of her life as far as freedom and frolic went. She walked, rowed, berried and dreamed to her heart's content; and when September came she was bright-eyed and alert, with a step that would have satisfied the Spencervale doctor and a heart full of ambition and zest once more.

"I feel just like studying with might and main," she declared as she brought her books down from the attic. "Oh, you good old friends, I'm glad to see your honest faces once more—yes, even you, geometry. I've had a perfectly beautiful summer, Marilla, and now I'm rejoicing as a strong man to run a race, as Mr. Allan said last Sunday. Doesn't Mr. Allan preach magnificent sermons? Mrs. Lynde says he is improving every day and the first thing we know some city church will gobble him up and then we'll be left and have to turn to and break in another green preacher. But I don't see the use of meeting trouble half-way, do you, Marilla? I think it would be better just to enjoy Mr. Allan while we have him. If I were a man I think I'd be a minister. They can have such an influence for good, if their theology is sound; and it must be thrilling to preach splendid sermons and stir your hearers' hearts. Why can't women be ministers, Marilla? I asked Mrs. Lynde that and she was shocked and said it would be a scandalous thing. She said there might be female ministers in the States and she believed there was, but thank goodness we hadn't got to that stage in Canada yet and she hoped we never would. But I don't see why. I think women would make splendid ministers. When there is a social to be got up or a church tea or anything else to raise money the women have to turn to and do the work. I'm sure Mrs. Lynde can pray ever bit as well as Superintendent Bell and I've no doubt she could preach too with a little practice."

"Yes, I believe she could," said Marilla drily. "She does plenty of unofficial preaching as it is. Nobody has much of a chance to go wrong in Avonlea with Rachel to oversee them."

"Marilla," said Anne in a burst of confidence, "I want to tell you something and ask you what you think about it. It has worried me terribly—on Sunday afternoons, that is, when I think specially about such matters. I do really want to be good; and when I'm with you or Mrs. Allan or Miss Stacy I want it more than ever and I want to do just what would please you and what you would approve of. But mostly when I'm with Mrs. Lynde I feel desperately wicked and as if I wanted to go and do the very thing she tells me I oughtn't to do. I feel irresistibly tempted to do it. Now, what do you think is the reason I feel like that? Do you think it's because I'm really bad and unregenerate?"

Marilla looked dubious for a moment. Then she laughed.

"If you are I guess I am too, Anne, for Rachel often has that very effect on me. I sometimes think she'd have more of an influence for good, as you say youself, if she didn't keep nagging people to do right. There should have been a special commandment against nagging. But there, I shouldn't talk so. Rachel is a good Christian woman and she means well. There isn't a kinder soul in Avonlea and she never shirks her share of work."

"I'm very glad you feel the same," said Anne decidedly. "It's so encouraging. I shan't worry so much over that after this. But I dare say there'll be other things to worry me. They keep coming up new all the time—things to perplex you, you know. You settle one question and there's another right after. There are so many things to be thought over and decided when you're beginning to grow up. It keeps me busy all the time thinking them over and deciding what is right. It's a serious thing to grow up, isn't it, Marilla? But when I have such good friends as you and Matthew and Mrs. Allan and Miss Stacy I ought to grow up successfully, and I'm sure it will be my own fault if I don't. I feel it's a great responsibility because I have only the one chance. If I don't grow up right I can't go back and begin all over again. I've grown two inches this summer, Marilla. Mr. Gillis measured me at Ruby's party. I'm so glad you made my new dresses longer. That dark green one is so pretty and it was sweet of you to put on the flounce. Of course I know it wasn't really necessary, but flounces are so stylish this fall and Josie Pye has flounces on all her dresses. I know I'll be able to study better because of mine. I shall have such a comfortable feeling deep down in my mind about that flounce."

"It's worth something to have that," admitted Marilla.

Miss Stacy came back to Avonlea school and found all her pupils eager for work once more. Especially did the Queen's class gird up their loins for the fray, for at the end of the coming year, dimly shadowing their pathway already, loomed up that fateful thing known as "the Entrance," at the thought of which one and all felt their hearts sink into their very shoes. Suppose they did not pass! That thought was doomed to haunt Anne through the waking hours of that winter, Sunday afternoons inclusive, to the almost entire exclusion of moral and theological problems. When Anne had bad dreams she found herself staring miserably at pass lists of the Entrance exams, where Gilbert Blythe's name was blazoned at the top and in which she did not appear at all.

But it was a jolly, busy, happy swift-flying winter. School work was as interesting, class rivalry as absorbing, as of yore. New worlds of thought, feeling, and ambition, fresh, fascinating fields of unexplored knowledge seemed to be opening out before Anne's eager eyes.

Hills peeped o'er hill and Alps on Alps arose.

Much of all this was due to Miss Stacy's tactful, careful, broadminded guidance. She led her class to think and explore and discover for themselves and encouraged straying from the old beaten paths to a degree that quite shocked Mrs. Lynde and the school trustees, who viewed all innovations on established methods rather dubiously.

Apart from her studies Anne expanded socially, for Marilla, mindful of the Spencervale doctor's dictum, no longer vetoed occasional outings. The Debating Club flourished and gave several concerts; there were one or two parties almost verging on grown-up affairs; there were sleigh drives and skating frolics galore.

Between times Anne grew, shooting up so rapidly that Marilla was astonished one day, when they were standing side by side, to find the girl was taller than herself.

"Why, Anne, how you've grown!" she said, almost unbelievingly. A sigh followed on the words. Marilla felt a queer regret over Anne's inches. The child she had learned to love had vanished somehow and here was this tall, serious-eyed girl of fifteen, with the thoughtful brows and the proudly poised little head, in her place. Marilla loved the girl as much as she had loved the child, but she was conscious of a queer sorrowful sense of loss. And that night when Anne had gone to prayer-meeting with Diana, Marilla sat alone in the wintry twilight and indulged in the weakness of a cry. Matthew, coming in with a lantern, caught her at it and gazed at her in such consternation that Marilla had to laugh through her tears.

"I was thinking about Anne," she explained. "She's got to be such a big girl—and she'll probably be away from us next winter. I'll miss her terrible."

"She'll be able to come home often," comforted Matthew, to whom Anne was as yet and always would be the little, eager girl he had brought home from Bright River on that June evening four years before. "The branch railroad will be built to Carmody by that time."

"It won't be the same thing as having her all the time," sighed Marilla gloomily, determined to enjoy her luxury of grief uncomforted. "But there—men can't understand these things!"

There were other changes in Anne no less real than the physical change. For one thing, she became much quieter. Perhaps she thought all the more and dreamed as much as ever, but she certainly talked less. Marilla noticed and commented on this also.

"You don't chatter half as much as you used to, Anne, nor use half as many big words. What has come over you?"

Anne colored and laughed a little, as she dropped her book and looked dreamily out of the window, where big fat red buds were bursting out on the creeper in response to the lure of the spring sunshine.

"I don't know—I don't want to talk as much," she said, denting her chin thoughtfully with her forefinger. "It's nicer to think dear, pretty thoughts and keep them in one's heart, like treasures. I don't like to have them laughed at or wondered over. And somehow I don't want to use big words any more. It's almost a pity, isn't it, now that I'm really growing big enough to say them if I did want to. It's fun to be almost grown up in some ways, but it's not the kind of fun I expected, Marilla. There's so much to learn and do and think that there isn't time for big words. Besides, Miss Stacy says the short ones are much stronger and better. She makes us write all our essays as simply as possible. It was hard at first. I was so used to crowding in all the fine big words I could think of—and I thought of any number of them. But I've got used to it now and I see it's so much better."

"What has become of your story club? I haven't heard you speak of it for a long time."

"The story club isn't in existence any longer. We hadn't time for it—and anyhow I think we had got tired of it. It was silly to be writing about love and murder and elopements and mysteries. Miss Stacy sometimes has us write a story for training in composition, but she won't let us write anything but what might happen in Avonlea in our own lives, and she criticizes it very sharply and makes us criticize our own too. I never thought my compositions had so many faults until I began to look for them myself. I felt so ashamed I wanted to give up altogether, but Miss Stacy said I could learn to write well if I only trained myself to be my own severest critic. And so I am trying to."

"You've only two more months before the Entrance," said Marilla. "Do you think you'll be able to get through?"

Anne shivered.

"I don't know. Sometimes I think I'll be all right—and then I get horribly afraid. We've studied hard and Miss Stacy has drilled us thoroughly, but we mayn't get through for all that. We've each got a stumbling-block. Mine is geometry of course, and Jane's is Latin and Ruby's and Charlie's is algebra and Josie's is arithmetic. Moody Spurgeon says he feels it in his bones that he is going to fail in English history. Miss Stacy is going to give us examinations in June just as hard as we'll have at the Entrance and mark us just as strictly, so we'll have some idea. I wish it was all over, Marilla. It haunts me. Sometimes I wake up in the night and wonder what I'll do if I don't pass."

"Why, go to school next year and try again," Marilla said unconcernedly.

"Oh, I don't believe I'd have the heart for it. It would be such a disgrace to fail, especially if Gil—if the others passed. And I get so nervous in an examination that I'm likely to make a mess of it. I wish I had nerves like Jane Andrews. Nothing rattles her."

Anne sighed and, dragging her eyes from the witcheries of the spring world, the beckoning day of breeze and blue, and the green things upspringing in the garden, buried herself resolutely in her book. There would be other springs, but if she did not succeed in passing the Entrance Anne felt convinced that she would never recover sufficiently to enjoy them.

CHAPTER 32

THE PASS LIST IS OUT

WITH THE end of June came the close of the term and the close of Miss Stacy's rule in Avonlea school. Anne and Diana walked home that evening feeling very sober indeed. Red eyes and damp handkerchiefs bore convincing testimony to the fact that Miss Stacy's farewell words must have been quite as touching as Mr. Phillips' had been under similar circumstances three years before. Diana looked back at the schoolhouse from the foot of the spruce hill and sighed deeply.

"It does seem as if it was the end of everything, doesn't it?" she said dismally.

"You oughtn't to feel half as badly as I do," said Anne, hunting vainly for a dry spot on her handkerchief. "You'll be back again next winter, but I suppose I've left the dear old school for ever—if I have good luck, that is."

"It won't be a bit the same. Miss Stacy won't be there, nor you nor Jane nor Ruby probably. I shall have to sit all alone, for I couldn't bear to have another deskmate after you. Oh, we have had jolly times, haven't we, Anne? It's dreadful to think they're all over."

Two big tears rolled down by Diana's nose.

"If you would stop crying I could," said Anne imploringly. "Just as soon as I put away my hanky I see you brimming up and that starts me off again. As Mrs. Lynde says, 'If you can't be cheerful, be as cheerful as you can.' After all, I dare say I'll be back next year. This is one of the times I *know* I'm not going to pass. They're getting alarmingly frequent."

"Why, you came out splendidly in the exams Miss Stacy gave."

"Yes, but those exams didn't make me nervous. When I think of the real thing you can't imagine what a horrid cold fluttery feeling comes round my heart. And then my number is thirteen and Josie Pye says it's so unlucky. I am *not* superstitious and I know it can make no difference. But still I wish it wasn't thirteen."

"I do wish I were going in with you," said Diana. "Wouldn't we have a perfectly elegant time? But I suppose you'll have to cram in the evenings."

"No; Miss Stacy has made us promise not to open a book at all. She says it would only tire and confuse us and we are to go out walking and not think about the exams at all and go to bed early. It's good advice, but I expect it will be hard to follow; good advice is apt to be, I think. Prissy Andrews told me that she sat up half the night every night of her Entrance week and crammed for dear life; and I had determined to sit up *at least* as long as she did. It was so kind of your Aunt Josephine to ask me to stay at Beechwood while I'm in town."

"You'll write to me while you're in, won't you?"

"I'll write Tuesday night and tell you how the first day goes," promised Anne.

"I'll be haunting the post-office Wednesday," vowed Diana.

Anne went to town the following Monday and on Wednesday Diana haunted the post-office, as agreed, and got her letter.

"Dearest Diana," wrote Anne, "here it is Tuesday night and I'm writing this in the library at Beechwood. Last night I was horribly lonesome all alone in my room and wished so much you were with me. I couldn't 'cram' because I'd promised Miss Stacy not to, but it was as hard to keep from opening my history as it used to be to keep from reading a story before my lessons were learned.

"This morning Miss Stacy came for me and we went to the Academy, calling for Jane and Ruby and Josie on our way. Ruby asked me to feel her hands and they were as cold as ice. Josie said I looked as if I hadn't slept a wink and she didn't believe I was strong enough to stand the grind of the teacher's course even if I did get through. There are times and seasons even yet when I don't feel that I've made any great headway in learning to like Josie Pye!

"When we reached the Academy there were scores of students there from all over the Island. The first person we saw was Moody Spurgeon sitting on the steps and muttering away to himself. Jane asked him what on earth he was doing and he said he was repeating the multiplication table over and over to steady his nerves and for pity's sake not to interrupt him, because if he stopped for a moment he got frightened and forgot everything he ever knew, but the multiplication table kept all his facts firmly in their proper place!

"When we were assigned to our rooms Miss Stacy had to leave us. Jane and I sat together and Jane was so composed that I envied her. No need of the multiplication table for good, steady, sensible Jane! I wondered if I looked as I felt and if they could hear my heart thumping clear across the room. Then a man came in and began distributing the English examination sheets. My hands grew cold then and my head fairly whirled around as I picked it up. Just one awful moment,—Diana, I felt exactly as I did four years ago when I asked Marilla if I might stay at Green Gables—and then everything cleared up in my mind and my heart began beating again—I forgot to say that it had stopped altogether!—for I knew I could do something with *that* paper anyhow.

"At noon we went home for dinner and then back again for history in the afternoon. The history was a pretty hard paper and I got dreadfully mixed up in the dates. Still, I think I did fairly well today. But oh, Diana, tomorrow the geometry exam comes off and when I think of it it takes every bit of determination I possess to keep from opening my Euclid. If I thought the multiplication table would help me any I would recite it from now till tomorrow morning.

"I went down to see the other girls this evening. On my way I met Moody Spurgeon wandering distractedly around. He said he knew he had failed in history and he was born to be a disappointment to his parents and he was going home on the morning train; and it would be easier to be a carpenter than a minister, anyhow. I cheered him up and persuaded him to stay to the end because it would be unfair to Miss Stacy if he didn't. Sometimes I have wished I was born a boy, but when I see Moody Spurgeon I'm always glad I'm a girl and not his sister.

"Ruby was in hysterics when I reached their boarding house; she had just discovered a fearful mistake she had made in her English paper. When she recovered we went uptown and had an ice-cream. How we wished you had been with us.

"Oh, Diana, if only the geometry examination were over! But there, as Mrs. Lynde would say, the sun will go on rising and setting whether I fail in geometry or not. That is true but not especially comforting. I think I'd rather it *didn't* go on if I failed!

> "Yours devotedly,
>
> "ANNE."

The geometry examination and all the others were over in due time and Anne arrived home Friday evening, rather tired but with an air of chastened triumph about her. Diana was over at Green Gables when she arrived and they met as if they had been parted for years.

"You old darling, it's perfectly splendid to see you back again. It seems like an age since you went to town and oh, Anne, how did you get along?"

"Pretty well, I think, in everything but the geometry. I don't know whether I passed in it or not and I have a creepy, crawly presentiment that I didn't. Oh, how good it is to be back! Green Gables is the dearest, loveliest spot in the world."

"How did the others do?"

"The girls say they know they didn't pass, but I think they did pretty well. Josie says the geometry was so easy a child of ten could do it! Moody Spurgeon still thinks he failed in history and Charlie says he failed in algebra. But we don't really know anything about it and won't until the pass list is out. That won't be for a fortnight. Fancy living a fortnight in such suspense! I wish I could go to sleep and never wake up until it is over."

Diana knew it would be useless to ask how Gilbert Blythe had fared, so she merely said:"

"Oh, you'll pass all right. Don't worry."

"I'd rather not pass at all than not come out pretty well up on the list," flashed Anne, by which she meant—and Diana knew she meant—that success would be incomplete and bitter if she did not come out ahead of Gilbert Blythe.

With this end in view Anne had strained every nerve during the examinations. So had Gilbert. They had met and passed each other on the street a dozen times without any sign of recognition and every time Anne had held her head a little higher and wished a little more earnestly that she had made friends with Gilbert when he asked her, and vowed a little more determinedly to surpass him in the examination. She knew that all Avonlea junior was wondering which would come out first; she even knew that Jimmy Glover and Ned Wright had a bet on the question and that Josie Pye had said there was no doubt in the world that Gilbert would be first; and she felt that her humiliation would be unbearable if she failed.

But she had another and nobler motive for wishing to do well. She wanted to "pass high" for the sake of Matthew and Marilla—especially Matthew. Matthew had declared to her his conviction that she "would beat the whole Island." That, Anne felt, was something it would be foolish to hope for even in the wildest dreams. But she did hope fervently that she would be among the first ten at least, so that she might see Matthew's kindly brown eyes gleam with pride in her achievement. That, she felt, would be a sweet reward indeed for all her hard work and patient grubbing among unimaginative equations and conjugations.

At the end of the fortnight Anne took to "haunting" the post office also, in the distracted company of Jane, Ruby and Josie, opening the Charlottetown dailies with shaking hands and cold, sinkaway feelings as bad as any experienced during the Entrance week. Charlie and Gilbert were not above doing this too, but Moody Spurgeon stayed resolutely away.

"I haven't got the grit to go there and look at a paper in cold blood," he told Anne. "I'm just going to wait until somebody comes and tells me suddenly whether I've passed or not."

When three weeks had gone by without the pass list appearing Anne began to feel that she really couldn't stand the strain much longer. Her appetite failed and her interest in Avonlea doings languished. Mrs. Lynde wanted to know what else you could expect with a Tory superintendent of education at the head of affairs, and Matthew, noting Anne's paleness and indifference and the lagging steps that bore her home from the post office every afternoon, began seriously to wonder if he hadn't better vote Grit at the next election.

But one evening the news came. Anne was sitting at her open window, for the time forgetful of the woes of examinations and the cares of the world, as she drank in the beauty of the summer dusk, sweet-scented with flower-breaths from the garden below and sibilant and rustling from the stir of poplars. The eastern sky above the firs was flushed faintly pink from the reflection of the west, and Anne was wondering dreamily if the spirit of color looked like that, when she saw Diana come flying down through the firs, over the log bridge, and up the slope, with a fluttering newspaper in her hand.

Anne sprang to her feet, knowing at once what that paper contained. The pass list was out! Her head whirled and her heart beat until it hurt her. She could not move a step. It seemed an hour to her before Diana came rushing along the hall and burst into the room without even knocking, so great was her excitement.

"Anne, you've passed," she cried, "passed the *very first*—you and Gilbert both—you're ties—but your name is first. Oh, I'm so proud!"

Diana flung the paper on the table and herself on Anne's bed, utterly breathless and incapable of further speech. Anne lighted the lamp, oversetting the match-safe and using up half a dozen matches before her shaking hands could accomplish the task. Then she snatched up the paper. Yes, she had passed—there was her name at the very top of a list of two hundred! That moment was worth living for.

"You did just splendidly, Anne," puffed Diana, recovering sufficiently to sit up and speak, for Anne, starry-eyed and rapt, had not uttered a word. "Father brought the paper home from Bright River not ten minutes ago—it came out on the afternoon train, you know, and won't be here till tomorrow by mail—and when I saw the pass list I just rushed over like a wild thing. You've all passed, every one of you, Moody Spurgeon and all, although he's conditioned in history. Jane and Ruby did pretty well—they're half-way up—and so did Charlie. Josie just scraped through with three marks to spare, but you'll see she'll put on as many airs as if she'd led. Won't Miss Stacy be delighted? Oh, Anne, what does it feel like to see your name at the head of a pass list like that? If it were me I know I'd go crazy with joy. I am pretty near crazy as it is, but you're as calm and cool as a spring evening."

"I'm just dazzled inside," said Anne. "I want to say a hundred things, and I can't find words to say them in. I never dreamed of this—yes, I did, too, just once! I let myself think *once*, 'What if I should come out first?' quakingly, you know, for it seemed so vain and presumptuous to think I could lead the Island. Excuse me a minute, Diana. I must run right out to the field to tell Matthew. Then we'll go up the road and tell the good news to the others.''

They hurried to the hayfield below the barn where Matthew was coiling hay, and, as luck would have it, Mrs. Lynde was talking to Marilla at the lane fence.

"Oh, Matthew,'' exclaimed Anne, "I've passed and I'm first— or one of the first! I'm not vain, but I'm thankful.''

"Well now, I always said it,'' said Matthew, gazing at the pass list delightedly. "I knew you could beat them all easy.''

"You've done pretty well, I must say, Anne,'' said Marilla, trying to hide her extreme pride in Anne from Mrs. Rachel's critical eye. But that good soul said heartily:

"I just guess she has done well, and far be it from me to be backward in saying it. You're a credit to your friends, Anne, that's what, and we're all proud of you.''

That night Anne, who had wound up a delightful evening by a serious little talk with Mrs. Allan at the manse, knelt sweetly by her open window in a great sheen of moonshine and murmured a prayer of gratitude and aspiration that came straight from her heart. There was in it thankfulness for the past and reverent petition for the future; and when she slept on her white pillow her dreams were as fair and bright and beautiful as maidenhood might desire.

CHAPTER 33

THE HOTEL CONCERT

PUT ON your white organdy, by all means, Anne,'' advised Diana decidely.

They were together in the east gable chamber; outside it was only twilight—a lovely yellowish-green twilight with a clear blue cloudless sky. A big round moon, slowly deepening from her pallid lustre into burnished silver, hung over the Haunted Wood; the air was full of sweet summer sounds—sleepy birds twittering, freakish breezes, far-away voices and laughter. But in Anne's room the blind was drawn and the lamp lighted, for an important toilet was being made.

The east gable was a very different place from what it had been on that night four years before, when Anne had felt its bareness penetrate to the marrow of her spirit with its inhospitable chill. Changes had crept in, Marilla conniving at them resignedly, until it was as sweet and dainty a nest as a young girl could desire.

The velvet carpet with the pink roses and the pink silk curtains of Anne's early visions had certainly never materialized; but her dreams had kept pace with her growth, and it is not probable she lamented them. The floor was covered with a pretty matting, and the curtains that softened the high window and fluttered in the vagrant breezes were of pale green art muslin. The walls, hung not with gold and silver brocade tapestry, but with a dainty apple-blossom paper, were adorned with a few good pictures given Anne by Mrs. Allan. Miss Stacy's photograph occupied the place of honor, and Anne made a sentimental point of keeping fresh flowers on the bracket under it. Tonight a spike of white lilies faintly perfumed the room like the dream of a fragrance. There was no "mahogany furniture," but there was a white-painted bookcase filled with books, a cushioned wicker rocker, a toilet-table befrilled with white muslin, a quaint, gilt-framed mirror with chubby pink cupids and purple grapes painted over its arched top, that used to hang in the spare room, and a low white bed.

Anne was dressing for a concert at the White Sands Hotel. The guests had got it up in aid of the Charlottetown hospital, and had hunted out all the available amateur talent in the surrounding districts to help it along. Bertha Sampson and Pearl Clay of the White Sands Baptist choir had been asked to sing a duet; Milton Clark of New-bridge was to give a violin solo; Winnie Adella Blair of Carmody was to sing a Scotch ballad; and Laura Spencer of Spencervale and Anne Shirley of Avonlea were to recite.

As Anne would have said at one time, it was "an epoch in her life," and she was deliciously athrill with the excitement of it. Matthew was in the seventh heaven of gratified pride over the honor conferred on his Anne, and Marilla was not far behind, although she would have died rather than admit it, and said she didn't think it was very proper for a lot of young folks to be gadding over to the hotel without any responsible person with them.

Anne and Diana were to drive over with Jane Andrews and her brother Billy in their double-seated buggy; and several other Avonlea girls and boys were going, too. There was a party of visitors expected out from town, and after the concert a supper was to be given to the performers.

"Do you really think the organdy will be best?" queried Anne anxiously. "I don't think it's as pretty as my blue-flowered muslin—and it certainly isn't so fashionable."

"But it suits you ever so much better," said Diana. "It's so soft and frilly and clinging. The muslin is stiff, and makes you look too dressed up. But the organdy seems as if it grew on you."

Anne sighed and yielded. Diana was beginning to have a reputation for notable taste in dressing, and her advice on such subjects was much sought after. She was looking very pretty herself on this particular night in a dress of the lovely wild-rose pink, from which Anne was for ever debarred; but she was not to take any part in the concert, so her appearance was of minor importance. All her pains were bestowed upon Anne, who, she vowed, must, for the credit of Avonlea, be dressed and combed and adorned to the queen's taste.

"Pull out that frill a little more—so; here, let me tie your sash; now for your slippers. I'm going to braid your hair in two thick braids, and tie them half-way up with big white bows—no, don't pull out a single curl over your forehead—just have the soft part. There is no way you do your hair suits you so well, Anne, and Mrs. Allan says you look like a Madonna when you part it so. I shall fasten this little white house rose just behind your ear. There was just one on my bush, and I saved it for you."

"Shall I put my pearl beads on?" asked Anne. "Matthew brought me a string from town last week, and I know he'd like to see them on me."

Diana pursed up her lips, put her black head on one side critically, and finally pronounced in favor of the beads, which were thereupon tied around Anne's slim milk-white throat.

"There's something so stylish about you, Anne," said Diana, with unenvious admiration. "You hold your head with such an air. I suppose it's your figure. I am just a dumpling. I've always been afraid of it, and now I know it is so. Well, I suppose I shall just have to resign myself to it."

"But you have such dimples," said Anne, smiling affectionately into the pretty, vivacious face so near her own. "Lovely dimples, like little dents in cream. I have given up all hope of dimples. My dimple-dream will never come true; but so many of my dreams have that I mustn't complain. Am I all ready now?"

"All ready," assured Diana, as Marilla appeared in the doorway, a gaunt figure with grayer hair than of yore and no fewer angles, but with a much softer face. "Come right in and look at our elocutionist, Marilla. Doesn't she look lovely?"

Marilla emitted a sound between a sniff and a grunt.

"She looks neat and proper. I like that way of fixing her hair. But I expect she'll ruin that dress driving over there in the dust and dew with it, and it looks most too thin for these damp nights. Organdy's the most unserviceable stuff in the world anyhow, and I told Matthew so when he got it. But there is no use in saying anything to Matthew nowadays. Time was when he would take my advice, but now he just buys things for Anne regardless, and the clerks at Carmody know they can palm anything off on him. Just let them tell him a thing is pretty and fashionable, and Matthew plunks his money down for it. Mind you keep your skirt clear of the wheel, Anne, and put your warm jacket on."

Then Marilla stalked downstairs, thinking proudly how sweet Anne looked, with that

One moonbeam from the forehead to the crown

and regretting that she could not go to the concert herself to hear her girl recite.

"I wonder if it *is* too damp for my dress," said Anne anxiously.

"Not a bit of it," said Diana, pulling up the window blind. "It's a perfect night, and there won't be any dew. Look at the moonlight."

"I'm so glad my window looks east into the sunrising," said Anne, going over to Diana. "It's so splendid to see the morning coming up over those long hills and glowing through those sharp fir tops. It's new every morning, and I feel as if I washed my very soul in that bath of earliest sunshine. Oh, Diana, I love this little room so dearly. I don't know how I'll get along without it when I go to town next month."

"Don't speak of your going away tonight," begged Diana. "I don't want to think of it, it makes me so miserable, and I do want to have a good time this evening. What are you going to recite, Anne? And are you nervous?"

"Not a bit. I've recited so often in public I don't mind at all now. I've decided to give 'The Maiden's Vow.' It's so pathetic. Laura Spencer is going to give a comic recitation, but I'd rather make people cry than laugh."

"THERE'S SOMETHING SO STYLISH ABOUT YOU, ANNE,"
SAID DIANA.

"What will you recite if they encore you?"

"They won't dream of encoring me," scoffed Anne, who was not without her own secret hopes that they would, and already visioned herself telling Matthew all about it at the next morning's breakfast table. "There are Billy and Jane now—I hear the wheels. Come on."

Billy Andrews insisted that Anne should ride on the front seat with him, so she unwillingly climbed up. She would have much preferred to sit back with the girls, where she could have laughed and chattered to her heart's content. There was not much of either laughter or chatter in Billy. He was a big, fat, stolid youth of twenty, with a round, expressionless face, and a painful lack of conversational gifts. But he admired Anne immensely, and was puffed up with pride over the prospect of driving to White Sands with that slim, upright figure beside him.

Anne, by dint of talking over her shoulder to the girls and occasionally passing a sop of civility to Billy—who grinned and chuckled and never could think of any reply until it was too late—contrived to enjoy the drive in spite of all. It was a night for enjoyment. The road was full of buggies, all bound for the hotel, and laughter, silver-clear, echoed and re-echoed along it. When they reached the hotel it was a blaze of light from top to bottom. They were met by the ladies of the concert committee, one of whom took Anne off to the performers' dressing room, which was filled with the members of a Charlottetown Symphony Club, among whom Anne felt suddenly shy and frightened and countrified. Her dress, which, in the east gable, had seemed so dainty and pretty, now seemed simple and plain—too simple and plain, she thought, among all the silks and laces that glistened and rustled around her. What were her pearl beads compared to the diamonds of the big, handsome lady near her? And how poor her one wee white rose must look beside all the hothouse flowers the others wore! Anne laid her hat and jacket away, and shrank miserably into a corner. She wished herself back in the white room at Green Gables.

It was still worse on the platform of the big concert hall of the hotel, where she presently found herself. The electric lights dazzled her eyes, the perfume and hum bewildered her. She wished she were sitting down in the audience with Diana and Jane, who seemed to be having a splendid time away at the back. She was wedged in between a stout lady in pink silk and a tall, scornful looking girl in a white lace dress. The stout lady occasionally turned her head squarely around and surveyed Anne through her eyeglasses until Anne, acutely sensitive of being so scrutinized, felt that she must scream aloud; and the white lace girl kept talking audibly to her next neighbor about the "country bumpkins" and "rustic belles" in the audience, languidly anticipating "such fun" from the displays of local talent on the programme. Anne believed that she would hate that white lace girl to the end of life.

Unfortunately for Anne, a professional elocutionist was staying at the hotel and had consented to recite. She was a lithe, dark-eyed woman in a wonderful gown of shimmering gray stuff like woven moonbeams, with gems on her neck and in her dark hair. She had a marvellously flexible voice and wonderful power of expression; the audience went wild over her selection. Anne, forgetting all about herself and her troubles for the time, listened with rapt and shining eyes; but when the recitation ended she suddenly put her hands over her face. She could never get up and recite after that—never. Had she ever thought she could recite? Oh, if she were only back at Green Gables!

At this unpropitious moment her name was called. Somehow, Anne—who did not notice the rather guilty little start of surprise the white lace girl gave, and would not have understood the subtle compliment if she had—got on her feet, and moved dizzily out to the front. She was so pale that Diana and Jane, down in the audience, clasped each other's hands in nervous sympathy.

Anne was the victim of an overwhelming attack of stage fright. Often as she had recited in public, she had never before faced such an audience as this, and the sight of it paralyzed her energies completely. Everything was so strange, so brilliant, so bewildering—the rows of ladies in evening dress, the critical faces, the whole atmosphere of wealth and culture about her. Very different this from the plain benches at the Debating Club, filled with the homely, smypathetic faces of friends and neighbors. These people, she thought, would be merciless critics. Perhaps, like the white lace girl, they anticipated amusement from her "rustic" efforts. She felt hopelessly, helplessly ashamed and miserable. Her knees trembled, her heart fluttered, a horrible faintness came over her; not a word could she utter, and the next moment she would have fled from the platform despite the humiliation which, she felt, must ever after be her portion if she did so.

But suddenly, as her dilated, frightened eyes gazed out over the audience, she saw Gilbert Blythe away at the back of the room, bending forward with a smile on his face—a smile which seemed to Anne at once triumphant and taunting. In reality it was nothing of the kind. Gilbert was merely smiling with appreciation of the whole affair in general and of the effect produced by Anne's slender white form and spiritual face against a background of palms in particular. Josie Pye, whom he had driven over, sat beside him, and her face certainly was both triumphant and taunting. But Anne did not see Josie, and would not have cared if she had. She drew a long breath and flung her head up proudly, courage and determination tingling over her like an electric shock. She *would not* fail before Gilbert Blythe—he should never be able to laugh at her, never, never! Her fright and nervousness vanished; and she began her recitation, her clear, sweet voice reaching to the farthest corner of the room without a tremor or a break. Self-possession was fully restored to her, and in the reaction from that horrible moment of powerlessness she recited as she had never done before. When she finished there were bursts of honest applause. Anne, stepping back to her seat, blushing with shyness and delight, found her hand vigorously clasped and shaken by the stout lady in pink silk.

"My dear, you did splendidly," she puffed. "I've been crying like a baby, actually I have. There, they're encoring you—they're bound to have you back!"

"Oh, I can't go," said Anne confusedly. "But yet—I must, or Matthew will be disappointed. He said they would encore me."

"Then don't disappoint Matthew," said the pink lady, laughing.

Smiling, blushing, limpid-eyed, Anne tripped back and gave a quaint, funny little selection that captivated her audience still further. The rest of the evening was quite a little triumph for her.

When the concert was over, the stout, pink lady—who was the wife of an American millionaire—took her under her wing, and introduced her to everybody; and everybody was very nice to her. The professional elocutionist, Mrs. Evans, came and chatted with her, telling her that she had a charming voice and "interpreted" her selections beautifully. Even the white lace girl paid her a languid little compliment. They had supper in the big, beautifully decorated dining room; Diana and Jane were invited to partake of this, also, since they had come with Anne, but Billy was nowhere to be found, having decamped in mortal fear of some such invitation. He was in waiting for them, with the team, however, when it was all over, and the three girls came merrily out into the calm, white moonshine radiance. Anne breathed deeply, and looked into the clear sky beyond the dark boughs of the firs.

Oh, it was good to be out again in the purity and silence of the night! How great and still and wonderful everything was, with the murmur of the sea sounding through it and the darkling cliffs beyond like grim giants guarding enchanted coasts.

"Hasn't it been a perfectly splendid time?" sighed Jane, as they drove away. "I just wish I was a rich American and could spend my summer at a hotel and wear jewels and low-necked dresses and have ice-cream and chicken salad every blessed day. I'm sure it would be ever so much more fun than teaching school. Anne, your recitations was simply great, although I thought at first you were never going to begin. I think it was better than Mrs. Evans'."

"Oh, no don't say things like that, Jane," said Anne quickly, "because it sounds silly. It couldn't be better than Mrs. Evans', you know, for she is a professional, and I'm only a schoolgirl, with a little knack of reciting. I'm quite satisfied if the people just liked mine pretty well."

"I've a compliment for you, Anne," said Diana. "At least I think it must be a compliment because of the tone he said it in. Part of it was anyhow. There was an American sitting behind Jane and me— such a romantic-looking man, with coal-black hair and eyes. Josie Pye says he is a distinguished artist, and that her mother's cousin in Boston is married to a man that used to go to school with him. Well, we heard him say—didn't we, Jane?—'Who is that girl on the platform with the splendid Titian hair? She has a face I should like to paint.' There now, Anne. But what does Titian hair mean?"

"Being interpreted it means plain red, I guess," laughed Anne. "Titian was a very famous artist who liked to paint red-haired women."

"*Did* you see all the diamonds those ladies wore?" sighed Jane. "They were simply dazzling. Wouldn't you just love to be rich, girls?"

"We *are* rich," said Anne stanchly. "Why, we have sixteen years to our credit, and we're happy as queens, and we've all got imaginations, more or less. Look at that sea, girls—all silver and shadow and vision of things not seen. We couldn't enjoy its loveliness any more if we had millions of dollars and ropes of diamonds. You wouldn't change into any of those women if you could. Would you want to be that white lace girl and wear a sour look all your life, as if you'd been born turning up your nose at the world? Or the pink lady, kind and nice as she is, so stout and short that you'd really no figure at all? Or even Mrs. Evans, with that sad, sad look in her eyes? She must have been dreadfully unhappy sometime to have such a look. You *know* you wouldn't, Jane Andrews!''

''I *don't* know—exactly,'' said Jane unconvinced. ''I think diamonds would comfort a person for a good deal.''

''Well, I don't want to be any one but myself, even if I go uncomforted by diamonds all my life,'' declared Anne. ''I'm quite content to be Anne of Green Gables, with my string of pearl beads. I know Matthew gave me as much love with them as ever went with Madame the Pink Lady's jewels.''

———— CHAPTER 34 ————

A QUEEN'S GIRL

THE NEXT three weeks were busy ones at Green Gables, for Anne was getting ready to go to Queen's, and there was much sewing to be done, and many things to be talked over and arranged. Anne's outift was ample and pretty, for Matthew saw to that, and Marilla for once made no objections whatever to anything he purchased or suggested. More—one evening she went up to the east gable with her arms full of a delicate pale green material.

''Anne, here's something for a nice light dress for you. I don't suppose you really need it; you've plenty of pretty waists; but I thought maybe you'd like something real dressy to wear if you were asked out anywhere of an evening in town, to a party or anything like that. I hear that Jane and Ruby and Josie have got 'evening dresses,' as they call them, and I don't mean you shall be behind them. I got Mrs. Allan to help me pick it in town last week; and we'll get Emily Gillis to make it up for you. Emily has got taste, and her fits aren't to be equalled.''

''Oh, Marilla, it's just lovely,'' said Anne. ''Thank you so much. I don't believe you ought to be so kind to me—it's making it harder every day for me to go away."

The green dress was made up with as many tucks and frills and shirrings as Emily's taste permitted. Anne put it on one evening for Matthew's and Marilla's benefit, and recited "The Maiden's Vow" for them in the kitchen. As Marilla watched the bright, animated face and graceful motions her thoughts went back to the evening Anne had arrived at Green Gables, and memory recalled a vivid picture of the odd, frightened child in her preposterous yellowish-brown wincey dress, the heartbreak looking out of her tearful eyes. Something in the memory brought tears to Marilla's eyes.

"I declare, my recitation has made you cry, Marilla," said Anne gaily, stooping over Marilla's chair to drop a butterfly kiss on that lady's cheek. "Now, I call that a positive triumph."

"No, I wasn't crying over your piece," said Marilla, who would have scorned to be betrayed into such weakness by any "poetry stuff." "I just couldn't help thinking of the little girl you used to be, Anne. And I was wishing you could have stayed a little girl, even with all your queer ways. You've grown up now and you're going away; and you look so tall and stylish and so—so—different altogether in that dress—as if you didn't belong in Avonlea at all—and I just got lonesome thinking it all over."

"Marilla!" Anne sat down on Marilla's gingham lap, took Marilla's lined face between her hands, and looked gravely and tenderly into Marilla's eyes. "I'm not a bit changed—not really. I'm only just pruned down and branched out. The real *me*—back here—is just the same. It won't make a bit of difference where I go or how much I change outwardly; at heart I shall always be your little Anne, who will love you and Matthew and dear Green Gables more and better every day of her life."

Anne laid her fresh young cheek against Marilla's faded one, and reached out a hand to pat Matthew's shoulder. Marilla would have given much just then to have possessed Anne's power of putting her feelings into words; but nature and habit had willed it otherwise, and she could only put her arms close about her girl and hold her tenderly to her heart, wishing that she need never let her go.

Matthew, with a suspicious moisture in his eyes, got up and went out-of-doors. Under the stars of the blue summer night he walked agitatedly across the yard to the gate under the poplars.

"Well now, I guess she ain't been much spoiled," he muttered, proudly. "I guess my putting in my oar occasional never did much harm after all. She's smart and pretty, and loving, too, which is better than all the rest. She's been a blessing to us, and there never was a luckier mistake than what Mrs. Spencer made—if it *was* luck. I don't believe it was any such thing. It was Providence, because the Almighty saw we needed her, I reckon.''

The day finally came when Anne must go to town. She and Matthew drove in one fine September morning, after a tearful parting with Diana and an untearful, practical one—on Marilla's side at least—with Marilla. But when Anne had gone Diana dried her tears and went to a beach picnic at White Sands with some of her Carmody cousins, where she contrived to enjoy herself tolerably well; while Marilla plunged fiercely into unnecessary work and kept at it all day long with the bitterest kind of a heartache—the ache that burns and gnaws and cannot wash itself away in ready tears. But that night when Marilla went to bed, acutely and miserably conscious that the little gable room at the end of the hall was untenanted by any vivid young life and unstirred by any soft breathing, she buried her face in her pillow, and wept for her girl in a passion of sobs that appalled her when she grew calm enough to reflect how very wicked it must be to take on so about a sinful fellow creature.

Anne and the rest of the Avonlea scholars reached town just in time to hurry off to the Academy. That first day passed pleasantly enough in a whirl of excitement, meeting all the new students, learning to know the professors by sight and being assorted and organized into classes. Anne intended taking up the Second Year work, being advised to do so by Miss Stacy; Gilbert Blythe elected to do the same. This meant getting a First Class teacher's license in one year instead of two, if they were successful; but it also meant much more and harder work. Jane, Ruby, Josie, Charlie, and Moody Spurgeon, not being troubled with the stirrings of ambition, were content to take up the Second Class work. Anne was conscious of a pang of loneliness when she found herself in a room with fifty other students, not one of whom she knew, except the tall, brown-haired boy across the room; and knowing him in the fashion she did, did not help her much, as she reflected pessimistically. Yet she was undeniably glad that they were in the same class; the old rivalry could still be carried on, and Anne would hardly have known what to do if it had been lacking.

''I wouldn't feel comfortable without it,'' she thought. ''Gilbert looks awfully determined. I suppose he's making up his mind, here and now, to win the medal. What a splendid chin he has! I never noticed it before. I do wish Jane and Ruby had gone in for First Class, too. I suppose I won't feel so much like a cat in a strange garret when I get acquainted, though. I wonder which of the girls here are going to be my friends. It's really an interesting speculation. Of course I promised Diana that no Queen's girl, no matter how much I liked her, should ever be as dear to me as she is; but I've lots of second-best affections to bestow. I like the look of that girl with the brown eyes and the crimson waist. She looks vivid and red-rosy; and there's that pale, fair one gazing out of the window. She has lovely hair, and looks as if she knew a thing or two about dreams. I'd like to know them both—know them well—well enough to walk with my arm about their waists, and call them nicknames. But just now I don't know them and they don't know me, and probably don't want to know me particularly. Oh, it's lonesome!''

It was lonesomer still when Anne found herself alone in her hall bedroom that night at twilight. She was not to board with the other girls, who all had relatives in town to take pity on them. Miss Josephine Barry would have liked to board her, but Beechwood was so far from the Academy that it was out of the question; so Miss Barry hunted up a boarding-house, assuring Matthew and Marilla that it was the very place for Anne.

''The lady who keeps it is a reduced gentlewoman,'' explained Miss Barry. ''Her husband was a British officer, and she is very careful what sort of boarders she takes. Anne will not meet with any objectionable persons under her roof. The table is good, and the house is near the Academy, in a quiet neighborhood.''

All this might be quite true, and, indeed, proved to be so, but it did not materially help Anne in the first agony of homesickness that seized upon her. She looked dismally about her narrow little room, with its dull-papered, pictureless walls, its small iron bedstead and empty bookcase; and a horrible choke came into her throat as she thought of her own white room at Green Gables, where she would have the pleasant consciousness of a great green still outdoors, of sweet peas growing in the garden, and moonlight falling on the orchard, of the brook below the slope and the spruce boughs tossing in the night wind beyond it, of a vast starry sky, and the light from Diana's window shining out through the gap in the trees. Here there was nothing of this; Anne knew that outside of her window was a hard street, with a network of telephone wires shutting out the sky, the tramp of alien feet, and a thousand lights gleaming on stranger faces. She knew that she was going to cry, and fought against it.

"I *won't* cry. It's silly—and weak—there's the third tear splashing down by my nose. There are more coming! I must think of something funny to stop them. But there's nothing funny except what is connected with Avonlea, and that only makes things worse—four—five—I'm going home next Friday, but that seems a hundred years away. Oh, Matthew is nearly home by now—and Marilla is at the gate, looking down the lane for him—six—seven—eight—oh, there's no use in counting them! They're coming in a flood presently. I can't cheer up—I don't *want* to cheer up. It's nicer to be miserable!"

The flood of tears would have come, no doubt, had not Josie Pye appeared at that moment. In the joy of seeing a familiar face Anne forgot that there had never been much love lost between her and Josie. As a part of Avonlea life even a Pye was welcome.

"I'm so glad you came up," Anne said sincerely.

"You've been crying," remarked Josie, with aggravating pity. "I suppose you're homesick—some people have so little self-control in that respect. I've no intention of being homesick, I can tell you. Town's too jolly after that poky old Avonlea. I wonder how I ever existed there so long. You shouldn't cry, Anne; it isn't becoming, for your nose and eyes get red, and then you seem *all* red. I'd a perfectly scrumptious time in the Academy today. Our French professor is simply a duck. His moustache would give you kerwollops of the heart. Have you anything eatable around, Anne? I'm literally starving. Ah, I guessed likely Marilla'd load you up with cake. That's why I called round. Otherwise I'd have gone to the park to hear the band play with Frank Stockley. He boards same place as I do, and he's a sport. He noticed you in class today, and asked me who the red-headed girl was. I told him you were an orphan that the Cuthberts had adopted, and nobody knew very much about what you'd been before that."

Anne was wondering if, after all, solitude and tears were not more satisfactory than Josie Pye's companionship when Jane and Ruby appeared, each with an inch of Queen's color ribbon—purple and scarlet—pinned proudly to her coat. As Josie was not "speaking" to Jane just then she had to subside into comparative harmlessness.

"Well," said Jane with a sigh, "I feel as if I'd lived many moons since the morning. I ought to be home studying my Virgil—that horrid old professor gave us twenty lines to start in on tomorrow. But I simply couldn't settle down to study tonight. Anne, methinks I see the traces of tears. If you've been crying *do* own up. It will restore my self-respect, for I was shedding tears freely before Ruby came along. I don't mind being a goose so much if somebody else is goosey, too. Cake? You'll give me a teeny piece, won't you? Thank you. It has the real Avonlea flavor.''

Ruby, perceiving the Queen's calendar lying on the table, wanted to know if Anne meant to try for the gold medal.

Anne blushed and admitted she was thinking of it.

''Oh, that reminds me,'' said Josie, ''Queen's is to get one of the Avery scholarships after all. The word came today. Frank Stockley told me—his uncle is one of the board of governors, you know. It will be announced in the Academy tomorrow.''

An Avery scholarship! Anne felt her heart beat more quickly, and the horizons of her amibiton shifted and broadened as if by magic. Before Josie had told the news Anne's highest pinnacle of aspiration had been a teacher's provincial license, Class First, at the end of the year, and perhaps the medal! But now in one moment Anne saw herself winning the Avery scholarship, taking an Arts course at Redmond College, and graduating in a gown and mortar-board, all before the echo of Josie's words had died away. For the Avery scholarship was in English, and Anne felt that here her foot was on her native heath.

A wealthy manufacturer of New Brunswick had died and left part of his fortune to endow a large number of scholarships to be distributed among the various high schools and academies of the Maritime Provinces, according to their respective standings. There had been much doubt whether one would be allotted to Queen's, but the matter was settled at last, and at the end of the year the graduate who made the highest mark in English and English Literature would win the scholarship—two hundred and fifty dollars a year for four years at Redmond College. No wonder that Anne went to bed that night with tingling cheeks!

''I'll win that scholarship if hard work can do it,'' she resolved. ''Wouldn't Matthew be proud if I got to be a B.A.? Oh, it's delightful to have ambitions. I'm so glad I have such a lot. And there never seems to be any end to them—that's the best of it. Just as soon as you attain to one ambition you see another one glittering higher up still. It does make life so interesting.''

CHAPTER 35

THE WINTER AT QUEEN'S

ANNE'S HOMESICKNESS wore off, greatly helped in the wearing by her weekend visits home. As long as the open weather lasted the Avonlea students went out to Carmody on the new branch railway every Friday night. Diana and several other Avonlea young folks were generally on hand to meet them and they all walked over to Avonlea in a merry party. Anne thought those Friday evening gipsyings over the autumnal hills in the crisp golden air, with the home-lights of Avonlea twinkling beyond, were the best and dearest hours in the whole week.

Gilbert Blythe nearly always walked with Ruby Gillis and carried her satchel for her. Ruby was a very handsome young lady, now thinking herself quite as grown up as she really was; she wore her skirts as long as her mother would let her and did her hair up in town, though she had to take it down when she went home. She had large, bright blue eyes, a brilliant complexion, and a plump showy figure. She laughed a great deal, was cheerful and good-tempered, and enjoyed the pleasant things of life frankly.

"But I shouldn't think she was the sort of girl Gilbert would like," whispered Jane to Anne. Anne did not think so either, but she would not have said so for the Avery scholarship. She could not help thinking, too, that it would be very pleasant to have such a friend as Gilbert to jest and chatter with and exchange ideas about books and studies and ambitions. Gilbert had ambitions, she knew, and Ruby Gillis did not seem the sort of person with whom such could be profitably discussed.

There was no silly sentiment in Anne's ideas concerning Gilbert. Boys were to her, when she thought about them at all, merely possible good comrades. If she and Gilbert had been friends she would not have cared how many other friends he had nor with whom he walked. She had a genius for friendship; girlfriends she had in plenty, but she had a vague consciousness that masculine friendship might also be a good thing to round out one's conceptions of companionship and furnish broader standpoints of judgment and comparison. Not that Anne could have put her feelings on the matter into just such clear definition. But she thought that if Gilbert had ever walked home with her from the train, over the crisp fields and along the ferny byways, they might have had many and merry and interesting conversations about the new world that was opening around them and their hopes and ambitions therein. Gilbert was a clever young fellow, with his own thoughts about things and a determination to get the best out of life and put the best into it. Ruby Gillis told Jane Andrews that she didn't understand half the things Gilbert Blythe said; he talked just like Anne Shirley did when she had a thoughtful fit on and for her part she didn't think it any fun to be bothering about books and that sort of thing when you didn't have to. Frank Stockley had lots more dash and go, but then he wasn't half as good-looking as Gilbert and she really couldn't decide which she liked best!

In the Academy Anne gradually drew a little circle of friends about her, thoughtful, imaginative, ambitious students like herself. With the "rose-red" girl, Stella Maynard, and the "dream girl," Priscilla Grant, she soon became intimate, finding the latter pale spiritual-looking maiden to be full to the brim of mischief and pranks and fun, while the vivid, black-eyed Stella had a heartful of wistful dreams and fancies, as aerial and rainbow-like as Anne's own.

After the Christmas holidays the Avonlea students gave up going home on Fridays and settled down to hard work. By this time all the Queen's scholars had gravitated into their own places in the ranks and the various classes had assumed distinct and settled shadings of individuality. Certain facts had become generally accepted. It was admitted that the medal contestants had practically narrowed down to three—Gilbert Blythe, Anne Shirley, and Lewis Wilson; the Avery scholarship was more doubtful, any one of a certain six being a possible winner. The bronze medal for mathematics was considered as good as won by a fat, funny little up-country boy with a bumpy forehead and a patched coat.

Ruby Gillis was the handsomest girl of the year at the Academy; in the Second Year classes Stella Maynard carried off the palm for beauty, with a small but critical minority in favor of Anne Shirley. Ethel Marr was admitted by all competent judges to have the most stylish modes of hair-dressing, and Jane Andrews—plain, plodding, conscientious Jane—carried off the honors in the domestic science course. Even Josie Pye attained a certain preeminence as the sharpest-tongued young lady in attendance at Queen's. So it may be fairly stated that Miss Stacy's old pupils held their own in the wider arena of the academical course.

Anne worked hard and steadily. Her rivalry with Gilbert was as intense as it had ever been in Avonlea school, although it was not known in the class at large, but somehow the bitterness had gone out of it. Anne no longer wished to win for the sake of defeating Gilbert; rather, for the proud consciousness of a well-won victory over a worthy foeman. It would be worth while to win, but she no longer thought life would be insupportable if she did not.

In spite of lessons the students found opportunities for pleasant times. Anne spent many of her spare hours at Beechwood and generally ate her Sunday dinners there and went to church with Miss Barry. The latter was, as she admitted, growing old, but her black eyes were not dim nor the vigor of her tongue in the least abated. But she never sharpened the latter on Anne, who continued to be a prime favorite with the critical old lady.

"That Anne-girl improves all the time," she said. "I get tired of other girls—there is such a provoking and eternal sameness about them. Anne has as many shades as a rainbow and every shade is the prettiest while it lasts. I don't know that she is as amusing as she was when she was a child, but she makes me love her and I like people who make me love them. It saves me so much trouble in making myself love them."

Then, almost before anybody realized it, spring had come; out in Avonlea the Mayflowers were peeping pinkly out on the sere barrens where snow-wreaths lingered; and the "mist of green" was on the woods and in the valleys. But in Charlottetown harassed Queen's students thought and talked only of examinations.

"It doesn't seem possible that the term is nearly over," said Anne. "Why, last fall it seemed so long to look forward to—a whole winter of studies and classes. And here we are, with the exams looming up next week. Girls, sometimes I feel as if those exams meant everything, but when I look at the big buds swelling on those chestnut trees and the misty blue air at the end of the streets they don't seem half so important.'

Jane and Ruby and Josie, who had dropped in, did not take this view of it. To them the coming examinations were constantly very important indeed—far more important than chestnut buds or Maytime hazes. It was all very well for Anne, who was sure of passing at least, to have her moments of belittling them, but when your whole future depended on them—as the girls truly thought theirs did—you could not regard them philosphically.

"I've lost seven pounds in the last two weeks," sighed Jane. "It's no use to say don't worry. I *will* worry. Worrying helps you some—it seems as if you were doing something when you're worrying. It would be dreadful if I failed to get my license after going to Queen's all winter and spending so much money.''

"*I* don't care,'' said Josie Pye. "If I don't pass this year I'm coming back next. My father can afford to send me. Anne, Frank Stockely says that Professor Tremaine said Gilbert Blythe was sure to get the medal and that Emily Clay would likely win the Avery scholarship.''

''That may make me feel badly tomorrow, Josie,'' laughed Anne, ''but just now I honestly feel that as long as I know the violets are coming out all purple down in the hollow below Green Gables and that little ferns are poking their heads up in Lovers' Lane, it's not a great deal of difference whether I begin to understand what is meant by the 'joy of the strife.' Next to trying and winning, the best thing is trying and failing. Girls, don't talk about exams! Look at that arch of pale green sky over those houses and picture to yourselves what it must look like over the purply-dark beechwoods back of Avonlea.''

"What are you going to wear for commencement, Jane?'' asked Ruby practically.

Jane and Josie both answered at once and the chatter drifted into a side eddy of fashions. But Anne, with her elbows on the window sill, her soft cheek laid against her clasped hands, and her eyes filled with visions, looked out unheedingly across city roof and spire to that glorious dome of sunset sky and wove her dreams of a possible future from the golden tissue of youth's own optimism. All the Beyond was hers with its possibilities lurking rosily in the oncoming years—each year a rose of promise to be woven into an immortal chaplet.

CHAPTER 36

THE GLORY AND THE DREAM

ON THE morning when the final results of all the examinations were to be posted on the bulletin board at Queen's, Anne and Jane walked down the street together. Jane was smiling and happy; examinations were over and she was comfortably sure she had made a pass at least; further considerations troubled Jane not at all; she had no soaring ambitions and consequently was not affected with the unrest attendant thereon. For we pay a price for everything we get or take in this world; and although ambitions are well worth having, they are not to be cheaply won, but exact their dues of work and self-denial, anxiety and discouragement. Anne was pale and quiet; in ten more minutes she would know who had won the medal and who the Avery. Beyond those ten minutes there did not seem, just then, to be anything worth being called Time.

"Of course you'll win one of them anyhow," said Jane, who couldn't understand how the faculty could be so unfair as to order it otherwise.

"I have no hope of the Avery," said Anne. "Everybody says Emily Clay will win it. And I'm not going to march up to that bulletin board and look at it before everybody. I haven't the moral courage. I'm going straight to the girls' dressing-room. You must read the announcements and then come and tell me, Jane. And I implore you in the name of our old friendship to do it as quickly as possible. If I have failed just say so, without trying to break it gently; and whatever you do *don't* sympathize with me. Promise me this, Jane."

Jane promised solemnly; but, as it happened, there was no necessity for such a promise. When they went up the entrance steps of Queen's they found the hall full of boys who were carrying Gilbert Blythe around on their shoulders and yelling at the tops of their voices, "Hurrah for Blythe, Medallist!"

For a moment Anne felt one sickening pang of defeat and disappointment. So she had failed and Gilbert had won! Well, Matthew would be sorry—he had been so sure she would win.

And then!

Somebody called out:

"Three cheers for Miss Shirley, winner of the Avery!"

"Oh, Anne," gasped Jane, as they fled to the girls' dressing-room amid hearty cheers. "Oh, Anne, I'm so proud! Isn't it splendid?"

And then the girls were around them and Anne was the centre of a laughing, congratulating group. Her shoulders were thumped and her hands shaken vigorously. She was pushed and pulled and hugged and among it all she managed to whisper to Jane:

"Oh, won't Matthew and Marilla be pleased! I must write the news home right away."

Commencement was the next important happening. The exercises were held in the big assembly hall of the Academy. Addresses were given, essays read, songs sung, the public award of diplomas, prizes and medals made.

Matthew and Marilla were there, with eyes and ears for only one student on the platform—a tall girl in pale green, with faintly flushed cheeks and starry eyes, who read the best essay and was pointed out and whispered about as the Avery winner.

"Reckon you're glad we kept her, Marilla?" whispered Matthew, speaking for the first time since he had entered the hall, when Anne had finished her essay.

"It's not the first time I've been glad," retorted Marilla. "You do like to rub things in, Matthew Cuthbert."

Miss Barry, who was sitting behind them, leaned forward and poked Marilla in the back with her parasol.

"Aren't you proud of that Anne-girl? I am," she said.

Anne went home to Avonlea with Matthew and Marilla that evening. She had not been home since April and she felt that she could not wait another day. The apple-blossoms were out and the world was fresh and young. Diana was at Green Gables to meet her. In her own white room, where Marilla had set a flowering house rose on the window sill, Anne looked about her and drew a long breath of happiness.

"Oh, Diana, it's so good to be back again. It's so good to see those pointed firs coming out against the pink sky—and that white orchard and the old Snow Queen. Isn't the breath of the mint delicious? And that tea rose—why, it's *good* to see you again, Diana!"

"I thought you liked that Stella Maynard better than me," said Diana reproachfully. "Josie Pye told me you did. Josie said you were *infatuated* with her."

Anne lauged and pelted Diana with the faded "June lilies" of her bouquet.

"Stella Maynard is the dearest girl in the world except one and you are that one, Diana," she said. "I love you more than ever—and I've so many things to tell you. But just now I feel as if it were joy enough to sit here and look at you. I'm tired, I think—tired of being studious and ambitious. I mean to spend at least two hours tomorrow lying out in the orchard grass, thinking of absolutely nothing."

"You've done splendidly, Anne. I suppose you won't be teaching now that you've won the Avery?"

"No. I'm going to Redmond in September. Doesn't it seem wonderful? I'll have a brand-new stock of ambition laid in by that time after three glorious, golden months of vacation. Jane and Ruby are going to teach. Isn't it splendid to think we all got through even to Moody Spurgeon and Josie Pye?"

"The Newbridge trustees have offered Jane their school already," said Diana. ''Gilbert Blythe is going to teach, too. He has to. His father can't afford to send him to college next year, after all, so he means to earn his own way through. I expect he'll get the school here if Miss Ames decides to leave.''

Anne felt a queer little sensation of dismayed surprise. She had not known this; she had expected Gilbert would be going to Redmond also. What would she do without their inspiring rivalry? Would not work, even at a co-educational college with a real degree in prospect, be rather flat without her friend the enemy?

The next morning at breakfast it suddenly struck Anne that Matthew was not looking well. Surely he was much grayer than he had been a year before.

''Marilla,'' she said hesitatingly when he had gone out, ''is Matthew quite well?''

''No, he isn't,'' said Marilla in a troubled tone. ''He's had some real bad spells with his heart this spring and he won't spare himself a mite. I've been real worried about him, but he's some better this while back and we've got a good hired man, so I'm hoping he'll kind of rest and pick up. Maybe he will now you're home. You always cheer him up.''

Anne leaned across the table and took Marilla's face in her hands.

''You are not looking as well yourself as I'd like to see you, Marilla. You look tired. I'm afraid you've been working too hard. You must take a rest, now that I'm home. I'm just going to take this one day off to visit all the dear old spots and hunt up my old dreams, and then it well be your turn to be lazy while I do the work.''

Marilla smiled affectionately at her girl.

''It's not the work—it's my head. I've a pain so often now—behind my eyes. Doctor Spencer's been fussing with glasses, but they don't do me any good. There is a distinguished oculist coming to the Island the last of June and the doctor says I must see him. I guess I'll have to. I can't read or sew with any comfort now. Well, Anne, you've done real well at Queen's I must say. To take First Class License in one year and win the Avery scholarship—well, well, Mrs. Lynde says pride goes before a fall and she doesn't believe in the higher education of women at all; she says it unfits them for woman's true sphere. I don't believe a word of it. Speaking of Rachel reminds me—did you hear anything about the Abbey Bank lately, Anne?''

''I heard that it was shaky,'' answered Anne. ''Why?''

''That is what Rachel said. She was up here one day last week and said there was some talk about it. Matthew felt real worried. All we have saved is in that bank—every penny. I wanted Matthew to put it in the Savings Bank in the first place, but old Mr. Abbey was a great friend of father's and he'd always banked with him. Matthew said any bank with him at the head of it was good enough for anybody."

"I think he has only been its nominal head for many years," said Anne. "He is a very old man; his nephews are really at the head of the institution."

"Well, when Rachel told us that, I wanted Matthew to draw our money right out and he said he'd think of it. But Mr. Russell told him yesterday that the bank was all right."

Anne had her good day in the companionship of the outdoor world. She never forgot that day; it was so bright and golden and fair, so free from shadow and so lavish of blossom. Anne spent some of its rich hours in the orchard; she went to the Dryad's Bubble and Willowmere and Violet Vale; she called at the manse and had a satisfying talk with Mrs. Allan; and finally in the evening she went with Matthew for the cows, through Lovers' Lane to the back pasture. The woods were all gloried through with sunset and the warm splendor of it streamed down through the hill gaps in the west. Matthew walked slowly with bent head; Anne, tall and erect, suited her springing step to his.

"You've been working too hard today, Matthew," she said reproachfully. "Why won't you take things easier?"

"Well now, I can't seem to," said Matthew, as he opened the yard gate to let the cows through. "It's only that I'm getting old, Anne, and keep forgetting it. Well, well, I've always worked pretty hard and I'd rather drop in harness."

"If I had been the boy you sent for," said Anne wistfully, "I'd be able to help you so much now and spare you in a hundred ways. I could find it in my heart to wish I had been, just for that."

"Well, no, I'd rather have you than a dozen boys, Anne," said Matthew patting her hand. "Just mind you that—rather than a dozen boys. Well now, I guess it wasn't a boy that took the Avery scholarship, was it? It was a girl—my girl—my girl that I'm proud of."

He smiled his shy smile at her as he went into the yard. Anne took the memory of it with her when she went to her room that night and sat for a long while at her open window, thinking of the past and dreaming of the future. Outside the Snow Queen was mistily white in the moonshine; the frogs were singing in the marsh beyond Orchard Slope. Anne always remembered the silvery, peaceful beauty and fragrant calm of that night. It was the last night before sorrow touched her life; and no life is ever quite the same again once that cold, sanctifying touch has been laid upon it.

—————————— CHAPTER 37 ——————————

THE REAPER WHOSE NAME IS DEATH

"MATTHEW—MATTHEW—What is the matter? Matthew, are you sick?"

It was Marilla who spoke, alarm in every jerky word. Anne came through the hall, her hands full of white narcissus,—it was long before Anne could love the sight or odor of white narcissus again,— in time to hear her and to see Matthew standing in the porch doorway, a folded paper in his hand, and his face strangely drawn and gray. Anne dropped her flowers and sprang across the kitchen to him at the same moment as Marilla. They were both too late; before they could reach him Matthew had fallen across the threshold.

"He's fainted," gasped Marilla. "Anne, run for Martin—quick, quick! He's at the barn."

Martin, the hired man, who had just driven home from the post-office, started at once for the doctor, calling at Orchard Slope on his way to send Mr. and Mrs. Barry over. Mrs. Lynde, who was there on an errand, came too. They found Anne and Marilla distractedly trying to restore Matthew to consciousness.

Mrs. Lynde pushed them gently aside, tried his pulse, and then laid her ear over his heart. She looked at their anxious faces sorrow-fully and the tears came into her eyes.

"Oh, Marilla," she said gravely. "I don't think—we can do anything for him."

"Mrs. Lynde, you don't think—you can't think Matthew is— is—" Anne could not say the dreadful word; she turned sick and pallid.

"Child, yes, I'm afraid of it. Look at his face. When you've seen that look as often as I have you'll know what it means."

Anne looked at the still face and there beheld the seal of the Great Presence.

When the doctor came he said that death had been instantaneous and probably painless, caused in all likelihood by some sudden shock. The secret of the shock was discovered to be in the paper Matthew had held and which Martin had brought from the office that morning. It contained an account of the failure of the Abbey Bank.

The news spread quickly through Avonlea, and all day friends and neighbors thronged Green Gables and came and went on errands of kindness for the dead and living. For the first time shy, quiet Matthew Cuthbert was a person of central importance; the white majesty of death had fallen on him and set him apart as one crowned.

When the calm night came softly down over Green Gables the old house was hushed and tranquil. In the parlor lay Matthew Cuthbert in his coffin, his long gray hair framing his placid face on which there was a little kindly smile as if he but slept, dreaming pleasant dreams. There were flowers about him—sweet old-fashioned flowers which his mother had planted in the homestead garden in her bridal days and for which Matthew had always had a secret, wordless love. Anne had gathered them and brought them to him, her anguished, tearless eyes burning in her white face. It was the last thing she could do for him.

The Barrys and Mrs. Lynde stayed with them that night. Diana, going to the east gable, where Anne was standing at her window, said gently:

"Anne dear, would you like to have me sleep with you tonight?"

"Thank you, Diana." Anne looked earnestly into her friend's face. "I think you won't misunderstand me when I say that I want to be alone. I'm not afraid. I haven't been alone one minute since it happened—and I want to be. I want to be quite silent and quiet and try to realize it. I *can't* realize it. Half the time it seems to me that Matthew can't be dead; and the other half it seems as if he must have been dead for a long time and I've had this horrible dull ache ever since."

Diana did not quite understand. Marilla's impassioned grief, breaking all the bounds of natural reserve and lifelong habit in its stormy rush, she could comprehend better than Anne's tearless agony. But she went away kindly, leaving Anne alone to keep her first vigil with sorrow.

Anne hoped that tears would come in solitude. It seemed to her a terrible thing that she could not shed a tear for Matthew, whom she had loved so much and who had been so kind to her, Matthew, who had walked with her last evening at sunset and was now lying in the dim room below with that awful peace on his brow. But no tears came at first, even when she knelt by her window in the darkness and prayed, looking up to the stars beyond the hills—no tears, only the same horrible dull ache of misery that kept on aching until she fell asleep, worn out with the day's pain and excitement.

In the night she awakened, with the stillness and the darkness about her, and the recollection of the day came over her like a wave of sorrow. She could see Matthew's face smiling at her as he had smiled when they parted at the gate that last evening—she could hear his voice saying, "My girl—my girl that I'm proud of." Then the tears came and Anne wept her heart out. Marilla heard her and crept in to comfort her.

"There—there—don't cry so, dearie. It can't bring him back. It—it—isn't right to cry so. I knew that today, but I couldn't help it then. He'd always been such a good, kind brother to me—but God knows best."

"Oh, just let me cry, Marilla," sobbed Anne. "The tears don't hurt me like that ache did. Stay here for a little while with me and keep your arm round me—so. I couldn't have Diana stay, she's good and kind and sweet—but it's not her sorrow—she's outside of it and she couldn't come close enough to my heart to help me. It's our sorrow—yours and mine. Oh, Marilla, what will we do without him?"

"We've got each other, Anne. I don't know what I'd do if you weren't here—if you'd never come. Oh, Anne, I know I've been kind of strict and harsh with you maybe—but you mustn't think I didn't love you as well as Matthew did, for all that. I want to tell you now when I can. It's never been easy for me to say things out of my heart, but at times like this it's easier. I love you as dear as if you were my own flesh and blood and you've been my joy and comfort ever since you came to Green Gables."

Two days afterwards they carried Matthew Cuthbert over his homestead threshold and away from the fields he had tilled and the orchards he had loved and the trees he had planted; and then Avonlea settled back to its usual placidity and even at Green Gables affairs slipped into their old groove and work was done and duties fulfilled with regularity as before, although always with the aching sense of "loss in all familiar things." Anne, new to grief, thought it almost sad that it could be so—that they *could* go on in the old way without Matthew. She felt something like shame and remorse when she discovered that the sunrises behind the firs and the pale pink buds opening in the garden gave her the old inrush of gladness when she saw them—that Diana's visits were pleasant to her and that Diana's merry words and ways moved her to laughter and smiles—that, in brief, the beautiful world of blossom and love and friendship had lost none of its power to please her fancy and thrill her heart, that life still called to her with many insistent voices.

"It seems like disloyalty to Matthew, somehow, to find pleasure in these things now that he has gone," she said wistfully to Mrs. Allan one evening when they were together in the manse garden. "I miss him so much—all the time—and yet, Mrs. Allan, the world and life seem very beautiful and interesting to me for all. Today Diana said something funny and I found myself laughing. I thought when it happened I could never laugh again. And it somehow seems as if I oughtn't to."

"When Matthew was here he liked to hear you laugh and he liked to know that you found pleasure in the pleasant things around you," said Mrs. Allan gently. "He is just away now; and he likes to know it is just the same. I am sure we should not shut our hearts against the healing influences that nature offers us. But I understand your feeling. I think we all experience the same thing. We resent the thought that anything can please us when someone we love is no longer here to share the pleasure with us, and we almost feel as if we were unfaithful to our sorrow when we find our interest in life returning to us."

"I was down to the graveyard to plant a rosebush on Matthew's grave this afternoon," said Anne dreamily. "I took a slip of the little white Scotch rosebush his mother brought out from Scotland long ago; Matthew always liked those roses the best—they were so small and sweet on their thorny stems. It made me feel glad that I could plant it by his grave—as if I were doing something that must please him in taking it there to be near him. I hope he has roses like them in heaven. Perhaps the souls of all those little white roses that he has loved so many summers were all there to meet him. I must go home now. Marilla is all alone and she gets lonely at twilight."

"She will be lonelier still, I fear, when you go away again to college," said Mrs. Allan.

Anne did not reply; she said good night and went slowly back to Green Gables. Marilla was sitting on the front door steps and Anne sat down beside her. The door was open behind them, held back by a big pink conch shell with hints of sea sunsets in its smooth inner convolutions.

Anne gathered some sprays of pale yellow honeysuckle and put them in her hair. She liked the delicious hint of fragrance, as of some aerial benediction, above her every time she moved.

"Doctor Spencer was here while you were away," Marilla said. "He says that the specialist will be in town tomorrow and he insists that I must go in and have my eyes examined. I suppose I'd better go and have it over. I'll be more than thankful if the man can give me the right kind of glasses to suit my eyes. You won't mind staying here alone while I'm away, will you? Martin will have to drive me in and there's ironing and baking to do."

"I shall be all right. Diana will come over for company for me. I shall attend to the ironing and baking beautifully—you needn't fear that I'll starch the handkerchiefs or flavor the cake with liniment."

Marilla laughed.

"What a girl you were for making mistakes in them days, Anne. You were always getting into scrapes. I did use to think you were possessed. Do you mind the time you dyed your hair?"

"Yes, indeed. I shall never forget it," smiled Anne, touching the heavy braid of hair that was wound about her shapely head. "I laugh a little now sometimes when I think what a worry my hair used to be to me——but I don't laugh *much*, because it was a very real trouble then. I did suffer terribly over my hair and my freckles. My freckles are really gone; and people are nice enough to tell me my hair is auburn now—all but Josie Pye. She informed me yesterday that she really thought it was redder than ever, or at least my black dress made it look redder, and she asked me if people who had red hair ever got used to having it. Marilla, I've almost decided to give up trying to like Josie Pye. I've made what I would once have called a heroic effort to like her, but Josie Pye won't *be* liked."

"Josie is a Pye," said Marilla sharply, "so she can't help being disagreeable. I suppose people of that kind serve some useful purpose in society, but I must say I don't know what it is any more than I know the use of thistles. Is Josie going to teach?"

"No, she is going back to Queen's next year. So are Moody Spurgeon and Charlie Sloane. Jane and Ruby are going to teach and they have both got schools—Jane at Newbridge and Ruby at some place up west."

"Gilbert Blythe is going to teach too, isn't he?"

"Yes"—briefly.

"What a nice-looking young fellow he is," said Marilla absently. "I saw him in church last Sunday and he seemed so tall and manly. He looks a lot like his father did at the same age. John Blythe was a nice boy. We used to be real good friends, he and I. People called him my beau."

Anne looked up with swift interest.

"Oh, Marilla—and what happened?—why didn't you—"

"We had a quarrel. I wouldn't forgive him when he asked me to. I meant to, after awhile—but I was sulky and angry and I wanted to punish him first. He never came back—the Blythes were all mighty independent. But I always felt—rather sorry. I've always kind of wished I'd forgiven him when I had the chance."

"So you've had a bit of romance in your life, too," said Anne softly.

"Yes, I suppose you might call it that. You wouldn't think so to look at me, would you? But you never can tell about people from their outsides. Everybody has forgot about me and John. I'd forgotten myself. But it all came back to me when I saw Gilbert last Sunday."

CHAPTER 38

THE BEND IN THE ROAD

MARILLA WENT to town the next day and returned in the evening. Anne had gone over to Orchard Slope with Diana and came back to find Marilla in the kitchen, sitting by the table with her head leaning on her hand. Something in her dejected attitude struck a chill to Anne's heart. She had never seen Marilla sit limply inert like that.

"Are you very tired, Marilla?"

"Yes—no—I don't know," said Marilla wearily, looking up. "I suppose I am tired but I haven't thought about it. It's not that."

"Did you see the oculist? What did he say?" asked Anne anxiously.

"Yes, I saw him. He examined my eyes. He says that if I give up all reading and sewing entirely and any kind of work that strains the eyes, and if I'm careful not to cry, and if I wear the glasses he's given me he thinks my eyes may not get any worse and my headaches will be cured. But if I don't he says I'll certainly be stone blind in six months. Blind! Anne, just think of it!"

For a minute Anne, after her first quick exclamation of dismay, was silent. It seemed to her that she could *not* speak. Then she said bravely, but with a catch in her voice:

"Marilla, *don't* think of it. You know he has given you hope. If you are careful you won't lose your sight altogether; and if his glasses cure your headaches it will be a great thing."

"I don't call it much hope," said Marilla bitterly. "What am I to live for if I can't read or sew or do anything like that? I might as well be blind—or dead. And as for crying, I can't help that when I get lonesome. But there, it's no good talking about it. If you'll get me a cup of tea I'll be thankful. I'm about done out. Don't say anything about this to any one for a spell yet, anyway. I can't bear that folks should come here to question and sympathize and talk about it."

When Marilla had eaten her lunch Anne persuaded her to go to bed. Then Anne went herself to the east gable and sat down by her window in the darkness alone with her tears and her heaviness of heart. How sadly things had changed since she had sat there the night after coming home! Then she had been full of hope and joy and the future had looked rosy with promise. Anne felt as if she had lived years since then, but before she went to bed there was a smile on her lips and peace in her heart. She had looked her duty courageously in the face and found it a friend—as duty ever is when we meet it frankly.

One afternoon a few days later Marilla came slowly in from the yard where she had been talking to a caller—a man whom Anne knew by sight as John Sadler from Carmody. Anne wondered what he could have been saying to bring that look to Marilla's face.

"What did Mr. Sadler want, Marilla?"

Marilla sat down by the window and looked at Anne. There were tears in her eyes in defiance of the oculist's prohibition and her voice broke as she said:

"He heard that I was going to sell Green Gables and he wants to buy it."

"Buy it! Buy Green Gables?" Anne wondered if she had heard aright. "Oh, Marilla, you don't mean to sell Green Gables!"

"Anne, I don't know what else is to be done. I've thought it all over. If my eyes were strong I could stay here and make out to look after things and manage, with a good hired man. But as it is I can't. I may lose my sight altogether; and anyway I'll not be fit to run things. Oh, I never thought I'd live to see the day when I'd have to sell my home. But things would only go behind worse and worse all the time, till nobody would want to buy it. Every cent of our money went in that bank; and there's some notes Matthew gave last fall to pay. Mrs.

Lynde advises me to sell the farm and board somewhere—with her I suppose. It won't bring much—it's small and the buildings are old. But it'll be enough for me to live on I reckon. I'm thankful you're provided for with that scholarship, Anne. I'm sorry you won't have a home to come to in your vacations, that's all, but I suppose you'll manage somehow."

Marilla broke down and wept bitterly.

"You mustn't sell Green Gables," said Anne resolutely.

"Oh, Anne, I wish I didn't have to. But you can see for yourself. I can't stay here alone. I'd go crazy with trouble and loneliness. And my sight would go—I know it would."

"You won't have to stay here alone, Marilla. I'll be with you. I'm not going to Redmond."

"Not going to Redmond!" Marilla lifted her worn face from her hands and looked at Anne. "Why, what do you mean?"

"Just what I say. I'm not going to take the scholarship. I decided so the night after you came home from town. You surely don't think I could leave you alone in your trouble, Marilla, after all you've done for me. I've been thinking and planning. Let me tell you my plans. Mr. Barry wants to rent the farm for next year. So you won't have any bother over that. And I'm going to teach. I've applied for the school here—but I don't expect to get it for I understand the trustees have promised it to Gilbert Blythe. But I can have the Carmody school— Mr. Blair told me so last night at the store. Of course that won't be quite as nice or convenient as if I had the Avonlea school. But I can board home and drive myself over to Carmody and back, in the warm weather at least. And even in winter I can come home Fridays. We'll keep a horse for that. Oh, I have it all planned out, Marilla. And I'll read to you and keep you cheered up. You shan't be dull or lonesome. And we'll be real cosy and happy here together, you and I."

Marilla had listened like a woman in a dream.

"Oh, Anne, I could get on real well if you were here, I know. But I can't let you sacrifice yourself so for me. It would be terrible."

"Nonsense!" Anne laughed merrily. "There is no sacrifice. Nothing could be worse than giving up Green Gables—nothing could hurt me more. We must keep the dear old place. My mind is quite made up, Marilla. I'm *not* going to Redmond; and I *am* going to stay here and teach. Don't you worry about me a bit."

"But your ambitions—and—"

"I'm just as ambitious as ever. Only, I've changed the object of my ambitions. I'm going to be a good teacher—and I'm going to save your eyesight. Besides, I mean to study at home here and take a little college course all by myself. Oh, I've dozens of plans, Marilla. I've been thinking them out for a week. I shall give life here my best, and I believe it will give its best to me in return. When I left Queen's my future seemed to stretch out before me like a straight road. I thought I could see along it for many a milestone. Now there is a bend in it. I don't know what lies around the bend, but I'm going to believe that the best does. It has a fascination of its own, that bend, Marilla. I wonder how the road beyond it goes—what there is of green glory and soft, checkered light and shadows—what new landscapes—what new beauties—what curves and hills and valleys further on.''

"I don't feel as if I ought to let you give it up," said Marilla, referring to the scholarship.

"But you can't prevent me. I'm sixteen and a half, 'obstinate as a mule,' as Mrs. Lynde once told me," laughed Anne. "Oh, Marilla, don't you go pitying me. I don't like to be pitied, and there is no need for it. I'm heart glad over the very thought of staying at dear Green Gables. Nobody could love it as you and I do—so we must keep it.''

"You blessed girl!" said Marilla, yielding. "I feel as if you'd given me new life. I guess I ought to stick out and make you go to college—but I know I can't, so I ain't going to try. I'll make it up to you though, Anne.''

When it became noised abroad in Avonlea that Anne Shirley had given up the idea of going to college and intended to stay home and teach there was a good deal of discussion over it. Most of the good folks, not knowing about Marilla's eyes, thought she was foolish. Mrs. Allan did not. She told Anne so in approving words that brought tears of pleasure to the girl's eyes. Neither did good Mrs. Lynde. She came up one evening and found Anne and Marilla sitting at the front door in the warm, scented summer dusk. They liked to sit there when the twilight came down and the white moths flew about in the garden and the odor of mint filled the dewy air.

Mrs. Rachel deposited her substantial person upon the stone bench by the door, behind which grew a row of tall pink and yellow hollyhocks, with a long breath of mingled weariness and relief.

"I declare I'm glad to sit down. I've been on my feet all day, and two hundred pounds is a good bit for two feet to carry round. It's a great blessing not to be fat, Marilla. I hope you appreciate it. Well, Anne, I hear you've given up your notion of going to college. I was real glad to hear it. You've got as much education now as a woman can be comfortable with. I don't believe in girls going to college and cramming their heads full of Latin and Greek and all that nonsense.''

"But I'm going to study Latin and Greek just the same, Mrs. Lynde," said Anne laughing. "I'm going to take my Arts course right here at Green Gables, and study everything that I would at college.''

Mrs. Lynde lifted her hands in holy horror.

"Anne Shirley, you'll kill yourself.''

"Not a bit of it. I shall thrive on it. Oh, I'm not going to overdo things. As 'Josiah Allen's wife' says, I shall be 'mejum.' But I'll have lots of spare time in the long winter evenings, and I've no vocation for fancy work. I'm going to teach over at Carmody, you know."

"I don't know it. I guess you're going to teach right here in Avonlea. The trustees have decided to give you the school.''

"Mrs. Lynde!" cried Anne, springing to her feet in her surprise. "Why, I thought they had promised it to Gilbert Blythe!''

"So they did. But as soon as Gilbert heard that you had applied for it he went to them—they had a business meeting at the school last night, you know—and told them that he withdrew his application, and suggested that they accept yours. He said he was going to teach at White Sands. Of course he gave up the school just to oblige you, because he knew how much you wanted to stay with Marilla, and I must say I think it was real kind and thoughtful in him, that's what. Real self-sacrificing, too, for he'll have his board to pay at White Sands, and everybody knows he's got to earn his own way through college. So the trustees decided to take you. I was tickled to death when Thomas came home and told me.''

"I don't feel that I ought to take it," murmured Anne. "I mean—I don't think I ought to let Gilbert make such a sacrifice for—for me.''

"I guess you can't prevent him now. He's signed papers with the White Sands trustees. So it wouldn't do him any good now if you were to refuse. Of course you'll take the school. You'll get along all right, now that there are no Pyes going. Josie was the last of them, and a good thing she was, that's what. There's been some Pye or other going to Avonlea school for the last twenty years, and I guess their mission in life was to keep school-teachers reminded that earth isn't their home. Bless my heart! What does all that winking and blinking at the Barry gable mean?''

"Diana is signalling for me to go over," laughed Anne. "You know we keep up the old custom. Excuse me while I run over and see what she wants.''

Anne ran down the clover slope like a deer, and disappeared in the firry shadows of the Haunted Wood. Mrs. Lynde looked after her indulgently.

"There's a good deal of the child about her yet in some ways."

"There's a good deal more of the woman about her in others," retorted Marilla, with a momentary return of her old crispness.

But crispness was no longer Marilla's distinguishing characteristic. As Mrs. Lynde told her Thomas that night.

"Marilla Cuthbert has got *mellow*. That's what."

Anne went to the little Avonlea graveyard the next evening to put fresh flowers on Matthew's grave and water the Scotch rosebush. She lingered there until dusk, liking the peace and calm of the little place, with its poplars whose rustle was like low, friendly speech, and its whispering grasses growing at will among the graves. When she finally left it and walked down the long hill that sloped to the Lake of Shining Waters it was past sunset and all Avonlea lay before her in a dreamlike afterlight—"a haunt of ancient peace." There was a freshness in the air as of a wind that had blown over honey-sweet fields of clover. Home lights twinkled out here and there among the homestead trees. Beyond lay the sea, misty and purple, with its haunting, unceasing murmur. The west was a glory of soft mingled hues, and the pond reflected them all in still softer shadings. The beauty of it all thrilled Anne's heart, and she gratefully opened the gates of her soul to it.

"Dear old world," she murmured, "you are very lovely, and I am glad to be alive in you."

Halfway down the hill a tall lad came whistling out of a gate before the Blythe homestead. It was Gilbert, and the whistle died on his lips as he recognized Anne. He lifted his cap courteously, but he would have passed on in silence, if Anne had not stopped and held out her hand.

"Gilbert," she said, with scarlet cheeks, "I want to thank you for giving up the school for me. It was very good of you—and I want you to know that I appreciate it."

Gilbert took the offered hand eagerly.

"It wasn't particularly good of me at all, Anne. I was pleased to be able to do you some small service. Are we going to be friends after this? Have you really forgiven me my old fault?"

Anne laughed and tried unsuccessfully to withdraw her hand.

"I forgave you that day by the pond landing, although I didn't know it. What a stubborn little goose I was. I've been—I may as well make a complete confession—I've been sorry ever since."

"COME, I'M GOING TO WALK WITH YOU."

"We are going to be the best of friends," said Gilbert, jubilantly. "We were born to be good friends, Anne. You've thwarted destiny long enough. I know we can help each other in many ways. You are going to keep up with your studies, aren't you? So am I. Come, I'm going to walk home with you."

Marilla looked curiously at Anne when the latter entered the kitchen.

"Who was that came up the lane with you, Anne?"

"Gilbert Blythe," answered Anne, vexed to find herself blushing. "I met him on Barry's hill."

"I didn't think you and Gilbert Blythe were such good friends that you'd stand for half an hour at the gate talking to him," said Marilla, with a dry smile.

"We haven't been—we've been good enemies. But we have decided that it will be much more sensible to be good friends in future. Were we really there half an hour? It seemed just a few minutes. But, you see, we have five years' lost conversations to catch up with, Marilla."

Anne sat long at her window that night companioned by a glad content. The wind purred softly in the cherry boughs, and the mint breaths came up to her. The stars twinkled over the pointed firs in the hollow and Diana's light gleamed through the old gap.

Anne's horizons had closed in since the night she had sat there after coming home from Queen's; but if the path set before her feet was to be narrow she knew that flowers of quiet happiness would bloom along it. The joys of sincere work and worthy aspirations and congenial friendship were to be hers; nothing could rob her of her birthright of fancy or her ideal world of dreams. And there was always the bend in the road!

" 'God's in his heaven, all's right with the world,' " whispered Anne softly.